INCONSISTENTLY
Inconsistent

Plausible Plots

Montana

First paperback edition July 2020

Cover design by Corey Hutchison

ISBN 978-0-578-70371-8 (paperback)

Also by Dana S. Harvey

Completely Indeterminate

*To those stalwarts working
in the trenches of rural medicine
without benefit of helmet, weapon or gas mask;
we salute you.*

Dana S. Harvey

TABLE OF CONTENTS

WAIT A FEW MINUTES

Five miles west of Bedlam, midway through the stretch of highway negotiating an undulating terrain of gullies and coulees, Ben Parker passed the faded, bullet riddled sign announcing that he had crossed a sovereign border and had entered the reservation. Once through the near treeless, windswept section of badlands, the landscape immediately flattened and the highway coursed its way straight towards the horizon. The railroad line to the south gently curved north and then westward, melding into a parallel route adjacent to the macadam. Harvested ground to both sides was covered with several inches of snow lingering from previous storms, the trees to the far south along the river banks stood starkly gray and barren.

The roadway was free of any accumulation of snow or ice, the barrow pits in the right of ways level with snow, burying the abundant highway refuse predominately composed of beer cans, liquor bottles and fast food wrappers. Roadside delineators marched by, their top mounted reflectors shining in the rays of the sun rising behind him. Ben periodically passed small white crosses affixed to red steel posts, usually a single cross, occasionally two or three clustered together, standing in the right of ways as stark reminders of motor vehicle fatalities. Ben had driven numerous Montana highways where American Legion Posts erected the white cross markers so this was not a unique sight. What had always provoked his curiosity were the numbers of crosses arrayed along seemingly innocuous straightaways, prompting him to surmise that speed, alcohol or boredom were the chief culprits. He knew that Montana was always in the top five for motor vehicle deaths involving alcohol.

Ben had just passed a small reservation town to the north, a virtual mountain of empty beer cans in the back lot towering above the roof of its lone drinking establishment. Ironically named Drought, the town had once been singled out as having consumed the most alcoholic beverages per capita in the United States. Although this was not an annual distinction, the claim was vigorously supported and pursued by resident enthusiasts, obviously in competition with towns claiming the largest ball of twine, the largest wind chimes and perhaps the fewest viable teeth in a population of 300 or more.

Leaving Bedlam that morning at 7 AM, Ben was traveling to Slipknot in clear, cloudless and temperate conditions, infrequent for mid-November. Tuesday was his scheduled day off from the clinic; however, due to Dr. Saroni's avoidance or reticence to spend time mentoring him, Ben had chosen to spend a number of his Tuesdays under the tutelage of secondary supervising physicians at other facilities. Today was being spent at the clinic in Slipknot with Dr. Molson, an internal medicine doctor who had been practicing for more than 20 years. Ben looked forward to his frequent changes of venue, especially with Dr. Molson, a sharp diagnostician, with a winning personality, who in addition to being a great instructor providing constructive criticism or praise, was well liked and respected by his staff and patients.

The morning weather forecast had confidently predicted a day time temperature hovering in the low forties with 0% chance of precipitation. A cold front with accompanying snow was pushing down from Canada and the glib television meteorologist, gesturing grandly at his colorful wall map, demonstrated that the pending storm would bypass their region, flowing over the Canadian border into mid and eastern North Dakota. Ben had long ago made the comparison that a meteorologist producing a reliable weather forecast had the predictability and outcome of someone attempting to herd cats. It was surprising to Ben that more people did not pursue careers in meteorology considering the high probability of an errant forecast coupled with the apparent unassailable job security. He had speculated as to the viability of medical facilities or perhaps casinos were they to rely on the same predictive percentages as weather forecasting. The legal system would eventually implode under the weight of malpractice suits and casino owners would soon be living in cardboard boxes under freeway underpasses. The radio broadcast of the day's weather promised a "beautiful and well-deserved break from our early winter here in Northern Montana" and "get out there and soak up the vitamin D!"

It was now 3:30 PM and Ben had been shadowing Dr. Molson since clinic had started at 9 AM. Having emerged from an afternoon spent in windowless clinic rooms, he was startled to see an outdoor landscape blanketed in snow. Through the office window he observed snow descending and accumulating at an alarming rate, with intermittent wind gusts blowing snow diagonally as bare tree limbs vibrated and swayed.

Ben had initially set 3:45 PM as his departure time since he was due to start call back in Bedlam at 5 PM. He realized his anticipated travel time might be increased and dialed the Bedlam Medical Center Clinic. In Ben's view, asking Dr. Saroni a favor was comparable to running a cheese grater over an open wound, however, he needed to swallow his pride and ask the doctor to please cover call in the event that he was late returning to town. Callie answered, attempted to bring Dr. Saroni to the phone, the doctor declining to take the call. "Sorry, Ben, he's dictating and said to call back." Ben asked Callie to please inform the doctor of his current predicament and assure him that Ben would call him back once on the highway. His second call was to the nurses' station at the hospital which was answered by Tara Buell the LPN on duty. He apprised her of his current situation and told her that Dr. Saroni would cover call until he returned to town.

He asked Tara, "Who is the lucky nurse on duty tonight?"

"We have a traveler scheduled for tonight and tomorrow night. I think they said she's from Billings or there about."

"Would you happen to know her name or if she's been here before?"

"Hang on a sec." Ben could hear Tara flipping through the scheduling binder. "Her name is Cecilia Warden. I don't recognize the name Ben."

"That's okay. Thanks for checking. I'm just being nosy as usual but I like knowing who I'll be working with. I'll call the hospital as soon as I get back into town."

"Thanks for the heads up. It's been snowing here for close to two hours so drive safe. Bye." Click.

Exiting the Slipknot clinic, he was surprised at the drastic drop in temperature. A steel gray sky provided the background for the blowing snow knifing across the parking lot. Using his jacket sleeve, he wiped the snow from his driver side window and door latch, struggled but managed to insert the key into a near frozen lock and climbed into the cab. Minute particles of snow wafted about the cab after he slammed shut the door. The truck was covered with several inches of snow and it muffled the outside sounds. His trustworthy engine turned over and started without cough or sputter. With the defroster running he sat for several minutes watching the vapor of his exhaled breath. Once convinced that the engine was warmed enough he exited, then used his snow brush and scraper to clear the windows, windshield and frontend, and then turned in his hubs in the event that he might need four wheel drive. Back in the cab, the defroster on high, he shifted into gear and headed toward the highway. As he neared the stop sign he gently pumped his brakes and felt his tires slide. He speculated that ice had formed after the initial snow melted on warm roadway followed by the plunge in temperature.

The snow continued adding to his estimate of four to five inches. Cars moving in town were few and traversing slowly, headlights now on as cloud cover descended and daylight diminished. He tentatively pulled out onto the highway's eastbound lane and his truck fishtailed slightly. He corrected and resigned himself to a slow tedious drive back to Bedlam. There was no indication that a snow plow, let alone a sanding truck had ventured out on the road and Ben anticipated that might be the case for the next 50 plus miles. With that thought in mind he reached down and shifted his transfer case into four wheel high.

As he left the city limits of Slipknot, Ben estimated visibility to be a few hundred yards at best. Snow blew into his windshield then shifted horizontally across from left to right as more frequent wind gusts streamed in from the north. For the next 20 miles, a slow advance towards Compton, he met with the occasional pair of headlights appearing out of the constant snow and fast approaching night fall. Ben would slow and drift slightly toward the right shoulder when the headlights and amber marker lamps of a semi-truck bore down towards him. Ghostly leviathans of the road sped on unflinchingly generating a trailing vortex of swirling snow that would blind and sometimes disorient motorists passing in the opposite direction. These were the times you gripped the steering wheel a little tighter and drove straight and true until vague landmarks, delineator posts or vehicle tracks reappeared and allowed you to reestablish your position on the highway. Motorists could not rely on the transverse grooves cut into the edge of a roadway's shoulder to warn them back into their lane since the grooves were an incomplete patchwork along literally thousands of miles of Montana highways.

Full darkness had fallen well before he entered Compton. The north wind was buffered on the main street by the array of two story buildings, most of them housing businesses on the first floor with small apartments on the second. Ben conjectured that the snow plowing crews were still drinking coffee while warming up their trucks, perhaps waiting until the snow and wind stopped or maybe until spring arrived. The streets were nearly deserted save for the trucks idling in front of the several drinking establishments spaced along the four block downtown district. Ben did not see any other moving vehicle as he passed through and continued down the highway towards Drought. The next 15 miles was relatively straight, the flat landscape offering little resistance or diversion to the steady, intermittently gusting winds. To his right, the railroad continued to parallel the highway and it dawned on him that considering the number of daily trains he had not observed any since leaving Slipknot. Even the engineers had more sense than to venture out in near blizzard conditions.

As he rolled into the limits of Drought, the eerily green hue of mercury vapor lamps illuminated the falling snow of the parking lot and the red and blue neon lighting of the bar sign advertised that the Keep on Tappin' Bar was open for business. Several snow covered pickup trucks were clustered by the front entrance, probably locals since no one else seemed willing to brave the weather and snow covered highway. A few dim house lights close to the highway were discernible. Ben knew the distance between Drought and Bedlam was close to 20 miles and glanced at his odometer making a mental note of his current mileage. The highway remained untouched by a plow and he continued on, his truck breaking trail through the nine to 10 inches of snow he estimated blanketed the roadway. He conceded the fact that until he reached Bedlam the only lights he would see were liable to be his own headlights.

Slogging along, several miles east of Drought, though visibility was severely limited, Ben knew that he was entering into the badlands as snow drifts across the highway became deeper and more defined. Where hillocks and swells dropped into coulees and ravines, north winds whistled down natural wind tunnels buffeting the truck. A lapse of attention combined with a patch of unseen ice could easily turn the truck catty-wampus sliding it towards unseen but understood drop offs. Guard rails were sparsely employed along any stretch of this roadway. Ben found himself leaning over the steering wheel, almost hypnotized by the swirling flakes, rationalizing that the extra two feet he gained in distance would improve his mostly obscured visualization of the roadway ahead. His gloves sat next to him on the seat; bare handed he had a better feel of the steering wheel allowing his white knuckle grip to maintain control. He discovered that he had been unconsciously wriggling, sucking in his abdomen and clenching his buttocks because his bladder was brimming.

Pulling over to urinate was not an option. He had not seen trailing headlights for at least 20, maybe 30 miles or more, yet he knew that as soon as he did pull to the shoulder a speeding, self-proclaimed bullet proof moron, without enough brain cells to formulate a death wish, would fly over a rise in the road and ram into the rear end of his truck. Ben pioneered on, the snow blowing and swirling in his low beams, knowing that the brightness and reflection of high beams would only create more distraction and disorientation. He searched ahead, one eye on the perceived roadway the other concentrating on the shoulder, delineators jumping out from the murk of snow and night. The white crosses with their red posts were obscured. The few road signs now unreadable from blowing snow having adhered to the flat surfaces. There were no vestiges of tire tracks to follow so he drove on often unsure of whether he had strayed over the center line or was about to slip off the shoulder and plunge head long into a rocky ravine.

He realized that he was ascending a long, slightly inclined grade and recognized that he had topped the last rise before the highway descended toward Bedlam. There was a momentary lull in the crosswinds and he glimpsed what he believed to be the lights of Bedlam. A random thought occurred to him as he headed down the grade that the power was still on in town, and then suddenly he remembered the possibility that the road barrier gates below may be closed. Shifting down to second gear Ben wondered if there was ice under the snow, hoping to avoid braking as he arrested his descent using only his transmission and the deep snow. His headlights reflected off the metal gates and warning signs that extended across the highway and he managed a graceful, sliding stop five feet short of the gates. A fleeting thought that the gates were not only chained but locked was assuaged as he clamored out of the truck and unlatched the restraining chain.

Ben pushed open the eastbound barrier, snow drifted to the bottom cross pipe. He estimated the snow depth on the level at 13 to 14 inches. The head lights projected out far enough to ascertain the road had been plowed some time ago, probably when the highway crew had closed the barrier gates. Standing in the middle of the highway, Ben emptied his bladder feeling his body muscles starting to relax. He pulled his truck through the barrier then swung the gate closed securing it with the chain. Once back in the cab, the defroster and heater blasting warm air, Ben sat motionless as a sense of relief was coursing through him. As if Mother Nature was acknowledging the end of his quest the snow and wind abated and ceased. Ben engaged his transmission and started toward town, smiling at an old axiom paraphrased from Mark Twain which he thought Montana meteorologists should adopt as their official mantra; "If you don't like the weather…just wait a few minutes."

POSTAL

It was nearing 6:30 PM when Ben parked his truck at the curb in front of the post office. He had alerted the hospital that he was back in town and Roxy, a young, enthusiastic CNA with at times questionable observational skills, had advised him that the roads in and out of Bedlam were closed and had admonished him to stay at home, that he should not be out driving around. He had thanked Roxy for the information and told her that he would take her recommendation under advisement. Roxy then added that Dr. Saroni had called three times since leaving the clinic demanding to know if Ben had yet returned to town. Ben cursed himself, remembering that he had neglected to call the doctor once he was on the highway headed back to Bedlam. When he dialed Dr. Saroni's home phone the doctor's wife answered, immediately scolding him for interrupting their dinner hour. She then commanded him to "schedule his time more strategically in the future so the doctor would not have to make accommodations for his poor planning." Ben was momentarily taken aback by Mrs. Saroni's harsh tone, bit his tongue and apologized before asking for the doctor. "He is trying to enjoy his meal, what is it you want?" He politely asked her to pass along to the doctor that he was back in town and now covering call.

"Finally," and then she added, "Do not let this happen again." Click. He concluded that the age old adage that opposites attract did not seem to be applicable in the Saroni household.

Outside the entranceway and again inside the vestibule on the floor mats, Ben stomped his feet ridding him of as much snow as possible. The vestibule and post office box area were minimally lighted. Brighter fluorescent ceiling lights illuminated the empty service lobby and unmanned service counter which were separated from the vestibule by plate glass windows and a heavy glass door securely and promptly locked at 5 PM. While kicking off the snow he glanced into the service areas and as expected saw no one. It was a rarity to see a postal employee anywhere in or near the building after 5 PM and he was sure that tonight would be no exception. The soles of his wet shoes emitted squishes and squeaks as walked to his post office box.

The post office boxes were arrayed on two opposing walls within a spacious, high ceilinged room. The small sized boxes were most predominant, obviously the cheapest to rent and most inconvenient to access. Ben had speculated that the size and positioning of the small sized boxes resulted from tests employing a height challenged individual with exceptionally small hands to determine the national standards. On a normal day he found the process of retrieving his mail one of precise shaping and positioning of the hand, careful insertion, pinching, squeezing, pulling, twisting, manipulating, cajoling, cursing and partial shredding of the box contents and skin of his hand while attempting to extricate his mail. He knew that he could rent a bigger box to accommodate his hand, but his volume of mail did not warrant it, and besides that, he was stubbornly too cheap to make the upgrade.

11

Ben removed his mail from his box incurring minimal injury and walked to the vestibule positioning himself adjacent to the locked, glass partitioned but better lighted service area. He began sifting through his few pieces of mail when the back of a postcard appeared. This immediately piqued his curiosity since postcards were so infrequently sent or received these days. He flipped the postcard over to the front and leaned up by the plate glass door to take advantage of the service area lighting. Upon first glance it appeared to Ben to be a poster reduced to postcard size. He could discern a map of Montana providing the background and someone's hand, he was positive it was a woman's, was superimposed, the hand forming a fist while prominently and defiantly displaying the middle or social finger. Upon closer examination he recognized a face superimposed over the fingernail of the middle finger; his own. Oh, this was not a good sign he thought. Turning the postcard over he immediately knew who had sent it; the hand writing was irrefutable. In actuality it was not handwriting or cursive, rather tiny, highly legible printing that belonged to an old girlfriend, Amy Greenfield. He had once or twice teased her that she could print an entire spy novel on the back of a postage stamp having enough glue left to stick it on an envelope. His humor had not been appreciated.

An artist and free spirit, Amy had stolen and imprisoned his heart for one summer many years ago. She had drifted into Montana in mid-June expecting to travel randomly throughout the state, pursuing her artistic passions of sketching, painting and photography, mixing them liberally with sightseeing and partying. Her passions soon expanded to include Ben after he rescued her from her dilapidated and much in need of repair Isuzu Stylus, perhaps the only one of its kind to have invaded Montana.

She had broken down on her way north from Yellowstone Park and never made it out of Southwest Montana. They had spent the summer together and although Amy's protestations were frequent and adamant that they were merely having a frivolous summer romance she had developed much more than a "passing fancy" for her "Montana Man."

By early fall Amy, though still in the throes of new romance, had become increasingly homesick for California. She wanted to return home, reassert her energies toward her art career and pursue her dream of opening her own gallery that she would name "The Crazed Eye." However, she was also determined to maintain and grow her relationship with Ben, believing it required him accompanying her back to California. At first her plan to influence him was through subtle inferences and enticements. When this approach failed cajoling followed, building into moderate demands, slowly escalating into sternly worded demands soon bordering on leveraged threats finally triggering tantrums and tears, but nothing could soften Ben's position and steely resolve to remain in Montana. As steadfast as Ben had been Amy had been just as resolute in returning to California, rebuffing every appreciable attempt Ben made to convince her to stay. They had a reached an impasse and Amy, angry and disappointed, had packed her Isuzu that Ben had painstakingly repaired and quietly disappeared one night under cover of darkness. That was 11 years ago.

Five or six weeks ago, Ben, in a moment of weakness, with a considerable lapse in judgment, fueled by a near overwhelming desire for female companionship and by his own admission "just plain horny as hell," had searched the internet, found an art gallery in California named "The Crazed Eye," and penned a letter to Amy. He recounted his past few years, his current locale and circumstances and had inquired of her that should she be currently unattached and unencumbered would she consider a trip to Montana to renew their friendship and possibly rekindle a romance. In other words, a thinly veiled appeal for sex of a noncommittal nature. He had mailed it to the gallery with the outside hope that it was indeed Amy's dream come true; however, Ben held no illusions that Amy would respond and afterwards rued the fact he had not held the letter for a day or two to reconsider mailing it. What had he been thinking? At least he hadn't been in the pathos of self-pity due to strong drink when he wrote the letter. He read the back of the postcard.

Roses are red
Violets are blue
You stomped on my heart
Now you're stalking me too?

Roses are red
Violets are blue
Sounds like depression
Perhaps Prozac for you

Roses have thorns
Draw blood with a prick
Violets are harmless
They don't own a dick

Roses are red
your balls must be blue
There's no way in hell
I'll be visiting you

Ben immediately recognized that he may have underestimated how acrimonious their breakup had been. Detecting that some deep unresolved issues remained he concluded that no amount of sniveling or groveling on his part would constitute an apology or begin to scratch the

14

surface toward reconciliation. Upon reflection, when declining her repeated invitations to join her in California, he should have refrained from referring to California as the land of fruits and nuts. As unappealing as it sounded, he would at this juncture in time, continue his monastic lifestyle and embrace celibacy until a more appropriate opportunity arose.

Ben was about to zip up his coat when he inadvertently dropped his mail. As he stooped to retrieve the scattered envelopes and post card he detected out of the corner of his eye, a slight movement, in the service areas. He quickly looked back over his right shoulder and spied Martin Kaplanic, the postmaster, standing in the shadows behind the service counter. Kaplanic looked back at Ben, surprise on his face at having been discovered. His mail collected, Ben straightened himself and turned to face the postmaster.

Mr. Kaplanic had scheduled a clinic appointment in late September complaining of a sore throat and fatigue. Ben had reviewed his chart before the appointment and found that Mr. Kaplanic visited the clinic about once a year, usually in the spring to review his lab results from the Health Fair. The only notable lab finding was his PSA, Prostate-specific-antigen, a test that helped portray the health of his prostate. Mr. Kaplanic's PSA level had consistently increased; last spring a recorded 6.8, a level for definite concern. There was no indication that he had ever undergone a physical exam of his prostate and Ben did find mention in two of Dr. Saroni's short notes that the exam had been recommended and declined. Otherwise Mr. Martin Kaplanic appeared healthy.

Soon after Ben had begun obtaining his patient's history he discovered the appointment was merely a pretext in an attempt to find out what Ben had seen Kaplanic's estranged wife for earlier that month.

Ben had informed him politely, "I'm sorry Mr. Kaplanic, but your wife's medical records are private and cannot be shared with you."

With authority Kaplanic responded, "I'm her husband and I'm entitled to see them."

"Again, sir, I cannot divulge any of your wife's medical records to you or to anyone else without her written consent."

"She already gave permission years ago."

"Mrs. Kaplanic may have consented on a past date however; her current wishes of nondisclosure are definitive and must be honored. To disregard them would constitute a HIPPA violation. The HIPPA laws are what protect your records from unauthorized scrutiny and prying eyes."

"Are you implying that I have prying eyes? Do I look like any schmuck or deviant off the street?" Mr. Kaplanic seemed a bit defensive.

"Certainly not Mr. Kaplanic," Ben said soothingly, attempting to diffuse the situation, "I am not at all implying that you have prying eyes."

"Then you're saying that I'm some schmuck attempting to do something illegal with my wife's records?"

Ben sensed where this was going and realized he needed to direct the discussion back to the initial reason for the appointment. "Mr. Kaplanic, I cannot share your wife's records with you. Let's discuss what brought you in today."

Mr. Kaplanic, now agitated and slightly surly sat straight backed with his arms tightly crossed across his chest, jaw tensely set, lips compressed. Ben believed his patient knew perfectly well about the restrictions and the true reason for his reaction was his failure to manipulate or bully his way to his goal. "I'm fine now. The only complaint I have is about you, and your lack of compassion and consideration for me, my wife, and my attempts to learn how I might be able to better support and help her with her medical problems."

Ben wondered how Marni had failed to mention passive aggressive in her behavioral report. He decided to redirect to an alternate tact. "I reviewed your lab results and find your elevated PSA level to be concerning. Dr. Saroni's notes indicated you declined a prostate exam. The combination of ..."

"Stop right there bud. I see where you're going with this, trying to divert my attention from my wife's plight by insisting that I get a finger wave. No way there bud. That is just not going to happen." Then he loudly blurted out, "Now then, getting back to my wife. We need to talk about her affair and who gave her that STD you treated her for."

Ben did not react but believed Marni to be spot on with the whack job perspective. He was not to be swayed. "Mr. Kaplanic, your PSA level warrants further investigation and I highly recommend a prostate exam whether it's me, Dr. Saroni or a referral to a urologist to perform it. This is noth..."

"What don't you understand about no? N-fucking-O. No! No one is going to stick any fingers or gizmos up my butt, especially you. Look at the damn size of those damn sausages you call fingers. No one has and no one will ever be lubing anything up then poking and waving it around in my bung hole."

Ben was thinking high drama mixed with homophobia with a big dollop of proctophobia. He excused himself, went to his office and returned with the name and number of a urologist who visited Sunnvale. When handing the slip of paper to Mr. Kaplanic he said, "In the event that you change your mind."

Kaplanic dropped it to the floor. "I bet you and that urologist charge even more to fondle my butt, you perverts."

"We're done here Mr. Kaplanic. Thank you for coming in and I highly recommend that you never make the mistake of scheduling another appointment with me." Ben adjourned to his office.

Kaplanic stepped forward out of the shadows though remaining behind the service counter with his arms casually crossed over his chest. He was staring at Ben, the look of surprise having morphed into a self-satisfied smirk. Obviously, he was delighting himself with some knowledge that Ben was not privy to. His head was slowly nodding and his smirk spread as Ben pondered what Kaplanic was enjoying at his expense. Suddenly the postmaster bent over, leaning to his right, his left hand on the counter helping to balance him. He appeared to be searching for something under the counter top. Straightening up he produced a blank postcard. Holding it by the corner between his thumb and forefinger, he held it up and began waving it at Ben, at the same time he burst into laughter. It finally dawned on Ben what Kaplanic was doing. He was taunting Ben, letting him know that he had read the postcard from Amy before Ben had retrieved and read it himself. Kaplanic was thoroughly enjoying the moment, knowing about the postcard content as well as being a magnifying source of Ben's discomfort and embarrassment. Ben understood that this was the type of circumstance that Kaplanic reveled in.

His initial reaction was shocked embarrassment and Ben considered walking away, recovering his dignity at a later time. However, knowing Kaplanic's personality, the postmaster would construe Ben's retreat or portrayed indifference as a weakness worthy of future harassment or belittling. Ben was a good boy scout, always prepared. During his boyhood years he had learned, initially at his parents' insistence, to always have easy access to a small flashlight and spare change. Over the years the compacted resources he carried in his coats and jackets had grown. He tucked his mail into his waist band and searched his left coat pocket until he located what he wanted. Turning away from the view of Kaplanic he was able to shield his actions. Ben suddenly whirled and thrust his right hand up and toward the smug postmaster.

His right hand was now gloved in a latex free glove and Ben made it a highly visual point to snap the cuff into position with his left hand. Making a fist, he extended his index finger straight at Kaplanic and began rotating and waving it back and forth as if stirring something, exaggerating the movement and surely making the impression that he wanted. Kaplanic almost instantly understood Ben's intent as his face blanched, his smirk vanished, and he took an unsteady step backwards. Ben looked directly at Kaplanic making and holding eye contact. He let out an exaggerated yet sinister laugh then slowly and distinctly, so there would be no mistake in Kaplanic's interpretation, he mouthed the words, "Sooner or later," a slight pause for effect, then "You're mine." Then Ben smiled, turned and exited the post office. He was thinking that now was the time for a bite to eat, to put his feet up for a while, to hit the sack early and if he was lucky grab a full night's sleep. My job here is now done.

Ben could vaguely hear the phone ringing as he rousted himself from sleep. He had fallen asleep in his canvas camp recliner, the television remained on as a newscaster quietly droned on in the background. He reached for the phone on the plastic crate next to the recliner.

Drowsily he answered, "Hello."

"Hi, Ben, it's Roxy at the hospital." There was a pause and Roxy began again. "Hello, Mr. Parker, it's Roxy. We have an ER for you."

"What's on tonight's menu Roxy?"

"A leg laceration. He fell on broken glass and someone from the bar dropped him off."

Ben glanced at his watch. "It's only midnight, not closing time yet."

"It is for him. He's passed out on the gurney in the ER."

"Who's with him?"

"The traveler."

He was still trying to clear his head. "I think it was Tara who told me Cecilia Warden."

"I'm not sure but it sounds about right."

"Okay then, I'll be right in."

Still dressed, Ben headed to the bathroom, splashed cold water on his face, quickly brushed his teeth and ran a comb through his hair. He still felt half asleep as he laced up his boots, slipped on his Carhart coat, and then grabbed his gloves and baseball cap. His pager was on the kitchen counter so he clipped it on his belt at the same time trying to remember when he had moved the phone into the living room. Once outside the cold air was like a slap to the face and he could see his breath. The skies remained cloud covered and siftings of light snow descended. The back steps and path to the garage had been shoveled but were now covered with several inches of newly fallen snow.

The neighborhood streets were deserted and remained unplowed as he slowly made his way towards the highway. The only sounds were his defroster and the compacting of snow under his tires. Snow had inundated yards and driveways, drifting against and covering vehicles, turning them into unidentifiable shapes and mounds. He had driven this street numerous times but tonight several of the houses appeared strangely alien. The snow fall was becoming heavier which, in concert with the largely obscured landscaping and piled high roofs was apparently distorting his perception. Ben must have been daydreaming because the drive in seemed unusually fast. He found himself parked in front of the hospital and walked in through the main entrance. No one was at the nurses' station and the nursing home hallways were dark and silent. At the end of the hospital corridor he spied the light on in the emergency room. Ben started down that silent hallway which seemed darker than usual. The doors to the patient rooms had all been closed and his footsteps created a slight unfamiliar echo.

Entering the ER Ben came upon a disheveled middle aged male sprawled on the gurney. A sheet covered his abdomen and legs, his stocking feet protruding out from under the end. His blue jeans had been folded and lay atop his wet shoes on the floor at the foot of the gurney. Ben snuck a quick peek under the sheet observing an impressive laceration to the right lower leg and had also concluded that by the lack of underwear the patient had inexplicably gone commando this frozen evening. He may have been imagining it but he thought he detected a strong mixture of stale beer, body odor and flatulence permeating the room. The traveler, dressed in Navy blue scrubs, shapely with dark shoulder length hair, stood at the counter writing, her back to him. She turned as he was introducing himself with, "Good morning. I'm Ben Parker the PA on duty."

Ben stopped abruptly, stood stock still, stunned into silence yet internally fumbling for his next words. The nurse was facing him. It was her. Rational thought would conclude that it couldn't be but there was no mistaking her. It was the woman of his dreams. Before she could speak Ben blurted out, "Cecelia Warden?"

She laughed. "No, I'm not Cecelia Warden. Where did you come up with that name?"

Ben answered hurriedly, his words literally spewing out in an unstoppable jumble. "The nurses. The nurses gave me your name but I can see that you're not Cecelia Warden. You're someone else. Yes, I know who you are, at least you look like someone I know, and I mean I don't know you as if we had previously met but I know you look like who you are or at least who you look like and I think you are. Are you who I think you are or am I wrong?"

The woman looked at him incredulously and again laughed, not at him but a laugh as if she was in on the joke. "Who do you think I might be?"

"Sela Ward?"

The nurse walked over to Ben and extended her hand. He reached out and took hers in greeting. Her voice was soft but carried well, with a slight Southern lilt. "Good morning Ben Parker. I'm Sela Ward and I'm your nurse tonight."

When Ben displayed the biggest shit-eatin' grin on his face it had the unexpected secondary effect of allowing his brain to once again function in what was for him a normal manner. "It's a pleasure making your acquaintance Sela Ward. Now, please tell me what you know about our stinky comatose friend here and we'll see what it is we need to sew up."

With that said, the two of them set to work reviewing the patient's chart from a previous ER visit, examining, cleaning, inspecting, numbing, irrigating, re-inspecting, sterilizing, suturing, re-cleaning, and dressing the wound, all undertaken as their sleeping beauty snorted and snored, farted, and periodically dribbled urine when coughing, prompting them to clothe him in an adult diaper. Ben having achieved an ethereal state, maintained his "I can't believe it's happening to me smile" as he worked and politely prompted the efficient and proficient Sela Ward RN to reveal why and how she had undergone a metamorphosis from Hollywood starlet to traveling nurse from Billings, Montana. Ben found her to be surprisingly candid and once when he was attempting clandestinely to glimpse her unadorned left ring finger she stopped her story, stated "divorced" and started back in where she had left off.

"Okay, good work here," Ben proclaimed as he stood up from his bedside stool and stretched his back and arms. As he gathered and disposed of his sharps he continued, "The chances of finding him a ride home tonight are next to none. Let's update his tetanus, give him a gram of Ancef, and tuck him in over in observation."

"I can make that happen," replied Sela.

"Thank you. I'll be right back to help you move him to observation."

Sela was drawing up the Tdap and smiled at Ben as he exited the emergency room.

Ben was washing his hands in the restroom by the rear entranceway to the hospital and try as he might, when he looked in the mirror he could not lose the goofy smile on his face. He returned to an empty ER, no patient, no gurney, and no nurse. He headed toward the observation room located by the nurses' station. The hallway was dimly lit and strangely someone had opened all of the doors to the hospital rooms during his time in the ER. He stopped outside the last hospital room on the left and stood quietly in the doorway. Finally entering the dark room, he stood, arms at his side, his eyes slowly becoming accustomed to the dim lighting filtering in from a street light illuminating the ambulance bay. He located a chair and set it down a few feet from the bed and sat down.

The patient was an elderly gentleman dying of congestive heart failure; his wife suffered her own medical maladies and had finally worn out caring for him at home. Lying on his hospital bed with his upper torso elevated, an oxygen mask on his face, he looked terribly frail and vulnerable. Ben sat there watching the shallow rise of his chest, listening to the steady hum of the oxygen concentrator, the ragged breathing and occasional gurgle originating in the old man's throat. He remembered meeting the wife and local clergyman, the discussion regarding hospice care, the doctor's recommendation of CPAP to augment the patient's breathing at night, and the patient declining CPAP but finally acquiescing to wearing a mask while asleep. At this moment, Ben found himself at a loss for the patient's name. His gaze shifted from the old man to outside through the large window across the room. The snow was drifting down in large, slowly undulating flakes. Occasional swirls of added snow slid off the roof indicating the wind was starting to gust again.

He felt a presence behind him, quiet, even breathing and then hands were gently kneading his shoulders. The room was at peace. Ben was sure who stood behind and it was confirmed as her cheek nuzzled the side of his head and Sela whispered, "Go home, Ben and get some sleep. Everything is good right now, the patients are safe. We got your back."

"I wanted to talk with you some more but; I know you must be tired of being pestered by infatuated fans."

24

"Do you know where the house is where the travelers stay?"

Ben nodded and said, "Yes."

"I get off shift at 6:30, so stop by around 7 or so. Think you can scrounge up a cup of coffee at that hour?"

"What? No fancy latte?"

"Don't spoil the moment smartass." She lingered for another minute her hands on his shoulders and her chin resting on top of his head. "I've got to check on Stinky, so I'll see you in the morning." She squeezed his shoulders one more time and was gone.

Ben continued to sit realizing that he felt drained and in need of some sleep. He heard the telephone ringing at the nearby nurses' station. It continued to ring and Ben wondered whether he was the only one that heard it. The ringing persisted and he was about to…

He sat bolt upright in his bed, the pager on his nightstand producing that obnoxious, piercing beeping. The beeping suddenly stopped and a voice took over. "Ben Parker please call the hospital. Ben Parker please call the hospital." He looked over at his alarm clock and the digital red display read 12:10 AM. Rolling out of bed, he headed to the wall phone mounted in the kitchen, bumping into the door frame in his still awakening state when the pager once again started its paging sequence followed by a second round of requests for him to call the hospital. He dialed the hospital number hoping it would be fast enough to forestall a third page. The phone was answered on the second ring.

"Bedlam Medical Center. This is Becca Trebek RN. How may I help you?"

"Becca, it's Ben. I thought you had a traveler on tonight."

"And a 'Hi, how are you, Becca? Great to hear your melodious and reassuring voice,' to you too."

"Sorry, Becca, I just wasn't expecting to hear your voice. How are you?"

"I'm doing just fine thank you, Mr. Ben Parker."

"So, to what do I owe this," he checked his kitchen clock, "12:15 AM adrenalin pumping page?"

"You're 10 minutes fast and the reason I paged you was you were not answering your phone, mister guy on call. You have, to use the expression loosely, a gentleman with a forehead laceration requesting your presence in the ER."

"Alcohol involved?"

"Would you have it any other way? C'mon, chop, chop, get your butt in here. That's why we pay you the big bucks."

"It's PA not MD, so can it on the big bucks. So again, I ask, why are you at work? I thought we had a traveler tonight?"

"I'm here because the traveler, one Cecelia Warden from Billings could not make it due to inclement weather and foul driving conditions, and the fact that I was stupid enough to answer my phone. Does that help?"

"Absolutely. You're always a wealth of information. I'll be right in. Goodbye."

As he was getting dressed Ben recounted his day yesterday starting with his alarm going off at 5:30 AM and finally meeting his dream girl, if only in a dream. Now, at midnight, he was headed back into work with a short nap under his belt and a lacerated drunk to sew up. He had wanted diversity in his career and for what it was worth his wish had been granted. He closed the back door and was greeted with a blast of cold air and gust of windblown snow. Every day was a new adventure and just like Cracker Jacks, there was a surprise in every box.

THANKSGIVING

Thanksgiving is not a moving target. At 7:30 AM Ben stood by the gas pump island at the Bedlam One Stop filling his pickup when the thought struck him. Thanksgiving is always observed on the fourth Thursday in November. Always. Consistent, unlike the perceived randomness of Easter, the fluctuating dates or days of the week of numerous other major holidays or the arbitrarily declared holidays that the government announces, reassigns, consolidates, decertifies or manipulates upon bureaucratic whim. The metallic hum of the pump droned on as he stared to the east, a muted sun rising in an overcast sky.

He hung up the pump handle and entered the convenience store, neither customer nor clerk in immediate sight. He stopped at the newspaper rack and selected both weekly papers, the Bedlam Bulletin and Reservation Review, knowing that the Great Falls Tribune was delivered daily to the hospital and available for his perusal. He selected lemonade from the cooler and at the unattended cashier counter he unfolded the front page of the Bulletin. In big bold print, the lead headline stretched across the page; "Broncos Broke In Playoff." An out of focus, black and white photograph displayed a dog pile of football players in varying shades of gray. Obviously bemoaning Bedlam High School's loss in the Class C football playoffs, the article also effusively described the team's extraordinary season and their foreshortened quest for glory.

The next bold but in smaller type headline read, "Pilgrim Play at Park," followed by an unwieldy, alliterative attempt at an explanatory subtitle. "PTA Presents Pilgrim Play at Park Picnic to Placate Pocahontas and Paleface Pals." Ben's most immediate thought was that this was wrong, oh, so wrong. What moron penned this drivel? The article alluded not only to an underlying conflict with an unnamed entity or individual but contained less than subtle prejudice against the local Native American community. The alliteration and verbiage smacked of pandering to the smug ego of a small town newspaper reporter with questionable journalistic skills and credentials. It appeared to Ben that both the editor and the reporter were adverse to research, historical fact checking and obviously not above personal editorializing when reporting the news. Ben was reminded of the similarities that many years ago prompted complaints by the NAACP and a subsequent investigation by the ACLU of a small town newspaper in Western Montana. He was a teenager at the time but remembered that the editor received a perfunctory slap on the wrist, printed a tongue in cheek apology nearly as offensive as the original article, all of which prompted his father to mention castration in the same breath as tar and feathering. The repugnant bent of the article smacked of Whip Acres.

His eyes were drawn to the lower half of the front page where a grainy photograph of a foursome, clothed in German festival attire, stood side by side, all holding decorative beer steins. It suddenly dawned on him that he was looking at an elaborately painted, probably plywood façade, where tourists stood behind the façade inserting their faces into the corresponding cut outs in the plywood. The frauleins were adorned with long, braided hair, cleavage revealing blouses with short, sexy Bavarian dirndl dresses and decorative knee socks characterizing the beer garden girls and serving wenches. The men were depicted as beer drinking yodelers wearing feathered alpine fedoras, embroidered suspenders, the colorful knee socks and of course, the mandatory lederhosen. Ben concluded that this was the German Oktoberfest rendition of a stateside boardwalk or carnival "we were here" slice of Americana. The photo was headed with "Bedlam's Best Attend Oktoberfest" and the caption underneath the photo identified Mr. and Mrs. Harmon Krum and Mayor and Mrs. Owen Boyle visiting the Beer Gardens of Oktoberfest while vacationing in Germany. Someone should have warned the German populace to hide their wallets, valuables and Hostess products.

"Morning, Ben." Ben had been engrossed with the newspaper and had heard someone approaching behind the counter but was unaware of who it was. "You know that's last week's newspaper?" was added rhetorically.

He looked up and smiled as he refolded the newspaper and said, "And a good morning to you, Frank. Happy Thanksgiving."

Frank began ringing up Ben's purchases and responded without enthusiasm, "Yeah, right, and a Happy Thanksgiving back at you." The down in the mouth response and body language were not lost on Ben.

"What's up sunshine?"

Frank bagged the items and slid them over to Ben. "I'm in a foul mood. I had to open this morning at 6 AM and I get to work 'til closing while everyone else has the entire day off. I'm tired of drawing short straw for all of the holidays and last minute call offs." Frank suddenly thrust his right arm with erect index finger high above his head and dramatically, if somewhat factitiously, proclaimed, "I've had enough. I've reached my limit. I've been here longer than most of the clerks and I'm still low man on the totem pole."

"I see you're getting comfortable with the use of Native American euphemisms."

"Smart ass. I am prepared to engage my persecutors and eradicate the discriminatory policies and practices promulgated upon the poor East Indian immigrant."

"Yes, a smart ass indeed. As much as I sympathize and support your position, you need to realize that dependent upon which tribe and culture you are referencing, the totem's vertical order of importance may be reversed, the more significant figures at or near the bottom."

Frank dropped his arm and muttered with a notably dejected tone, "Oh for Christ's sake, Ben, can't you just let me enjoy wallowing in my pity pot of low self-esteem?"

"Sorry, Mujibar, would you rather that I further denigrate, abuse and add to the stereotypical racial profiling?"

"I'm quite comfortable with my current seat on the pot. Go profile some patients."

He waved from the door. "Adios, Frank. I hope you have a better day. Don't forget to flush."

Ben poked his head in Salty's door. "Morning, Salty. Happy Thanksgiving."

A broad smile spread across Salty's face. He was sitting up in bed cradling a steaming cup of coffee in his hands. "Grab the board Parker," motioning with his head towards the cribbage board on his small dresser. "I hope you brought lots of cash."

31

Ben was about to answer when he felt a gentle tap on his shoulder. He turned to face Stella the RN on duty. "No cribbage yet. You've got an ER."

He stuck his head back in, "Sorry, Salty, I've got someone in the ER and then I have to make rounds."

"We still on for turkey day dinner?"

"And your Green Bay Packers?"

"You bet. See you later."

Stella and Ben walked down the corridor side by side, Ben commenting, "He seems upbeat today."

"Yes. Noticeably so. I haven't been on duty for a few days but last time I saw him I thought he was a bit depressed." She looked over to him as they walked, "You're good medicine for him, Ben."

Ben didn't respond. "So, what have we got in the ER?"

"A difference of opinion on how to take a temperature." Ben eyed her as they continued walking, a look of expectation on his face. She didn't take the bait but added nonchalantly, "We run into these things periodically."

They entered the emergency room, a man and woman, probably both in their early 40s, sat side by side on the gurney. The woman looking fit, brown hair in a short pony tail, dressed in blue jeans, a white T-shirt and full-length apron leapt up and off the gurney positioning herself off to the side. Her eyes bespoke of earlier tears. Remaining seated, the man was dressed in faded fatigue pants, an army green T-shirt under his full length kitchen apron. He too looked to be in relatively good shape, a hint of gray invading his temples and a small patch in front. Noting that the aprons matched but the lettering in front did not, Ben read hers, "Chief Cook, just ask him." His read, "Chief Bottle Washer, just ask her." A silk screen representation of their faces together appeared below the printing. There was a small amount of blood on his apron corresponding to his abdomen. The man's left hand, wrapped in a kitchen dish towel displaying a small splotch of blood, lay cradled in his lap.

"Ben, this is Earl Staley and his wife Ruth." Ben stepped over, shook Mrs. Staley's hand as he introduced himself and repeated the action with Mr. Staley. "What brings you in Mr. Staley?"

Stella moved forward and carefully unwrapped Mr. Staley's left hand. Before Stella could prevent it, he held up his left hand, palm toward Ben and slowly turned it 90 degrees and then back. A metal meat thermometer appeared to be clasped in the palm; however, the pointed probe was protruding out the back of his hand. Ben reviewed the chart, took note of the vital signs and began examining the patient, questioning him as he proceeded. Initial bleeding? Pain level? Tetanus status? Right or left hand dominant? Prior injuries to left hand? Numbness or tingling? Tobacco use? Medications? Allergies to medications? A litany of questions followed as the exam continued.

"I realize it's morning but I thought I detected the odor of alcohol. Was alcohol involved here?"

Both the Staley's looked somewhat chagrined. "Yes," said Mr. Staley, there's a lot of wine in her dishes."

"Any sampling by chance?"

"Yes, quite a bit actually. It's traditional."

Ben pointed at the thermometer impaled in his patient's hand. "I'm assuming that this is not traditional placement?"

"I had inserted the thermometer in the turkey and noticed some resistance so I made mention that the turkey wasn't entirely thawed. Fran pointed out that if I had followed her instructions on when to take the turkey out of the freezer it would have been thawed. Then she came over and said, 'That's not the right spot,' and pulled the thermometer out." Ben looked to Mrs. Staley who rolled her eyes and looked up to the ceiling. Mr. Staley continued, "We began arguing about how long it takes to thaw a 14-pound turkey and the proper placement of the thermometer. I made the unfortunate," his eyes drifted to Mrs. Staley, "but true comment, that maybe if she'd thaw out a little a poke in the right place might do her a world of good and bam," he now looked at his left hand, "I realized my mistake too late." Focusing directly at his wife he offered, "I am truly sorry honey. I was way out of line and I hope you can forgive me."

Mrs. Staley burst into tears, darted over insinuating herself between Ben and her husband, and threw her arms around her husband's neck repeating 'I'm sorry, I'm sorry, I'm sorry.' Mr. Staley winced and bit his lower lip.

"Stella, I'll write some orders for a Tetanus shot, one gram of Ancef IM one time dose, and an X-ray of his left hand with a copy made for the patient." He confirmed that the patient had no medication allergies and had had no adverse reactions to pain medications or anti-inflammatories. "Let's give Mr. Staley 60 mg of Toradol IM one time dose in the buttock of his choice and after X-rays we'll fully immobilize the thermometer. I'll call the ER in Sunnyvale and see if they have ortho on call." To the Staleys he explained, "I'm sorry but I will not be able to remove the thermometer here. I will find an Orthopedist to evaluate and remove it. We will treat and stabilize the hand so as soon as I do locate an Orthopedist I will have you on your way." Ben wrote the orders and spoke to Stella who was busy drawing up medications, "I'll be across the hall making some calls." He turned to the Staleys as he reached the ER doors, started to say something, thought better of it, nodded and walked across the hall thinking, "Next year they might consider the Butterball turkey with the pop-up thermometer."

Ben slid Salty's bedside table over, lowered it, placed the cribbage board down and unwrapped a new deck of playing cards.

Salty eyed the new deck and asked, "They give you a raise?"

Having pulled up a chair, Ben sat down and began shuffling the stiff, slick new cards. "No, just figured you've had more than enough time to mark and memorize the last deck. Ready to part with your retirement?"

"You're a bit cocky today considering you haven't beaten me yet."

"Yeah, well, even a blind squirrel occasionally finds a nut." He stuck the pegs in the starting holes and dealt out two six card hands then slapped the deck down on the table.

"All done with rounds Mr. PA?"

"Done did. I had to finish the ER paperwork since I had to refer the patient on, but all is good."

They both scanned their respective hands and discarded two cards each to make the crib. Salty cut the deck and Ben flipped over the top card. It was the Jack of Spades.

"Hah! His nobs, a good omen. Jack for two," as he pegged two holes. "When does your Green Bay game start?"

Salt studied his watch and said, "I think it might have already started."

Ben arose and walked over to the TV suspended from the wall and once turned on he skipped through the channels until the familiar green and yellow uniforms of the Packers came into view. He resumed his seat and restudied his cards. "Looks like they're playing the Lions."

Salty led with a seven. "Detroit always plays on Thanksgiving."

Ben played an eight. "Fifteen for two."

"Twenty four for three."

"Thirty for four."

"Go."

"And one."

Salty counted eight. Between Ben's hand and crib he pegged 16. "I believe your streak is ending old man."

"You need to learn some humility punk." Salty assembled the deck and began shuffling, his eyes glued to the television screen.

"You going to deal or watch TV."

Salty began dealing. "Personally, I can multi task. You though, seem more one dimensional."

Ben was arranging his cards having trouble deciding on which two to discard. "You do realize that I have access to anesthetics, needle and thread. You could wake up one morning unable to verbally harass the nurses and I would have their undying gratitude."

"Discard and cut the cards."

They could hear the surprised excitement in the commentator's voice as he announced that Detroit had just scored a touchdown and taken the lead. Salty let out an almost imperceptible groan.

"You know Ben, you've been picking my brain for the past few weeks and I've been giving up my darkest secrets. I believe that today will be tit for tat. Fifteen for two." Each played a card.

"Fire away but there is nothing too exciting or dark. Go."

"Thirty one for two. I never hear mention of girlfriend or wife."

"That's because I have neither."

"Salty displayed a devious smile. "Lack of opportunity or motivation? Fifteen two, fifteen four, fifteen six and a run for four."

"Quite frankly I've been too tied up with a new career. Hold your horses Salty, I count first."

"You can do better than that."

"Yes, actually I can. I'm pegging 12."

"I mean women wise."

"Now you can count your hand. You know Salty, I've had my share of relationships and…"

There was a knock on the open hallway door. Ben turned his head and Salty looked up from his cards to see Stella smiling at them. "Sorry to interrupt your high stakes game fellas but Ben you have an ER."

"What have we got?"

"Turkey day special. Turkey versus carver, round one."

Outside of Salty's room Ben stopped Stella. He stared back towards the nurses' station where there was flurry of voices and two nursing home residents bundled up, sitting in wheelchairs accompanied by a number of unknown faces.

"Mrs. Mueller and Mrs. Sculpaski are being picked up by their respective families for a day out."

"Good for them." He added almost wistfully, "We all need to get away from here more often." He turned back to Stella, "So what's this turkey versus carver, round one?"

"I said round one because we usually have two or three ER's on Thanksgiving where the turkey carvers get a bit tipsy, cavalier or frisky with their knives and the turkeys are a bit resistant to their advances. You get to sew them up."

"What am I walking into with this one?"

"Young man exercising his rite of passage into manhood was carving his first turkey and his father, who apparently felt the angle to be wrong or the pace too slow, attempted to intercede."

"So, we have a kid with sliced fingers."

"No. We have a dad with diced fingers thanks to the recently purchased electric carving knife."

"What about the kid?"

Ben sensed that Stella was trying to keep a straight face. "He's fine. Presently home carving the family turkey. Grandpa brought in the injured party so, I believe, he could tell the tale and rub it in."

They reached the doors and Ben held one open for Stella emergency room to enter first all the while whispering, "And that is why we revere our elders."

Salty was reclining in his bed, eyelids drooping heavily. The commentators were presenting the wrap up of the Green Bay, Detroit game. Salty startled awake, smiled at Ben and said, "You're back."

"Sorry for the delay Salty but we had round one and two, back to back ER's."

"You ready to eat? I had the aide hold our dinners until you got back."

"Yes, let's eat, I'm famished. In fact, I will run, rescue our dinners from the kitchen while you set the table and make the drinks."

Salty laughed. "No need. I've got some pull around here." He held aloft his call button and pressed it with a flourish. "Plus, if you hadn't noticed, they've already brought in an extra dining table and will serve our Thanksgiving meal with their finest china and place settings."

"Are you two gentlemen ready to eat?" It was Sydney the CNA at the doorway. Salty waved her in. She disappeared and a meal cart wheeled through the door pushed by Sally from the kitchen staff, followed by Sydney. Sally, a quiet but pleasant young woman, dwarfed Sydney in height and if positioned correctly might provide enough shade for the remaining three in the room. Ben arose and moved to help. He was abruptly and firmly stopped in his tracks by Sally's hand warning then motioned to assume his seat. Both Sally and Sydney silently and efficiently set out the meals and water glasses as Salty and Ben commented several times on how wonderful the meal looked and smelled. Finished, the two ladies started rolling the cart from the room. In unison Ben and Salty thanked the two of them profusely, Sally waving them off and Sydney nodding and producing a toothy smile as they retreated through the door.

They each had their own small dining table, a large plate of turkey, mashed potatoes laden with gravy, stuffing, carrots, Brussels sprouts and cranberry sauce. A small dish with a jiggling jello fruit salad. A small plate with dinner rolls and butter. Another small plate with a slice of pumpkin pie and a square of apple cobbler, each topped with a dollop of whipped cream.

"Brussels sprouts?"

Salty shrugged as he tucked his napkin into the neck of his gown, "They must have run out of green beans with roasted almonds."

"Maybe they thought you needed more fiber."

"Screw the fiber. It gives you gas."

"Apparently you do have some pull here. I'm very impressed with the service and table settings."

39

"I requested the Wal-Mart collection."

"I believe both Emily Post and Martha Stewart would be duly impressed, if not humbled."

Salty ignored him as he sampled the fruit salad. Ben was savoring a mouthful of turkey and potatoes but managed to relay between chews, "You throw a hell of a nice party." They busied themselves eating. Ben was aware that his dinner companion was picking more than transferring food into his mouth. No wonder he was looking gaunter these days. In between bites Ben pointed out, "Your Packers lost to the Lions 22 to 14."

"You're a real ray of sunshine Ben."

"The Cowboys and Dolphins are on next. Do you want to watch?"

Salty nibbled and continued to push food around his plate, perhaps thinking that if it were rearranged no one would notice how little he had eaten. He pushed away his dinner plate, repositioned his cobbler and spooned some whipped cream into his mouth. "Yeah, let's tune in the game. Keep the volume low so I can hear all about your lost love." He nodded his head up and down, pointing down to the cobbler with his spoon, his mouth filled with the last of the whipped cream. "Pretty damn good, you better try some."

Ben studied Salty as he alternated bites of pie and cobbler. His face appeared thinner, more tired, his eyes not quite as bright and inquisitive. He had shaved this morning, not an everyday occurrence as of late. His Adam apple more pronounced. Still sporting a sparse head of grey hair, Ben bet it had been trimmed last night with the assistance of the night aide. The octogenarian's upper body mass was waning, his arms beginning to waste, and his left upper arm USMC tattoo a bit more shriveled. He was reminded of his dad, certainly healthier then Salty, though not nearly as robust as even three to four years ago.

"So, how about we get back to the game."

"So, how about you get back to your lost love story."

"I forgot where I…"

"I've had my share of relationships and dot, dot, dot."

"This only goes to prove you lie through your teeth when you claim short term memory loss."

"Begin." He sat back into his bed pillows making himself comfortable, smugly grinning at Ben.

"Okay. So, we dated for over two years and I was beginning to think that she was a keeper, that she was the one. She worked for the state and I was even willing to move to Helena." Ben stopped and took a sip of water. "How about a cup of coffee?"

Salty picked up his call button and with the same previous flourish pressed the button. Then he gestured for Ben to continue. "So, what happened?"

"I don't think she was ready, maybe not willing to fully commit."

"That's not the whole story."

"Okay. So, I, so I was discovering she was a bit reticent to commitment. I realized that she had some control issues. She was higher maintenance then I was initially aware of. I was beginning to suspect she had higher social expectations and sometimes I had the thought she was embarrassed… of me? For me? Maybe, well, sometimes to be seen with me around her friends? I don't know, just a feeling I had once in a while. Anyway, things were going along okay and one day we get back to her place after hiking up near McDonald Pass. It was hot, a slight late afternoon breeze and she stretched out on her back on the floor of the porch, and just like that she's out like a light. I sat there looking at how relaxed, how peaceful she looked. Just the hint of a smile, maybe a smirk on her lips. Once in a while a quiet snore. Her elbows beside her on the floor, her hands flat on her belly. She looked so damn beautiful; I just couldn't take my eyes off of her. I'm not sure how…"

There was a knock at the door; Sydney the CNA. "Did you press your call light Salty?"

"Yes, young lady. Any chance you could rustle us up a couple cups of coffee?"

"Sure thing. I'll be back in a minute."

"On second thought Sydney, I'm going to pass on the coffee. Thank you anyway."

"Okay then, one cup for Salty. I'll clear your dishes when I return." Then she was gone.

Salty stretched his arms out in front of him as if doing a pushup with fingers interlocked. He adjusted himself in bed. "Please, continue."

"She woke up and saw me watching her, sat right up and asked if I had been watching her. I said yes and told her how beautiful and serene she had looked. She immediately got up and said, 'That's weird, that is just plain creepy. How long were you watching me?' I don't know, a while. She repeated, 'That's creepy.' I was definitely confused over her reaction. She demanded to know if I'd done that before and I said yes, I think so, probably, but I could not remember the exact circumstances. She went into the house and acted distant until I left for home that night."

"Did she finally figure out that it was okay, and not creepy or abnormal?"

"As a matter of fact, no. Things seemed to get more strained between us afterward and I confronted her about it.

And this is when I thought it got more than a little odd. I didn't realize that women, and from the way she revealed it, most women will periodically get together and in due course discuss their dates, relationships, quirks, sex , whatever. Sometimes one on one, sometimes in a small group."

"Some kind of informal forum?"

"I'm thinking, well, not exactly, but she told me that she had asked four of her friends about what happened and that every one of them agreed that it was weird, creepy behavior."

"Does this have Oprah's stamp of approval?"

"Christ, Salty" the sound of exasperation in Ben's voice.

"I'm sorry Ben. I don't know why I said that. I know this is serious shit for you. Sorry, go on. Did she tell you who these friends were that she consulted with?"

"All four of them."

"And you know them all?"

Ben nodded yes. "She apparently has total confidence in their opinions. That's what worried me."

"How so?"

"Well, one of them was single, works in real estate, goes to AA meetings to meet men and had been stalking one guy for a couple of years. Another one was married, four kids, held down two jobs while her unemployed husband was defining himself as an artist."

Salty just politely listened, nonplussed, no expression on his face.

"One of them was younger, worked in some state inspector's office. She had a proclivity for saturation drinking, dancing on bars and showing off her tits at the drop of a hat."

That seemed to put a small glimmer in Salty's eyes.

"The last one was married and had sworn off sex, completely frustrating her husband, and had no clue that he had been hitting on my girlfriend."

"Seriously?"

"Seriously. She had politely, but categorically refused his advances. She felt sorry for him but didn't want to spill the beans to his wife because they were best girlfriends. She had begged me not to say anything so I swore myself to secrecy."

"Jeez, so much for romance as we know it." Almost morosely Salty added, "If this is the state of romance who indeed reads or needs Blake or Byron or Shelley?"

Ben nodded silently.

"And this was your former girlfriend's relationship think tank, her love council per se?"

"Sadly, yes."

Salty suddenly and brightly asked, "So where's the rub? Sounds like a truly well rounded, high caliber, insightful group from whom to garner direction and worldly advice."

Ben stared at Salty trying not to laugh out loud. "You're an old prick, don't you know."

"I've been told."

Ben stood up. "I've got to stretch my legs but I'll be back shortly to finish our cribbage game."

"No, you won't," said Stella as a matter of fact from the door. "Sydney's here with a cup of coffee for Salty and you've got an ambulance coming in."

"Okay then, as I said, I'll be back sooner or later."

Salty motioned him over and pulled him down by the sleeve to whisper in his ear. "Keep the faith in romance Ben. Don't over think it; just listen to your heart. That's what will endure, that is what will set you apart in your medicine, your love and your life. Trust me." He reached over with his other hand and patted him on the cheek. "Now go pretend you know what you're doing and let me have my coffee."

Twilight. Red warning lights alternately flashing at the door. The wheels of the gurney spinning along linoleum tiles. Bag valve mask assistance a tad too fast. Faces of EMTs with a sense of purpose. Spousal hysterics, tears and hyperventilating not uncommon. Unresponsive patients always up the ante, and the adrenalin.

"Stella, all hands on board. Let's get vitals, IV access, bedside glucose, call lab. Hook up high flow O2 with the BVM. We'll need an EKG. I'll assess for airway management."

"Roger that."

The EMT's wheeled the gurney into the ER and ably transferred the patient to the ER gurney. Ben was approached by Zina, the EMT holding the transport clipboard ready to provide a verbal report about the patient. Zina, an attractive, raven haired Goth child in her mid-20s, had been employed at the hospital as a CNA until her makeup, wardrobe and demeanor became so unacceptable that she was given the choice of making the appropriate adjustments to maintain her job or seek employment elsewhere. She opted out of Bedlam Medical Center, currently works a couple of part time jobs in town and continues to volunteer as an EMT on the local ambulance. Today she was scrubbed clean and attired in a long sleeved shirt, black tactical pants and EMT jacket with reflective stripes.

"Hi Ben, 46-year-old male was unresponsive upon our arrival at his home. No injury or trauma. He was sitting in the living room recliner. His wife reported that he had not been breathing; however, we found a depressed, very shallow respiratory effort and a slow, near bradycardic heart rate. No history of MI or stroke. Blood pressure 106/70, heart rate 64, definitely palpable radial pulse, respirations were 8 and shallow, SaO2 was 90% on room air. The patient did not appear to be in distress. The wife was extremely agitated and emotional so it was hard to understand what she was trying to convey. We believe she was claiming to have hidden Ativan in his desert as well as in the desert of two other lethargic but responsive men who are coming in by private vehicle."

Ben looked over at the patient's wife who stood a few feet away, trembling and continuing to sob, though apparently in better control of her faculties. He looked back to Zina standing placidly amidst the numerous personnel moving quickly about the patient. "What's this about two additional patients coming in?"

"There were two other males in the living room, both sitting on a couch. Both men were lethargic but were verbally responsive to our questions. No respiratory distress and vitals were stable. Their spouses were present, however, not nearly as agitated or emotional as this patient's wife. They admitted to having served the three men apple pie laced with Ativan."

Ben shook his head incredulously. "We'll talk more about this later. You started bagging him?" Zina nodded in affirmation. "Did you try an oral airway?"

"Not tolerated, he had an intact gag reflex. His airway was open, unobstructed, no wheezing or strider, slow, shallow respirations so we decided to augment with the BVM."

"Good choice. Good report." He looked over to the EMT who continued to operate the Bag Valve Mask. "Who's the young guy bagging?"

"Dave Kelly. He's an Army Reservist who lives in town and started on the ambulance in the fall."

Ben approached Dave, introduced himself, and asked, "Dave, any resistance?"

"No sir. Good seal. Good flow. Good breaths. No gastric distention."

"Great job. Try to keep it at 12 per minute, no more than 15.

"Yes sir."

Stella was starting an IV in the patient's right arm as Allyssyn the LPN was at the patient's left side obtaining a full set of vital signs. Dave continued assisting the patients breathing with the BVM now attached to supplemental oxygen. Ben quietly asked Zina, "What is his name?"

Zina whispered, "Art Crumley."

Again quietly, "And the crying woman is his wife, Mrs. Crumley?" Zina nodded yes.

Picking up a box of facial tissues off the counter, he approached Mrs. Crumley and introduced himself. Ben spoke calmly but firmly. "I need to ask you some questions so please," he held out the box of tissues, "I need for you to take a deep breath." Her green, gold and tan ensemble was slightly disheveled, light brown bangs matted to her forehead, crying having streaked her mascara and puffed out her face. "We need direct answers so we can treat your husband quickly and appropriately. We'll sort out the details later."

"Whatever you need."

"Are you okay Mrs. Crumley?"

She nodded, dabbing her eyes with tissues, appeared to be composing herself then blurted out, "I, oh God, I'm so sorry. I never meant for this to happen."

Ben interrupted her. "We all understand that you meant your husband no harm but please, I need you to focus on my questions. Can you tell me what happened to your husband?"

"I put Ativan on his pie. I put Ativan on all of the men's deserts so they would go to sleep and we could watch a movie instead of their damn football games. Oh God I'm so sorry, I…"

"Do you have any idea how much Ativan you gave him?"

"No. But I gave him more than the others because he's bigger."

"Do you know how much he weighs?"

"He'll say 190 pounds, maybe 195, but I know it's more like 220 or 225."

"Lab's here."

Ben turned to find Sandi, the new laboratory tech standing expectantly, rocking back and forth on her feet, test tray in her hands. "Good. Sandi, I need a CBC, CMP, Cardiac Markers, ETOH and tox screen."

"Okay Mr. Parker. You want a Complete Blood Count, Complete Metabolic Panel, Cardiac Enzyme Panel, Blood Alcohol Level and a Urine Toxicology Screen. Is that correct?"

"That is correct. If you would fill out the lab sheet I'll sign it before you go. Stella, IV?"

"Yes, flushed and patent."

"Could we get a 12 lead before we administer any meds?"

"Roger that." Ben noticed Dave smile.

"How are Mr. Crumley's vitals?"

Allyssyn piped up, "Stable," then read them aloud.

"Did you say sating at 98%?"

"Yes. 98%. Bag Valve assist with 10 liters."

48

"How are you doing Dave?"

Dave looked up, "We're good here."

To no one in particular Ben addressed a continuing evaluation and treatment plan. "Dave, continue with what you're doing and report any changes. Allyssyn, vital signs and mental status check every 10 minutes, report any changes. Stella, we'll need the EKG. As soon as Sandi is done drawing labs and I review the EKG, administer Romazicon, wait…" He looked to Stella and mouthed "Romazicon, right?" "Hold on here." Ben flipped through his pocket pharmaceutical reference and confirmed the medication and dose. "Okay. Romazicon 0.2 mg IV, one time dose. It should start having effect in less than five minutes so we'll reevaluate for effect after five minutes and repeat the dose if needed. Everyone good with that?" Ben heard four separate voices and responses; "Yes, affirmative, yes Mr. Parker and roger that." Stella repeated the orders back as Ben recorded them on the ER chart.

"Ben, the other two patients are here." Sydney's head was poking around the partially open ER door.

"Thanks, Sydney. Are they upright?"

"Upright and talking."

"Good deal. Would you put them across the hall in the little ER and grab a set of vitals for each one? I'll be over there shortly."

Ben removed the otoscope from the charging cradle and grabbed his stethoscope. He completed a quick head to toe physical evaluation of Mr. Crumley. He thought to himself; outside of Mr. Crumley probably being gorked on Ativan there isn't anything jumping out at him…but let's not jump to any hard and fast conclusions. He returned to Mrs. Crumley and explained to her that for the sake of expedience he would ask some questions that would probably only require yes or no or very short answers. She voiced her understanding. He began with current medications, allergies to medications, alcohol beverages today, and tobacco use. He queried history of head injury, diabetes, heart disease, MI, stroke, lung disease, until he was satisfied with the extent of information Mrs. Crumley provided.

"Zina, you're our utility man, ah, person. You're on point to help anyone who needs it." He looked directly at Zina, his eyes shifting towards Mrs. Crumley as he mouthed, "Please keep an eye on her."

Zina replied with smile, "Aye, captain."

Ben responded with, "Make it so number one," then exited the ER trauma bay and made his way to the little ER across the hall where his other two patients were waiting with their wives. He had a fleeting thought that it would have been a hell of a lot cheaper to pay the movie rental late fee.

There was a light rap on the door and Stella stepped in handing Ben Mr. Crumley's EKG. He excused himself and joined Stella in the hallway. He reviewed the EKG and could not find anything that appeared to be an acute abnormality. There was no previous EKG for comparison.

Stella offered, "Romazicon?"

"Yes, 0.2 mg IV, one time dose. I'll be right over."

Ben returned to his current patient continuing his examination. Several minutes later there was another light rapping on the door and once again Ben joined Stella in the hallway.

"Mr. Crumley opened his eyes. His breathing has improved and his respiratory rate is now 16. We stopped bagging him and put him on a nasal cannula. He's sating at 100% on four liters. He's talking, aware of where he is and so far, has not asked for a second helping of pie."

"You, Stella, are on a roll today."

"CBC and Troponin are back and look normal. The rest of the labs should be back soon. I've got some added insight regarding the Crumleys."

"Oh, do tell."

"Mrs. Crumley finally reached the end of her all American, good natured, codependent, husband facilitating rope. That of course is me editorializing. Since their two children moved away for college and work, she has been hosting Thanksgiving Day dinner for their two best friend couples. They're all good friends and the husbands are hunting buddies. When the men are not eating, they're watching TV, monopolizing the communal television in the living room. She's been asking him and he's been promising for five years that he would buy a second TV so the women had their own entertainment source. But and this is a huge but every year he has blown the money on new hunting equipment. A duck blind, or a rifle, or new camouflage clothing or, well you get the picture. Of note; His mother passed away last spring and Mrs. Crumley cleaned out the medicine cabinet, finding and keeping a couple of medications, including as you might now have guessed, Lorazepam, unknown mg. This year when he failed to buy the TV she had had enough.

So, she devises a plan that will allow the ladies their afternoon entertainment and this morning she shares her plan with the other two women who willingly become coconspirators. After dinner the men adjourn to the living room, let out their belts, settle in to watch football and eat their desert. Usually she makes a pumpkin and an apple pie but this year only an apple pie. Why, you may ask? Because she knows they don't want it a la mode, rather they will want that Wisconsin Green Bay Packer thick slice of cheese melted on top. She grinds up a number of tablets, she can't remember how many, and sprinkles the Ativan on the pie, and covers it with cheese which she then melts per their usual request. The women serve the pie to their unsuspecting husbands and wait.

The boys zonk out; the ladies pull up some chairs and pop in their movie, the husbands never the wiser. About an hour or so into the movie one of the other wives gets up for a bathroom break and notices that Mr. Crumley does not appear to be breathing. That's when all hell broke loose and they called 911, and you know the rest of the story. "Ben..." He saw concern on her face and in her voice.

"What's wrong Stella?"

"Does anything strike you as off or odd during this whole scenario?"

"You're thinking that something must be off since there hasn't been yelling or volcanic eruptions from the husbands?"

"There you go."

Ben tried to sound hopeful. "Yeah, the thought did not elude me. I'm counting on the probability that the husbands really love their wives and, on some level, knew they've been pricks for too long. That and the calming effect of some residual sedation."

Stella nodded, "Let's keep our fingers crossed."

"And this action is based on empirical evidence?"

She glared at him. "Same basis as your lucky rabbit's foot."

He replied contritely, "Sorry, you're right, we can't predict, only hope for what might happen once they leave. I'm voting for a peaceful solution. What's your take on possible fallout?"

Stella grinned recognizing he was attempting to appease her. "Call me crazy, maybe a closet romantic but I'd like to agree with you on this one."

"I need to mark this day down."

"You just can't help yourself, can you?" Stella stood expressionless.

Ben was weighing the intent of her response as either exasperation or silently laughing though begrudgingly resigned. He chose the latter. Now the question was should he let this lie, respond in defense, or press his luck? He silently shook his head, gravely looking past Stella, pondering the situation. "What do you think the chances are now for the second TV?" Stella punched him in the shoulder, called him a dork, but before she could flee he responded with, "Was it a chick flick or a good shoot-em-up?"

"You, Ben Parker, are incorrigible."

In the trauma bay Ben introduced himself to Mr. Crumley and ordered a liter of Normal saline started. He reassessed the patient, found no focal neurological deficits and found the patient to be much improved in all aspects. The lab results arrived, positive for Benzodiazepines confirming the Ativan that Mrs. Crumley had reported, and a level of alcohol one might expect to see after two or three beers consumed several hours earlier. All the other lab results were normal. Ben explained to the Crumleys that he would not be ordering additional Romazicon to reverse the effects of the Ativan. He was recommending Mr. Crumley remain on supplemental oxygen, receive a liter of fluid and be monitored for the next couple of hours before considering discharge home or overnight observation. Mr. Crumley said he understood but was adamant that he would be going home after the fluid was in. Period. No further discussion. Ben smiled and said, "Let's see how you are after the fluids."

He wrote orders for Mr. Crumley, advised Mrs. Crumley to consider catching a ride home with the other couples so she could retrieve their family vehicle. Both Ben and Stella assured her that Mr. Crumley was stable and improving; it might be a good opportunity for her to take a few minutes for herself before returning. Ben finished up in the little ER, discharging the other two patients into the care of their highly apologetic wives who voiced their gratitude that their husbands were alright, as one voiced, "no worse for wear." They agreed to drive Mrs. Crumley home and stay with her until she returned to the hospital. Ben took a quick stroll down to Salty's room, his friend snoring peacefully as the Cowboys were losing to the Dolphins. He turned off the TV and was about to douse the lights as he spied the cribbage board on Salty's bedside nightstand. Finding Salty's mail pile on the bureau, Ben plucked out an empty envelope. On the back he wrote, "Does falling asleep constitute surrender?" He removed a cribbage peg, placed the envelope on the board and punched the peg through to anchor it down. That should stir the pot he thought as he doused the lights and closed the door behind him.

Karmma Mason, the night nurse appeared in the open doorway of the ER office. "Knock, knock."

Head and shoulders bowed, Ben sat in his chair deep into fatigue induced sleep and snapped awake immediately attempting to orient himself.

"Do they pay you to sleep on duty Mr. Parker?"

Still a bit groggy, Ben found himself lacking a quick retort. "What's up?"

"Mr. Crumley. Fluid is finished. Vital signs are stable. Neuro and mentation are good. Mrs. Crumley is bedside and he is chomping at the bit to go home."

Picking up the discharge orders he had written prior to falling asleep 20 minutes ago, he handed them over to Karmma. "Let's go see the Crumleys."

In the emergency room, Karmma disconnected and removed the IV access as Ben evaluated Mr. Crumley. He reviewed a last set of vital signs, observed his patient standing and taking a few steps and pronounced Mr. Crumley "good to go." They shook hands and Mrs. Crumley jumped up giving Ben a big hug and thank you. Karmma reviewed the discharge orders with the couple, providing them a copy, and the Crumleys filed out of the ER doors.

Ben peeked around an ER door and watched as the couple embraced in the hallway. "I'm so sorry Art, can you ever forgive me?"

"No, no, no it's my fault honey. I've been a selfish ass. I'm so sorry, can you forgive ME?" She was weeping and he wiped her tear with his thumb. "I'm going to Wynot tomorrow and buying you that new TV. I promise no new hunting gear for at least a year."

They hugged each other again until Mrs. Crumley said, "Zip up your pants and lets go home."

Ben continued to watch as they walked side by side to the exit doors, her index finger finding a rear belt loop, her thumb hooked over the top of his pants, gently tugging them up. His hand giving her derriere a gentle pat, then settling in the small of her back. He held the door open for her as they exited. Ben quietly walked out into the hallway staring out the exit doors thinking, "By God, there is still a flicker of life left in romance."

Ben sat in the quiet darkness of his office staring at the two small packages lying on his desk. When he had entered the hospital earlier the dim lighting of the clinic hallway had stood in stark contrast to the Saturday morning sun reflecting off the overnight coating of new snow in town. He had purposefully left the overhead light off in the office and found the subdued effect of indirect lighting from the hallway relaxing, almost soothing. Although he had been afforded an unusual seven hours of uninterrupted sleep he continued to feel sleep deprived and was hoping, though unrealistically, that the day would be relatively slow, maybe providing time for a short afternoon nap. Then again, he thought that he would definitely have a better chance of contracting a tropical disease here in sub-arctic Montana.

With great dexterity, an almost delicate touch, Ben began the process of peeling away the wrapping on one of the small packages. After several attempts to separate a tightly sealed seam he then rotated the package to tackle one end by separating the wrapping with a deft tearing motion. It would not yield and the more he struggled the greater his frustration until he finally clenched the edge of the cellophane in his teeth and almost vehemently ripped open the packaging spilling one of the Twinkies which, now teetered precariously on his left knee. He quickly rescued his Hostess prize before it fell to the floor and then found himself looking to his doorway with guilty pleasure.

He had finally admitted to himself that over time he had begun to secretly covet Tara's confectionary temptations. Today, when purchasing a newspaper at the Bedlam One Stop he had succumbed to the colorful display of empty calorie, preservative laced snack cakes, fully aware that they would provide relatively little nourishment and short lived satisfaction. Yet, after a short internal struggle weighted heavily towards denying him this one time spontaneous lapse of judgment, purchase them he did and then smuggled them into the hospital within the pockets of his bulky winter coat. Bringing the blond, cream filled confection to his mouth he suddenly had a vision of Harmon Krum inhaling Hostess products while driving his black Suburban, chocolate smudges on his fingers and steering wheel, vestiges of cream filling dried at the corner of his lips and a variety of cake crumbs anointing his lap. Ben's hand abruptly stopped, poised in midair, he found himself once again having a strong reservation. Then rationalizing that he, Ben Parker, was nothing like Krum, that just this once he could indulge himself and no one, especially Krum would be any the wiser. His was not a weakness, not a character flaw, merely an exercise in curiosity, and with that thought in mind took a bite of the Twinkie, attempting to savor what millions had tasted before.

He was about to take his second bite when his desk phone rang. He let it ring several times before answering; hoping that it did would not involve the emergency room. "Hello, this is Ben."

"Did I interrupt you from doing something that you may have regretted doing?" It was Stella.

He experienced a flash of paranoia as he thought, "Had she seen him earlier at the convenience store," but immediately realized that she could not have left the hospital without another RN being on the premises. "No, but if you have any suggestions I will take them under advisement. What's up?"

"Tara just fielded a call from a gentleman who wanted to know which provider was on call and dutifully followed protocol telling him that it was hospital policy not to divulge the provider's name but assured him that a skilled provider would see him in the emergency room. She said that he had attempted to schmooze her but to her credit, she held her ground. Then he asked to have medication for his gout dispensed without an ER visit. Tara told him that she believed that the provider would insist on seeing him before prescribing anything. Now he began, in her words, "getting pissy" and claimed that he was a long time patient of Dr. Saroni, that in the past the doctor had dispensed medication without a visit and would probably be greatly displeased if he knew that one of his patients was being treated this way. Tara must have her big girl pants on today because she didn't back down telling him politely, she says, that he would have to come in to the emergency room."

"Is he coming in?"

"Couldn't say for sure. Tara says that he mumbled something that rhymed with witch and hung up."

"We are known for our exemplary clientele. Who was it?"

"He didn't say. I'll let you know if he shows up."

"Thanks. I'll be out there shortly to do rounds."

"No rush, finish what you're up to even if we wouldn't approve. Bye."

Ben knew that Stella didn't have a clue but certainly had his number. He stared at the partially consumed Twinkie and its twin lying on his desktop. Somehow, they did not hold the same unexplainable allure of just several minutes ago. He considered wrapping them in some paper towels to disguise them, disposing of them in the biohazard container in the ER, no one any the wiser. Without hesitation he quickly consumed the Twinkies and thought "they're not so bad." Secreting the package of cupcakes in the very back of the bottom right draw of his desk, he them submerged the Twinkie packaging at the bottom of his trash basket confident that his onetime indulgence would remain his secret, alone.

At the nurses' station he was greeted by Tara who held several emergency room records in one hand and a partially eaten caramel, fudge nut bar in the other. Ben held his tongue, refraining from applauding her choice of adding protein to her diet, considering the poor food selection that he had just consumed. Stella, in her stealth mode, appeared unexpectedly at his right with what appeared to be a clinic chart.

"Any word from out mystery caller?"

"As a matter of fact, yes. He called back shortly after you and I talked, asked Tara for her supervisor and I had the privilege of listening to his demands, then his whining sense of entitlement and finally his verbal assault upon my nursing and administrative credentials."

"I take it that he will not be coming in."

"Au contraire, mon frère. I told him flat out that he would have to be seen in the emergency room, and paraphrased our hallway sign outlining that at a Critical Access Hospital Emergency Room he could not be turned away and is entitled to be evaluated by a medical provider. I did add, however, that the posted sign does not assure that he would receive dispensed medications." With a hint of self-satisfaction Stella continued, "And on a personal note I interjected that were he to impugn my integrity or disparage my credentials again, I would make his hospital visit an extremely drawn out affair and unforgettable experience. He apologized and said that he would be coming in shortly; apparently, he's worried about missing some televised football game. We took the liberty of pulling his charts. He has not darkened our hospital or clinic doors for the past three and one half years."

Ben looked back and forth from Stella to Tara expectantly waiting for them to disclose their mystery caller.

Tara, with an unmistakable look of distain announced, "Harmon Krum is our mystery caller."

Ben could not quell his reaction when he closed his eyes, bowed his head and quietly breathed, "Of course it is."

Stella looked at him, concerned. "Ben, are you okay? You look a little pale."

"Yes," he said resignedly, "Just something I ate."

Ben had positioned himself by the emergency room doors waiting to see if either of the two scenarios he projected would come to fruition. The first, and most preferable was Krum opts not to come to the ER, the second, Krum enters the hallway outside the ER, spies Ben, realizes that Ben is the provider on call, promptly turns on his heel and leaves. In either scenario, Krum returns home, suffers through his football game, and then drives to another town's ER for treatment, thus releasing Ben from the odious duty of spending time with the giant blue Smurf.

Stella joined him at the door. "Any sign of him?"

"Not so far." Ben chose not to editorialize further.

A large black vehicle, possibly a Suburban, pulled up onto the concrete apron and stopped. Two large figures, the driver and front seat passenger, emerged. The intense autumn sunlight reflected off the vehicle and the entranceway glass hampering their view of the two people approaching. As the two figures entered the hospital doors the obscuring glare lessened and Ben instantly identified the lumbering man in the lead as Harmon Krum Jr., clad in his usual all black ensemble. Ben heard a sudden intake of breath by Stella as they both witnessed an apparition appearing from out of the sun's glare; a corpulent visage, dressed from head to toe in Kelly green. Kelly green stocking cap with insignia, Kelly green long sleeved sweatshirt and matching sweatpants both with insignia, green socks and green sneakers, which might very well have comfortably fit a yeti. Green tinted sunglasses shaded his eyes. A chronic alcoholic who has endured the hallucinations of withdrawal might conclude that they were experiencing a flashback; a sane and sober individual might fanaticize that this is what a hallucination might look like. Ben realized that the ND insignia did not represent North Dakota, rather the University of Notre Dame, and this was not a mutant Kermit the Frog but a limping, immensely disproportionately sized facsimile of the leprechaun mascot. Krum's dower expression was punctuated by grimaces as he placed his ample weight upon his right leg. Obviously, happiness and good health were not synonymous with color coordination.

Ben whispered out through the side of his mouth, "This would make Knute Rochne whimper like a little girl."

Stella elbowed him in the ribs before moving forward, introduced herself to Krum and Krum Jr., and escorted them into the emergency room. Krum did not acknowledge Ben as he passed but Ben observed Krum diverting his eyes away as a sign of recognition. Krum Jr. walking in lock step followed his father in. Ben walked over to the office across the hall, checked the lab and X-ray call sheet and called both technicians alerting them that their services would be needed. When Ben entered the ER Krum was seated on the side of the gurney in Bay One as Krum Jr. announced that he was leaving in search of a vending machine for something to eat, purposely brushing into Ben's shoulder as he exited the ER. Stella was unwrapping an extra-large blood pressure cuff from around Krum's bared left upper arm, his sunglasses gone, his green sweatshirt off and a Kelly green T-shirt unable to contain his abdominal girth.

"I checked his blood pressure in the right arm and got 106/72, seemed a little low so I checked the left arm and registered 108/72. He took his Losartan and HCTZ this morning. Heart rate of 104, SaO2 is 88% on room air, respirations of 18 and temperature of 97.6." She looked a bit concerned and perplexed at the same time. "He takes Nexium, Synthroid and has been gobbling ibuprofen for the past week. Approximately 10 days ago he went to a Doc-in-the-box in Sunnvale and was diagnosed with bronchitis. They prescribed a Z-Pak and Albuterol inhaler."

"Look, do we have to go through all this mumbo-jumbo? I came in because I got the gout in my right knee. All I need is some of that inflammatory medicine and I'll be good." Krum looked directly at Ben and glowered. He slowly emphasized his next words, "I...do...not...intend...on...missing...the...football game." Then with a loud, angry snarl, "Let's get a move on." His jowls quivered. Krum's pasty complexion had turned paler as he broke into a coughing fit which, caused him to be short of breath. Stella had quietly attached oxygen mask tubing to the wall outlet and held up the mask for Ben to see.

In a calm but firm voice Ben looked Krum in the eye and began speaking, "Mr. Krum, I understand your desire to return home, however, I believe that you are more ill than you might realize. Please allow me to ask some questions and examine you so we can figure out what's going on and how to treat it. Your oxygen level is low so if you will allow us to we'll give you some oxygen through the mask that Stella is holding. It should make you feel a bit better as we continue your exam." Krum had stopped coughing, appeared physically spent and silently nodded his head "yes." Stella applied the mask and told Krum to breathe in and out with normal breaths.

"I know that you were recently treated for bronchitis Mr. Krum; would you say that you improved on the medications, remained the same or worsened?"

Krum appeared to be thinking, undecided, then said, the mask muffling his voice, "No, not really any improvement."

"Are you a smoker?"

Krum shook his head, no.

"Does your chest hurt? Any pain?"

Krum nodded, yes. He reached up and pulled the mask away with his right hand. "Here on the right side," he said as his left hand rubbed the upper and mid-right side of his chest.

"Steady or intermittent?"

"Steady."

Ben pointed to a pain chart on the wall, describing levels of pain with a corresponding number. "What is your level of pain on a scale of 1 to 10, 10 being the worst pain you have experienced in your life?"

Krum studied the chart, shrugged his shoulders and said, "I don't know, maybe a six, no a seven."

"Does it hurt more when you cough?"

Krum thought for a minute, "No, it's been steady and getting worse the past two or three days."

"I'm going to examine your leg in a minute but first let me listen to your heart and lungs." Ben began listening with his stethoscope, first listening to Krum's heart and then his lung fields, front and back, instructing Krum to take a deep breath with each new position. When he was finished Stella repositioned the oxygen mask, centering it on Krum's face. Ben looked at Stella, "No wheezes or rhonchi, maybe some crackles but that might be a reach. The bases seem diminished, right more so than left. I've got to consider pneumonia, so let's figure on some labs and a chest X-ray, PA and lateral." Krum's demeanor appeared to have slightly relaxed and his complexion not quite as pale. Stella checked his oxygen level with the finger monitor and Ben saw a 91% displayed. At 10 liters of oxygen flowing through the mask he thought "not much of an improvement."

Ben began asking Krum a series of questions regarding his right knee and his history of gout. He learned that Krum had had gout attacks for 8 to 10 years, usually in his big toes, occasionally in his ankles and once in his left knee. His right knee had begun to ache a couple of weeks ago and had become worse over the past several days. He thought at first that he may have pulled a muscle in his calf slipping on some ice, but a few days later, when it began hurting behind his knee he suspected the gout. The pain had continued to worsen in both his calf and knee, admittedly not quite the pain symptoms of the gout attack of his left knee. Ben bent down, kneeling on his right knee, removed Krum's sneakers and socks, immediately regretting not having put on the exam gloves. He could see Stella smirking as she pulled a pair from the wall mounted glove dispenser and handed them to him. He said thank you avoiding her grin. With some difficulty he pulled the green sweat pants up over both knees. Now gloved, he examined Krum's lower legs and found that the right mid and upper calf to be significantly warmer than the left. He palpated the right calf with moderate pressure and Krum pulled away. Ben apologized yet continued, Krum admitting to more than uncomfortable tenderness extending up behind the knee to the lower thigh. Ben grasped Krum's right forefoot bending the foot upwards from the ankle.

"Jesus, that hurts." Krum was grimacing.

"Where?"

"My calf and behind my knee."

Ben continued the examination and completed it by checking Krum's ankle and foot pulses. As he arose he noticed Sandi, the laboratory technician had arrived and was standing next to Stella. He said a good morning. Krum Jr. reentered the ER holding a cup of coffee, Ben recognizing that the mug came from the nurses' station private stash. He wondered briefly if Tara knew that it was missing; the staff was very protective of their personal property. The young man's combination lumbering saunter was something that Ben knew he couldn't begin to mimic. That black clothing seemed only to embellish an apparent black mood.

Krum Junior loudly said to apparently no one in particular, "We about done here? I need to get going, it's the next to last day to shoot something." He was flipping a cigarette between the index and middle finger of his coffee free hand.

"Put a sock in it Junior, and please take your coffee and cigarettes outside." Stella apparently hadn't warmed to Krum Junior and Ben couldn't help from smiling, quickly assuming facial neutrality before returning to the case at hand. Junior lumbered without the saunter out the ER doors, tail dragging.

"Mr. Krum, besides your slip on the ice and a possible strained calf muscle, have you had any other recent injury or trauma? Recent surgeries? Recent travel where you sat for extended periods of time without stretching or walking?"

Krum was slumped forward staring at his lap as he shook his head "no." Ben suddenly remembered the news article in the local paper about Krum's travels to Germany.

"Mr. Krum, did you travel to Germany in the last few weeks?"

His head shot up to attention, suspicion in his eyes. "How would you know that?"

"It was on the front page of the Bedlam paper."

"Oh jeez, that's right...yeah, me and the missus traveled to New Jersey on business, then to Germany for Oktoberfest, and then we toured Europe for a few weeks. We got home, oh, a little over two weeks ago."

"Sandi, I need to order some labs but I'm wondering, did you ever get set up to do D-Dimers yet?"

"No. We're still waiting for administration to give us the go ahead and allocate the money."

Ben was now gloveless and Stella handed him the chart. "X-ray is ready when you are."

He wrote down the labs he wanted along with the X-ray order.

'Mr. Krum, I do not believe that you are having a flare of your gout. We need to get some lab tests and a chest X-ray because I'm very suspicious of a DVT or blood clot in your right leg and I'm also worried that your bronchitis may have progressed to pneumonia. At any rate, you will need a Doppler ultrasound of your right leg to determine if you have a clot and how extensive it is. Do you have a preference as to where we send you for the testing? Sunnvale or Wynot are the closest choices."

Krum looked almost apoplectic. "What? And miss the game? You need to do this later. Tell you what, I'll go home, watch the game and then I'll come back for the tests or go wherever you want me to go."

Ben responded to this outburst head on. "Mr. Krum, you need to have these tests done ASAP. You are very ill and we need to act now, waiting may only worsen your condition."

Expecting another postponement plea, another denial over the seriousness of the situation, Ben was surprised when Krum suddenly related, "Okay, okay, let's get this done. I feel like shit so okay, I'll go to Sunnvale."

Ben walked across the hall to the office and dialed up the Sunnvale Hospital Emergency Room. He waited as the receptionist transferred him to Dr. Stokes, the ER Physician. "Hello Dr. Stokes, I'm Ben Parker the physician assistant at Bedlam Medical Center...No, Dr. Saroni is out of town until Monday...Yes sir...thank you for taking my call." Ben presented his patient's demographics, pertinent medical history, and signs and symptoms as briefly and concisely as possible. "Yes, Dr. Stokes...I'm suspicious of a right lower leg DVT and pneumonia...No, unfortunately we don't have D-Dimer available...He's probably on his way or in X-ray as we speak...No, we do not have a Cat Scan...Yes, we do...yes, he's aware that he needs additional imaging...I believe Lovenox is one mg per kilogram...Okay, we'll start with the Lovenox, get him loaded up and headed in your direction...I'll fax the labs and ER notes.........Yes, Thank you Dr. Stokes...Yes sir, goodbye." Ben hung up.

Back in the ER, Ben reviewed Krum's chart, found the stated weight, and wrote an order to administer Lovenox, a clot dissolving medication, then handed the chart back to Stella. "I called dispatch to page the ambulance for a transfer to Sunnvale." Stella raised her eyes in question. "He needs a chest CT as well. He may very well have a pulmonary embolus rather than pneumonia."

"Oh, that makes sense. Good pick up Ben."

"No, not me. It was staring me in the face and I missed it completely. It was Dr. Stokes who clued me in. Potential Deep Vein Thrombosis, elevated heart rate, dropping blood pressure, chest pain, lung sounds, and oxygen levels; all the signs were there and though they weren't adding up PE didn't cross my mind."

"Don't beat yourself up Ben, you called for the consult, Dr. Stokes walked you through it and now we'll get Krum where he needs to be."

Ben did not look convinced but accepted her rationalization. "I'll look over the labs when they arrive and make copies. In the interim, since you have established a warm and fuzzy relationship with him, would you round up Krum Junior so we can bring him up to speed? When Krum gets back from X-ray I'll fill him in if you would administer the Lovenox."

"You can be such a smartass sometimes, and then on occasion trump that with 'prick,' but that is only one person's observation." Stella was not able to keep a straight face.

"Sorry."

"No, you're not."

"Is this when you lecture me with that old saying, "Familiarity breeds contempt?"

"No need. You and I both crossed that line months ago. Now it wouldn't feel right if we attempted to revert back to civility and political correctness."

They were both laughing as Sandi delivered the lab results, asking if they would need anything else. Both Stella and Ben said "no, but thank you," so Sandi left apparently not feeling the need to question the reason for their good humor.

"Thanks for the good words and having my back." Ben was sincere.

Stella smiled and headed out to locate Black Bart, alias Krum Junior.

Ben and Stella stood just inside the entrance way doors as John Bersted, one of the EMT's on Krum's transfer, folded up the step at the back of the ambulance and closed the rear doors. He turned to face them, grinned expansively as he gave a slight bow before walking to the side door of the ambulance and climbed in. A minute later the ambulance pulled off the apron, Krum secured to the gurney, paperwork on board, a 45-minute trip to the Sunnvale Hospital Emergency Room, dependent on road conditions. John had talked briefly with Ben relating that his sister Paula was in Houston, but still intended on having him over for dinner one of these fine days. He reported that his mother's cancer had returned and Paula accompanied her to Houston while she was receiving treatment. Ben expressed his best wishes and prayers to John and asked him to please share them with Paula, "Providing me with a free meal should be the least of her worries." They shook hands and John returned to attending to Krum.

"Good job Ben."

"Back atcha Stella."

"Ready to do hospital rounds?"

"I was hoping that you had done them for me."

"Yeah, right. It won't take too long and then you can grab something to eat."

"Let me finish my notes and fax them to Dr. Stokes, then we can do rounds, and then I'm heading home for a nap. Perhaps later, I might turn on the Notre Dame, Stanford game since they're playing on the West coast."

"You are a Notre Dame fan?"

"No, but I thought I'd be kind to Krum. Actually, I'll probably tune in the Bobcat game tonight; they have a playoff game with Northern Iowa."

"You're a true mensch Ben Parker."

"I could have sworn I spied a crucifix dangling from your neck Stella."

"I'm fluent in several languages. Finish up your notes and I'll meet you at the nurses' station."

"Sounds like a plan, and Stella thanks, Harmon Krum is not the most pleasant individual to deal with."

"You two have a history?"

"Unfortunately, but I'm not going to share right now."

"You are a man of mystery, of many secrets I'll bet." Then Stella leaned in and in a conspiratorial voice said, "Like your affinity for Hostess Twinkies."

Ben's mouth literally dropped open, his eyes almost bug-eyed in surprise. "What do you mean?" Then realizing that he couldn't deny or sidestep her comment he resignedly said, "How did you know?"

"You know that little white piece of cardboard that the Twinkies are usually stuck to in the wrapper?" Ben nodded, trying desperately to remember if he had hidden it in the bottom of his wastebasket. "It was stuck to the heel of your shoe when you first came out to the nurses' station."

Ben knew he had been caught red handed. "You got me." He produced a sheepish smile, "Our little secret?"

"My lips are sealed, but next time you might consider bringing a package in for me."

PAUL REUBENS TO GO

"Home in one piece but you may have missed your *Lawrence Welk Show*." Marni managed a sliding stop in the alley, precariously short of rearranging the corner of Ben's garage.

"Four hundred and fifty miles of blowing snow and icy roads, with you behind the wheel is more adventure than one man should be allowed to have."

She turned to face him, the left side of her face starkly illuminated by the headlights reflecting off his white garage door. "You will be eternally thankful at your next trauma that I hauled your ungrateful ass to Fargo for ATLS training."

"The problem with Advanced Trauma Life Support is that you can't perform it on yourself after your driver puts you upside down and catty-wampus in the interstate median."

"That is why, my friend, that you wear seatbelts and put your faith in the hands of a higher power." Ben could see a slightly twisted smile belying the innocent concern in her voice. "Look at you Ben, your color is already returning to normal."

He had his thermos in hand, a Navy watch cap warming his head, gloves in his lap as he scanned the passenger side floor.

She was studying him. "Got everything?"

71

Sitting back upright in the seat he stared out through the windshield at the falling snow beginning to dissipate. "I believe so. Looks like the snow is letting up."

"Good course, huh?"

"Excellent. Well worth the bullshit it took to get everything arranged to go." He looked to see if Marni was still watching him. "Saroni was not a willing participant in all of this. Remember he stonewalled me for months about trading weekends."

"Yeah, but he did relent, you have to give him that."

"Surprising as it may seem, after he agreed to trade he was unusually accommodating and helpful, almost pleasant the whole month of November, and now it's the second week of December. This behavior is highly abnormal for him so somehow I think that he has something in store for me." He attempted and failed miserably at a Danish accent, "Fie, I say, something smells rotten in the state of Denmark."

Marni responded lightly, "Oh ye of little faith, though you never can be sure about him. You know that he just signed a new three year contract on Wednesday?"

"No. No, I had no clue."

"Yep, he'd been negotiating with the Hospital Board for the past six, maybe eight weeks, and from what my sources say it was a plum deal."

"Your sources?"

Sounding a bit offended Marni continued, "Yes, I have sources. Pretty damn good sources if you need to know."

"Care to share?"

"Carol Whitlow for one," with some attitude.

"And Carol Whitlow is…?"

"The wife of the Hospital Board chairman."

"The hell you say. You do have sources." Ben could see a smug look on her face, "You know that all of this gives Saroni more leverage."

"Yes, it does. It's easier to find pigs flying out of someone's butt then to entice a new doctor to these parts. I think the board was deathly afraid that he'd leave if he didn't get what he wanted."

"I'm not sure if Saroni is purposefully malicious, unaware of how inappropriate his actions are, or what would be most disturbing, a grand manipulator with sociopathic tendencies."

"My vote is outright narcissist."

"You're probably right." Ben began to open his door and involuntarily shivered as he was met with a blast of frigid air. He climbed out and gingerly secured his footing on the icy alleyway. He released the lock and hinged the seat forward to access his coat. "If the past six or so weeks were a demonstration of model behavior to secure his financial future, then I would expect him to revert back to his usual behavior patterns in the very near future."

"Ben, it sounds like your treading on the brink of paranoia."

With his coat now on he grasped the handle of his overnight bag, "Just because you're paranoid doesn't mean that someone isn't after you. You want to come in for some coffee or something hot?"

Marni laughed, "Be prepared is the scout motto. Thanks, but I better get home before Michael thinks that I've abandoned him."

"Thanks for everything Marni. I'll see you on Wednesday."

"You bet. Good night."

Inside Ben dropped his travel bag in the living room, flipped on the floor lamp and turned on the television. Back in the kitchen he stooped slightly, peering into the open refrigerator and reached in for a bottle of beer. As he was closing the refrigerator door his land line rang.

"Hello."

"Hello, Ben. It's Becca at the hospital."

"Yes Becca, I recognized your voice." What now? They can't need me tonight. "What's up?"

"Well I, ahh, I need to, ahh…please Ben, don't kill the messenger."

Ben detected a sincere apologetic pleading in her voice. It can't be that bad he thought. "There is no murder in my heart, at least at the moment. What's going on?"

"Dr. Saroni called in and said that he has the flu. He'd like you to cover his weekend call until he's feeling better."

And now the shoe has dropped.

"How long ago did he call?"

"Two hours ago, and his wife has been calling every 15 minutes to confirm that we got hold of you."

Persistent when she wants to be. "I guess that I can't very well say no so if you would give them a call and tell them that I have his call covered I'd be very appreciative."

"Sorry Ben. Thank you."

Not as sorry as I am. "It's okay Becca, I'm too tired to kill anyone. Goodbye."

He hung up the phone, replaced his beer in the refrigerator, grabbed a can of pop and trundled off to the living room, cursing Saroni and amazed that the Lawrence Welk Show was still being aired.

Ben was pulling on his blue jeans grumbling, "so much for a night away from the emergency room." He had hoped for a night of blissful slumber, to be punctuated only by the sound of his alarm at 6:30 in the morning. Whoever said, "Sleep is overrated, that there would plenty when you were dead," had apparently never covered emergency room calls in rural Montana.

Once in his truck he had realized another skiff of snow had fallen since he had gone to bed, the icy roads more treacherous to navigate. Subsequently the intense ache in his right buttock and elbow proof positive that footing in the hospital parking lot was just as compromised.

The overhead lighting of the nursing station was dimmed after the residents went to bed and as he approached he found it to be unattended. He was limping slightly as he reached the counter. Midway down the darkened north resident hall a vertical shaft of light shone across the hallway, otherwise the hallways of the hospital were either dimmed or dark. He entered the nursing station, knowing that there was a bottle of ibuprofen in one of the drawers. A partially eaten, now cold, supper sat in its plastic tray, the packaging setting alongside indicating that someone was attempting to lose weight with a pre-packaged diet meal plan. Ben, having out of curiosity once sampled a similar product, had determined that the cardboard packaging probably tasted better and provided more nourishment.

A personal disc player close by the half eaten meal continued to play a movie and Ben stood staring at the screen for a short span, found the power button and shut it off. He located the ibuprofen, shook out three tablets and swallowed them with water from the supply room sink, aggravating his now moderately throbbing elbow. Favoring his right leg, he walked down the hallway towards the doorway emitting light. He could hear quiet voices inside that room and knocked lightly on the partially open door. A few seconds later Becca, the night nurse that had wrested him from his sleep, fully opened the door. Tonight, he noticed, her hair tint and eye makeup appeared to have a sepia tone. He wondered if she knew that sepia was Greek for cuttlefish, trivia that he had no memory of ever having heard. "Hello Ben, come on in."

Ben entered; saw Sheena the CNA sitting alongside Mrs. Betty Schtupe on the side of her bed. Dressed in her dark green flannel night gown, Mrs. Schtupe was staring down at her malformed, discolored toenails, wiggling her toes as she slowly and alternately swung her feet in and out. Mrs. Schtupe, who had her hair done every Wednesday when one of the local cosmetologists from town donated their time and expertise, looked disheveled, her hair in disarray. A bulky, protective Kerlix bandage was wrapped midway down her right forearm.

Becca began her report, "Mrs. Schtupe apparently started getting out of bed and had a fall. She did not press her call button for assistance, something she is normally good at remembering to do. We found her sitting by the side of her bed. The only visible injury is a skin tear on her right arm, which, we cleaned up, applied a Tegaderm and a Kerlix dressing. No fever and vital signs are stable. She seemed a little confused but as I said no visible signs of head injury. We performed a quick head to toe, helped her to her feet and were able to obtain a urine sample. Urine dip indicated probable UTI. I checked her chart and she is allergic to Sulfa."

"Of course she is. Was there anything in the day shift notes mentioning confusion, incontinence, urine odor or increased frequency? Any thoughts leaning towards a urinary tract infection?"

"Not that I could find. She has had UTI's in the past with slight confusion but I thought you would want to check her out and make sure she was safe to be put back to bed."

Ben introduced himself, once again, to Mrs. Schtupe, asked her a few questions to establish her mental acuity, receiving short, and only two times rather vague replies. He stifled a laugh when she named the present president "Bushwhacker." A concise, head to toe exam was performed and he borrowed Becca's stethoscope to listen to Mrs. Schtupe's heart and lungs. As he thanked her for her patience she smiled weakly and asked, "Can I go back to sleep now?"

"You sure can Mrs. Schtupe. Sheena will help get you settled in." Sheena nodded and stood as Ben said a quiet "Thank you." To Mrs. Schtupe, "If you need anything else Mrs. Schtupe just let us know by pressing the call button." She looked around the bed, found the cord, followed it to the button, held it up in her hand and smiled.

Ben and Becca started for the doorway and stopped just outside in the hallway. "I'm thinking Nitrofurantoin, a Urinalysis and to promote oral hydration."

"Would you like me to write it up so you can go home and sign off in the morning?"

"No, but thanks. I'm already here so I'll write up the treatment and lab orders. I'll add a culture to the Urinalysis."

They started down the hallway and Ben realized that the ibuprofen was taking the edge off of his elbow and buttock discomfort. "Sooo, Becca, when I got here I saw something interesting at the nurses' station."

Becca stopped. "Such as…?" she questioned.

"There was a large black man wearing nothing but a tool belt vigorously fornicating with a petite white woman who was bent forward over the edge of what appeared to be a kitchen sink."

Becca blanched near white, "Oh, shit. I must have forgotten to shut it off. Oh, Christ, I am sorry."

Ben was laughing, more loudly than intended, "I had no clue the hospital provided such late night entertainment." He was slowly walking backwards towards the nurses' station, turned to walk forwards and motioned with a wave of his arm for Becca to follow. She quickened her pace and caught up.

"Really Ben, I'm sorry. There's normally no one up this late and…" she paused, "I was wrong to bring it in. It won't happen again."

"Becca, no harm, no foul, but for your own sake keep them out of the hospital. You never know who might wander in or for that matter someone you work with might be offended and report you."

They arrived at the nurses' station, Ben taking a seat to enter into Mrs. Schtupe's chart and Becca removing the disc from her disc player, then snapping it shut in a disc case that she produced from her handbag.

"Becca, could I see that for a second?" She handed the case over to him. He read, "The Plumber's Snake, A Cautionary Tail," the cover was otherwise blank except for the words, "Rental, Contains Anti-Theft and Copy ware." "Out of curiosity, where do you rent porn in this county?"

"Adult Entertainment, not porn." She momentarily clenched her lower lip between her teeth. "That's not a very well-known secret."

"That is the point of a secret, isn't it?"

"Well, yes, you've got a point there."

"So where is this secret porn, er, Adult Entertainment rental outlet?"

She rolled her chair closer and in a near whisper said, "You didn't get this from me but... Susie's Sandwich Shop."

"Jeezzz, Becca, don't make such a big deal out of it. Almost every nurse and aid in here rents adult movies at Suzie's." Sheena's quiet return to the north counter of the nurses' station had gone unnoticed. Becca stared at her with a glare that would pierce armored plate. Sheena continued, "If you want to rent an adult movie you go up to the order counter and say, "I want a Paul Reubens to go."

"A what?"

"A Paul Reubens to go. Remember to say it just that way and someone will show you to the secret room behind the regular videos."

Ben burst out laughing, "You have got to be kidding me. Right? A Paul Reubens to go at Susie's? "Holy crap, I never would have guessed."

Becca was still shooting daggers at Sheena but added, "Neither did I until I went in the first time, but that is the password." Sheena went scuttling off down the west nursing home corridor.

"How damn appropriate is that?"

"What do you mean?"

"Do you know who Paul Ruebens is?"

"Some porn star I suppose."

Ben found a piece of scrap paper, wrote something on it and handed it to Becca. "This surprises me, but then again sometimes nothing in Bedlam surprises me."

Becca frowned when she read the scrap of paper, "Am I supposed to know this Pee Wee Herman?"

"Look him up on the Internet. Okay, the orders are written, signed off and I am out of here."

Becca nodded and added, "I'll try not to bother you again this morning."

"No bother, Becca. I'm hoping that Dr. Saroni recuperates quickly and reclaims his call tomorrow so I can kick back for a night."

Becca arched an eyebrow. "Do you want to borrow the DVD?" She held it out to him; a shiny red apple replete with snake.

"No thank you Becca, though tempting as you make it I believe someone here needs to uphold some sense of decorum, at least for the next 24 hours or so. If I change my mind I will visit Susie's and ask for a "Reubens to go.""

"Paul Reubens to go."

"Exactly."

"So, what's the plan Ben?

"I'm going to call Saroni and ask him to over read the EKG." He glanced down again studying the EKG in his hands as if an imperfection he had missed would jump out at him.

They were standing in the X-ray reading room across and down the hallway from the emergency room and Karmma, the day RN, normally taciturn, though pleasant, appeared to be slightly out of sorts today. With a hint of sarcasm she stated, "He might be a little owly today since he called off sick."

"'Owly' being a medical term?" Ben asked innocently.

She rolled her eyes. "Are you just prodding the sleeping bear to elicit a reaction, Ben?"

"Granted he did call off but he is in town, he gave no instructions not to be bothered, he has his own fax machine at home and it will take him all of two minutes to review the EKG."

"You're overlooking one thing."

"And that is?"

"We're talking about Saroni here."

"Point taken but let's live dangerously. I'm pretty sure there's nothing acute going on with her heart, however, I would like a second opinion." Ben paused for a minute contemplating his options. "Okay, let's review what we have here. We have an 82-year-old female patient, an unrestrained passenger in a pickup truck that slid off the road and sideways down an approximate 15 foot embankment. She was exposed to sub-freezing temperatures for approximately 90 minutes before transported. No loss of consciousness or altered mental status. She complains of sub sternal chest pain that can be reproduced with movement and deep breaths. No other signs or symptoms lending to a cardiac event. History of prior Myocardial infarction, cardiac stent, Diabetes type two, Hypertension and Hyperlipidemia. Chest X-ray is negative, labs indicated slight dehydration but otherwise within normal limits. Hemoglobin A1C indicates that her Diabetes seems to be well controlled with oral medication. Myoglobin shows minor elevation but all other cardiac enzymes are normal. EKG appears to have a normal sinus rhythm, indications of an old inferior infarct, and without any acute changes that I can readily observe. Is there anything I missed or that you would like to add?" Ben looked to Karmma for comment.

"That pretty well sums it up. I can't think of anything to add at this time. What if you can't reach Saroni?"

"I'll call Billings and have someone there review it. If the EKG is normal then we'll give her fluids, repeat the enzymes and EKG in two, then four hours and keep her in observation until her son makes it up here from Bismarck to pick her and her grandson up. What do you think?"

Karmma was quick to answer, "I believe that you have a very workable plan, Ben." With her thumb and forefinger, she plucked the EKG from Ben's hands and headed down the hall to the fax machine.

He called after her, "How's her grandson doing?"

"I think he was more shaken up over the possibility of injuring his grandmother than his bouncing around in that truck cab. He's doing fine, just hovering over his grandmother."

"Good. I'll be down in a minute to call Saroni."

Ben walked out of the X-ray reading room to the entrance doors leading out to the ambulance pad. Staring out at the wintry landscape he could imagine the frigid cold; it just looked cold. The snow that had been banked at the edges of the pad and rear parking lot he estimated at five feet or more, testimony to snow falls that had started accumulating in late October. The steel gray sky thickly blanketed with dark clouds obscured any hint of the sun, even shadows having disappeared, fleeing the deep freeze.

He had harbored a feeling since Thanksgiving that he couldn't quite fathom or shake. It wasn't homesickness, depression or loneliness. There were disappointments, sure, sometimes with the lack of sleep a feeling of being adrift, occasionally tentative and unsure, and never fearless. His dedication and drive were a boon to him when he periodically felt abandoned, "tossed to the wolves" by Dr. Saroni. Ben had known that he was immersing himself in a grueling and highly demanding career, and though he would never wallow found himself hoping for the occasional security of an anchored lifeline. He was unwilling to lay all of the blame at Dr. Saroni's feet though Ben could not help but to believe that Saroni was a major contributor. Naiveté was not a sin or a failing though it most certainly had placed him at center stage with the possibility to fail. He held close his privacy and private thoughts, choosing to spare his few friends in Bedlam his fleeting thoughts of insecurity and uncertainty. Fear of failing is disconcerting, yet quite often a most motivating factor. It was time to motivate.

He met Karmma in the office and she was entering a phone number into the fax machine. "I've sent the cover sheet and fax twice and received a fax failed notification both times. I'm hoping the third time is the charm."

"Before you send it again let me try calling Saroni's home and cell numbers."

Karmma canceled the fax and took a seat, leaning back as she folded her hands in her lap. Ben looked at the laminated phone listings taped to the desk and dialed Dr. Saroni's home phone and listened. "Dr. Saroni, it's Ben Parker at the hospital. It's 1:15 on Sunday afternoon, please call me as soon as possible. Thank you. Goodbye." Ben dialed the cell phone number and ended up leaving the same message.

He looked at Karmma who shrugged and asked him, "So, do you have a plan B?"

Ben thought for a minute. "Dr. Molson may have ER call this weekend in Slipknot. Would you be willing to call the Slipknot Emergency Room and check while I duck into the men's room?"

As he dried his hands he caught a glimpse of himself in the mirror. "You look tired Parker, do yourself a favor, take a PTO day and get some sleep." He walked into the office and Karmma held the phone out to him covering the mouth piece with her free hand. It was the first time that he had seen her smile all day; a smug, self-satisfying, cat caught the canary smile.

"Dr. Molson is not on duty today but they have a locum on duty that they have paged to the phone."

"Did they give you the doctor's name?"

"Dr. Arman Saroni."

Ben's unabashed look of surprise slowly morphed into a broad grin as he slowly shook his head back and forth in disbelief. "That son of a bitch. Sorry."

"My sentiments exactly. Would you like me to fax the EKG to the Slipknot ER?"

"Why yes, Karmma. That would be most thoughtful of you." The grin never left his face as he accepted the phone and punched the speaker button on the phone console. Ben could see Karmma smiling, head bobbing up and down as she entered the phone number into the fax machine.

"I was under the impression that the Hospital Board and Westergard didn't want him to moonlight."

"You are absolutely correct. Last spring, they told me that Saroni would no longer be taking on any locum work that his sole interest was to this hospital only."

The voice from the phone console was loud enough, however, sounded distant, "Hello, this is Dr. Saroni."

"Hello, Dr. Saroni, this Ben Parker." There was an extended pause. Ben was imagining the doctor's surprise, hoping he was uncomfortable.

"Why you call here? He sounded irritated but tentative.

"I was hoping that you would over read an EKG on a..."

"Why you call? I am not home."

Karmma held up a sheet of paper printed from the fax machine and handed it to Ben as she made the "OK" sign with her fingers. The fax had gone through.

"Apparently not. I left voice messages on your home and cell phones. Again, I was hoping..."

"If no answer why persist? Why you call here?"

"Actually, I was trying to reach Dr. Molson…"

"He not here so why you call me?"

"Dr. Saroni, will you please review the EKG that we just faxed to you?"

"No one is home. Fax machine is off."

"We know that. The EKG was faxed to the Slipknot Emergency Room."

"How you get that number?"

Ben ignored the question, however was pre-empted before he could speak.

"How you know I am here?"

Karmma imitated a gun with her hand, inserting her forefinger barrel into her mouth and flexing her thumb as the trigger.

"I didn't, I thought you were home with the flu."

"Obviously not."

"You called the hospital and said you were ill."

"When I say that?"

"Yesterday, last night."

"No, I am here."

"No, the Bedlam hospital. You said that you had the flu."

"I am recovered."

"Then why didn't you call me and take over the call?"

"I am on call."

"I'm talking about here in Bedlam."

"How? I am not at home."

"I know…"Ben paused, closed his eyes and pretended to drive a pen into his ear canal, continuing on into his brain. Karmma nearly had her entire fist wedged inside of her mouth to stifle a laugh. "Will you review the EKG we faxed to you in Slipknot?"

"Fax machine not working. Call Billings."

"We have confirmation that the fax was delivered."

"Possibly out of paper, maybe ink. Call Billings."

"How convenient."

"No, inconvenient."

Karmma was pretending to beat her head against the desktop all the while rapping the underside of the desk in unison with her fist. Ben decided to take a different tact, one which might produce future, if not immediate consequences.

"Does Mr. Westergard or Chairman Whitlow know that you are moonlighting?"

"None of your or their business."

"Probably not. Okay, I give up. I'm going to call Westergard and see if he can read EKG's"

Karmma looked up at Ben with a shocked expression while Ben stood placidly, belying his somersaulting stomach as the line remained virtually silent for over a minute.

"The EKG is normal, no new changes. What is your plan?"

"IV fluids to rehydrate, cardiac monitor, repeat EKGs and cardiac enzymes in two hours, again in four hours and observe her until her son arrives from Bismarck."

"That is satisfactory. No Westergard." Click.

Karmma stood up, a look of relief on her face as she held up her right hand for a high five. "Ben Parker, it's good to know that you got a pair." With that she exited and headed across the hall to the ER.

"A Reuben sandwich to go, please." As Ben stood in front of the order counter the squeaky voiced blond smoothly sidestepped to her right. A broad, practiced smile appeared as her arms arose, her left arm raised high with palm poised in offering of the subdued pastel yellow menu board.

Her high pitched voice stated the obvious, "As you can see sir, we do not offer a Reuben sandwich; however, we serve everything you see on our menu board."

Ben immediately realized his mistake. "I'm sorry. What I meant to order was a Paul Reubens to go, please."

The thin blonde's face assumed neutrality as her arms dropped to her side. "Excuse me sir, I will be right back." She made a quick, deliberately paced walk to the kitchen door and disappeared inside. In short order she reappeared followed by Susie who was in the process of doffing her pastel purple hairnet with one hand while untying her apron with the other. A definite look of surprise was evident as she walked up to Ben.

"You're just full of surprises Mr. Parker PA," she purred as she took his arm and guided him over to the first window booth. At 8 PM, the room otherwise empty of customers, they stood at the end of the table. "I always meet with anyone ordering the Paul Reubens to go for the first time, especially the horny, good looking ones. She could not hide that trademark twinkle in her eyes.

Slowly shaking his head as in disbelief, Ben responded with a faux air of judgment. "I just had to see for myself. I could not imagine a shy, reserved woman of your moral convictions pandering in smut."

Susie's deep throated laugh produced a smile from Ben. "You'd be surprised what people do around here to make ends meet."

"Have you no respect for the Sabbath?"

"People screw every day of the week, regardless. Are you hungry?"

"Not really." Ben paused rethinking his answer. "Well maybe a tad bit."

"It's time to close this joint but how about we share a Philly cheese steak? A real one, not that atrocity that you normally order."

"You're on. Just a warning though, I'm on call and may have to leave abruptly."

Susie started to say something, thought better of it and gave Ben a gentle nudge so he would get the idea to take a seat, which he promptly did. At the counter she grabbed a drink cup and tossed it over to Ben. "I'll be back in a few shakes" and as she turned, and in true form rocked her hips back and forth until she disappeared into the kitchen. Ben filled his drink cup with ice and root beer at the fountain, found a well-read Sunday paper and settled into the booth's bench seat. He read the paper as the blond girl walked about the restaurant policing and wiping down tables. When Susie emerged from the kitchen she slid a platter on the table containing two halves of a cheese steak and a mound of French fries. She returned with a steaming cup of coffee then wriggled her way onto the opposite bench. They were alone now, the young woman having made her own way back into the kitchen.

Ben started off with several fries as Susie blew on her coffee, her eyes upturned giving him a questioning glance before asking, "Did you really want a Paul Reubens to go?"

"No. I just found out about your secret porn society last night and felt obligated to give you a ration of crap."

"Ben, the correct phrase is, 'a ration of shit.' It's probably made its way into Webster's College Dictionary by now."

"I didn't want to offend your delicate sensibilities."

"Busy at the hospital?"

"They do keep me hopping. Keeps me off the street and out of the bars"

Susie nodded as she took a bite out of her cheese steak half. They sat in silence as they ate.

"So, when was the last time you got laid, Ben?"

He began choking with his eyes tearing up. A look of concern formed and she began to arise but Ben held up his hand as he took a sip of his root beer. He coughed and then squelched a belch with his fist. He wiped his eyes with his napkin, arched his back, stretching his shoulders backwards as he took a deep breath. Settling back into his bench seat he laid his forearms on the table and leaned forward.

"Why do you insist on tossing out those questions while I'm eating?"

"You okay?"

"Yes, I'm okay."

"So, I asked you, when was the last…"

"Too damn long."

Susie smiled almost deviously. The subtle tone of a vixen insinuated her voice. "You're a good looking guy Ben with a cute little butt. Hell, if I wasn't in a committed relationship I'd toss you a mercy fuck."

"I don't take charity," Ben snapped sharply.

"Sure, you would and we both know it," she retorted, and then added apologetically, "And it wouldn't be charity."

"You're right I would. But only once, so you'd know what you'd be missing afterwards."

Susie was now contrite. "Touché, Ben Parker. Touché. I'm willing to admit that was my relationship to fail…" She allowed her statement to trail off, unfinished. The two of them polished off the French fries smirking at each other between bites.

"Where are the Paul Reubens kept?"

"Back room behind the regular videos. Why? You want to see?"

"No, another time maybe." He paused briefly as he slid out of the booth, stood and reached into his back pocket for his wallet. "Only if it gets to the point that I'm calling out for mercy."

Susie reached over and stayed his right hand as she alighted from her seat. "My pleasure Ben."

Ben nodded as he briefly covered her hand with his left, "I agree. Always a pleasure, Susie."

She walked him to the door as he adjusted and zipped his coat, then pulled on his gloves. She gave his butt a quick squeeze as he stepped out into the cold, closing the door behind him. He smiled knowingly to himself as he navigated his way over the icy parking lot thinking that his outlook on life was a damn sight better having her as a friend.

CHRISTMAS

Ben leaned in bracing himself with both hands on the bathroom sink, staring into the mirror, trying to remember the last time that he had awoken after a disturbing dream with an erection and a near overwhelming urgency to urinate. For the past six months his dreams have been intermittent and vaguely forgettable. In comparison, this one had been a Technicolor extravaganza. He could remember snippets of his dream but similar to his dream there was no continuity to the slide show that he was attempting to replay.

There was an attractive blond haired woman that he did not know, who he recalled embracing and kissing while standing on a dilapidated third floor balcony. The sky behind her was amber, red and smoky. She wore a waist long duck colored Carhart winter coat and nothing else. An unseen man had shouted, "You have to go. We don't need your help." It had seemed forever finding his way out of the building's convoluted warren of hallways and passageways into a thick woodland of trees and suddenly emerging from a tangle of forest undergrowth. He ran across a barren baseball field littered with pairs of old work boots and several dead rattlesnakes. There was a test that he was late for and he ran helter-skelter along sidewalks on a college campus that he did not recognize, passing and dodging people who were running in the direction from which he came. He could not remember where he needed to be. A bright white classic Ford Thunderbird convertible had run into a tree, his high school football coach and Mrs. Kapanski from the Bedlam Motor Court, both motionless and bloodied, were sitting in the front seat, a still smoking cigarette in her mouth. Mr. Pasacovich, a friend of his father, sat on the ground by the passenger rear tire holding a hand gun in his right hand, his other forefinger pointing at Ben, a crooked smile on his face. Ben had looked down and realized that all he was wearing were white underpants. He could not remember anything else. Such is the nature of dreams. Ben knew that dream interpretation was not a science but someone would surely have a field day with this one.

Ben did not view this odd, disturbing dream as a portent of the week to come, however, were he prone to any degree of paranoia or foreshadowing he might contrive last night's emergency room patient as the start of a Holiday Season of melancholy, depression, or manic if not violent activity. He knew that by statistical studies any increase of this type of behavior during the Christmas holiday was usually attributed to an increased use of alcohol and drugs rather than planned homicide or suicide. Marni had been scheduled for an out of town appointment yesterday so they had traded their regular ER call nights. She managed a full night's sleep and Ben had been confronted with a volatile psyche patient, proving once again that no good deed goes unpunished.

A 39-year-old, power lifting, white male with a history of mental health issues and multiple arrests for domestic and felony assaults, often turbocharged with alcohol and mind altering drugs, had been brought to the emergency room by ambulance, hand cuffed and secured to a backboard with a multitude of straps and by Ben's estimation, at least two large rolls of duct tape. Deputy Babcock, the county's "ginormous" sheriff's deputy had accompanied the patient on board the ambulance and now stood sentry in the emergency room. Ben had noted that Deputy Babcock's normally spotless and placid deportment was not in evidence as his shirt was not tucked in, there were tears in his shirt pocket and the left knee of his duty pants, and his jaw was clenched so tightly Ben feared the deputy would crack a tooth. EMT's had reported that the man had not appeared lucid, screaming unintelligibly with short spurts of profanity as he had been apprehended and subdued while dismantling a sheriff's department cruiser with his bare hands.

The patient continued to struggle mightily against his restraints. Deputy Babcock, against the advice of, but with the unspoken relief of the EMT's, had wrapped several loops of duct tape over the patient's mouth circling the backboard. Ben had taken some trauma shears to cut loose the tape over the mouth when he had been warned by everyone in unison, "He bites!" It appeared to be a near impossibility for obtaining lab specimens due to the continued squirming and thrashing attempts. When Ben called Dr. Saroni for a consult regarding appropriate sedation Mrs. Saroni answered and refused to wake the sleeping doctor, all the while Becca was by his ear repeatedly whispering, "B52." After hanging up the phone he asked Becca, "What's a B52, besides a high altitude bomber?"

"I can't remember the drug combination but was hoping that you did. All I know is that it works."

Considering that he was not positive of any drugs on board, Ben contemplated whether or not Ativan would be the most appropriate and effective drug for sedation. Ben called Wynot, the closest facility equipped and staffed for psychiatric patients. When he presented his patient to Dr. Savage the physician on duty, Dr. Savage said, "Hit him with a B52 and send him over." Ben had asked what constituted a B52 and was told, "a cocktail of 50 milligrams of Benadryl, 5 milligrams of Haldol and two milligrams of Ativan." It worked like a charm. With the tape removed and supplemental oxygen being administered to the peacefully dozing patient, he was loaded back onto the ambulance. Deputy Babcock climbed aboard and off they drove to the Wynot Emergency Room.

Over the past eight months of practice, Ben had regrettably become aware of the woefully inadequate availability of acute mental health services and treatment within the state of Montana. Most rural Critical Access Hospitals were ill equipped and understaffed to treat these patients and quite often locating a facility to accept transfer of care usually required long hours of monitoring within the ER, extensive long distance phone calls, bargaining, cajoling, leveraging and literally selling one's soul to secure a bed, sometimes a couple hundred miles away. Thankfully, last night had been an inordinately smooth transfer.

Thursday was Dr. Saroni's regularly scheduled weekday off, however, he was starting a 10 day vacation on Friday morning and rumor had it that Westergard had pressured the doctor to work today and tie up any possible loose ends. At the nurses' station, after morning hospital rounds, Dr. Saroni waved last night's ER paperwork in Ben's face and confrontationally asked, "What is this B52?" Ben explained the sedating cocktail and the resulting desired effect. Dr. Saroni gave a dismissive wave of his hand, "Why you not call me?"

"I did but your wife said that you were sleeping and would not awaken you."

Dr. Saroni now replied sharply with a defensive tone in his voice, "You are mistaken. This I have discussed with her. I would be awakened."

"Perhaps you need to revisit that discussion," Ben replied flatly.

Dr. Saroni stormed off through the lobby and disappeared around the corner to the hallway leading to the clinic rooms. Since Ben had caught Saroni moonlighting the doctor had not been any friendlier but definitely less confrontational. Ben looked in the nurses' station at Karmma and remaining straight-faced merely shrugged his shoulders. He smiled at Myra as he said good morning, passing by the receptionist's window and stopping at the gaily decorated community bulletin board. Scanning the Christmas signup sheets and announcements he estimated a dozen posted, including Bedlam Childrens' Christmas Presents, Christmas Eve Carolers, Nursing Home Resident Gifts, Cookie Exchange and even a raffle announcement for a gift wrapped AR-15. The only ones missing that he glibly thought of, yet knew to be inappropriate, were a fruit cake raffle and perhaps a Christmas Cheer Liquor Basket Drawing. He was aware of but not focused upon the hushed voices of two women just around the corner. Averting his attention from the bulletin board he could now discern the women's conversation.

Woman 1, with a tone of insider knowledge, "You know that the Saroni's are personal friends of Imelda."

Woman 2, equally knowledgeable, "Yes, indeed, Mrs. Saroni has alluded to their relationship, of course only in confidence. Have you ever appreciated her flair for fashionable shoes and her impeccable taste in clothing and accents?"

Woman 1, slightly envious, "And with the doctor's new three year contract she should definitely be able to maintain appearances. We are so blessed by their presence. They add an international distinction to our community, I do so hope they remain long term and not return to the Philippines."

Woman 2, in agreement, "A cosmopolitan flavor. My husband sometimes has trouble with the Doctor's accent and still thinks he's from Indonesia; however, I know he is fully appreciative of the Saroni's contribution to our little burg."

Ben had never met Mrs. Saroni, let alone had an opportunity to admire her footwear, the doctor fulfilling any and all needs and expectations for further intercourse with the couple. Ben broke free from his eavesdropping position, briskly turned the corner startling two middle aged women as he offered "good morning," leaving them in silence as he continued on down the hallway.

"Callie, why is this guy written into my schedule for 3:30? Wasn't he on Dr. Saroni's schedule?"

"That would be because Dr. Saroni left a few minutes ago at 3."

"He just up and left?" Ben sounded incredulous.

"You sound surprised."

Ben's sarcasm was evident, "Behavior so unlike the good doctor."

"Your patient just got here so I'll let you know when he's roomed and ready."

"Thank you, Callie."

Just before he knocked on the clinic door Callie forewarned him that his patient was far more ill than the son's phone call had initially led her to believe. Knocking lightly Ben entered the room to find his patient, 65-year-old Warren Calhoun sitting in the clinic's wheelchair, his son standing next to him with his hand on Mr. Calhoun's shoulder as if steadying him. The son looked to Ben expectantly. Mr. Calhoun raised his head, passively indifferent, and then his chin slumped back down to his chest. Ben introduced himself. Immediately the son, smartly dressed in sport coat, tie and sharply creased pants, launched into a brief history, "Dad lives by himself and I usually stop by every few days but I was away on business and haven't seen him for about a week. This morning when I dropped by Dad said that he hadn't been feeling too good for the past couple of days. He looked a little pale to me and he told me that his belly was bothering him. Usually he goes to the VA but I thought we might get in here faster. I'm glad you were available 'cause quite frankly I don't think Dad would have been willing to see that camel jockey doctor."

While the son was presenting what Ben was weighing to be an excuse he was silently apprising his patient making note of his physical appearance. Mr. Calhoun was yellow. Not pale. Yellow. His skin was sallow, taut, and yellow. The white sclera of his eyes were yellow. His hands trembled as did his head and neck. Having been changed into a loose fitting hospital gown, Ben could still ascertain that his breathing was relatively shallow with a moderately rapid rate and his belly was definitely bloated, protuberant. His lower legs were hairless and his ankles and feet were more than moderately swollen by fluid retention. Mr. Calhoun appeared disheveled, unshaven and unkempt. A strong odor of urine and an underlying scent of alcohol were evident and he apparently hadn't bathed for at least several days. Ben believed Mr. Calhoun to be disoriented, obtunded, rather than disinterested, not slightly ill but in need of aggressive evaluation and treatment, and to top it off his son was a bigot.

Kneeling directly in front of his patient, Ben reintroduced himself, "Mr. Calhoun, my name is Ben Parker. I am the physician assistant on duty today. Do you know where you are?"

Mr. Calhoun barely lifted his head, his eyes dull and unfocused.

"Mr. Calhoun, do you know where you are? Can you tell me who brought you here?"

His head slightly bobbed up and down from his trembling as he mumbled something unintelligible.

Ben turned to the son and said, "Your father is severely ill so please remain with him while I call the nurse and forewarn her that we are headed up to the emergency room."

On his way back to his office, Ben poked his head in the doorway of Callie's office, "Mr. Calhoun is on his way to Sunnvale. He is jaundiced and has severely impaired liver function with extensive abdominal ascites, dehydration, congestive heart failure, electrolyte imbalances and altered mental status. I haven't seen that much abdominal fluid since my internal medicine rotation. Dr. Baumgartner accepted him at the ER and of notable irony the physician on hospital duty this weekend is Dr. Gandapur."

"The internal medicine doctor from Pakistan?"

"None other, which, should immensely please Mr. Calhoun's son who so embraces cultural diversity in modern western medicine."

Batting her eyelashes with a look of glowing admiration Callie responded sweetly, "Ben Parker, you make us all better human beings." She immediately resumed filling out a form on her desk and without looking up added, "I'll need his chart when you're done with your ER notes. Would you pull the door closed behind you?"

In the corridor outside of the closed door of Callie's and the main clinic office Ben could make out an intermingling of several elevated, though muffled, female voices. He determined that there were five in total, all of which seemed universally stressed, each with its own sense of fervor and immediacy. Holding Mr. Calhoun's chart in one hand, he knocked quietly on the door with the other, however, the dissonance continued unabated. Again, he knocked, slightly louder with yet again no response from those within the office. He gently turned the doorknob and pushed the door open slightly, enough to allow him to peer in at five women employees, Callie, Cora the transcriptionist, Helen, Irene and Eleanor from the business office, who had formed a loose, standing circle in the center of the office. It was a highly charged atmosphere of animated, agitated conversations, with a constant flow of interjections, comments and opinions, as each lady attempted to have her voice heard, regardless of who was also attempting to seize and hold the floor. Ben was not following the conversational fine points but had determined the central topic was Dr. Saroni. Considering himself an unwelcomed interloper he attempted to unobtrusively place the chart on Callie's desk when he was spotted by Cora, whose surprised gasp alerted the women of his presence as he was starting to strategically withdraw. The room abruptly became silent, their faces affixing wane, if not tormented smiles.

"Hey Ben, get in here and join us." Callie was waving him in.

"Really ladies, no disrespect intended here, I wasn't eavesdropping or trying to interrupt."

Callie and Irene both waved him in, coaxing him to join them. Cora spoke directly to him, "No, come in. This affects you as much as any of us, probably more in some cases."

He set the chart down on Callie's desk and joined the ladies, they having formed more of a semi-circle to allow him in. Helen reopened the formally vociferous discussion, "Have you seen the latest office protocol changes?"

Ben's eyes darted around the semi-circle, "No, I can't say..."

Irene chimed in, "...another change to the child fever treatment protocol. It's the fourth one in the past two weeks. Saroni changes it faster than we can type it up..."

Eleanor interrupted, "...and today he told the business office that he wants to be alerted by written notice, rather than verbally, of any coding discrepancies or billing changes regarding his patients and if it involves Ben then we..."

Ben found himself nodding in agreement or sympathy rather than taking a chance by opening his mouth.

Now Callie joined in, "Once again the doctor has changed his scheduling preferences. I can't begin to remember how many changes this makes since midsummer. Twenty minutes rather than 30 minutes, majority in the morning then majority in the afternoon then spread evenly throughout the day. Now, starting January first, he wants all of his patients scheduled for 15-minute appointments, all in the morning when he's," she makes quotation signs with her fingers, "fresh"..."

The voices were ramping up in volume and intensity. Ben turned to Cora who was starting to vent, "...today he complains to Westergard that his dictation transcriptions are late and incomplete. He starts and stops his Dictaphone in the middle of words and a sentence, never makes mention of corrections, rarely enunciates and if you've ever listened to his accent on tape he's like..."

All at once the five women unleashed a fusillade of complaints and opinions, hints of invective beginning to insinuate themselves into the comments, Ben finding it all but impossible to follow. He stood facing the semi-circle of five women, "Okay, okay now. Please, I need everyone to take a deep breath and let it out slowly counting down from four." The room was once again silent, a variety of facial expressions emerged, from quizzical to skeptical but everyone complied. "Now, please, let's as a group try an exercise in stress reduction and mental relaxation. Soooo, everyone remain standing in place, feet slightly spread around shoulder width, back straight, shoulders back, knees slightly flexed, abdomen relaxed. He demonstrated creating an "O" with his thumbs and forefingers, an okay sign by adding the additional three fingers of each hand, and then rested his pinky fingers on the top of each hip bone. "Close your eyes and continue deep breathing, a count of four when inhaling followed by a count of four when exhaling. No fair swaying. Now when you exhale let's softly chant "OOHHHMMMMMM." Slowly, almost shyly, they all joined in and together repeated the chant several times. He could detect some faint smiles appearing. "I would like everyone to slowly repeat after me, Arman Fubar Saroni. Good, now let's repeat only drawing it out. Arrmmaann Fuubaarr Saarroonnii, Arrmmaann Fuubaarr Saarroonnii. No, don't look at each other, head straight ahead eyes closed, and join in with me. Arrmmaann Fuubaarr

Saarroonnii." Tentative at first, soon all five women were chanting in unison. "That's it, excellent, now five more times." At this point everyone was smiling and he detected the atmosphere relaxing as a few giggles began to break out. "Okay, you may open your eyes. Does everyone feel a bit more relaxed? More at 'one' with themselves?"

"Uh, huh."

"Yeesssss, thank you."

"Definitely."

Giggling, "That was fun."

"What does 'fubar' mean?"

The other four formed a chorus, "Yeah, what does 'fubar' mean?"

Ben attempted to stifle a smile of embarrassment, "Excuse my French ladies but fubar stands for fucked up beyond all recognition."

There was wide eyed shock, then recognition and then laughter. Relaxed, loud, raucous, unabashed laughter. Ben walked out of the office, closing the door behind him and thinking, "My work here is done."

"Damn it Becca, I'm not cranky and I'm sure as hell not on call."

"Well, you sound cranky and unfortunately you are on call."

"It's 4:30 in the morning so I'm not quite on my game but when I left the hospital last night at 7 Dr. Saroni was on call."

"I hate to be the bearer of bad news Ben but technically you went on call at 1700 hours yesterday. Saroni's name is crossed out and yours is written in. So, quit whining, put on your big boy pants and get a move on. You've got lives to save and babies to deliver."

"You are so right Becca. Thanks for that pity pot wake up call." Ben's words literally dripped with sarcasm.

"You, Mr. Parker, are most welcome. Please make haste as your patient is a teenage female with abdominal pain."

"Now I know you're pulling my leg. First you bait me with Saroni dumping his shift and then embellish it with the potential minefield of a teenage female with abdominal pain; that is over the top. So what's really up?"

"One, Saroni did dump his shift and two, be happy that the weather is good in case you have to ship out our little cheerleader. Have you ever known me to screw with your head?"

"Only when it suits your agenda or when you're just in the mood to toy with me."

Becca responded with feigned disappointment, "You hurt me to the quick Ben."

"Okay, okay, I believe you. I'll be in shortly. Goodbye."

"Ben, this young lady is Genevieve Doltzimmer and she is complaining of right lower quadrant pain. No injury or trauma. Pain started around midnight and is now a nine out of 10. No fever and vital signs are stable. Occasional nausea, no vomiting. The lab has been notified. Would you like me to start an IV?"

"Thank you, Becca, let's hold off on the IV for now. Good morning, Genevieve, I'm Ben Parker the physician assistant on duty." He scanned the patient chart that Becca had handed him. When Ben had entered the emergency room he had made a quick study of his patient and his initial impression of Genevieve was a pretty teenager in no apparent distress. Her appearance suggested she had dressed for a public appearance with clean, pressed designer blue jeans decorated with ruby rhinestones on the pockets and seams, a conservative white blouse, the top button unfastened, and a red silk scarf loosely tied around her neck. To Ben, her makeup was applied rather heavily for her perceived age, lacquered nails matched her lipstick and her blond hair was severely pulled back into a pony tail. A pair of fur topped winter boots stood upright at the foot of the gurney. Her face had been neutral, seemingly unperturbed, arms folded across her chest and legs crossed at the ankles. Trying not to be judgmental he failed miserably; high maintenance with more than a hint of entitlement.

Ben was about to ask a question when Genevieve's hands dropped to her right lower abdomen and her face registered an intense grimace. Instead he asked, "Is your pain getting worse?"

"No, not worse, just ah, maybe more frequent."

"Is it sharp, dull, or burning?"

"Yes."

"Which?"

"Mostly dull but occasionally sharp for a few minutes."

"Lab is here, Ben. What do you want them to draw?"

"Ben looked at Becca and calmly said, "Let's hold off a couple of minutes."

Back to his patient, "Genevieve, you came to the hospital by yourself, correct?" She nodded yes. "Your date of birth indicates that you are 15 years old. We need permission from a parent or guardian to treat you. Is there someone that we can call?"

"Can't you treat me now and we call my grandmother afterwards?"

"I wish that were allowable but I can't. If you have your grandmother's phone number we can call her for permission."

"Isn't there some paper or waiver or something I can sign?" She was sounding more anxious.

"Again, I'm..."

Becca interrupted, "Why don't we get some labs started while you sort out permission?"

Ben was now getting irritated and said, "No labs until we talk with her parents or grandmother."

"Maybe a urine sample?"

"Who can we call, Genevieve?"

"My parents are in Missoula bringing my brother back from college for Christmas break." There was a whine insinuating itself. "I really don't want to bother my grandmother." She grimaced again and her hands pressed down on her right lower abdomen.

"We should start an IV and give her something for pain."

Ben shot Becca a glaring look that said, 'What are you doing?' "Not yet."

"Well, if no IV, how about a Lortab or something?"

He excused himself from his patient, stepped away from the gurney, motioned to Becca to follow him and walked through the doors to the hallway."

"What the hell is going on, Becca?" He continued before she could get a word in. "I know that you want to feel in charge, that you like to make the decisions, that you believe that I will defer to you so there's no dispute in front of the patient, but this time just let me do my job, today let's just pretend that I know what I'm doing and that I'm the one in charge."

Becca was tightlipped with an intense stare. A moment later she morphed to chagrin and her icy look melted. "Sorry, Ben, sometimes I just can't help myself. You guys have all the fun. You're right, sometimes I want to diagnose, to give orders, not just take them, you know, be in charge."

"Believe me, Becca, at times I've felt the same way. Right now we're a team but I get to be the coach. Kabeesh?"

"Kabeesh."

"Okay. Before we go back in I would like you to fill me in on what she told you before I arrived. I know you Becca; I know that you always chat up the patient before I arrive."

"She's a cheerleader at Bedlam High School. The basketball team had an away game last night and after they got back to town a group of cheerleaders, ball players and friends got together and drank some beer at a home where the parents are away. When she got dropped off at home, grandma had already fallen asleep. The pain started around 1 and first she thought it was menstrual cramps but the timing is off. She's scared because a couple of weeks ago she stayed at a friend's house who hosted a party when her parents were out of town. Genevieve got really drunk and woke up naked next to a basketball player she has the hots for. She thinks that she passed out but isn't sure what really happened. She snuck out this morning, borrowed grandma's car and came here to get checked out. Most of all she's in mortal fear of her mother."

"You are a wonder, Becca. Without you we'd still be at square one sorting out what prompted her to come."

"What are thinking Ben?"

He frowned, "A 15 year old high maintenance, rebellious, teenage female with attitude, raging hormones and right lower quadrant pain. Her purported pain is disproportionate to her physical demeanor. She may or may not have a substance on board altering her mentation or physical response to pain." Ben shrugged his shoulders, "With these symptoms there are only 267 possible maladies to choose from, give or take a few. I'm not going to speculate so let's convince her to call grandma."

When they reentered the ER Genevieve was listening to her cell phone, a sullen expression as she sat wiggling her toes, apparently examining her nail polish. She spoke into the phone, "My stomach still hurts. They keep saying that I need permission from a parent or..." Her expression did not change; she added a rolling of her eyes to the heavens above. "No mom, he's a physician's assistant. The doctor is..."

Ben wanted to interrupt, "There is no apostrophe s in physician assistant," but refrained.

"Why can't you listen to me for a minute? Some of us got together after the game and..." She grimaced, bent forward, straightened up, pushed a button on her phone and held it up at arm's length.

"I'm betting that you and all of your so called friends were drinking, that's why you were late getting to your grandmother's and I'm sure that two weeks ago you were drinking the night you called to say that you were staying over at Cynthia's. I'm sure..."

Ben was surprised to hear how loud the cell phone speaker was and sheepishly thought that he didn't know if his phone had that feature. He shook his head at Genevieve in an effort to have her shut off the speaker phone and the voice that could literally cut glass. Genevieve had a smug, satisfied look on her face as she continued to broadcast her mother's diatribe.

"...you could make more of an attempt to develop quality relationships, and use better taste and judgment when choosing your friends, especially when it comes to that punk basketball player, that Harper kid, who is probably of the same ilk as his low life father and…" there was a pause and then with increased fervor, "you didn't screw him did you? Did you? If you screwed that Robbie Harper I swear that I'll put his balls in a vice and have him arrested, and then we will pack up your shit and you will be attending school in North Dakota at Our Lady of Perpetual Flagellation…"

Ben was attempting to signal her to turn off the speaker phone by slashing his neck with his forefinger; however she was ignoring his overtures. Genevieve looked embarrassed but still held the phone out for all to hear.

"…and another thing, I want you to tell this ER guy that you are to be seen by a 'real' doctor, not some assistant or apprentice or whatever they call him, probably some guy that washed out of a second rate Caribbean school where they also teach auto mechanics or truck driving, so you tell him to call your grandmother and arrange for you to be seen by the doctor. You hear me, Genevieve? Well, do you?"

"We all do mother, loud and clear."

"What the hell do you mean by that?"

"We can all hear you mother, I have you on speaker phone."

Silence.

The voice that could strip paint off a Navy warship was replaced by one that mimicked syrup slowly gliding and dripping down the sides of a stack of pancakes. "Genevieve, honey, would you please be a dear and allow me to speak with the gentleman please?"

A smirking Genevieve mouthed, "It's my mother", as she handed the phone to Ben. Her smirk was erased by a grimace from pain.

"Hello, Mrs. Doltzimmer, I'm Ben Parker the physician assistant on duty. I'd be glad to evaluate your daughter Genevieve if you would grant permission."

"Please identify again, Mr. Parker," the voice remaining silky smooth, "your level of medical expertise."

"I am a physician assistant."

"Sooooo, not a medical doctor. No offense Parker..." there was a hint of sharpness in her voice. Ben was desperately searching for the button to deactivate the speaker. "...but nobody's assistant," intoned with condescension, "is going to lay a hand on my daughter. Call the doctor in to see her."

Ben spoke through gritted teeth, "The doctor is unavailable Mrs. Doltzimmer. I am the medical provider on duty and we have an excellent staff that..."

"You're not catching my drift Parker," now full blown condescension and sarcasm sharply edged, "so no wonder you are only an assistant. I want her evaluated by a "real" doctor. Read my lips; no one...but...a...doctor...touches...my...daughter....If you can't roust the doctor up, then call her grandmother to pick her up and have her taken to Sunnvale."

Ben was inwardly seething when he covered the phone with both hands. Genevieve looked mortified. Becca appeared angrily embarrassed for all of them.

"Genevieve, does your grandmother have a second vehicle?"

She shook her head and mumbled, "No."

"Becca, do you think that Dwight has made it to work yet?"

"I can check. Why?"

"He might be able to pick up her grandmother, bring her to our ER and then she'll have her car to drive to Sunnvale."

109

He uncovered the phone and spoke calmly and clearly, "Mrs. Doltzimmer, your daughter drove her grandmother's car to the hospital. She shouldn't be driving whether or not she might have a driver's license. I'm going to hand you off to Becca Trebek, the registered nurse on duty. She's going to give you our hospital's phone number so you may call back since cell phones are verboten in our emergency room. She will help you sort out who is driving whom while I call Sunnvale to alert them that your daughter will be arriving at their ER and that they should expect a very unpleasant woman to call granting permission to treat and to provide insurance information."

They could all hear Mrs. Doltzimmer attempting to interrupt; to no avail.

"And, Mrs. Doltzimmer; offense taken." He handed the phone to Becca, nodded to Genevieve, and walked out of the ER.

Ben emerged from the office, walked across the hall and entered the ER. Becca had stripped down the gurney and was wiping the mattress down with disinfectant.

"Where's Genevieve?"

"We were out of AMA (against medical advice) forms so I stepped out to get some from the storage closet in X-ray and when I got back, Poof!, she was gone like the brides pajamas."

Ben laughed, "You know how to turn a phrase Becca. So, who is driving whom?"

"Dwight was going to pick up grandma and bring her here. I just called his cell phone and told him to be on the lookout for Genevieve headed to grandmas. He's going to wait there."

"I gave Dr. Benson a quick report and he said to send her along. He's going to call me later to let me know what he finds with Genevieve."

"Mrs. Doltzimmer, she's a piece of work." Ben could tell that she was hedging around and waited. "She was so fucking out of line and you handled it so well." Becca hesitated, "Ahhh, Ben, you okay?"

"Yeah, I'm good, I'm okay. Thanks. You know Becca, in retrospection I should have let you have your way and let Doltzimmer think that you were in control here." He made it sound so sincere.

She was smiling broadly, "No, Ben, you made the right call. It's just about time to hand off to Myrna so when you're done with the chart would you please drop it off at the nurses' station? Besides, it will give you a chance to check out the decorations that we added last night." She sounded very pleased with herself.

"No problem. I'm sure it's a tasteful and aesthetically pleasing celebration of the pending Christian holiday."

"When you put it that way maybe we need to add some more lights."

"Thanks for all of your help. I'll give you a call later with Dr. Benson's report."

Ben finished off his ER note and walked down to the nurses' station, yesterday tastefully decorated with subtle seasonal colors and ornaments, now a garish landscape of blinking multicolored icicles, a scale model of Santa's sleigh and reindeer suspended above the inner station, a nativity scene on the counter crowding the nursing home sign in book, bubble head elves nodding incessantly in every nook and cranny, and a life size inflatable Santa Claus, hands on hips, positioned in front of the counter jovially laughing, "Ho, ho, ho, Merry

Christmas," when someone walked by activating its motion detector. Myrna stood behind the counter looking none too happy and Ben made a silent projection that by noon Santa would have a new home on the rear stoop, laughing at any smoker who ventured out.

"Good morning, Myrna."

Her eyes moved left and without rotating her head looked at him briefly, then returned to a blank stare, seemingly lost in thought. She responded flatly, "Good morning Ben, I heard that your cheerleader bolted AMA."

"I'm sure that she and her grandmother are on route to Sunnvale and the excellent care of Dr. Benson." His voice softened, "I don't want to meddle but is everything okay?"

"Yah. Yes, thank you, I'm good, Ben. Just having a lost moment."

"Need to talk?"

"Later, maybe."

"Hey, I can't say that I've seen Skylar lately, what's up?"

Myrna displayed a toothy grin, "Gone. She gave her two week notice on December 1st and," Myrna snapped her fingers, "she was gone like a fart in the wind; never showed up for any of her last shifts. I would imagine that daddy is paving her way into law school with a boatload of healthy donations." Myrna sounded a bit glib, "Just as well; I think that more than a handful of the nursing staff were itching to smack her upside the head."

Ben looked surprised but merely nodded and smiled in agreement, "Law school at least spares the Peace Corps the embarrassment of her triggering an international incident."

A glint of light caught Ben's attention and he located a narrow viewport amid the extensively applied spray frosting and watercolor Christmas murals obscuring the plate glass windows of the lobby. A relatively new extended cab pickup had come to a stop in the parking lot and the driver's door opened. A tall figure emerged and there was enough illumination from the street light to recognize the nephew of Raymond Light Feather a resident who was admitted to the nursing home last fall. The rear driver's side door opened then closed, the tall Native American now walking towards the hospital, something slung over his left shoulder and a duffle of sorts grasped in his right hand. Ben felt Myrna's presence to his right.

As if reading his mind she responded quietly, "His name is Norman Strong Tree, Mr. Light Feather's nephew."

Mr. Strong Tree entered the lobby wearing a subdued dark gray calf length wool coat which struck Ben as being tasteful and very warm. Strong Tree immediately turned to his left and proceeded to pass by the west side of the nurses' station. Their eyes met momentarily, a glint of recognition registering in Strong Tree's eyes. Ben said, "Good morning," but no reciprocal salutation was made, rather, the whistled strains of Garryowen were almost immediately heard as he passed by and turned down the west resident hallway.

Myrna ventured, "There is something hinky about Strong Tree."

"How so? Besides his apparent affinity for the Seventh Cavalry's marching tune?"

"Every Friday he's here at 0715 sharp carrying Mr. Light Feather's freshly laundered clothing, enters Mr. Light Feather's room, closes the door and then leaves within 30 minutes."

"And this is hinky because?"

"Mr. Light Feather may be elderly but he is a creature of habit. He's in the cafeteria at 0700 hours every morning, eats breakfast, socializes and returns to his room at 0800 hours. They never see each other on Fridays."

"Okay, I agree a bit odd but hinky?"

"Every Friday a line of five little Indians files in..."

Ben interrupted, "Five little Indians?" He looked at Myrna with a questioning eye. "All in a row?"

"There may be a hint of bias."

"A hint?"

Her voice rose and was sharper. "What would you prefer Ben, five little apprentices? Five little braves? Five junior medicine men? Five Native Americans of questionable repute?"

"Are they?"

"Are they what?"

"Of questionable repute."

"They raise a flag or two."

"How so?"

"I can't put my finger on it but my gut tells me so."

Ben sounded supportive when he said, "Your gut has served you and your patients well." He was encouraging her to continue when he added, "I trust it."

"As I have said, Mr. Light Feather is a creature of habit. After a light lunch he usually takes a short nap between 12:30 and 1. I think he has a built in alarm clock because he is always ready for afternoon activities that start at 1. Friday is bingo at 1300 hours and Mr. Light Feather loves his bingo. Every Friday at quarter after one these five," well enunciated, "men, troop into his room, close the door and usually leave within a half hour. I believe that they also lock or block the door."

Ben was surprised, "I thought Westergard addressed the lock when Mr. Light Feather was admitted."

"Dwight removed that slide lock and has removed a couple more since. They might also be using a wedge at the base of the door. Essentially, Strong Tree, Light Feather nor the five young men see one another at all on Fridays. I think that the only time that they are all together is one or two Sunday evenings a month. Since I do not work Sunday nights everything I hear is second hand. I understand that there is some prayer chanting and incense burning but again that is all hear say."

Standing motionless, Ben pondered this new information. "Myrna, let's keep the five little Indian thing between the two of us, okay? And quietly watch Mr. Strong Tree and company a little closer."

She nodded in agreement. "About before Ben," said with a sigh of resignation, "I am biased, prejudiced. I cannot seem to get by it."

Ben spoke softly and carefully, "You don't have to say more Myrna."

She was silent, weighing her thoughts. "That lost moment? It was about my younger sister, Emily. She was 10 years younger than me, a wild child to be sure. She had a tendency to make bad, sometimes grotesquely bad choices. Emily was a party girl and went to a bar on the reservation to score some dope, sampled too much, stayed on too long, and was assaulted and raped by several...Native Americans. It was a downhill spiral after that until five years ago," Myrna paused, continued, "She committed suicide on Christmas Day."

He was searching, at a sudden loss for the right words to say, "I am..."

Myrna knowingly interrupted, "I appreciate the thought Ben but you do not have to say the words. I, ahhh, I tried some counseling, grief therapy, a grief group and ended up quitting them all. I've read quite a bit but I'm not sure that I have it right. Maybe it's racial transference, or stereotyping, guilt, or a combination of everything. Sometimes it's a struggle to be kind, to find the compassion at this time of the year. I think that I'm getting better but then there are times I believe I've backtracked to square one." She stopped and they both remained silent.

Ben looked out to the winter darkness and gently laid his hand on her shoulder.

She gave him a quick hug, whispering, "Thank you for not judging me Ben."

"Believe me when I tell you Myrna that I am the last one that should be casting dispersions or the first stone."

When she released him she said, "Clinic opens in a half hour Ben. Go home, take a shower for God's sake," she laughed, "you're starting to stink."

It was early afternoon when Ben found the yellow post-it note on his office desk. The note was unsigned; however, he thought that he recognized Tara's handwriting. He pealed it off of his desk blotter, read it and puzzled over the message:

Dr. Benson from Sunnvale called.
Your patient has middle Smurf.

He burst out laughing, sat down and scrolled down the hospital employee roster for a phone number. While dialing the number Ben continued to chortle to himself.

A sleepy but irritated voice answered, "Hi. What?"

"Becca, it's Ben. Our cheerleader has Mittelschmerz."

"What was that?"

Ben slowly and overly enunciated, "Mittelschmerz."

"I've heard that somewhere before but right now I can't put my finger on it."

"Painful ovulation. It's usually one sided pelvic and lower abdominal pain and I think that it's usually between menstrual cycles."

She was still a bit groggy but the irritation was gone, "Well good for Genevieve. No immaculate conception."

"I'm sure that there is still hell to be paid in that house hold."

"I suppose we can hope that it scares the pants off her, ehhh, wait, scares her to keep her pants on."

"Have a good weekend Becca."

"Thanks Ben. I'll pray for some immaculate prevention for your weekend call."

"...And Ben, you need to get a move on if you want a place to park."

He thought Stella's comment odd, "Did the parking valet quit?"

"See you shortly, goodbye."

As he rose from his recliner he shut off the television. He had no idea what program was on having lost interest after watching the 6 PM news and weather report. It was 7, the drop in temperature and freezing rain event predicted to start after midnight. The projected change in tonight's weather was, by all appearances, the precursor to a severe winter storm front rushing down from Canada anticipated to blanket Montana, Idaho, North Dakota and points south with frigid temperatures, high winds and unprecedented snow accumulations. While listening to the news he had been salvaging his left over chicken from the oven, heard the phrase blizzard of a lifetime and thought what a lucky bastard he was to have call over the next week.

He knew that he was responding to a 75-year-old woman with chest pain who had an extended history of angina, high blood pressure and diabetes so he did not dawdle, however, he was completely taken by surprise by the ER parking lot being full and the ambulance on the loading pad being completely surrounded by a half dozen vehicles. Parking below the emergency room approach ramp he walked up and was even more surprised by the fact that some moron had parked a black Lincoln Town car directly in front of the ambulance. As he entered the emergency room hallway he was in for another surprise as he viewed the crowd of people congregated and blocking the emergency room doors. One or two people took a passing notice of him as he walked up and hung his hat and coat in the ER office across from the ER entrance. When more than gentle pushing and cajoling with polite "excuse me," "pardon me" failed to motivate the crowd, his more aggressive "make a hole" and physical jostling created a pathway. Once in the emergency room he was met with another half dozen people hovering around the patient on the gurney.

Stella and Trudi, the lab tech, were by the counter and motioned him over. EMT's John Bersted and Zina Crane stood in the far corner by the bathroom door; they both waved at him. Ben was about to speak when Stella subtlety put her forefinger to her lips and motioned him to follow her further down the counter. As Ben passed by Trudi he whispered a hello; she nodded and remained where she stood.

"Where did all…"

"I tried to warn you, Ben, the Mormon community has a much more efficient and effective calling tree than the hospital could ever dream of having. Tonight we happen to have Muriel Schaefer, the beloved wife of a church elder, on center stage. The man holding her left hand is her husband and the man holding her right hand with both of his is the bishop. Everyone else surrounding the gurney is a relative. The crowd is a collection of Latter-day Saint lookie-loos and late arriving or estranged relatives." Stella sounded slightly irritated. "They keep coming like locusts and I haven't been able to keep them at bay. Mrs. Schaefer has a history of angina, HTN and diabetes. Her cardiologist is Dr. Ramono in Billings. Chest pain started approximately 30 to 40 minutes ago and she took two nitro tablets before the ambulance brought her in. She claims that it's just her angina acting up but lasting a little longer than normal. She also took an extra 'water pill' tonight because she thought her ankles were a little swollen.

Vitals are currently stable; heart rate 92, blood pressure 110 over 72, SaO2 95% on room air, respirations are 18. Reported minor headache, however, she says that is normal when she uses her nitroglycerin. No radiating chest pain to shoulder, back, neck, jaw or upper extremities. No numbness or tingling. She denies shortness of breath, nausea or vomiting. Last meal at 1700 hours. Glucose is controlled with long acting insulin at bedtime and sliding scale with meals. Wynter is getting her chart and as with so many of our patients neither she nor her husband has a clue as to the names of her medications. I've got her on a nasal cannula with four liters of oxygen and an IV in the right AC."

Ben caught Trudi's eye, gave her a please come hither motion with his hand and thanked Stella for the report. "Okay, this is the game plan. I'm going to introduce myself, thin out the hovering mass at the gurney and then we're going to work. Serial vital signs every 15 minutes, an EKG, labs per cardiac protocol but let's add a BNP, magnesium and hemoglobin A1c. Let's hold off on the chest X-ray for a little while until we sort out what is going on. Hang a bag of normal saline but don't start it; that's precautionary before we give her any additional nitro. I'll do a quick head to toe while confirming her history." The two EMTs had been quietly listening. "John and Zina can help out if we need any additional hands." They both nodded in agreement. "Any questions? Anything to add? No? Well let's get to work." Just then, Wynter pushed her way through the crowd in the doorway and walked over with a chart at least two inches thick. She held it out to Ben who hefted its weight, "Thank you, Wynter. There may be more to this patient than what meets the eye."

Ben positioned himself at the foot of the gurney, the low din of conversations continued. "May I have everyone's attention please?" Those around the gurney glanced at him but continued their conversations. His patient's eyes never left her husband's. Stella had managed to get her into a gown and Mrs. Schaefer lay there, frail, calm, blanket pulled up to her neck. He raised his voice above conversational level. "May I have your attention please?" Now everyone on and around the gurney looked to him. As Ben looked left to the people at the ER doorway, a continually growing, standing room only crowd of concerned and expectant faces, the need for stadium seating crossed his mind.

"I am Ben Parker the physician assistant on duty. Our emergency room staff is RN Stella Rasniki, CNA Wynter Erskine, and our laboratory technician Trudi Downes. EMT's John Bersted and Zina Crane are here to lend a hand if needed." Ben had never made this type of introduction before but for some reason felt compelled to do it tonight; maybe it's connected to the stadium seating. "We would appreciate your consideration in regards to affording Mrs. Schaefer her privacy and the ER staff room to carry out their tasks. Two, I repeat, two family members may stand at bedside and rotate in as we can accommodate and we ask everyone else to exit the emergency room and stand a few feet back into the hallway so that staff has easy access in and out of the ER. Also, of the utmost importance; anyone parked on or around the ambulance apron, especially the black Lincoln Town car blocking the ambulance, please move those vehicles immediately." Ben saw an involuntary twitch of the bishop's head. Quietly and seemingly to no one in particular he mumbled, "That would be my car." 'Of course it would' thought Ben. A young man at the doorway strode up and offered to move it for the bishop, who thanked him but said that he would go out and move it shortly.

Immediately an even louder conversational din started and no one moved; apparently all thinking that obviously he couldn't have meant them. Ben thought to himself, "screw this," and began moving around the gurney tapping people on the shoulder and firmly directing them towards the ER doors. The looks he got were none too happy but they begrudgingly complied. Making a pushing gesture with both hands, he began coaxing people back so that he could close the ER doors. He then insinuated, almost having to wedge himself, between the bishop and his patient, and then reintroduced himself. "Mrs. Schaefer, your husband will remain by your side but we need room to evaluate you. You may choose one other person to stay at bedside." She smiled glowingly and looked at the bishop.

Ben began by eliciting a brief medical history as he performed a physical exam. Wynter obtained a set of vital signs, Stella prepared to perform an EKG and Trudi drew several vials of blood and left for the lab, bulling her way through the crowded hallway. "We'll eventually need a urine sample. Heart has a regular rate and rhythm, lungs are clear and there is no lower extremity edema. Let's hold off on the chest X-ray for a while." He began to step away and immediately the bishop moved forward. Ben asked him to step back for a few more minutes. Thankfully, both Mr. Schaefer and the bishop remained a couple of steps back to allow the staff unfettered access to the patient. Ben met Stella at the counter. "She's still wearing her..." he paused, "...I forget what they call them."

"Magic underwear. She and the bishop fought me tooth and nail not to remove them, so I gave up and put the gown on over them."

Ben smiled, "Religious undergarments; apparently effective against slings, arrows and Satan's minions..."

"...but not the errant internal workings of the human body," Stella finished.

They smiled to each other. "I swear, Ben; your humor gets a shade darker with every passing week. Let me get you your EKG."

He walked over to John and Zina who were conversing quietly in the corner. "Thanks for sticking around; we'll sort this out shortly."

Zina smiled, "Largest gathering in Bedlam on a Friday night even without alcohol being served."

John laughed and added, "The closest competition is the Dirty Shame's Christmas gala. By the way, Ben, my sister is flying back for Christmas. Mom is holding her own but chose to stay in Houston with her sister for the holidays. You should expect a call and a dinner invite within days."

"I'd love a home cooked meal but I'll have to play it by ear since I'm on call next week and have a short vacation planned soon afterward."

"Better jump on the opportunity if you want a free meal. Believe me; Paula will make it happen, eventually."

"Maybe one of you should sneak out while you can and grab a couple of sandwiches or something."

John looked over at the ER entrance, "Right, and fight our way through that mob?"

Zina tapped on the bathroom door, "We can duck out through the X-ray room if needed."

Excusing himself, Ben returned to the foot of the gurney and Stella handed him the just completed EKG. He briefly studied it, "I don't see anything acute going on but I'll compare it with any old EKG's in her chart. I'm going to take her chart and go across the hall in case I need to fax it or call her cardiologist." Moving to Mrs. Schaefer's right he asked her, "Are you having any chest pain Mrs. Schaefer?"

"Not really, doctor."

"Mrs. Schaefer, just a reminder, I am a physician assistant. Are you having pain at all?"

"You're my doctor tonight. Every now and then I have a little twinge; much better than it was, thank you."

Ben retrieved the chart from the counter and quietly told Stella, "If her pain returns we'll consider a Nitro tablet or maybe paste but let's check her blood pressure first so we don't bottom her out. I will definitely call Dr. Romano or his counterpart after Trudi sends up the lab results. Be back shortly."

"I'm good here, as long as the hordes behave."

He slowly made his way through the hallway crowd a few unidentified people asking questions; "How is she?," "Is she going to be okay?," "What's wrong with her?" none of which he could nor would he answer. "I'm sorry I cannot discuss Mrs. Schaefer's medical information." Finally making it to the office he entered and gratefully closed the door behind him.

While burrowing his way through the crowd at the ER doors he found that they had again bunched in the doorway, the doors were reopened and now the living mass was bulging into the ER. Inside the emergency room he found the gurney once again surrounded by the bishop, Mr. Schaefer, and an additional six people he assumed to be relatives. Stella wormed her way out from behind the head of the gurney and met Ben walking back to the counter. Starring straight forward, her lips puffed out expelling an extended breath. Ben reached out and gently tapped her right upper arm.

"You okay?"

"Yeah, just peachy," more than a hint of exasperation in her voice.

Ben coaxed her to midway down the counter. "What's going on Stella?"

"Nothing," in resignation.

He looked her in the eye, raised his eyebrows, gave a near imperceptible, "let's hear it," nod.

"For some reason tonight I'm suddenly over working in front of the entire tabernacle choir and negotiating with the patient and her husband and the bishop into letting me do my job."

A quick look over his shoulder at the doorway and then at the gurney reinforced that they were being overwhelmed and patient care could very well become compromised. Then he noticed John and Zina standing in the far corner and motioned for them to join him and Stella. Wynter, who had been standing by the second bay gurney entering vital signs into the patient chart walked over. Ben reviewed the chart and found the vital signs to be stable. Addressing John and Zina he observed, "You're still here. I thought one of you was going out for food."

"Zina had good intentions but the Lincoln is still blocking us in."

John's partner nodded, tightlipped.

Ben bristled. "I spoke to Dr. Romano, Mrs. Schaefer's cardiologist. We reviewed her labs and EKG and although there is nothing glaringly wrong he's worried that her angina is becoming unstable. He wants her flown to Billings so he is contacting the fixed wing medical transport. Right now I'm going to address our noncompliant visitors and then we'll notify Mrs. Schaefer of Dr. Romano's wishes and prepare her for her flight. Zina and John, once we empty the ER would you maintain the door security?"

"No problem."

"With pleasure."

He removed the ER phone from its cradle and positioned himself between the doors and the gurney. Skipping formalities he launched into his announcement at a level he was sure would gain everyone's attention. "I have asked politely for everyone to observe some basic rules, provide Mrs. Schaefer with the privacy that she deserves and to make room for the ER staff to do their work. I also asked to have all vehicles blocking the ambulance and the emergency room access ramp moved. You have ignored our requests and shown no consideration to our patient, so now I am ordering everyone out of the emergency room except for staff and Mr. Schaefer. If you would like to stay in the hallway then please stand against the walls so the staff may move freely. Everyone needs to start moving now and I want those vehicles moved immediately." Ben held up the phone for all to see, "I have absolutely no problem calling the sheriff's department and requesting a deputy to help with crowd control and to ticket or tow any vehicle hindering access to an emergency vehicle."

There was a low murmur, a shuffling of feet but no definitive movement. Ben waited an additional 10 seconds and said for all to hear, "You leave me no choice." He punched in 911 for all to see, put the phone to his ear and waited for dispatch to answer.

Suddenly he detected movement as the bulge of people began to recede into the hallway. Relatives around the gurney expressed fond wishes and promised to wait in the hallway. "911, what is your emergency?"

"Hello, this is Ben Parker at the Bedlam Hospital." He covered the receiver with his hand, "John, Zina, would you close the ER doors?" Staring directly at the bishop who had stood fast, Ben made a motion as if he were turning a key in an ignition. The bishop whispered something in Mrs. Schaefer's ear and exited the ER. "Yes, dispatch," he walked over to the counter out of earshot, "I'm calling to notify you that we will be transferring a cardiac patient to Billings, Montana. We are expecting a fixed wing aircraft to be landing at the local airport in approximately 90 minutes. The Bedlam Volunteer Ambulance is currently here and manned by two EMTs and will not need to be dispatched...Yes, Ben Parker the physician assistant...thank you. Goodbye.

The ambulance was currently transporting the flight crew and the Schaefers to the airport. Trudi had just pulled out headed for home. Wynter and Roxy, the other CNA on duty, were checking on nursing home patients. Stella was completing her charting. The ER hallway was empty. Ben stood on the far edge of the ambulance pad noting the drop in temperature, the crisp night air still not hinting at the predicted precipitation. A waning crescent moon hung in the sky and he could easily identify Orion and Cassiopeia.

"Give a guy a little encouragement and viola, next thing you know he's a raging, power hungry tyrant. Okay, maybe a benevolent dictator who also wrestles the local clergy into submission."

"You may bow in adulation and kiss my ring; however, I really do prefer cash."

"Ya done good tonight, Ben."

"Thanks, Stella. The whole team did well."

They both stared up at the crystal clear night sky, comfortably oblivious as to what Mother Nature had in store for their near future.

This does not bode well. Ben stood staring out his front picture window at the ever deepening snow accumulating on his porch and front yard. The wind was unrelenting forming pockets and riffles along the west row of lilacs and around the two struggling Black Hill Spruce trees in his front yard. While sweeping snow into impressive drifts along his steps and porch, the wind was also drifting and layering snow onto the trees and bushes defining his east property line. The blizzard had started in the early morning hours and gave no indication of abating. Earlier today he had shoveled the front porch, a path to the garage and the drifts that had accumulated against his garage doors prior to driving to the hospital to make rounds at 9. The town roads were untouched by plows. He broke trail on the empty streets estimating that were the snow on the level it would measure a good 8 to 10 inches in depth.

Daytime visibility had been at best 100 feet, maybe at times closer to 75 feet and he had thought that he had been driving prudently for the conditions yet, he hadn't accounted for the ice layers under the snow prior to sliding his truck through the first intersection. After slowing to a crawl he had still found traction to be at a minimum and attempts at plowing through drifts were tenuous. A pickup truck had been abandoned in the center of the highway, perpendicular to normal traffic flow and at the corner where he would turn off to the hospital a car had overshot the corner and was nose down in the barrow pit, rear wheels suspended well above the tire tracks that had almost completely been filled in by the blowing snow. There did not appear to be anyone in the older Chrysler product as he carefully navigated the turn, his rear tires sliding momentarily and then regaining traction. At the hospital Dwight was bundled up and laboriously at work with his snow blower clearing sidewalks by the main entrance as Ben pulled into the parking lot and slid on the snow covered glare ice before the curb brought him to a stop.

Karmma was at the nurses' station which, had been considerably culled of the most flagrantly commercial Christmas decorations and now presented a more subdued but festive holiday look.

"How cold is it Ben?"

"It's a bit brisk." Ben used a rule of thumb handed down from his father and grandfather. During the winter months 32 degrees and warmer was "spring like," zero to 32 was "brisk," zero to 30 below was "cold," and less than minus 30 was "fucking cold." Any temperature below zero with severe wind chill factors was considered "getting western."

He had reviewed the charts of his three hospital patients before he and Karmma made rounds. "I don't see the lab reports on our pneumonia or CHF patients."

"The lab tech hasn't made it in yet. You know they closed the highways about an hour ago?"

"No, I didn't." Karmma had sat down at her computer and pulled up the Montana Travelers Information Site Map. Almost all of the roads in the state of Montana were colored purple for ice or black ice, broken red lines for severe driving conditions or solid red for closed. Bedlam was surrounded by solid red for at least 80 miles and more. Ben looked at the Southwest section of the map and saw almost every road south of the Interstate, extending south to the borders of Idaho and Wyoming, was colored broken red. After lunch he'll call his father and find out how he's doing.

A high functioning octogenarian, Ben's father was self-sufficient with an unyielding stubbornness and who flawlessly played the role of aging curmudgeon. Ben was more worried about his father's proclivity of involving himself in Good Samaritan scenarios that required more physicality and stamina than the demands of his daily life. A number of underprepared and ill-informed new neighbors had moved into the area oblivious to their shortcomings, their caviler attitudes and actions periodically placing life, limb or property in jeopardy. Ben knew that his father did not suffer fools gladly, however, could not ignore their plights and would not let them fail under the weight of their own ignorance. His father was one to offer up his own shirt to someone who had lost his; however, it was not unknown for him to unabashedly inform them that they were a moron for having lost their shirt in the first place. Ben loved his dad, often hoping that there was more that he could do to protect his dad from his own good intentions.

"Thank you Karmma. Let's go do hospital rounds and hope that everyone stays at home and behaves because we won't be able to ship anyone who gets themselves into a real jackpot."

"Hello, Dad."

"Hiya Ben. You short on cash again?"

"Ha! You think that you're so damn funny. I'm financially stable but if you've got extra you have my address. I just called to see how you were faring. The travel map was showing the roads down there were a bit dicey."

"The what map?"

"It's online, Dad. When you break down and buy yourself a computer I will show you. Better yet, I'll bring my laptop with me when I come and give you a brief tutorial."

"I don't need a computer. I've got pens, paper, a typewriter; I can read, write, multiply and divide, read a map and compass and own a TV. Why on earth would I buy a computer?"

"I don't know, Dad. Maybe to try something different, challenge yourself?"

"It's a challenge often enough to get these old bones moving. So what's on your mind besides my being technology challenged?"

"What have you been up to today?" Ben was hoping that he didn't hear the word shovel.

"Drinking coffee and shoveling. I was getting ready to go over to Pasacovich's and help him get his snowplow mounted since he's so Johnny on the spot every winter."

Ben had a fleeting flashback to his recent dream; Pasacovich must have made bail. "Just you two old farts?"

"It's not rocket science…" Edward Parker sounded indignant, "…plus he has that engine hoist that will handle the weight. I help him mount the plow and he clears my driveway all winter; fair deal."

130

Ben knew not to say "be careful." "I'm only teasing, Dad."

"If you're going to tease then make it about something I have no control over like," he paused, "why I haven't found that good looking, rich widow lady, yet. Again, what else is on your mind Ben?"

"Really, Dad, just checkin' in and getting your weather report."

"How bad is it up there in the hinterland?"

"Pretty damn foul. It started with freezing rain around two AM on Saturday morning followed by a few inches of snow in the early morning. It warmed to above freezing in the afternoon with some melting but everything froze solid again Saturday night. The temperature kept dropping and the blizzard blew in during the early morning hours and continues in full force. That's it in a nutshell."

"You have somewhere to go for Christmas?"

"I'm on call so I'll probably come in for rounds and play some cribbage with Salty."

"That old jarhead? Give him my regards."

"Will do. I'll call you on Christmas."

"Stay safe son."

"You too, Dad. Bye."

He awoke in pitch blackness, reached for the bedside lamp and turned the switch. Nothing happened, so he turned the switch off and back on again. Crap, the bulb is out. The phone continued to ring. Ben noticed that his digital alarm clock numbers were not glowing. Shit, the power must be off. By reflex he located his phone. "Hello."

"Power's off."

"Stating the obvious will not make the situation better, Stella."

"No, but stating the obvious puts you on alert before you stumble around blindly trying to locate your pants."

"Why am I looking for my pants?"

"Because Mr. Thorsten died and we have an interesting situation developing."

Mr. Thorsten was a 90-year-old nursing home resident with advanced heart, lung and kidney diseases who had been slowly losing ground to his pneumonia, "the old man's friend," drifting towards the great unknown.

"Sorry to hear that he's gone. So I need to bring my thinking cap?"

"That, along with your flashlight and cold weather gear. The temperature has dropped to 10 below."

"See you shortly."

"Take your time Ben, besides you may have to shovel your way out."

Ben dressed appropriately stuffing a balaclava and an extra pair of gloves in his coat pockets and turned the kitchen faucet to a trickle hoping that it was enough to prevent his pipes from freezing solid. Opening the back door he realized that Stella was right; he grabbed his shovel knowing that the garage doors would be drifted in.

"Who dares to ruin my beauty sleep?"

"Sorry to wake you Dwight. It's Ben Parker."

"What's shakin' doc?" There was a pause followed by, "can't find my watch, what time is it? Zero dark thirty?"

"Are you available? We need your expertise at the hospital."

"Care to clue me in?"

"When you get here, it's a sensitive issue. And warm up your snow blower."

They sat at one table in the dimly lit cafeteria, a pot of coffee being divided amongst them; two CNA's, Stella and Ben. Dwight had made another trip to check the generator building and now joined them at the table. Stella poured a cup of coffee and slid it over to Dwight who smiled a thank you as he brought the cup up to sip. His nose and cheeks were ruddy red from wind and the snow it drove horizontally at a near continuous 20 miles per hour, his lips looked chapped. Snow caught in the treads of his boots was now melting and creating a puddle around his feet. Stella scolded him amicably, "Wear your scarf ninny, so you don't catch your death."

Ben began, "So, here is the current state of the state…"

Earlier, after entering Mr. Thorsten's room and attesting to his demise, Ben had sat in his office for some time reviewing and contemplating the numerous unusual circumstances that had by chance promulgated this ethical and time sensitive dilemma. Considering the dignity and care of Mr. Thorsten's remains, his family, the residents, patients and staff of the hospital, Ben had weighed the narrowed possibilities afforded after gathering information, reviewing the resources at hand and then discussing additional options and suggestions as presented by Stella and Dwight. He had mentally listed pros and cons, dissecting each carefully and assigning merit until he had settled on a plan. After a final review he had concluded that at this juncture in time he had no other recourse but to implement the plan.

"…Mr. Thorsten died. In all likelihood, the pneumonia he was battling finally overwhelmed his already highly compromised cardio, pulmonary and renal systems. The moment he died he technically became a bio hazard. Normally we would contact the family, the national donor registry, the funeral home and coroner's office if warranted. Stella has notified the donor registry. The family has been contacted but unfortunately, though maybe fortuitously considering the circumstances, is currently stuck in Minnesota. There are no funeral home employees in the local vicinity, their planned overlap of vacation and travel times are in complete disarray due to the storms. The nearest funeral home employee is sitting in the air terminal in Salt Lake City. The sheriff, our county coroner, is snowed in on the reservation somewhere north of Slipknot and has only sporadic radio communication with dispatch. I've spoken with Deputy Stalcup, the deputy county coroner, who is up to his neck directing local emergency services and he has put his blessing on my plan. If we have any extenuating problems we may contact him and he will stop in as able. The roads are closed in every direction out of Bedlam and the power is out in all of the adjoining counties. This means the funeral home has no power, no proper storage for the remains of any deceased, and dispatch believes that the sheriff has their set of the funeral home keys.

We are on generator power, which, Dwight estimates provides 50-60% of our normal demand. We cannot allow Mr. Thorsten to remain in his room for an unlimited period of time, nor can we store him in the kitchen cooler, potentially contaminating the food stores. Dwight has determined that we cannot cool down the basement and jeopardize the general stores, the mechanical room and any exposed water and sewage lines. The only safe sanctuary in which to place Mr. Thorsten is the maintenance shed in back of the hospital, behind the gazebo. I located several body bags in general stores so the plan is that Dwight and I will blaze a trail from the rear door of the north wing out to the maintenance shed while

Stella, Roxy and Wynter prepare and place Mr. Thorsten into a body bag and transport him on a spare gurney to the rear door. Dwight and I will carry him out to the maintenance shed where he will remain until he can be transferred to the funeral home. This decision is mine and mine alone, so I accept all responsibility and will deal with any potential repercussions." Ben looked at everyone individually and asked, "Any questions? Any suggestions? Anything that I may have overlooked?"

Roxy and Wynter looked at each other and back to Ben, concern in their eyes.

"Why can't we just leave him where he is, and, you know, just open the windows or something?" Wynter sounded anxious when she added, "Is this even legal?"

"What if we put him in the body bag and then in his bathtub," Roxy paused, thought for a minute and continued, "and we can cover him in ice and put 'duck' tape all around the door." She looked expectantly and seemed rather pleased with her idea.

Stella looked both women in the eye. "We have to protect Mr. Thorsten's dignity yet at the same time protect the health of all of our patients and residents. Sometimes we need to employ extraordinary measures and this is one of those times. Roxy that is an imaginative idea. Unfortunately, Mr. Thorsten has a shower, no bathtub. Looking directly at Wynter, "and yes Wynter, it is legal. Let hop to, we can discuss this further as we work. "Ben, Dwight, are we ready?"

Roxy piped up, "Don't we need to ask Mr. Westergard or Dr. Saroni about this whole thing?"

Stella sent her a look that would blister paint. Roxy appeared oblivious to her melting mascara.

Ben responded directly and firmly, "Westergard is on vacation in Hawaii and Saroni is god knows where. We are it, the staff on duty, and responsible for the safety and health of our patients and residents and quite frankly, even if we could contact Westergard and waited for a decision, well, let's say it is better that we act in good faith and ask for forgiveness rather than wait for permission."

As Dwight arose from his chair he chimed in, "Okay then, lets tag 'em, bag 'em, and cool 'em out."

Ben rolled his eyes but kept his mouth shut. They all headed off to their appointed tasks.

As Ben shoveled the rear door clear of a three foot drift of snow, Dwight attempted to quietly roll the snow blower down the north hallway past the closed doors of the sleeping residents and Alzheimer's patients. Ben held open the wide, wheelchair accessible outside door as Dwight maneuvered over the threshold.

"This machine is pretty loud but maybe the wind will help to deaden the sound." Dwight was nearly yelling to be heard through the wool scarf protecting his face and above the howling wind gusts. Snow continued to blow by horizontally. "You'd think with this wind all the snow would end up in South Dakota."

He nodded as Dwight worked at starting the snow blower. They spent the next 30 minutes cutting, blowing and shoveling a narrow swath through the 70 feet of drifted snow to the maintenance shed. Dwight had turned on the flood light above the rear door and the lights of the sidewalk leading to the gazebo, however, most of their scant illumination was supplied by Dwight's head lamp, their flashlights and a small headlight mounted on the snow blower. Any shadows that may have been thrown were obscured by the windblown snow which also partially filled in the path behind them as they progressed. There was a thick layer of ice under the snow that made footing tenuous at times. Ben shoveled and then chipped ice at the base of the shed doors in order to free them. Once the right side door was free Dwight entered and Ben, his fingers starting to numb, continued to free the other door. When he finished he swung open the left hand door and joined Dwight inside. As he eyed the contents and confines of the shed the wind blew that door shut and rattled the other. There was a waist high work bench extending across the back of the shed.

"Not much room in here but I cleared the bench and floor area the best I could. We should be able to lay him on top of the bench"

Tools, gardening implements, spare lawn mower parts and several boxes were stacked in the corners, stuffed under the bench or hung on the side walls. "This should work Dwight. Let's go get Mr. Thorsten." Dwight pushed open the wind closed door and wedged a set of hedge clippers in the corner of the door jam in an attempt to keep it open.

Stella opened the door when they arrived; a zippered body bag strapped to an emergency room backboard lay on the gurney. "It might be easier to carry him on a rigid backboard than slung between the two of you. Do you want a hand carrying him?"

Ben and Dwight had each taken an end of the backboard and had easily lifted it up. "No thanks Stella, we can manage okay. The backboard is a great idea." They gingerly walked down the pathway, the blown in snow packing under their combined weights yet, sliding on the hidden ice. They lifted Mr. Thorsten onto the work counter, loosened the straps and slid the backboard from under the body bag. Ben remarked, "Pretty tight quarters in here but it will suffice. He won't be in here for long."

"Hopefully, but after a day in here we won't need the backboard to stiffen him up."

Ben didn't answer, instead he was offering up a short prayer. He and Dwight stepped out and together muscled close the doors against the harsh, frigid wind and secured the hasp and padlock. Ben found himself yelling just to hear himself in the wind, "Dwight, do you have an extra key in case you're gone somewhere?"

"And just how far do you think I might get?"

"Point taken, smartass."

Stella had removed the gurney and held the door as Ben and Dwight maneuvered the snow blower into the small foyer. Stella stood sentry as they stomped the snow off their boots and shook themselves free of snow.

"I'll leave the snow blower in here; it will be easier to start when I come to clear the sidewalks in the morning."

"Thank you for all of your help Dwight."

"No problem. You do know what your nickname is, don't you doc?

"Stop, I don't need to hear it tonight." Ben looked at his watch and declared, "I'm going to head home, catch a couple hours of sleep and take care of Mr. Thorsten's paperwork before the clinic opens."

"Not so fast, Ben. Mrs. Skulaski just threw up and has a 101 degree fever. Would you mind taking a quick look at her before heading home?"

In resignation Ben answered, "Sure Stella, give me a minute to warm up and I'll meet you in her room."

"Take your time. She hasn't got any pressing travel plans."

Dwight smiled at Stella and spoke to Ben, "I knew there was a reason that I liked this woman."

"Callie, good morning, it's Ben Parker. I found your message and...Sure...No problem Callie...I...Uh, huh, is there...Okay...Alright, I don't see that...No, no don't worry about…Yes, again that's…Who?…You have enough on…Okay, by me…Yep, I'll just…Uh, huh…sure, that works for…well then call when…no don't apologize, the…Please take…Alright, be safe and…Let us know if we…Yep, okay then…Yes, goodbye, Callie." He slowly laid the receiver back into the phone cradle.

"You are quite the conversationalist Mr. Ben Parker." Myrna and Ben sat in his office, Ben staring at his Duck Boy wall calendar, the battered and bandaged Grizzly Bear Insemination Team staring back at him, as he confirmed that it was indeed Monday, December 22, the fourth day of his eight day stretch, and feeling more like it was a state of incarceration rather than working at his chosen profession. Myrna sat, a repeated Christmas tree, wreath, ribbon, ornament and garland motif on her scrubs, one leg crossed over the other, resting her coffee mug on her knee. She was studying his blue Viagra wall clock. "I like what you have done with the room." Nodding in appreciation she added, "Early cellblock?"

"Callie is wound around the axel this morning, what with being drifted in over half a mile from the highway, which, itself is closed, 30 below temperature, a number of cows spread from hell to breakfast, the water line to the barn and corral frozen, her husband cursing the heavens as he tries to get the tractor with the plow started, and her two teenagers already sniping at each other. And to top it off her coffee maker went on the fritz. Obviously she will not be making it into work this morning. She wanted to make some calls and locate someone to fill in for her but; I'm not exactly sure which one of us decided that the hospital staff would handle it. She will call with updates. I'm open to any ideas, Myrna."

"We can rotate the nursing staff throughout the day. They can answer the phones, pull charts, and take vitals. If they get into a bind I can come help out. I don't see a problem with this."

"Good plan, thank you Myrna. It's what? Twenty five, maybe 30 below and the roads are closed, so maybe we may have a light day."

"Don't get carried away here and use the Q word."

They tapped coffee mug to Pepsi can, took a gulp and headed out to face the day.

Ben lifted the receiver and answered, "Bedlam Rural Health Clinic, Ben Parker speaking."

"Hi Ben, it's Callie. How are you doing?"

He was sitting at Callie's desk, a stack of clinic charts at his left, nursing home charts to his right, and three ER charts staring him in the face. A minor headache, abnormal for him, was currently being treated with ibuprofen and he was attributing it to lack of sleep and mild dehydration. Living on coffee and soda pop, both diuretics inducing more frequent urination, had also provided him with enough caffeine to stay functionally awake.

"Great, Callie, the crew all rotated through so we did fine."

"You sound tired Ben, are you okay?"

"I'm doing okay." He wanted to defer the questions. "Did you get things turned around out there?"

"Yes! Mark and I almost have a handle on things. His brother snowmobiled out to help and things are definitely looking up. We got the…"

Ben was quietly making a mental list of his patients today as he listened without hearing Callie's ranch report. In the emergency room, two people with near identical non-displaced wrist fractures were splinted and stable until they could travel to see an Orthopedist, and a middle aged women with a painful but non-fracture hip injury. The hidden ice was taking its toll on pedestrians. In the clinic, two acute bronchitis's, a strep throat, three viral upper respiratory infections, a urinary tract infection, gout pain and a refill for a depression medication. Five nursing home residents now had the as yet unidentified gastro-intestinal virus and everyone was hoping that the gown, glove and room isolation protocol would slow the spread among the residents. The hospital patient with pneumonia had improved enough to return home but Ben felt that it was prudent to keep him another day since he lived 10 miles out of Bedlam. A slow clinic day had certainly helped to balance the demands of the hospital, nursing home and ER.

He and Myrna had been discussing the need to closely monitor the hospital pharmacy inventory, when they were coincidently interrupted by a phone call from an absent Heidi Lafevbre who was "stuck out of town" at an undisclosed location and calling to impress upon them the need to closely monitor the hospital pharmacy inventory. "The pharmacist lives in Sunnvale and there's no telling when he'll be able to return to town and open the Bedlam Pharmacy." Leaving Myrna to continue the phone call with the DON on her own, he had retreated to the relative silence of the clinic office.

"...and Mark and his brother should have us plowed out to the road tonight so hopefully I should make it in tomorrow morning."

"Good to hear everything is going better for you two. Don't worry about getting in here in the morning if the weather gets worse tonight. Myrna and the hospital staff rotated through and we can do it again tomorrow if needed. Callie, sorry, but I have to get out to the nurses' station and write some orders." He felt bad telling the white lie but he needed a few minutes to decompress.

"Okay Ben, thanks for being so understanding. I'll see you tomorrow. Bye."

"Good night, Callie."

Ben was asleep in his recliner when the phone rang. It was once again pitch black as he pressed the button on his watch to illuminate the face thinking, "They can't possibly be calling me again so soon," and confirming that he had arrived home a mere 45 minutes ago. He had eaten half a box of wheat thins and must have fallen asleep. As he attempted to awaken from his fog of exhaustion he felt certain that he had turned on the floor lamp and now turned the switch twice. He realized that the power most be off again, having been off more than on during the past 24 hours. He located the phone, "This better be something I can take care of from the comfort of a partially warm home."

"Good evening Ben, sorry to bother you but as you know you are the only game in town."

"Stella? When I left, Pammula was on duty. What's up?"

"I was dumb enough to answer the phone. Pammula's babysitter came down sick with the same stomach virus that her kids have so she called me to 'Paaleasssssse' come in and cover her shift. I said sure and 10 minutes after I got here Mr. Schumacher died."

"Mr. Schumacher? He wasn't ill."

"No, he wasn't, but apparently while he was sleeping his poor 92-year-old body decided to give up the ghost."

"Crap. I mean, forget I said that, I mean I'm sorry to hear that. Any chance the funeral home is back in business yet?"

"Dispatch confirmed that the roads are still closed, the sheriff is still among the missing, rather still out of town with the keys, and the weather is the status quo. The power is off, temperature is now 22 below, snow is horizontal and Dwight is on his way in. He has now verbally expressed the sentiment that he now agrees with everyone else that you my friend are a shit magnet."

"Thank you for that Stella. You have managed to turn the last holdout, perhaps the only person left in the hospital who may have had a modicum of faith in me, into believing me to be a medical pariah."

"Don't try to pin that on me Mr. PA certified. You have earned that title all on your own."

"Maybe, but you certainly didn't make much of an attempt to give me plausible denial."

"So, are you coming in or what?"

"See you shortly."

"Need I remind you to dress warm and wear you mittens?"

The nursing home census had been one male resident less than full prior to Mr. Thorsten's death, his room being a double and housing only Mr. Thorsten. During the day hospital staff had carefully boxed and stored Mr. Thorsten's belongings in a basement storage room and industriously cleaned, disinfected and readied the room for its next resident admission. Mr. Schumacher had a roommate and tonight's CNA's, Tyraa and Sydney had with care and compassion moved the roommate to Mr. Thorsten's former room, which now his temporary quarters. Once Ben and Stella together had confirmed Mr. Schumacher's death Ben had officially pronounced for the record at 1232 AM. Several photos hung on the wall of Mr. Schumacher and what Ben surmised to be his wife, son and daughter. Other framed photos appeared to be of extended family and friends. Of late, the frail gentleman who was relegated to wheelchair transport was but a shadow of the once healthy and smiling visage in the photos.

"Mr. Schumacher's wife passed away several years ago, they lived together here in the Nursing Home. He has one son in Texas and one daughter in Arizona. I need to call the donor registry and then I will call the two children. The daughter holds power of financial and medical attorney. I gave Tyraa and Sydney a briefing on what transpired yesterday with Mr. Thorsten but told them that when you arrived you would make the decision on the disposition of Mr. Schumaker's body."

"Thank you Stella. I really don't see that we have any other option but to place Mr. Schumacher outside with Mr. Thorsten. Do you?"

Stella shook her head, "No, I don't think we have a choice. Do you want to meet in the cafeteria when Dwight finishes gassing up the snow blower?"

"Yes. I'll go to the basement for a body bag if you would round up Tyraa and Sydney. I'll see you in the cafeteria."

"Hiya doc, just like day ja view all over again."

Ben had met up with Dwight in the lobby on his way to the cafeteria. He could see Stella, Tyraa and Sydney sitting at the far end of the cafeteria, a pot of coffee and cups set on the table top. "You're in a good mood for someone who had their beauty sleep interrupted again. You didn't happen to start a pool on which patients weren't going to make it to Christmas, did you?"

"Hell no doc." Ben couldn't tell if Dwight was faking his indignant tone. "I have principles, though I have been thinking of starting a pool for when you clean Saroni's clock."

Ben looked at him with fire in his eyes.

Dwight put up his hands in protest, "Just kidding Ben, just kidding."

"Let's go join the ladies in the cafeteria. We are faced with pretty much the same scenario as yesterday with Mr. Thorsten so you can have a cup of coffee while I give Tyraa and Sydney a briefing."

"I'm curious doc, but is stacking bodies in a maintenance shed something they look for in a resume?" Dwight said in all innocence, though a smirk was lying in wait.

"Leave it to you Dwight," Ben could not keep a straight face between his exhaustion and increasing level of black humor. "Truthfully, I can't say that I've run across that question or for that matter this particular set of circumstances. However, you may use me as a reference and I'll write you a glowing letter of recommendation."

"You're all heart Ben, but I was actually thinking of you. Let's get some coffee."

"Is it my imagination or is it darker, colder, windier and the snow deeper than our first polar expedition?"

Dwight turned off the snow blower, the path now cleared to the maintenance shed yet filling back in with blowing snow. "What?" the wind literally screamed at times, "What did you say Ben? I couldn't hear you," Dwight's words unintelligible from the scarf covering his mouth and the gusting wind.

Ben realized that the combination of wearing a balaclava, a wool watch cap covering his head and ears and the fierce wind, it would be impossible to hear any conversation. He had the snowdrifts shoveled clear of the shed doors so he lifted the padlock with one hand and shined his flashlight on the key hole. Dwight produced his key, unlocked the padlock and both of them opened the doors. After stepping inside they pulled the doors shut, each of them holding on to an inside handle to keep them from blowing open from the wind. Dwight drew his scarf down under his chin and Ben folded his balaclava up over his face and cap. Clouds of vapor were exhaled with each super chilled breath.

Ben started, "Mr. Thorsten can remain on the bench but we'll have to lay Mr. Schumacher flat on the floor."

"Agreed. Once they're stiff, if not frozen, we can stand them up if needed."

"Jesus Dwight, that's rather undignified and disrespectful." A violent shiver ran up and down his spine and he stuffed his hands into his armpits.

"More so than storing them in a body bag in a tool shed at 30 below zero?"

"Point taken but we should at least let them lay."

"Might I point out the rule of threes?"

"You too? You're anticipating a third poor soul will give up the ghost during this cold spell?"

"I'm just saying."

"Alright, I'll keep that in mind. Let's go get Mr. Schumacher."

Stella was waiting for them inside the rear door foyer, the body bag containing Mr. Schumacher was strapped to a backboard, as had Mr. Thorsten been secured.

"Room enough for Mr. Schumacher?"

"Yes, and our MVP here," pointing at Dwight brushing the snow off himself, "and to clarify, most vocal pessimist, has already pre-planned the shed space for a

146

third poor soul since he's an adamant believer in the rule of threes."

Ben and Dwight had positioned themselves at either end of the backboard and were about to lift when Stella laughed and said, "I wish we could dispel that myth but I hate to think of how many times it has proven true."

"Hey you two don't be dissin' me. It's not a myth or black magic and I'm not a pessimist. It's a proven fact and universally accepted. The rule of threes exists; otherwise they wouldn't have made it one of Murphy's Laws."

Stella held open the door. "Safe sledding gentleman."

"Stella, I'm beat. Dwight headed home, Mr. Thorsten and Mr. Schumacher are safely though temporarily laid to rest, everyone in the hospital is tucked in, and all the orders for our nursing home patients with the stomach virus are complete. I'm tired of driving the roads of this winter wonderland so I'm going to catch a few zees in the little ER."

"Good choice, Ben. If you need anything call the nurses' station, otherwise I promise not to disturb you."

"Ben," her voice was soft but firm, "Ben, you need to wake up. Ben," she gently shook his shoulder staying at arm's length. "Ben, wake up Ben."

Ben woke up in a startled response, immediately sat up; her hand remained steady on his shoulder. "What? Oh, hey there, what's up Stella?"

"Sorry Ben, but Mrs. Milic had a fairly nasty fall and…"

Considering recent history, Ben reacted by thinking worst case scenario, "She's dead? She isn't dead is she?"

"No, no Ben," Stella tried to sound reassuring, "but given her age, anti-coagulation therapy and her complaint of hip pain I have to follow protocol and notify the provider on call. I think that she's more scared than anything."

"Okay, okay." He shook his head, rubbed his face with both hands and unconsciously scratched the back of his head. Now he looked at Stella with disappointment in his eyes, "You promised me Stella, you promised that you wouldn't wake me up and I believed in you."

Stella, with a sympathetic voice and a sly smile replied, "Yes Ben, I know I promised and if it's of any solace, you still have Leprechauns, the Easter Bunny and Santa Claus."

"Are you contagious Ben? You look like crap." Marni stood in the main lobby, in front of the nurse's station, bundled in a bulky, florescent orange snowsuit, snowmobile helmet tucked under her arm, red nose and ruddy cheeks revealed as she unwound a wool scarf from around her lower face, with melting snow and ice in rivulets forming puddles around her snow mobile boots. Oversized, waterproof mittens adorned her hands and a pair of sneakers dangled from her hand by their laces.

"Between the arctic survival suit, helmet hair and the frozen snot above your upper lip, any chance that you just arrived off the deck of a Coast Guard icebreaker?"

"Always the charmer, Ben. I was feeling sorry for you so I came in. I could just as easily return home with my handsome chauffeur and spend the day in my little French maid outfit entertaining my husband." She motioned towards Michael who was now entering the lobby doors dressed in similar attire.

Ben blushed, recovered, waved at Michael and said, "I didn't expect you here. I thought you two had gone to

148

Seattle for Christmas. That being said, I'm glad to see you."

"Saturday night we were on the road headed for Seattle when Michael's brother called from Missoula and told us that the weather in northern Idaho was foul and headed east and south. He recommended that we consider turning around rather than being stranded out in the middle of nowhere. We thought about it and Bedlam sounded as good as nowhere so here we are."

"How bad are the roads out of town?"

Myrna joined them. She took Marni's sneakers and the two of them exchanged smiles.

"They're still pretty dicey but the Travelers Information Map shows some of the surrounding areas opening up to emergency traffic only. I'll bet by noon we'll have the same rating. Our road hasn't seen a plow yet so we flipped a coin between snowmobile and horseback. Guess what won." Michael sidled up next to her. "Actually I wanted to ride in yesterday afternoon but Michael couldn't get the snowmobile started so last night he worked on it and I helped." Marni was sounding more animated and pleased with herself. "We were out in the barn and holy crap it was cold. First he took off the dealy bob, opened up the hoopla and blew out the watch-a-ma-callit. Then he found that the fripnut was splayed and rebuilt that. The thing-a-ma-jig needed tweaking and a tab had snapped off the who-se-whats-it so he stole one off of his old sled..." Ben stole a look at Michael who was rolling his eyes skyward and trying hardily to suppress a laugh. "...jerry rigged it with a slip dibbet that he filched off of the fan belt determinator, then cambered and sniggered the jay bolt and muffler bearing, sucked the gas out, refilled with high test super sled octane and viola, it started." She looked at

Michael who looked as if he was biting his tongue, "Did I miss anything Michael?"

"No, honey, you pretty much nailed it."

"See? I'm not just a pretty face, I know my mechanics."

"You sure do, sweetie. I can't ever fault you for that."

Marni had a smug look as she bowed to her small audience and then addressed Ben. "How is our shit magnet faring?"

"Jesus, Marni, I expect better from you." Ben sounded disappointed.

"What other moniker would you deem appropriate Ben? Leading the employee's down a dubious road of disrespect for the good Dr. Saroni, harassing innocent cheerleaders, casting dispersions upon our Native American neighbors, alienating the Mormon community, forcing your hospital staff to perform double duty by covering the clinic, unleashing a Norovirus on the nursing home residents, and worst of all coercing poor Dwight into helping you stack bodies in the maintenance shed? You Ben Parker should be ashamed." Marni was taking delight in teasing Ben and he damn well knew it.   Ben looked at her and with a poor attempt at sounding angry asked, "Who the hell have you been talking to?" He turned to Myrna who shuffled behind Michael in an attempt to be less of a target.

"I've got my sources and don't you be blaming Myrna or anyone else." She next spoke to Myrna, "How much sleep has he had over the past few days?"

Myrna stepped back from behind Michael, "I would bet that during one stretch of 48 hours maybe three hours, four tops. Ben has been hammered since Saroni left on vacation. Maybe he might catch a few hours of sleep with you here today."

If anything, Ben looked to be a bit embarrassed, "I'm too tired to joust with you this morning."

"So, go home, I've got this."

"I can't just up and leave everything to you."

"Sure, you can. I'm a big girl now and I don't need any hand holding." She sounded defensive.

"I apologize Marni. That came out wrong, I meant no offense. On second thought I could use a short break and a couple hours of sleep so if you don't mind I'll take you up on your offer. Let's adjourn to my temporary office," Ben gestured with a sweeping arm towards the nurses' station, "and let me fill you in on the past few days. A strange and at times a sordid tale of intrigue, plague, death, salvation, and survival on the frozen tundra."

Myrna eyed Marni, raised an eyebrow and loudly whispered, "He's been vacillating between rapid mood swings, delusions of grandeur, flights of fantasy and hallucinations. Should we send him home or sedate him right here?"

"Home, for sure, otherwise we'll be responsible."

Ben ignored both of them. It just now registered with him that Michael was holding an overnight bag. "Marni, are you planning on spending the night?"

"It is my regular night for ER call. So, the answer is yes, I am staying the night."

"At the traveler's house?"

"Not if you have any rooms left open here."

Ben reached out and coaxed the bag away from Michael, "Let's see what's left here at the Inn and get you registered."

"You're early Ben; I thought you might try sleeping in."

Ben had just entered the hospital and joined Marni at the nurses' station front counter, "And a Merry Christmas to you as well Mrs. Capelletti. Since you were kind enough to come in and take call I considered it reasonable to come in early enough today so you could enjoy Christmas morning with your hubby."

"Merry Christmas to you as well Ben. Thank you for thinking of us. Michael was planning on picking me up at 10. Did you finally get some sleep?"

"Like a rock. I feel like I can face the world again. So, fill me in; what's the state of the state?"

Tara was sitting at the inside counter of the nurses' station wearing a green elf hat with white trim. Its pointed peak drooped considerably probably due to the heavy bell she had fastened to the top. There was a dark brown smudge on the fur trim riding over her forehead. A large Bismarck, slathered in chocolate and decorated with red and green sprinkles was poised at her mouth when she noticed Ben and Marni watching, "What?" Then almost begrudgingly she asked, "Would you like one?"

Marni replied quickly, "No thanks. I enjoy watching someone who so loves her pastry."

Tara motioned silently at Ben with the Bismarck.

"I would love one Tara, thank you."

She placed a half empty bakery box on the counter and Ben chose a twisted cinnamon crueler, said thank you and with a flourish took a big bite. "Damn tasty," said with a smile of satisfaction, "You were about to say…"

"Yesterday, the roads were opened up to emergency travel. The sheriff and the funeral home director showed up and I gave them the document file you had left for them. We paged Dwight and he met us at the north wing exit door carrying a shovel. I don't think that he particularly cares for the sheriff because he handed the funeral home director the key to the shed, the shovel to the sheriff and said, 'I'm sure you know how to operate this, it works the same on snow as bullshit.' To me he said, 'I'll be in the generator shop working on the snow blower,' and left. The sheriff will be calling you today or tomorrow. Neither of the families of the deceased has as yet made it to town. I discharged the pneumonia and CHF patients home with medications and instructions to follow up with Dr. Saroni on Monday. No new cases of Norovirus, I cured that problem." She was sounding self-assured and a little cocky. "The clinic was slow; the pharmacist made it to town, opened his pharmacy, restocked the hospital pharmacy and promptly closed at noon. I saw one sprained ankle and one case of sciatica in the emergency room. Hell, Ben, you could have covered yesterday standing on your head." She paused, gathered her thoughts and then continued. "This morning I had Myrna hold the dressing change on Salty's feet so you could examine them. Both his feet, especially the right, are looking pretty grim. What's the current plan?"

"The visiting orthopedist from Sunnvale was supposed to be here this past Monday but obviously didn't make it, so next Monday. I believe that eventually he will lose the right foot and several toes on the left, if not his forefoot. What Saroni has or has not told him is anybody's guess, however, knowing Saroni he'll leave it up to Orthopedist to deliver the prognosis."

"Poor guy. Between the Diabetes, his heart disease, declining kidney function, pulmonary fibrosis and poor lower extremity circulation he probably won't be returning home."

"I hate to say it but I agree; not much chance of that happening. Let's go take a look at his feet."

"Now I'm being tag teamed by Lucy and Ricky Ricardo?"

As she and Ben positioned themselves at his feet Marni replied, "Typhoid Mary and Mr. Hyde couldn't make it so you are stuck with us."

"As I would prefer; Merry Christmas Marni, Ben. What's shakin' on the lord's birthday?"

"We wanted to take another peek at your feet before Myrna dresses them."

"Better look now before the ortho doc has his way with them."

Ben and Marni gloved up and gently removed the sterile drapes covering his lower legs and feet. Ben gently palpated Salty's feet, examining and checking for color, temperature, circulation, edema and tenderness. His lower legs were discolored with brown lesions and the scabs of superficial ulcerations as a result of his venous insufficiency. The deep ulcerations, wounds and skin discoloration of Salty's right and left feet were the status quo, deep, dusky, and without indications of improvement."

"Any pain today, Salty?"

"Oh, some generalized aches everywhere but my feet. It's similar to having a couple blocks of wood attached to my legs."

They gently replaced the drapes and discarded their gloves into a red bio hazard receptacle.

"As I told you on Monday, Salty, the Orthopedist called when he could not make it up here. He wants me to call him if anything worsens, otherwise he will be seeing you on Monday."

"What's your opinion Ben?"

Salty was putting him on the spot and Ben thought he knew why, though it made him extremely uncomfortable. "I'm not an Orthopedist Salty; I don't have anything close to that level of expertise."

"Don't bullshit a bullshitter Ben; give me an honest opinion."

"You will probably lose the right foot and at least a few toes on the left." He felt terrible, and had the unshakable feeling that Saroni had not discussed this possibility at all.

Salty looked stoic, "See, was that so bad?"

"We'll continue the antibiotic treatments, the daily wound care, dressings and close monitoring, and concentrate on improvement."

"Okay, Doc, I'm with you." Ben interpreted Salty's tone more as resignation than hope.

Marni squeezed Ben's arm, a signal to go. "Salty, I'm going to steal Ben away to finish filling him in on everyone before I leave for home. I'm sure that he'll come back later."

"Before you two go, humor me and listen to a story."

Marni and Ben looked expectantly.

"Okay, you have my undivided attention."

Marni nodded her ascent as well.

"I have a Christmas story..." He looked relaxed, more at ease, "...with what I regard as religious overtones though others might find bordering on the sacrilegious."

"I'm good with that," Marni motioned with her hands to quicken the pace.

"Okay then. A priest died and the old bishop of the diocese was to choose a replacement. He first considered a number of well established, you know, veteran priests but then told his staff to bring him three novices as candidates to interview. They ushered in the first and the bishop said, 'Sit down son. Would you please tell me the true meaning of Christmas?'"

"'Yes, I can father. Christmas is a holiday when people erect and decorate an evergreen tree, drink spiked eggnog to excess and pass out under the tree.'"

Marni rolled her eyes having realized that she had been sold a bill of goods.

Salty continued, "The old bishop scratched his chin and said, 'I'll let you know son, I will let you know.' He had the second novice brought in, offered him a chair, and asked the same question, 'Would you please tell me the true meaning of Christmas?'"

"'Yes, your eminence. Christmas is when colored outdoor lights and nativity scenes are displayed and a large white rabbit delivers chocolate eggs.'"

"The old bishop smoothed what little hair he had left and said, 'I'll be in touch, thank you.' He thought, 'What are they teaching these days at the seminary?' He had the third novice escorted in and was struck with a new idea. 'Son...' 'Yes Bishop?' 'Can you tell me the true meaning of Easter?'

'Yes, I can father. Jesus sat with his disciples and had the last supper, he was betrayed, arrested, tried, was crucified and died on the cross, was buried, and on the third day he rose, rolled the rock away from the entrance of the tomb, saw his shadow and there were six more weeks of winter.'"

Marni burst out in laughter, Ben smiled broadly and Salty pointed a separate forefinger at each of them.

"That wasn't just sacrilegious, Salty; it was borderline blasphemous, and a damn good joke. Thank you, Merry Christmas, and I am out of here." She pulled Ben by the arm towards the door.

Marni's contagious laughter had prodded Ben's broad smile into laughter, "Good one, Salty, good one. Merry Christmas. I'll stop by later."

Marni had her overnight bag in hand and was waiting as Michael approached the entryway to the hospital.

"I hope that you have a mellow day Ben."

Tara was busy licking chocolate frosting off of her fingers and casually interjected, "Oh, it should be fine. Christmas Day is always quiet."

Everyone looked at her in disbelief; the Q word had been invoked.

Myrna had just joined them, "Well there you have it. Tara has just assured us a nonstop day of ER fun and frolic." Her next words were well enunciated with sarcasm, "Thank you, Tara."

All three continued to stare at Tara who suddenly stopped licking her fingers, had that "what did I do now" expression pasted on her face, and then her faux pas dawned on her. "Oh, shit...ah, sorry...oh, crap, I'm so sorry. Can I say something to take it back? You know, cancel it?"

"Tara, nothing short of throwing yourself on a funeral pyre will reverse today's course of events." She allowed Michael to take her overnight bag, slipped her hand through his crooked arm and as she proceeded to the door tossed over her shoulder, "Ta ta all, call me if you elect to build a bonfire."

The phone at the nurses' station was ringing and Myrna answered it, listened and Ben could see her making notes as he overheard her conversation. "What is your name sir...your phone number...and your son's name...and how old is he...when did this happen...did he lose consciousness...have you called 911...I would strongly suggest we dispatch an ambulance...yes, our provider is here...alright I will tell him that you are on your way in." Ben looked at her expectantly. "Ten year old male running with his new snow saucer slipped on the ice and face planted. Bleeding profusely from the nose and chipped his top front teeth. No loss of consciousness. His father, Fred Warburton, is bringing him in by private vehicle and should be here in about 10. She gave Tara a short twisted frown and turned back to Ben, "And so it begins."

"Ben, if you're done here I can go over the discharge instructions and walk Steven and Mr. Warburton out."

"We're finished here Myrna, but I can go over the instructions."

"Actually, you should let me do that Ben because you have Mr. Thorsten's family members waiting for you at the nurses' station."

"Phone call Ben, one of Dr. Saroni's patients wants an antibiotic for a possible urinary tract infection but doesn't feel that she needs to see you." Tara was loosely grasping the phone receiver in her hand as Ben was passing the nurses' station on his way to the emergency room, "I got her on hold."

"What did you tell her?"

"That she would have to come in."

"So, what's the problem?"

"She wants to talk directly to you."

"Please tell her that she can come in or I'll call her after I'm finished in the ER. You may add if you would like that I will be recommending her to come to the ER in any event."

Myrna bent over and whispered in Ben's ear, "Your mom is on the phone."

Ben looked up, surprised, "Would you get her number and tell her that I will call her back when I'm done with this patient?"

Smiling, Myrna said, "No problem Ben." To Ben's patient, the 30-year-old owner of a new pair of ice skates who was having his chin sutured up, "Looking good Stan, you're in good hands with Ben. He's the star pupil of the local quilting club." She directed her next comment to Ben, "Stan, here, is one of my neighbors." She then asked Stan, "What possessed you to buy new ice skates?"

"I didn't, Carol did."

"You might check to see if she recently took out a bigger life insurance policy on you."

"Myrna, I'm going to take 10 and call my mother back. I'll be in the little ER office."

"I'm headed back to the nurses' station and I'll try not to bother you."

Ben settled into the office chair and punched in his mother's number. It was busy. He thought, a good time to call his father and wish him a Merry Christmas. He punched in the number by memory. It rang three times and the answering machine picked up. "Hi, Dad. Merry Christmas. Sorry that I missed you so I'll try again later. The weather and roads have been horrendous but I'm still planning on getting home to visit. Vacation is supposed to start on Friday night but if for some reason my relief does not show up I'll have to cover the weekend. If I do I will probably go to Missoula first and then head down to your place. I hope that you're having a great day and we'll talk later. Bye, Dad." He leaned back in the chair to relax for five minutes. The overhead page crackled with its tinny static before a voice broke in, "Ben Parker, sheriff's department on line two, Ben Parker line two please."

"Do you want me to call X-ray in or wait till the patient gets here?"

"Repeat again how the patient described his forearm."

"He said it looked like the wing on the plane his grandfather flew in World War II. He thought that it was called a gull wing."

"A Navy Corsair, very distinctive. Yeah, call X-ray, it's most likely broken."

Ben was about to enter Salty's room when Tara caught his eye and held up the phone in the nurses' station.

"Hello, this Ben Parker."

"Ben, it's Tucker Labek."

Ben hesitated for a moment then recognized the name and voice of the veterinarian, "Hello Tucker, Merry Christmas. What can I do for you?"

"I've got a horse that got caught up in some barbwire and is pretty cut up. I've run out of tetanus. Any chance that you can loan me some?"

Ben thought, "He's direct, pragmatic, yet no time for a season's greeting?" "Is human and equine tetanus interchangeable?"

"I believe so. The dose for a horse is 1.0 ml."

"How about two 0.5 ml vials? Will that work?"

"Absolutely. You can have the hospital bill me."

"Not so fast guy. You never called me to help preg test so I'm holding the tetanus hostage until you give me the story on the guy with the snake that you treated."

"You're right, my bad. Sorry, I completely spaced it out. You interested in some night calving instead?"

"Just come in and I'll trade you the tetanus for the story of snake man."

There was a hesitant pause, "You don't deliver?" Another short silence, "I'll be there in 20."

"Okay, I'll see you shortly unless I get called to the ER and then you get to wait."

"Fair enough. Adios and Feliz Navidad."

Ben was in the X-ray reading room reviewing the films on the shoulder dislocation that he was currently treating in the emergency room. The overhead paging system crackled again, its poor quality created a garbled voice of mystery with most pages which had prompted numerous complaints apparently falling on administration's deaf ears. "Ben Parker, line two. Ben Parker, line two, please."

There was a knock on the door and he could hear Tara outside. She knocked again. "Ben, there's someone at the nurses' station that wants to talk with you."

Ben stayed silent hoping that Tara would give him a few minutes of peace.

She knocked on the door, "Ben, can you hear me? Someone wants to talk to you."

"Hold your horses, I…will…be…out…in…a minute." He knew that he sounded terse. "Give me a minute to wash my hands and I'll be right out."

She must have heard the toilet flush and either chose to be silent or had walked away.

Maybe a bonfire is not out of the question.

Finally. Ben had found a minute to visit with Salty and was standing next to his bed. He was about to ask him how he was faring today when Myrna stuck her head inside the partially closed door, "Sorry to interrupt you two conspiracy buffs but Ben you've got another walk in at the Emergency Room. Salty, I know that parting is such sweet sorrow but deal with it; I need him more than you do right now."

"I'll try again later, Salty. Sorry."

"Just a second, Mom, the nurse is at the door. I'm going to put you on hold."

Karmma was standing in the clinic doorway, "Sometimes you are a hard man to find."

"I thought I could disappear for 10 minutes and nobody would notice..." Ben glanced at his watch having realized that if Myrna had been relieved by Karmma then it was after 6 PM, "...obviously I was delusional." He looked slightly frustrated, "What have we got now?"

"Twins, three year old twin girls. Their 12-year-old brother got a BB gun for Christmas. Want to guess what happened?"

"He shot them when aiming for the apples balanced on their heads."

"Surprisingly, no. They found his box of BB's and apparently started filling up each other's ears and perhaps some other bodily orifices."

"Probably all gummed up in earwax or nasal mucous. Any place else and they will eventually work their way out."

"That would be my guess."

"Do we have some Debrox and maybe a wire loop for foreign bodies in the eye?"

Karmma looked confused, "I get the Debrox to loosen up the wax but the wire loop?"

"Some of the wire loop handles have a magnet in the handle. I'll go out to my truck and find the magnet I use for retrieving small screws and meet you at the ER."

"Ten-four boss."

"Hey mom, I'll have to call you back tonight or tomorrow...right...okay...gotta' go now, Merry Christmas...yep...I love you too mom...sure...Goodbye."

"Got a minute, Ben?" Karmma was standing in the door way of the ER office.

Ben was sitting at the desk completing a note on his most recent patients, "What's up Karmma?"

"Someone to see you."

He dropped his pen and flipped the pages face down, "Sure, show them in."

Karmma stepped away and Susie appeared; all smile, ruddy cheeks, wearing a bulky, multi-colored sweater. Red, green, white, blue, black, and yellow were vividly blended into a confusing jumble of ornaments, elves, reindeer, evergreens, gingerbread men, candy canes, so many Christmas themed items that he lost count. She held a small pizza box with a large red bow on top.

"Merry Christmas, Ben."

"Merry Christmas, Susie." Unabashedly he stared at her sweater. "Wow. Are you attending an ugly Christmas sweater party?"

"My grandmother knitted this sweater." She was not smiling.

Ben suddenly felt extremely small. "I am so sorry Susie. That was horribly callus of me. Really, when looking at it again I can appreciate the intricate work and detail that went into its making. Truly a magnificent sweater, a beautiful gift from your grandmother."

"That's more like it, apology accepted. I will pass that complement on to the hospital foundation second hand store where I found it. Grandma would have burned something like this, let alone knit it."

"You just…"

"You are so easy." She was laughing as she handed him the pizza box. "Merry belated Christmas Ben, you weren't here last evening when I brought pizza for the night crew. Marni said that she had sent you home to get some sleep."

"It's been a bit busy here for the past few days." Now that he had set the pizza on the desk Susie motioned for him to open the box. The aroma was already filling the small office. As he lifted the lid the fresh baked smells were intensified. A savory combination of meats, vegetables and cheeses were beckoning him to try a slice. "This is grand, thank you Susie." He leaned to his right to pull up the extra chair in the room.

"No, don't Ben." She was waving off the chair. "I'm sorry but I can't join you tonight. Enjoy your Christmas present and we'll catch up another night." Susie took a step forward to give him a hug and he reciprocated.

"One question before you go and if you choose not to answer I will understand."

She raised her left eyebrow suspiciously and then nodded yes. "Okay, Ben, be my guest."

"Tucker needed to borrow some medication from the hospital today to treat an injured horse and he was hesitant to come in to pick it up and once inside he appeared to be uncomfortable. What does he have against the hospital or is it someone working here?"

Susie took a deep breath, tucked her lower lip under her upper teeth, and looked at Ben as she slowly exhaled. "Tucker had a 12-year-old son. Years ago, the boy was brought here after being hit by a car while riding his bike. The doctor that treated him missed an internal bleed and a ruptured spleen and he died before he could be transferred. Several months later the doctor left the hospital supposedly for a better position elsewhere. He ended up dying in a motor vehicle accident in Wyoming and apparently was under the influence of prescription drugs. There was suspicion that he may have been impaired while working here but there was never anything officially released to substantiate the rumor. It severely affected Tucker and he's been jaded about this hospital and its providers ever since. For some reason, I believe he trusts you."

"I probably have you to thank for that."

"No, he reads people well."

"Thank you, Susie. I will keep this strictly confidential. That does help to explain his initial reaction to me last Labor Day."

"That and the fact that he was best friends with my older brother and Tucker always had a little crush on me."

"Older brother?"

"Another time." Susie coaxed Ben into the chair, sidled up behind him, put her hands on his shoulders and swiveled his chair so that he was directly facing his gift. "Eat, before it gets cold."

"I'm sorry that I don't have anything prepared for you Susie."

"I consider our friendship gift enough." She bent down and kissed the top of his head, "Oh, look, did you know Ben that you have a cute little bald spot?" She darted out the door. "Adios my friend, I'll see you soon." And she was gone.

Ben nudged the door further open and peered in. Salty was lying back, propped up by pillows, eyes closed, his hands resting on a closed book lying on his stomach. Ben recognized the book as one that he had given Salty a month or so ago. He looked at peace so Ben began to draw the door closed.

"Come in, I'm just resting my eyes." He stretched to his right to lay the book down on his nightstand.

Ben entered, pulled a chair up to bedside as Salty shifted his weight and sat up straighter as Ben repositioned the pillows. "How are you doing Salty?" He asked as he was pulling a small gaily wrapped package from a plastic shopping bag.

"I'm doing alright today. Good food, everyone one seems to be in good spirits, temperature above zero, no more bodies getting stacked in the back shed." That produced a wry smile on his face. Ben thought, "Damn, who doesn't know?" Salty sighed, "Personally, I'm getting tired, losing some traction." He suddenly looked wane, the wry smile faded. "I guess I had some greater expectations."

Ben was concerned. His friend and patient sounded more than tired, his voice held a suspicion of bone deep weariness, if not depression. "What expectations?"

"Going out with a bang rather than a whimper."

"What do you mean with a bang?"

"I don't know, maybe a skydiving accident? Perhaps getting hit by a train as I save a trussed up damsel from sure death on the tracks? Better yet while getting laid by some lithe, overly sexed coed?" He must have noticed the look of concern on Ben's face, "I'm only waxing nostalgic Ben, maybe wondering where the years went that flew by, coming to grips with my small victories and larger failures and a life of promise only partially fulfilled. I suppose making light of my fears and the occasional fantasy that I tucked away in the back of my head. Please, don't worry about me; the big bang is not a metaphor for sticking a gun in my mouth. God no, I may have my misgivings and vestiges of Christian guilt but I'm not about to do myself in leaving behind a gawd awful mess. Okay, I'm done with my little rant. What's in the package?"

"You're an old dog, Salty. Sometimes we change priorities and temper expectations. Give me something that I can work with."

"Like I said Ben, what's in the package?" Effectively signaling and solidifying the change of subject.

Ben handed Salty the small package. "Merry Christmas my friend."

Salty brightened up, "What have we here?" He quickly tore the wrapping off, obviously without intention of saving the paper. "What the hell...?" There were two decks of cards.

"The Disney approved Mickey Mouse Deck is for when you coerce the nurses into playing card games and the deck with the bare breasted babes is for you and the reprobates that visit you to play poker, hustle your money and ogle the nurses. Maybe they'll be distracted enough where you might win a hand or two."

"Hey now, that's a little harsh." He was attempting to look offended without much success.

"But true. I have eyes everywhere." Ben began to remove a second package from the bag.

"Hold your horses." Salty leaned over towards Ben and with his left hand pointed under the hospital bed. "There's a bag down there, would you grab it?"

Ben pulled a brown paper bag from under the bed and was about to hand it to Salty. Salty shook his head no,

"Inside. There's something for you but I was a bit short on wrapping paper."

He extracted a thick, dark green hard covered book. "The Home Physician and Guide to Health." Ben turned the first few pages, "Copyright 1923." The book was in excellent condition. "Those who ignore the laws of health die prematurely." Weighing the statement, he began opening to random pages, "Fomentation...Feeble Mindedness...Constitutional Diseases...hell, I'll bet this even covers dwindles, the vapors and bloodletting by leeches." Ben reached over and Salty offered his hand back and they shook hands with vigor. "Thank you Salty, I can't think of a better gift that I have ever received." Salty couldn't have looked happier.

Ben drew another package out of his bag and handed it to Salty.

"What? You'd think that this was Christmas or something."

"Open it."

He tore the paper off balling it up and launching it at the wastebasket across the room missing it by a wide margin. "Okay, so Larry Bird I'm not." Tilting his head back he focused his bifocals on the title, "*The Great American Novel* by Philip Roth." Now he raised his eyebrows and tilted his head questioningly at Ben.

"It's about baseball. A good story, different, a fun read. I think that you will like it."

"You bet your ass I will. Thank you Ben." Salty lifted the book on his night stand. "*Catch 22*. I'm enjoying the hell out of it. It took a couple of chapters to warm to it but then it grabbed me. I'm sure I'll like this one just as well." Salty transferred *Catch 22* over to his lap. "I cogitated over the premise and finally got a reasonable grasp of what *Catch 22* is; a situation or circumstance for which you can never win. If you claim to be crazy in order to avoid combat you are automatically deemed sane because wanting to avoid combat is not crazy."

Ben smiled and nodded in agreement. He was thrilled that Salty had embraced the book. "Now, I'm going to stir the pot here, for whatever good it usually does. Remember this is purely hypothetical. A guy is going to die of cancer and his doctor has given him a prognosis that he has three months to live. He is his own power of attorney. He is well aware that his last months will be debilitating and painful. The doctor has told him that he will be provided excellent comfort care and pain control. The man has witnessed a similar progression of treatment and death with his father and would prefer to have more control over his destiny and a more dignified death. He contemplates suicide or assisted suicide and broaches the topic with his doctor who says that either act would be illegal and that he would not help to facilitate it. If the man chooses the route that the doctor says is legal then he will incrementally lose his strength, cede his declining ability to care for himself to others and become more and more dependent on pain control which will eventually leave him addled, devoid of control of his bodily functions, and in all probability near or completely comatose prior to death.

Were he to express a wish to end his life on his terms after starting the doctor's prescribed treatment, such as declining all fluids and nourishment, his having become dependent on others to care for him and medication to control his pain, he is confident that he would be diagnosed as depressed or with a dependency on pain control medications inducing confusion and impaired thinking. By either account the doctor would determine that the man indeed has an altered mental status and incapable of making valid or cognizant decisions. The doctor would assume all medical decisions and the man will die in the projected three months, more or less, enduring much the same course that he had wanted to avoid. Personally, I would say that this was his medical catch 22. What do you think?"

Ben was feeling uncomfortable about Salty's analogy and was weighing the possibility that his friend was projecting this as his own self-fulfilling prophecy.

"Remember Ben, this is something I was tossing out, not in any way addressing my own plight."

Ben was not convinced but was not going to press him about it at the moment.

"So, a catch 22 as I perceive it is a no win situation. Not exactly a conundrum or caught between a rock and a hard place, so Ben, my question is; what did they call a catch 22 before Joseph Heller wrote *Catch 22*?"

"Bedlam?"

VACATION

Ben felt it, recognized it, and understood it. Relief. Not in the sense that you're the lone ranger, the solitary soul up to your ass in alligators before the cavalry arrives, rather the muscle tension edge of your seat sleep with one eye open release type of relief one should experience after 10 days straight of work and emergency room call. 1900 hours on Sunday, frozen roads open to tenuous travel and finally the appearance of Calvin Wright, the locum tenen physician assistant scheduled to start work and ER coverage two days previously.

Ben gave Calvin a handoff, a verbal synopsis of the acute and swing bed hospital patients currently admitted, nursing home residents to keep an eye on and patients seen in the clinic that would be returning for follow up appointments or in some manner had triggered a cautionary flag to be waved; be aware but not alarmed. He added to his report that Dr. Saroni was to resume clinic hours tomorrow although no one, at least to Ben's knowledge, had received any confirmation regarding the doctor's travels or anticipated return. Ben admittedly was unable to muster any level of concern regarding the doctor's whereabouts; rather he was fixated on his recliner, one or two cold beers, an hour or two of mindless television programming and an uninterrupted stretch of sleep, thankfully in his own bed. In his fatigued state he was repeatedly justifying that he was due his well-earned time off. The start of his postponed vacation was official and his departure to Missoula would in all likelihood be Tuesday, dependent on sleep, Mother Nature and road conditions.

Whistling Bachman Turner Overdrive's, "Taking Care of Business," Ben took one last cursory, light-footed stroll down the hospital hallway, peering in on his patients with his last stop at Salty's partially open door. He heard subdued voices and poked his head in after he had determined that they were electronically generated from a talk radio station. Salty laid on his back, eyes closed, chest gently rising and falling, and a quiet snore accompanying his slumber. Ben entered and at Salty's bedside contemplated awakening him to say goodbye, see you soon. He looked too peaceful to disturb so Ben opted to quietly say, "Happy New Year Salty, see you when I get back." Without further ado, Ben exited the room, slipped on his coat, gloves and hat, and to the staff at the nurses' station facetiously repeated the rodeo queen's salute as walked backwards out the main door.

Having departed in the winter darkness of 7:30 AM, Ben had navigated the predominately snow packed and icy rises and dips of the highway, past coolies and swales channeling moderate northern wind gusts, an uninterrupted steel grey pallor blending the horizon into the clouds. Three hours west of Bedlam, his progress barely over 100 miles, he was encountering unfamiliar territory never having driven on these particular stretches of highway. The landscape was definitively flattening out, yet visibility to the north and south remained limited. Usually streaming, occasionally swirling, crosswinds carried captured Canadian snow destined for southern Montana and Wyoming. Windswept, the roadway appeared shiny, almost reflective, as if freshly buffed. It was common knowledge that some highway maintenance departments would not sand specific areas of icy roadway when constant winds were blowing, the sand acting as a scouring agent, polishing the highway into a more treacherous condition. He continued with his attempts to wrap his head around the fact that this trip would be a tedious assault on his attention span. Speed was not going to be an option.

Midafternoon he slowed to take a left hand turn in the small farming community of Chester, anticipating that he would shorten his route by driving south to Great Falls via Fort Benton. His original plan had been to short cut south from Havre down through the Rocky Boy Indian Reservation to reach Great Falls; however, Route 87 was closed and barricaded to travel. Today's second stretch of 100 miles had been plodding and uneventful. He had encountered no more than a dozen cars passing him eastbound, one westbound. Slowing as he had approached questionable roadside conditions or a distant unidentifiable roadside hulk, he had passed by four abandoned cars on either side of the road, the windows marked with yellow after having been inspected by the Highway Patrol. At three additional scenes it appeared vehicles had slid off the road and were being tended to by State or County law enforcement and wrecker trucks. There had not appeared to be any injuries.

He proceeded through the western end of Chester for several city blocks. After passing the community's small hospital he encountered homes on either side of the road, smoke rising from their chimneys, immediately curling, flattening then dissipating in the unrelenting wind. Just past the thinning residential area he was confronted with barricades and a Highway Department Road Closed sign. He saw the faint tracks left by several vehicles that had swerved around the barricades. Blowing snow was filling and obliterating the faint vestiges of the southbound tire tracks. He considered for a moment tempting the fates and Boreas the North Wind God, then decided not, his bravado slacked. He could almost picture the abandoned vehicles ahead, the stark, stiffened extremities of hapless travelers protruding from frozen drifts, those who unadvisedly had fled mired or disabled cars to seek help. Staring ahead through the windshield he knew the blued fingertips pointing skyward would soon disappear, covered by the cruelly relentless wind driven snow. Ben knew, absolutely, that his sense of propriety was forever jaded by the black humor inherent to survival in medicine.

Backtracking into town and the highline highway, he pulled into a service station to fill his gas tank and review his map. He was met by a locked door at the service station restroom and he concluded from the darkened and frosted office windows the restroom key would not be readily available. Ben bet that the owner had closed early, likely thinking that there were not enough traveling idiots to cater to. Having relieved himself behind the building he climbed back into the truck and sat for a few minutes to warm up. The last of his hot chocolate filled roughly half of the thermos cup and was lukewarm. Sipping it slowly, his thoughts drifted to his planned New Year's reunion in Missoula with his two friends from the PA program and then a few days back home visiting with his father. Ben finished off the hot chocolate deciding that he did not have the luxury of burning what daylight was left daydreaming about what lay ahead tomorrow.

As he pulled out onto the roadway he spied a portable digitalized highway sign positioned at the end of town. The signboard was lighting up, alternately displaying two messages. A plywood sheet with block lettering sat at

174

the base of the highway sign facing westbound motorists. Ben decelerated from slow to crawl as he approached the signs. A message blinked on; Caution: Blowing Snow and Crosswinds, followed by a second message; Hazardous Conditions Next 43 miles. Snow was drifting across the base of the plywood sign and starting to stick to the untreated wood; "Abandon all hope, ye who enter here." He laughed aloud remembering that he had wanted to hang a similar sign over Dr. Saroni's office door after his first work day in Bedlam. He sped up to 35 mph as a wind gust buffeted his truck and crystallized snow blew across his hood and windshield. The decision was made to hold steady at the current speed, at least for a while.

Back in Chester, his review of the map had shown Shelby 43 miles ahead where he could access Interstate 15 and proceed south. Ben had settled on an arbitrary goal of 100 miles to complete the day's journey and at that distance Choteau was the most likely to have a motel. Ben read 4:15 PM as he glanced at his watch. Calculating his current rate of speed with the pending onset of darkness he wondered how long and far he was willing to chase his headlights. Anywhere along the route he could pull the plug and institute plan B. By Ben's standards of operation, one must logically have a plan B if not a C and D. In these conditions, should all else fail, there was a sleeping bag, blankets, flashlights and snack food stowed behind the seat and in the camper shell. It was dark upon reaching the muted but welcoming lights of Shelby. He had been tempted, and briefly considered stopping for the night, however, just as quickly he opted to continue south on I 15 towards Choteau. Thirty eight miles south of Shelby, halfway between Conrad and his proposed exit, his hands almost cramping from his death grip on the steering wheel, he cursed himself for not having stayed put in Shelby.

The snow streaked by horizontally from the west. Intermittently severe gusting winds from the west combined with the gale force vortex created by insanely speeding semi-trucks passing on the left, alternately slid him half way across his driving lane. Visibility had dangerously deteriorated prompting him to keep his right tires on the shoulder rumble strip for orientation. Ben kept looking for an exit sign or a pull out, any safe haven off the interstate where he could hunker down in his sleeping bag within the confines of his cab or camper shell. No apparent safe haven was readily presenting itself and despite his cautious speed and apt attention to the roadside he almost missed his exit to Choteau. At 7:30 PM, seven miles west of the Interstate on a secondary highway he turned off into a crowded parking lot, produced a credit card and secured the last vacant motel room in town. Ben did not recall vacations having had the effect of draining one's life blood, at least not within the first 48 hours.

Sandwiched between a gaudily refurbished second hand clothing store and a constantly evolving art gallery of mediocre local artisans, the bar's frontage was austere; one small Kelly green sign attached to the massive, darkly stained oak front door announcing "Herald's Pub." No neon in the tinted plate glass windows, rather Gaelic lettering again simply stating "Herald's Pub." The dark tinting of the windows prevented one from easily viewing the inside of the pub, perhaps with the intent of providing greater privacy to the patrons or to intentionally add an air of mystique to the faint of heart uncertain of entering an unknown entity. Herald's was a destination, not a place of casual discovery.

Ben pried back the cuff of his leather glove and glanced at his watch: 1330 hours; considering the traveling conditions he was only a half hour late for lunch with his two classmates from his physician assistant program, Shane McHale of Victor, Montana, and Alan Parsons who hailed from Kalispell. Both Shane and Alan had visited Herald's previously; Alan with his father, a construction foreman and Shane with his father, a former lineman for Montana Power. Shane had an intimate knowledge of Missoula having attended the University of Montana for three years until he ran out of money, then worked in the local plywood plant until finally enlisting in the Navy and becoming a corpsman. Alan had received his initial medical training while serving in the United States Army.

According to Shane, Herald's was a blue collar bar that also served breakfast and lunch, catering to the tastes and appetites of the railroad crews, millworkers, lumbermen and transient tradesmen staying in or passing through Missoula. For over 90 years its massive front door had opened at 6 every morning, closing at 2 AM to allow the swampers to clean and restock. Herald, an Irish immigrant of questionable background who was initially funded by some disreputable sources, had opened his pub in 1910 and reportedly the only times the doors had been locked in daytime hours were during the burial of a son, a casualty of Iwo Jima, and the funerals of FDR and JFK. It continues to be owned and run by the Herald clan.

Mounting the plowed mound of snow banked up to the curb, Ben gingerly traversed over a thin layer of new snow hiding extensive patches of ice covering the side street. Someone had shoveled a narrow passage through the snow bank in front of Herald's, the only gap along the street that Ben espied. Entering through the heavy oaken door he stamped the snow from his boots on a thick rubber mat all the while balancing his sunglasses on his forehead allowing his vision to adjust to the darker interior of the pub. He quickly scanned the establishment's interior, surprisingly deep and narrow with high ceilings composed of stamped tin, ceiling fans slowing turning and suspended lights providing a dim illumination. A rounded corner of the L shaped bar started approximately eight feet in front of him, extending almost the length of the room and making a 90 degree turn meeting the wall perhaps 10 feet to his right. There was a worn wooden bench against that wall and two small chest high tables immediately in front of the tinted plate glass window, apparently for waiting customers or standing room only. He was immediately drawn to two framed pictures hung on the wall over the bench. Satisfied that his boots were relatively snow free, Ben walked over to inspect the enlarged black and white photographs as he removed his coat.

The greatly enlarged and faded photo on the right pictured several men, most with arms folded across their chests, some wearing vests, bowties, garters on their arms, and waist aprons, the other men in full aprons with shirt sleeves rolled up to mid-forearm. A universal theme was slicked back hair and bushy or handlebar mustaches. All stood in front of what Ben recognized as Herald's Pub, circa pre-World War I was his guess.

Not so much hearing as sensing someone standing behind and to his left, he looked over his left shoulder and momentarily caught his breath. He estimated five foot six inches. She had thick, curly auburn hair, shoulder length, not wild but casual with no discernible design. Her eyes were alive, a vibrant dark brown that held his, now transfixed. A tentative smile blossomed into radiance, her entire face beamed. Light freckles dotted her upper cheeks. He found not a trace of makeup in evidence. When she smiled several fine lines appeared at the corner of her eyes and mouth suggesting that she might be closer to his age then he had originally thought. Ben was enraptured.

"Are you Ben?" A gentle lilt combined with full lips only added to the entrancement.

Ben heard her, it registered, yet he found himself so enthralled with her eyes, her radiant smile, the sound of her voice and an instant attraction that his response was delayed and relegated to an inarticulate, "Huh? Ahhh, yes. Yes, I'm Ben...yes I am."

"I'm Lindsay." She stepped up next to him and there was an electricity that was invigorating though somewhat unsettling. "I believe that the photo on the right was taken out front of the bar in 1912. The tall man in the middle with the full apron is Bryce Herald who opened and originally owned Herald's Pub, and the two men to either side are cousins. The other men are most likely employees. She motioned with her left hand at the other enlarged photograph. "You must recognize President John F. Kennedy. The man to Kennedy's right is my uncle Connor Herald and on Kennedy's left is my dad, Daniel Herald. My uncle served with Kennedy in the Pacific. He was a Lieutenant JG on another PT boat in the same squadron. Dad was a paratrooper who fought in Europe. The picture was taken in June 1960 at the Placer Hotel in Helena when Kennedy was running for president."

"Wow that is some history." Damn, he thought, could he be anymore lame? Let's try to redeem myself. "Does your uncle still run Herald's Pub?" Christ, the guy must be in his eighties, why would he still be subjecting himself to that? Where is my brain?

"My uncle passed in 1980 and now his oldest son runs it."

"How about your dad, is he a part owner?"

179

"He should have been considering how much of his paycheck he spent in here. No, he was a logger until he was injured in the woods and then he ended up working in the pulp mill. He comes in for a beer every once in a while."

Ben was about to ask another question but refrained.

She must have read his mind. "You're wondering if I have a financial interest in the bar."

"I've already asked too many personal questions."

Lindsay laughed, an easy, engaging laugh, "I fill in here when needed. I go to school part time, work part time and rein in a 13-year-old daughter full time. Your friends are waiting so let's go get you fed."

She pointed to the opposite wall by the doorway, "You can hang your coat over there."

He watched her walk down the aisle between the bar and dining booths on the left or east wall. She had an athletic physique, not too lean, rounded in all of the right spots, a comfortable gait with just the appropriate sway to her hips. Ben took his time, a leisurely stroll, his head on swivel as he scrutinized and admired the antique back bar, the bar itself and the comfortable dining booths. The back bar was true to the craft and artisanship of a bygone era. Intricate, inlaid scrolls and carvings, extensive mirrors, raised and etched glass panes within the cabinetry all caught his eye. Bar notices and pictures were framed, set on the ornate shelves or on the counter rather than taped to wood or glass. Two gleaming National Cash Registers sat on the back bar counter dividing the back bar into thirds.

A shined brass foot rail ran the length of what Ben estimated to be 30, maybe 35 feet of dark stained, well preserved, polished bar. Wooden bar stools with minimally padded seat backs were spaced to accommodate the expanding breadth and girth of middle aged bar patrons.

There was a shine to every square inch of wood and mirror. The bartender, a spitting image of the employee's in the 1912 photograph, however, albeit hair since his head was shaved smooth, stood against the counter in his vest, pinstriped shirt, garters, waist apron, and handlebar mustache reading the newspaper. Two older men, wearing their wool caps and vests, sat side by side near the far end quietly talking, half-finished beers and empty shot glasses sat before both of them.

Along the opposite wall, high, straight backed seating divided the booths. A forest green, rather than the expected Kelly green, Naugahyde material covered the seat backs and cushions. The tables were three inch thick wood planks smoothed by resting elbows. Framed photos and portraits of notable Missoulians and Montanans appointed the wall; Ben surmised that they would all be of Irish lineage. He caught up to Lindsay who stood by the booth occupied by Shane and Alan.

"I'll give you a couple of minutes to decide on what you would like to eat," and walked away.

Shane and Alan both displayed broad smiles and stood awkwardly bent forward against the table extending their hands. Almost in unison they asked, "How the hell are you Ben. Great to see you."   Ben shook each hand firmly and took a seat next to Shane where a third place setting had been prepared, "I'm doing great guys. Just happy to see you guys and to be off of the road."

Alan immediately poured him a glass of beer; they touched glasses, and drank to their own good luck and health. Ben listened as his two friends filled him in on their travels to Missoula as he perused the menu. It sounded as if he had faced the most challenging and adverse conditions but down played them when he recounted the past two travel days from Bedlam.

Lindsay appeared; order book and pen at the ready. They decided on community grazing on a plate of French fries and one of deep fried onion rings. A section of the menu just said "Burgers. Fresh ground certified Black Angus beef. Choose your size and customize. Size; Wimp, Regular, Big, Bigger, Biggest, Coma." A long list of toppings and add on's followed. Shane and Alan customized regular sized burgers. Ben looked up at Lindsay and asked, "I can add anything that I want to my burger?"

She met his eyes directly, smiled and answered, "You may order anything that you would like, Hun, just as long as I don't have to make a trip to the grocery store."

"Big burger, double bacon, Swiss cheese, mushrooms, grilled onions, green pepper, lettuce tomato, mayo, no pickles. Is that doable?" He looked at her hopefully.

"Excellent choice, Ben. I'll add a side order of Pepto-Bismol and a wheelchair." There was a growing familiarity between the two of them that he had not anticipated but which excited him. There was something about this woman that made his pulse accelerate and which, slightly unnerved him, made him, for lack of a better adjective, "stupid." She headed back to the kitchen.

Shane piped up, "Are we still planning to have the best story contest? Winner takes the pot and losers buy his lunch?"

"I drove 600 death defying miles just for that opportunity, so yes, most odd or obscure medical case with the most absurd circumstances wins."

"I'm in," Alan added, "but who's going to decide the winner?"

Ben suggested, "Maybe Lindsay would volunteer, however, I think it only fair that she gets to split the pot with the winner."

182

Shane and Alan looked at each other and then to Ben, "Split?"

"Only fair."

"50/50?"

Ben nodded, he was not relenting.

Shane observed, "You drive a hard bargain but okay." Alan nodded yes in agreement.

Their food arrived along with a fresh pitcher of beer. She set down a stack of large napkins, "You're going to need these boys," and winked at Ben. This again set his heart aflutter.

As they ate they caught up on life, love and the myriad of experiences they had encountered as new physician assistants. Shane was recently engaged and Alan had moved in with his girlfriend. Shane reported that the hospital where he worked was busy and well-staffed. There were four doctors and two PAs and he had weekend call every six weeks with one doctor always available for consultation or to come in to help. Alan's medical group was comprised of four doctors, two nurse practitioners and two physician assistants. One of the PA's was a bit of a cowboy and had been disciplined for exceeding his scope of practice and one of the NP's, a recent grad as was Alan, was pushing an independent practice agenda so hard that she was steadily alienating the physicians. Alan had emergency room call once every eight weeks and for the first six months a doctor always came in on his calls. He was never without adequate back up. Both agreed that they were enjoying their jobs and were learning a great deal.

Ben was torn as to whether to vent about or gloss over the difficulties that he had encountered in his work place. He chose a midline recitation. "Bedlam Medical Center is definitely frontier medicine. There is one doctor, myself and another PA who comes one day a week for clinic patients and to cover ER call for that same night. The doctor and I split the vast majority of Emergency call. Quite often I don't know if he is actually available for consultation or back up. On occasion he will come in and instead of discussing or mentoring he just takes over. When I was being interviewed he blew a lot of smoke up my skirt about mentoring, teaching, demonstrating procedures but essentially, once I hired on, he tossed me to the wolves. I spend a lot of my days and weekends off at other hospitals to gain more experience and mentoring that I'm not getting at my own facility. The most frustrating aspect is his inconsistency, and then, just when you think that things have assumed an even keel, bam, inconsistency again runs rampant.

Alan and Shane both appeared to be sympathetic but were both stymied as to what to say. They all continued eating in silence.

Ben started, "Maybe…"

Shane immediately interrupted, "Maybe you should call Cousin Guido and have him pay the doctor a visit?"

"Or," Alan interjected, "Look for another job."

Ben asked, "You do know the definition of insanity?"

Alan perked up, "Doing the same thing over and over again and expecting a different result?"

"Exactly. So, what do you call doing something over and over again and each time getting a totally different and unexpected outcome?"

"Government oversight? An exploding universe? A girlfriend?"

Ben turned to see Shane trying not to burst out laughing, "I still vote for Cousin Guido."

They finished their meals. Lindsay had stopped by twice asking if everything was okay, did they need anything. Anticipating that she would soon return Ben slid out and approached her at the waitress station. Before she could speak he said, "Everything was great, the food, the service, we are all ready to burst at the seams. I'm here on behalf of the three of us to offer you a proposal."

Lindsay said flatly, "I'm not that type of girl." Ben gasped. Then her eyes sparkled, "I'm just messing with you Ben. What's your proposal?"

Relief barely described what he felt. The last thing that he wanted to do was to upset her or toss a huge wet blanket over the past 60 minutes. Ben described the contest that he, Shane and Alan were proposing and the need for an impartial party to decide the winner.

"I didn't realize that all three of you were physician assistants." She pondered and paraphrased his words, "The most interesting medical case with the most absurd set of circumstances...you, Ben, have piqued my curiosity. Yes, I would be honored to be your impartial party."

"A state trooper brought a guy into the emergency room. He looked to be around 70, in actuality he was 50, and definitely intoxicated. There was a two inch laceration to his right forearm, a deep uneven laceration, a gash, just posterior to his left temple, and an avulsion and wide puncture wound to the back of his left hand. He told us that he had been drinking and fell down some stairs. It appeared to be pretty cut and dried, no pun intended. We were going to start a quick neuro exam and order a head CT," Alan looked at Lindsey and said, "Cat scan," she nodded that she understood, "When he asked, 'If you get hit on the head can that screw with your eyesight?' Well that put a whole new spin on things. The doctor asked the patient how his vision had been affected, you know, blurring, double vision, vision loss?" Alan pauses and slowly lifts his glass of beer, examines it under the light, and takes a leisurely swallow.

"Oh, for Christ's sake Alan," Shane sounded exasperated, "quit with the theatrics and get on with it."

Taking another drink of beer, Alan looked at Shane and smirked, "Don't rush me, I'm on vacation."

Ben chanced a glance at Lindsay and saw her looking directly back at him, attempting to suppress a smile. It made him nervously happy.

"So, as I was saying, the doctor asked him how his vision was affected. He said that he had been blind in his left eye for the past five years after falling off a scaffolding and hitting his head. Now he could see out of it again, pretty blurry, but he could see. That gained the doctor's attention."

It also pricked the attention of the other three in the booth.

"We determined that his left eye acuity was 20/100 and the doctor was performing an eye exam when this wild haired, disheveled women barged into the ER, imbalanced, and by the look and smell of it she'd had a snoot full. She loudly asked, 'how are ya' honey?'"

The patient yelled, "That woman is trying to kill me!" and the trooper, who was just outside the door, grabbed her arm and kept her from going any further.

The trooper looked at the patient and said one word, "Explain."

Our patient said, "She attacked me. She's trying to kill me."

"Did she have a weapon?"

"She's wearing it." He pointed at her shiny black stiletto heels that she was teetering on.

The doctor sounded incredulous, "She did this with a high heel shoe?"

The guy went on to detail the attack. "We were both drinking, got into an argument, and she attacked me with her shoe. I blocked her first swing with my arm," he pointed to the laceration on the top of his right arm. "But when I grabbed my arm," he demonstrated clamping his left hand over his right arm laceration, "she clocked me on the side of the head and I quick put my hand up," he demonstrated by laying his left hand gently over his left temple. "Then she drove the damn shoe into the back of my hand. I don't remember just how I got away but this cop found me and brought me here."

"The wife was escorted out, we ended up repairing his wounds and he allowed a cursory eye examination which was inconclusive of any definitive injury. He refused the head CT, telling us that 'I got enough radiation from my dental fillings.' That one left us all scratching our heads."

"That's it? That's all you got, Alan?"

"I don't think he's done, Shane."

Alan gave Ben a nod of thanks and Shane a look of distain. "Four months later a friend brought him into the ER disoriented with a good sized laceration to the top of his head. Immediately we thought his wife had attacked him again. The friend was witness to the event and reiterated what had happened to our patient. The patient and his wife, yes they were still together, lived in a second floor apartment over a bar with an outside staircase and balcony walkway. The apartment is very small so they keep a chest freezer out on the balcony. They had again been drinking. He's down on street level, she's on the balcony walkway, the two of them are screaming profanities at each other and she started tossing frozen packages of meat down at him. He started picking up packages as he continued egging her on. He bent over to pick up a package and she hit him on the head with what was probably a five pound roast. It knocked him colder than a wedge. He woke up dazed and bleeding from the head so his friend brought him in. In the ER our patient complained of a bad headache and that he's once again blind in his left eye. This time he gets a CT of the head and they can't find anything suspicious. He left AMA with a concussion, blind in one eye and to the best of our knowledge he and his wife remain in blissful wedlock."

Shane was the first to speak, "So, you never saw this guy again?"

"No, never again darkened the door of our emergency room."

Ben chimed in, "No clue as to the reason for his blindness? Trauma? Retinal detachment? Stroke or TIA? Glaucoma? Psychogenic? Clot? Uveitis?"

"All considered but nothing jumped out at us considering the limited exam and testing that the patient allowed us. I really can't add anything further." Alan turned to Lindsay, "What do you think Lindsay, good story?" He sounded hopeful.

"I have no medical background; however, it is definitely thought provoking, and an odd relationship to say the least." Ben thought that she was hedging, trying to be noncommittal. "Good story though." Looking directly into Ben's eyes she said, "Time for Ben to dazzle us with his medical malady."

"I wasn't on ER call that day but the nurse on duty called me at the clinic and told me to come to the ER, that the doctor was becoming unglued and that I had to see this. I hustled to the ER and when I got to the hallway outside the ER I saw the ER staff backed up against the opposite wall and the doctor hopping up and down performing St. Vitus's dance in the hallway, wringing his hands and yelling at a man retreating backwards toward the outside

188

entrance. The man appeared to be in his twenties, a construction worker. There's a two foot piece of house siding and a three and one half foot long snake dangling from his left hand and he is pointing at the doctor calling him a hack and hurling a few four letter expletives. Later, I got a report from the local veterinarian who ended up initially treating the guy.

The patient was part of a construction crew doing roofing and siding renovations at a house outside of town. He was in the backyard cutting shingles for the roofers and siding for the carpenters when a snake, a racer, a nonpoisonous species slithered out from under a nearby stack of firewood." Ben had been rotating his gaze from Alan, to Shane, to Lindsay who briefly appeared to be cringing. "He thought that he'd have some fun with his co-workers so he blocked the snake's path with a board and then with his left hand intending to grab hold of it with his right hand. This variety of snake is normally not aggressive...unless cornered, frightened or being attacked but in this case it struck out and latched onto the flesh between the thumb and forefinger," Ben pointed to the vee in his own hand, "and did not quickly let go. The guy immediately slapped his hand flat against a one by six siding board, picked up a pneumatic staple gun and fired a two inch staple behind the snake's head to kill it. Unfortunately, one leg of the staple hit a knot so one leg went through the snake and the wood and the other leg rebounded up at an angle through the snake's jaw, the guys hand and up and out of the snake's head, thereby securing the board, hand, and snake together. One of his co-workers was willing to cut the board shorter and brought him to the hospital in the back of a pickup truck, because the co-worker was also fearful of snakes, dead or alive.

The veterinarian, a colorful character in his own right, anointed the victim with the choice nickname of "Brain Dead the Snake Charmer" and called him everything but a white man for being so stupid. He numbed up the hand, managed to free the board, clipped and removed the staple freeing the dead snake from the guy's hand. Cleaned him up, gave him a shot of Penicillin in his butt and sent him on to Sunnvale for additional treatment. About a month later Brain Dead the Snake Charmer stopped by the Veterinary Clinic to pay his bill, brought along a case of beer for the vet, and filled him in on the subsequent IV antibiotic treatment he received because of an infection. He thanked the vet profusely and swore off any future attempts at "snake charming."

"Jesus, Ben, that one's a bit farfetched." Alan was emphatic. "You sure you didn't make that up or at least embellish a little?"

"Embellish a little?" Ben sounded affronted. "We didn't question the veracity of your case Alan, so give it a rest; besides you just can't make this shit up."

Lindsay shivered and interjected, "I agree with Ben. Who would be capable of making these stories up?"

Ben was inwardly ecstatic, "Whoooo, boy, she had agreed with and defended him...that had to be a good sign...but wait, don't read too much into that, maybe she was just being polite...but then again, maybe..." He smiled broadly at her and she returned it. Suddenly he had a disturbing thought; what if he had food stuck between his teeth. Closing his mouth, he consciously ran his tongue over his teeth.

"Now, for the coup de gras," announced Shane, "my case will ultimately prove to be THE most thought provoking and absurdly interesting thereby assuring me the winner's circle and victory lap."

"Regale us, Mr. Eloquent, with your wondrous story."

Shane looked directly at Lindsay and as if making a pre-emptive disclosure, "I hope that this story does not offend your delicate sensibilities. The nature of…"

"Shane, I grew up with two older brothers, a blue collar father and an uncle who owned this bar. What would give you the idea that my sensibilities were delicate?"

"Sorry, my mistake, I shall sally forth. Late one evening the ambulance was paged out to an unspecified medical emergency, a man reportedly in distress. The ambulance crew responded, picked up a man who lived alone, radioed in vital signs, confirmed that the emergency was not cardiac or respiratory in nature, however, provided no additional information. When they arrived at the hospital they rolled the gurney into the emergency room, the patient completely covered up with blankets, save his head. A large vertical bulge under the blanket at groin level was evident; a grimace of pain and embarrassment enveloped the patient's face. Before the ambulance crew could give a report the doctor introduced himself and unceremoniously stripped down the blanket. Everyone in the ER sucked in their breath at the same instant."

Shane reached for his glass of beer, lifted it to his lips, took a deep gulp and consciously set it back within the condensation ring on the table top.

"Okay, Shane, I'm calling you on this like you harassed me. Don't be creating more drama, just relate the case and let it stand on its own merit. I'm sure Lindsay doesn't have all day for our BS."

Ben lifted his glass and said, "You heard the man," and finished off his beer.

"The patient was holding an empty two liter plastic Coke bottle with his penis stuck more than half way inside the opening of the bottle." Shane looked around the table for effect. Lindsey, Alan, and Ben all had that "What the fuck?" expression on their faces. "The penis was approximately two thirds inside the bottle, extremely swollen and turning a deep purple. His hands were shaking; therefore, the bottle was vibrating adding to his admitted pain. The doctor told the nurse on duty to get the hospital's other doctor on the phone while simultaneously the patient attempted to explain why his penis was stuck in a soda pop bottle. Between the distraction of pain and mounting anxiety the patient was not faring well with his rendition. One of the paramedics related the history that the patient had told them on route.

The patient had a long history of kidney stones and with the onset of pain, when he believed one of the stones was starting to move or he thought that one might be exiting his bladder, he would place the pop bottle over the end of his penis and forcibly squeeze the bottle forcing a big puff of air into his urethra. He reported that this technique had worked in the past without any problem and believed that the puff of air dislodged the stone. Tonight, however, he did not remove the bottle quickly enough; the vacuum and expanding bottle sucked his penis in.

The doctor consulted with our other doctor over the phone as everyone else was brainstorming. They discounted a ring cutter, scalpel, trauma shears, and oral medications. Evacuating the blood by needle aspiration did not appear a viable option. At one time the nurse suggested punching a hole in the bottom of the bottle, pouring in baby or olive oil and, I'm quoting here, she said, 'Just lube it up and that puppy will pop right out of there.'

Shane realized what he had said and with great chagrin apologized, "I am so sorry, I…"

Lindsay looked nonplussed. "Continue."

"Immediately the doctor gave the nurse the stink eye, she turned bright red and excused herself for a few minutes. We ended up giving him some valium, pain medication, something to lower his blood pressure, and sent him to a surgical center."

Alan interrupted, "Did they manage to save his manhood?"

Ben could see Lindsay slowly shaking her head in disbelief, a smirk hiding below her slightly bowed head.

"Apparently everything turned out well. He was referred to a urologist and told to put on boxing gloves if he were ever tempted to repeat his old treatment procedure."

Everyone at the table stared blankly at Shane.

"Sorry, I just couldn't resist." Shane looked to Lindsey and asked, "Did I win?"

With an air of seriousness Lindsay folded her hands in front of her, resting them on the table, and appeared to be self-engrossed, probably recounting the three scenarios she had just listened to. "I am relying upon you three being honorable gentlemen who will stand by the veracity of their stories." All three nodded quickly while making verbal affirmations as well. "I found the patient stories to be compelling, absurdly interesting, and oddly enough, believable. I have also concluded that all three of you own a unique, if not slightly twisted, sense of black humor." Ben found that he was enthralled with Lindsey's voice, and sensed that she was doing her utmost to appear serious considering the nature of this farcical enterprise. "Without going into detail or fanfare, I choose Shane's patient as today's luncheon winner."

Shane's arms shot up into the air accompanied by a self-congratulatory cheer.

Lindsay burst out laughing. Hers was an unabashed, throaty laugh that pleasured Ben's ears. "I loved all of them, guys. Thank you so much for including me."

Alan looked slightly disappointed. Ben laughed and thanked Lindsey profusely for her patience and for putting up with the three of them. "I hope that we didn't embarrass you too terribly."

"No, not at all," She started to slide out of the booth, "It was my pleasure but I need to get back to work. Would you gentlemen like anything else? Another pitcher of beer?"

The three men universally shook their heads, no.

"I'm good thank you," Ben stated, "I have a couple of errands yet to run today."

Shane asked, "If you would be willing to bring us the bill these two will settle up while I rest upon my laurels."

"I'll be back in a couple of minutes with the bill." Ben gazed up at her and their eyes met; his pulse quickened. Her dark brown eyes drew him in and he knew that were he ever given the chance; he would be mere putty within her hands. She turned and walked towards the rear of the bar. Oddly, he felt elation and sadness at the same time. Believing that there was an intangible, yet strong attraction between the two of them he was buoyed and then suddenly deflated that it would all soon end. He watched her as she made her way down the bar. Shane and Alan had divided up the pooled money into two shares; the winner's share to Shane and the judge's share to Lindsay.

"Ben. Ben. Hey Ben. Earth to Ben." Alan was trying to gain his attention. Ben finally heard him and turned. Alan set Lindsay's share and additional money for the meal on the table in front of him. "Go pay the bill Ben, give Lindsey her share and get her phone number Romeo. She has a thing for you."

He felt his face reddening, knowing that these two would not let it go.

"Go, Ben, I agree with Alan. Don't leave here without professing your undying love."

Ben elbowed Shane eliciting an "Oommppfffff!" collected the money, slid out of the booth and walked down to the waitress station. "It was really a pleasure meeting you Lindsay." She had just tallied the bill so he pulled out his wallet and matched Alan's money leaving her a handsome tip.

"That's way too much, Ben," she attempted to return a portion.

"No, Lindsay, not near enough for putting up with the likes of us."

Again, he heard that throaty laugh that he loved. "You gentlemen are a walk in the park compared to some of our occasional clientele."

He handed her the judge's share of the pot, "This is the judge's share of the pot."

She attempted to refuse it. "You keep it Ben; spend it on your girlfriend."

"Even if I had one I would not consider spending your well earned money on her. Please...do something fun for yourself or with your guy." Ben knew that he was fishing. "Thank you for doing that favor for us."

"It was my pleasure and I really enjoyed meeting you." He recognized that she had emphasized the "you" but also accepted that Lindsay had not risen to the bait; she probably has a boyfriend. "How long are you three in town?"

"I'll be headed home tomorrow to see my dad and those two will probably head back to their jobs in the next couple of days." Ben lingered, started to open his mouth to ask for her phone number, and instead thought better of it. He felt like hitting himself for being so helpless.

"Well you travel safe Ben." Lindsay smiled and in a quick motion gently touched his arm. "I hope you drop by here again in the future."

Ben returned the smile and walked away. It did not feel right asking for her phone number knowing that he would soon be gone and returning to the edge of the world plus he did not want to be rebuffed should she have a beau. Alan and Shane were waiting at the front door for Ben, having already donned their winter gear. "Go ahead guys; I'll meet you at the motel. I have a couple of errands to run."

Shane put his hand to his ear, thumb and pinky extended, mimicking a phone, "Got her number, did ya?"

"Get lost; I'll see you two later." Alan and Shane exited but not before allowing a frigid blast to enter. Ben stared at the two photos that had garnered his attention when he first arrived and as he slipped on his coat, hat and gloves he sensed someone behind him. It was Lindsey.

She extended her hand, "Happy New Year Ben." He removed his glove and as he went to take her extended hand she slid a folded piece of paper into his palm. "I would like to think that the two ships quietly passing in the night occasionally find the same safe anchorage."

Ben could feel his heart pounding. He said the only thing that immediately came to mind, "Longfellow?"

She laughed, "You're a fan?"

His brain was doing flip flops, "Does the Wreck of the Hesperus count?"

"It won't if you manage to lose that paper Ben."

They shook hands and held on much longer than was needed for a proper goodbye. He grinned and arched

196

his eyebrows, she smiled and demurely batted her eyelashes and then they parted.

Ben stopped midway while crossing the street. The street was devoid of vehicle and pedestrian traffic and he noted but a few vehicles parked along its length, crowded against snow banks that literally forced them half way out into the driving lane. He speculated that this street would remain cold on most winter afternoons due to being in perpetual shadow. Exhaled breath created clouds of vapor fogging his sunglasses which, he now perched on his forehead. A short lived gust of frigid wind sent a shiver through him. Ben removed his glove to enable him to unfold the tightly creased paper.

I so hate snakes.
I am not known for turning a blind eye.
I occasionally enjoy a good penis story.
You are cute, I believe a rare find.
You though, will not find me easy.
You should have asked for my number.
Take a chance anyway, Please call.
Lindsay Daniels 406-555-1212

Ben looked back at the tinted windows of Herald's, wondered briefly if she might be watching him and quickly decided that no, she would be bussing the booth that they had just vacated. There would be an afternoon crowd of regulars to ready for or those looking to get an early start on a New Year's celebration. There was no gust of wind yet he felt another strong shiver and knew that it wasn't from the winter cold.

Jump on the grenade, Ben. Jump on the grenade. Ben stood under the vapor lights of a bar parking lot, the cold of packed snow and ice beginning to penetrate through the soles of his shoes. Thinking that he would be spending most of his time inside tonight he had opted for casual shoes instead of his insulated boots. A feather light snow sifted down as he felt an increasingly frequent shiver accentuating this evening's other questionable decision; an insulated but lighter coat. Starring absently at his motel across Reserve Street he could also see the large digital display sign of the bank on the adjoining corner. "Time to Open a New IRA" streamed by followed by "-10 degrees Fahrenheit" 8:15 PM, then "Happy New Year, Buckle Up and Drive Safe." A moderate flow of New Year's Eve traffic passed by, the vehicles producing the dull sound of compressing snow under their cold tires.

He removed his right glove, fished his cell phone out of his coat pocket, half expecting a message to appear on the display, like a kid's Magic 8 Ball answering questions with portents floating up from its fluid filled core. "Make the call you Wimp," "Forget about it Loser," or even "Grow a pair" streamed through his head, similar to the bank sign across the street. Having already memorized the phone number over the past several hours he began thumbing in the digits, then midway hesitated, reminded himself that this was a good thing, and finished punching in the phone number.

"Hello, Daniels residence."

Ben did not recognize the woman's voice and almost apologized for a wrong number, then realized that he did recognize the last name and responded tentatively with, "Hello. I was trying to reach Lindsay Daniels."

"Just a sec."

He could hear the woman calling out, "Lindsay, phone call. Lindsay, you've got a call." Ben could also hear in the background the strains of what sounded like the

Beach Boys singing *Santa Claus is Comin' to Town*. Whoa, they recorded a Christmas album too? The woman began talking again, muffled this time as if attempting to cover the phone with her palm, "It's a guy, Lindsay. You been holding out on me?" At full volume he heard, "No, it's not your ex..."

Her slightly husky voice greeted him, "Hello, this is Lindsay. May I help you?"

"Hi, Lindsay, it's Ben. Ben Parker."

In a flat unaffected voice, he heard, "Well, Mister Ben Parker, what can I do for you?"

Ben stood silently shivering in the parking lot, phone to his ear, searching for the right response, "I, ah...I um...I'm, oh jeez, Lindsay, I'm sorry I was under the impression that I should call." He was desperately wondering if he had misinterpreted her intent and began searching his pocket for her note to reread.

Her throaty laugh resounded in his ear, "I'm sorry Ben, I couldn't resist. I was hoping that phone number was burning a hole in your pocket and you couldn't resist calling me sooner."

Ben was immensely relieved, noticed that his clenched teeth were on the verge of chattering, "Damn, you had me worried there for a minute. I didn't take you as a sadist."

"My apologies, Ben. I am so glad that you called. I don't normally put myself out there like today and I hate to admit it but ever since I left Herald's I was hoping that you would call. I was beginning to think that maybe you were getting cold feet."

Ben looked down at his shoes which were now sporting a thin coating of snow, "There might some truth to that."

"Sometimes I can have that effect on people. Where are you?"

"I'm standing in a bar parking lot on Reserve Street freezing my keister off."

"Is there any reason that your cute little keister isn't inside where it's warm?"

"It's starting to get fairly drunk out and the decibels are increasing accordingly."

"And your friends?"

"My cohorts in crime are inside with a major head start on tomorrow's hangover. I finished my errands, took a nap to digest all of that excellent food, and I've been behaving myself. Originally I was to be tonight's designated driver, however, Shane and Alan have developed a strong attraction to this bar and as luck would have it, it is right across the street from our motel."

"Soooo, since you don't have to drive tonight you are going to imbibe heavily?"

"It wasn't my intent, especially not if I had a better offer." He was hopeful but did not want to sound overly so.

"Do you have a pencil handy?"

"Right now, I don't believe that I can pry my frozen fingers from around this phone so I will memorize whatever you say before the neuro-pathways of my brain shut down."

"Go warm up your vehicle and call me back. My address will be the same 15 minutes from now."

"What motivated you to become a physician assistant? Your dad? Your mom?"

"I don't believe that it was any one thing." Ben tilted his head and shrugged his shoulders. "Our family has always been involved in community service in one form or another. Right after high school I became a volunteer fireman and that evolved into a volunteer EMT. When I finally decided on college I also took Paramedic training and worked for an ambulance service in Bozeman part time to make some money. It evolved into a life of its own and after I returned home I continued as a volunteer and talked with a good friend of mine who is a physician assistant. He was great at what he did and I wanted to do it as well. I shadowed him and a couple of other doctors in the county. I realized that as a Paramedic or an EMT I was often responding to people who were having one the worse days of their lives. They needed someone with a relatively cool head to intervene, to help them through their pain, to help them prevail. I believed that I could do that."

"And the puzzles." Ben became more animated. "The puzzles of medicine. I was enthralled with the concept of figuring out what was going on and how could it be fixed. No, treated, treated is a better word. The thought of practicing medicine became my focus. The doctors that I shadowed gave me insight as to what lay ahead and what I should gear myself up for. One of them said, 'If you want to see trauma and to train for treating trauma go to a reservation or a big city.' Another doctor told me, 'In Montana, if you want a variety of emergency medicine and trauma go to a reservation, and if you want pathology go to a VA hospital but if you want vanilla, go into dermatology.' My friend, who has been practicing rural medicine for many years, told me that you will find interesting pathology everywhere, however, just more frequently in the bigger communities. He related that most of the time his days were routine, almost mundane, punctuated with moments of sheer terror. I knew what I wanted to do. I may have challenges in the environment that I work in but I do love my work."

Lindsay looked at him with a smile that morphed into an expectant look; there appeared to be an invitation pending. "It's almost midnight, let's go outside and watch the new year come in. There are usually a few small firework displays in the neighborhood and if we don't freeze our derrieres off first you might have a chance to bring in the New Year with a kiss."

Ben smiled broadly, helped her into her coat and whispered in her ear, "I'd be crazy not to accept that offer."

She murmured back, "Yes, you would, Ben Parker Yes, you would."

Ben filled two paper coffee cups at the motel office. He had knocked on the door and rang the bell repeatedly until an unshaven, apparently hung over desk clerk unlocked the door and allowed him in. Then, standing by patiently he watched the clerk shakily fill and start the coffee maker, and spread a bag of mini-donuts on a paper plate. He claimed his room receipt and 10 minutes later, having filled the coffee cups, he headed towards the two rooms his friends were still sleeping in. While knocking on Alan's door he held no great expectations that either of his friends were yet awake at 6:30 in the morning nor would either of them be functioning at a high level of mental acuity. He was not to be proven wrong.

As each door was eventually opened he greeted them by handing over a cup of coffee and was greeted in return by an individual suffering from sleep deprivation and the morning after haze induced by the over indulgence of alcohol. Thanking them for a great time, he assured them that he would be in touch and wished them the best in life and love. Ben apologized for having to leave early but explained that he had to get on the road in order to get home in time to watch the Rose Bowl with his dad. He neglected, however, to mention his pending breakfast plans with Lindsay prior to him heading south. One at a time he left them in the doorway on the verge of shivering, both only clad in a T-shirt and shorts, the bank sign across the street displaying -4 degrees Fahrenheit. He knew both Alan and Shane would at the least be nursing headaches and though sympathetic Ben was extremely happy with how fortuitous it was that his own evening had turned out so differently than originally planned.

He found a supermarket open on Reserve Street and as he cruised the isles his mind streamed random thoughts; Why would anyplace be open this early on New Year's Day...should he add some medium hot salsa to the omelets...why would any place actually open its doors at all on New Year's Day... what kind of cheese should he get...oh crap was she lactose intolerant...wait, no, there was an empty pizza box in the trash...there seems to be a shortage of store help this morning...probably manned by managerial staff since everyone called in with the 86-proof flu.

Ben pulled up in front of Lindsay's house at 0730 hours with the only illumination within the winter's darkness provided by the cones of halogen lighting directly below the street lamps. Few houses showed indications of life within, a meager number of windows emitting muted light from behind drawn curtains or window shades. Lindsay's front windows were alit as was her porch light. He arrived earlier than the appointed hour, happily nervous, disappointed that he could only stay for breakfast but ecstatic that he had been invited back. The engine was still running, pumping heat into the cab as he punched in her phone number.

"Good morning, Ben, is that your truck running out in front of my house?"

"And a Happy New Year to you also."

"Happy New Year, Ben, you're early."

"Is that a bad thing?"

"No, prompt is good, early is better. It indicates great enthusiasm and future expectations. You better turn off your truck and come in."

"I'll be in, in two shakes. I've got breakfast to cook."

"You're just full of surprises but I guess my expectations would be for nothing less."

Ben was folding over a three egg omelet filled with Swiss cheese, diced mushrooms, green peppers, onion and sausage topped with a layer of medium hot salsa, when he asked, "What's your goal when you finish your master's?"

"Didn't I tell you that last night, Ben?"

"No, you were building up to it when you distracted me with fireworks and your extraordinary lips. You kept deferring my questions with your own. I know that you majored in art history and minored in graphic design, and are currently finishing up your master's in business management; however, I'm curious as to what's next." He turned over the simmering bacon strips and dropped an English muffin into the toaster.

"I don't have any preconceived ideas or needs of being wealthy, just enough to make my daughter and me comfortable. There is a hope to open a graphic arts studio and eventually a gallery to promote local artisans. The biggest challenge will be the start up finances."

Ben had arranged the omelets, bacon and buttered English muffins on plates and now delivered them to the table. "Please, eat up. We can eat and talk between bites because unfortunately I have to leave at 9, 9:30 at the latest if I want to make it home on time. Fair enough?"

They ate periodically pausing to talk, sometimes animatedly, and after breakfast they continued their conversation over coffee and hot chocolate until 9:15 when Ben dejectedly announced that he had to head home. There was contemplative silence as each pondered what to say. Lindsay broached the topic of the elephant in the room. "Where do you want this to go, Ben?"

"I want this to continue on, Lindsay, long distance or not, I want for us to give it our best shot. How about you?"

Lindsay demurred before answering, "I agree, Ben Parker. I believe that you definitely have potential." She laughed and ventured, "How often do we communicate? Monthly? Weekly? Daily? Phone, e-mail, U.S. postal service?"

"Yep, all that you mentioned but I don't know how frequently I'll be able to call or write."

She looked warily disappointed, "What do you mean by how frequently?"

Ben replied as a matter of fact, "I'm not sure that I can do it any more than two, maybe three times a day."

"You are a shitbird, Parker, you know that don't you?"

"So, I've been told."

He stood and headed for the coat rack in the living room, Lindsay accompanying him. Before he could slide his coat off of the hook he found her hands locked behind his neck and they became embroiled in a long passionate kiss. Their embrace lasted for several minutes until she whispered up into his ear, "Call me when you're safe at home."

The interstate turned out to be in much better shape than he had anticipated. Granted the majority of the passing lane remained snow packed and icy, the right hand lane, having experienced substantially more vehicle traffic, was moderately cleared of ice and snow. The stretch of road between Clinton and Drummond, with its curves, bridges, and the extensive shadowing created by steep hillsides bracketing the roadway was generally treacherous with ice during winter storms. Having driven this snaking roadway numerous times during the winter months he had grown to equate it to a carnival ride with a pucker factor, an interstate sleigh ride fueled by a lemon enema.

The secondary roads south of Butte still required that one pay attention to the conditions but the appearance of the sun, traversing low across the southern horizon, and the dearth of windblown snow greatly enhanced visibility. He made reasonably good time, pulling into his dad's driveway and shutting off the engine with time to spare before the Rose Bowl kickoff. There was a lot more snow pushed into piles at either end of the driveway than in recent years, testament to this winter's cold and precipitation. Normally housed inside the garage in the winter, his father's truck was parked outside at the far end of the driveway and Ben could see the garage doors drifted shut by snow. This gave him pause; his dad might be slowing down more than he cared to admit.

Stamping his feet free of snow on the porch Ben entered the kitchen door and was met by his father. "You made it, son," Edward Parker was grinning widely, "Kickoff's in 10 minutes."

Ben set his duffle bag down on the hardwood kitchen floor and they shook hands. Hugging or embracing was not usually part of the greeting or departure ritual for the men of the Parker family. It was a rare but remembered occasion.

"You hungry Ben?"

"Yes sir, what have you got?"

"I've got some cheese, sausage, herring, clam dip, onion dip, chips and beer for the game. Rib eyes for tonight's supper. There's leftover meatloaf and some bacon if you want to make a sandwich. Anything healthier than that you'll have to forage for."

"I'll pass on the sandwich; the game fare and beer should cover the four food groups. Should we fire up the grill tonight for the steaks?"

"Outside grilling is a year round sport in Montana. Take off your coat and stay a while, Bub."

Ben slid out of his coat and as he hung it on one of the wall pegs he studied his father who was now busy removing tinfoil covered plates and bowls from the refrigerator. He looked thinner, his flannel shirt hanging loose from his shoulders. A bit more stooped at the back and shoulders, Ben thought his pallor a little lighter as if he had not been outside battling the winter elements as often as usual. Ben realized his father had grown older but when you haven't seen one another for six months or more the aging process appeared more evident.

"Let me give you a hand with that, Dad."

In the past an offer like that would have elicited a polite but gruff refusal of, "I've got it, I've got it handled. You think I can't carry a couple of plates? Go grab a seat and make yourself to home."

"Sure Ben, you take the plates out and I've got the rest handled."

Ben did not know if his dad was secretly acquiescing to advancing age and infirmity or if it was a gesture made to make Ben feel needed and welcomed back home. "You bet."

His dad had a wry smile on his face when he asked, "Who are you betting on?"

Ben new that his father wanted Michigan so he said "I'll bet you five on Southern Cal."

"A fin? A lousy fin, mister moneybags? Sweeten the pot and make it a sawbuck."

Laughing, Ben shook his head and responded with "Mister Moneybags? You seem to forget that it's PA now MD. Okay, 10 bucks it is old man."

"Good. Let's go watch some football."

"Hey, Ben, your oatmeal's getting cold," Ben's dad was loud but not yelling.

Ben called back from the living room, "I'll pass Your oatmeal could substitute for building mortar."

"Okay wiseass, the eggs are done so get a move on.

The opening strains of Gene Pitney's 24 hours from Tulsa began resonating from the living room as Ben walked into the kitchen singing along, "Dearest, darling, I had to write..."

Edward Parker stood by the small wooden kitchen table a heaping plate of scrambled eggs in one hand, a plate piled high with sourdough pancakes in the other, a look of stunned surprise morphing into an elated grin. He set the plates down. "What the hell is going on here? What have you been up to Ben, that old stereo hasn't worked for a good 15 years. And where on earth did you find Gene Pitney?" He was still the picture of surprise and at a loss as to what to do with his now empty hands so he folded his arms over his chest.

"Merry belated Christmas, Dad," then more softly, "Merry Christmas, Dad."

"Back atcha Ben, Merry Christmas." He took a seat at the table and waved Ben over, "Dig in before everything gets cold and give me a couple of answers."

They began filling their plates as Ben explained, "Right after the Fourth of July you drove Mr. Pasacovich up to Fort Harrison for his appointment at the VA and I had Nick Smoltz stop in and see if he could repair that old relic of a stereo. He told me that it belongs in the Smithsonian but yes he could fix it if he could locate the parts. So, when you and Mr. Pasacovich went to the Grizzly game in Missoula last September Smoltz came over and repaired it."

"You let that old horse thief in my house?" Edward had lost a partial mouthful of egg as he started laughing, coughed, caught his breath and said, "Thank you son. What a great gift. Where did you find Gene Pitney?"

"The same place that I located Johnny Cash and Mantovani. I called Rockin Rudi's in Missoula and they managed to find the three albums that I requested."

"I couldn't have asked for anything better. Thank you son."

"You still love Johnny Cash don't you?"

"I do but he's not for everyone."

"Oh? Such as?"

Edward looked down at his coffee before he took a gulp and said, "Such as your mother."

"What do you mean? You guys had Cash and Marty Robbins and Hank Williams playing all of the time."

"She tolerated it, just like I tolerated her choices of Blondie, U2 and those Fleetwood guys."

Ben and his father quietly sat eating eggs, pancakes, bacon, hash browns and toast as the melodious voice of Gene Pitney sang songs with a lilt of melancholy and angst. Mr. Parker suddenly arose, excused himself, disappeared to another part of the house and returned shortly with two envelopes. He placed them on the table. One was white with a thin green ribbon running from opposite corners with a flattened red bow in the middle. The other envelope was a bland tan. Ben's father sat, hands folded on the table, fingers intertwined and began talking, "After your mother left you consistently cut her out of your life but she wouldn't give up hope that someday you would relent and let her back in. I'm happy that you did last summer. Every Christmas and for your birthday she mailed a card here with a check so that you might buy something that you really wanted and you left them unopened. I tossed them in my dresser draw and told your mother that you had refused to open them."

He stopped, stared off above Ben's head for a moment and then continued once again locked in eye to eye, "She loves you Ben and couldn't give up so she salted the money from each check in an account she started for you. For over 20 years she's been hoping for reconciliation, for forgiveness." Edward tapped her finger on the envelope, "This is not a bribe for your affection. It represents grief, contrition, a plea for forgiveness and most of all love." He slid the decorated white envelope to Ben, "She wants you to have it, to spend it, however that you may choose."

Ben felt conflicted as he picked up the envelope and contemplated opening it and what it would indicate if he did; was it an appeasement, a surrender of principle or surrender to greed, or a show of forgiveness and acceptance. "I'm not turning it down and I'm not ready to open it right this minute but I will give her a call when I do."

His father pulled a slip of paper out of his shirt pocket, set it down next to the envelope and said evenly but with conviction, "That's your mother's new address. You open it Ben and she deserves more than a phone call."

"Agreed."

Ben picked up the tan envelope and held it up to his forehead, closed his eyes as if reading the contents via a transcendental thought process or perhaps osmosis. "I see cash money to purchase whatever my little heart desires."

His father sipped his coffee and remained impassive.

Ben opened the envelope and found a Christmas card which contained a gift certificate for a new television at Costco. His eyes lit up. "That's way too much money, Dad."

"Are you saying that you don't want it?"

"No, what I'm saying is that it's a great gift and thanks a million but you spent way too much on me."

"Perhaps. That old TV that you have has got to be at least 15, maybe 18 years old so I figured that it was time to buy a new one before yours craps out in East Podunk."

Ben reached over and they shook hands, "Thanks, Dad, thank you very much."

"My pleasure. What's on your schedule today?"

"Spending it here with you. I'll shovel out your garage doors and whatever else you need a hand with. Then we can listen to the Mantovani album with all your favorites like the theme song to *Patton*, *The Bridge Over the River Kwai*, and of course your all-time favorite, *Star Wars*."

Edward Parker just shook his head. "And Saturday? Did I hear you tell that gal on the phone that you were going to meet her in Anaconda on Saturday?"

"I didn't know you were listening in, Dad. I guess your claimed deafness is merely convenience of hearing. Yes, I'm going to Anaconda to meet Lindsay but I'll be back by late afternoon."

"Good. You can tell me about her while I'm cooking ribs and then we can talk before you head back on

Sunday." He slipped a $10 bill out of his pants pocket and slapped it on the table, "Here's your 10 bucks big spender. You should have bet more 'cause 10 bucks won't get you too damn far."

"You better get that wallet out again because shoveling snow is getting more expensive by the minute." Ben gave his best sinister laugh, "Let's clean this mess up because I can smell money burning a hole in your pocket."

Ben sat in his truck as it idled in the parking lot of the Chinese restaurant at the east end of Anaconda, the heat set on low but enough to keep the windshield defrosted and his feet warm. His was the only vehicle in the parking lot and periodically he looked up from his book to scan for any new arrivals. The outside temperature had warmed up to a tropical 15 degrees and the roads had improved since his trip home two days ago. This was due to change Sunday as they kept forecasting a new arctic front descending down from Canada. He looked up at the sound of tires crunching on compacted snow and ice, a mid-90s Chevy pickup truck pulling into the space to his left. A glance out of his driver side window revealed a smiling Lindsay, dark sunglasses, a burgundy Montana Grizzly baseball cap, her hair in a pony tail snaking out the rear opening of the cap. He returned the smile as he rolled his window down. She reciprocated by lowering hers.

He shut off his engine and he could hear that she had followed suit, "Hola, sweet lady, you're early."

"Not by much. You obviously made it here earlier Mr. Eager Beaver. How are you?"

"Just dandy, now that you're here. That and a little hungry."

"What gave you the idea to eat Chinese at lunch time?"

"The food here is good but how many people do you know that eat Chinese in the middle of a cold winter day?"

"Honestly, the thought never crossed my mind."

"And there you are. Shall we go inside?"

They both rolled up their windows. Ben allowed Lindsay to exit first and then hopped out closing his door in one fluid movement. Between the trucks they took an instant to take stock of each other and in the next they were embracing and exchanging a lingering kiss.

"Was that a shiver from cold, or tremble from passion?"

Ben bent his neck back looking Lindsay in the eye, his arms still embracing her closely, "Don't be trying to take credit; neither of us is wearing a coat."

"But I would give you credit for being a great kisser."

"Okay, I'll grant that you project an irresistible force that leaves me occasionally weak in the knees. Now let's get something to eat."

"I suggest that we get it to go and sit in your truck."

"And fog up the windows?"

"Don't get ahead of yourself. I was thinking we could eat lunch and talk in privacy."

"Look around the parking lot; we're the only customers here. How much privacy do we need?"

She gave him a look of faux disappointment, "You would rather settle for vanilla when you could opt for a cold weather adventure with the chance of fogging up the windows? We only have a short time with hopefully plenty to talk about."

"Lead on, you've talked me into it."

"You still warm enough Lindsay?"

They had been conversing incessantly, their food spread between them on the bench seat and she was currently finishing off a now cold pork eggroll as she nodded yes. She swallowed and said, "As toast, thank you." She glanced up at the windshield, "See? We still managed to fog up the windshield without any unseemly display of affection."

Ben retrieved a red bandana from his back pocket and wiped the misted window revealing the snow covered city park that they had chosen for a luncheon site. The wind had picked up, the evergreen boughs swaying in the gusts as skiffs of snow skimmed across the surface of the frozen white landscape.

"What time do you have to be at your sister's?"

"I told her that I'd be there around three." Lindsay glanced at her watch, "Wow, we've been yakking since before noon and it's a few minutes after two. I hate to say it Ben but I have to be leaving soon."

"Damn, I knew that it was too good to last. We manage to let the food go cold, fog up the windows without a hint of mischief and now you're abandoning me. What's Phillipsburg, 30 miles?"

"About 30, maybe 35."

"Then we better get you on the road. As I recall Deer Lodge County was never overly aggressive with snow plowing and hadn't quite figured out what sand was used for. The last time I was over that road to P-burg in the winter that Springhill grade was a skating rink."

He started up the truck as Lindsay bagged up the leftover food. She slid over the bench next to him. The tires were pushing through the unplowed parking lot. "What? You're making no attempt to foist your manly charm on me in hopes of passionate kissing and befogging the windows?"

Ben attempted a serious tone, "You had your chance woman. Now we need to get you on the road so you don't disappoint family."

After backing in beside Lindsay's truck she slid her hand off of his as he slipped the truck out of gear and applied the emergency brake. He turned to her and was caught by surprise as she leaned in to kiss him. Holding up an index finger she said, "Wait here," and she exited the cab, ran around and opened the door to the passenger side of her own truck. Quickly returning she set a cardboard box down on his bench seat. "Something to remember me by. Don't open it till you get home and don't let it slide off of the seat." She closed the door and walked around to his driver side door, motioning for him to roll down his window. Standing on her toes their lips met as he leaned out, his hands cradling the lines of her jaw, hers entwined behind his neck. There was intensity behind the kiss that sparked an involuntary shudder between his shoulders and down his spine. Ben was unprepared yet, not completely shocked that a kiss from this woman could elicit such a response. It also triggered the thought that he was not prepared to let her go.

A semi-trailer truck, speeding along on the still patchy snowpack and ice of the Interstate's passing lane, blew by him momentarily rocking his vehicle. The rear view mirrors were now clear of vehicles so he tried her cell phone number knowing that he would probably lose reception near the Fairmont exit.

"Well that didn't take long. Did 'we' forget something?"

"No, the box is still safe and sound and emitting an odor oddly reminiscent of apple pie, but I just suddenly missed your voice."

"You Ben are a true romantic," she paused, "and mind reader. I was missing yours as well. Keep your cotton picken' hands out of the box."

"How did this happen and why do I feel like a giddy little school boy?"

"I have this power over men."

"Soooo, why choose me?"

"Actually I had no control. It was Kismet."

Ben knew that he was grinning ear to ear when he said goodbye.

Edward Parker stood, stretched his arms while arching his back, hoisted his empty coffee cup and asked, "Anything for you Ben?"

"Maybe a beer please. You out did yourself, Dad, the ribs were excellent."

Ben's father refilled his cup and plucked a bottle of beer from the refrigerator door as Ben cleared the supper dishes from the table. Setting the beer down, Edward sat back down in is chair. "I forgot to ask you while we were cooking the ribs; how did your date go today?"

"Good, Dad. Good." He was not effusive.

"Good? You drive crappy roads for 100 miles one way to see a girl and that's all you have to say about it?" He sounded more hurt than prying.

Having had a few relationships fail over the years, Ben had grown reticent in providing too much information to his father early on, hoping to avoid any embarrassment to either of them should something not pan out. "Okay, Dad, it was better than good. We ate Chinese, talked a couple of hours and promised to communicate frequently. She sent me home with an apple pie for our dessert."

"At least she knows your favorite pie. I'm glad that you made it back. I wasn't relishing the idea of eating six pounds of ribs by myself."

The two men sat in silence sipping their respective beverages.

"How's your friend Salty faring these days?"

Ben was slowly rotating his bottle by the neck as it sat upright on the table.

His reply bordered on the edge of sadness, "He's losing ground steadily. I'm afraid that some major procedures are in his future that will only prolong the inevitable. Talking with him only seems to confirm that although he has accepted his mortality he's still somewhat depressed."

"Sorry to hear that Ben. He's made a strong impression on you."

"Salty is a good person, a character in his own right. He told me that he was in the First Marines and had received his wounds on Peleliu but like you, he never revealed anything else about his deployment. I mentioned that you were a Corpsman attached to the First Marines on Peleliu and Okinawa. He laughed and said it could have been you that saved his bacon."

"Do you form that kind of bond with many of your patients?"

Ben was quick to answer, "No, no I'm not inclined to do so but for some reason we just hit it off. In some ways he reminds me of you."

Edward cleared his throat, "So how are things in general? You doing okay?"

After taking another gulp of his beer Ben set the bottle down and slowly rolled it back and forth between his palms. "I like what I do, Dad. I truly love medicine. The nursing staff and ancillary crew are great and the community is very supportive. I've made a few friends but I rarely go out because of my schedule and sometimes I just need time away from any human beings. The country is definitely alien compared to here but has its own interesting beauty."

His father leaned back, interlocked his fingers behind his head, "So you're good. No problems, just as fine as frog hair." There was just the hint of sarcasm in his voice.

Ben laughed, "You and your expressions." He shifted in his chair as if uncomfortable in his position rather than uneasy with his thoughts. "There are always assholes in every community, I accept that but damn, Bedlam has got its share and I've been embroiled with several of them."

His dad raised an eyebrow.

"Yes, I've had words with a few with possible downstream consequences. A football coach with a problem with alcohol who uses his players to assuage his ego. There's a businessman and real estate broker that has the morals of Saddam Hussein and is in cahoots with the mayor who has no scruples and leaves the proverbial slime trail wherever he goes. I've discovered city workers of dubious character working at the behest of the mayor to promote his agenda and then there's a relentless and unprincipled newspaper reporter who may be dealing drugs on the side. Unfortunately the citizens are either truly uninformed or unaware or choose to ignore the obvious and accept their collective fates.

His father unfolded his hands from behind his head, leaned forward and refolded them to rest on the table top. "And the doctor? You have indicated some concern, if not displeasure, regarding his behavior and actions."

Ben semi-dramatically threw up his arms, "I haven't got a handle on him, Dad. I do know that he's a chauvinist, an egotist, if not a narcissist. He frequently belittles the staff yet, shows favoritism to patients and the community hierarchy, unethically accepts gifts, and politics with the hospital administrator and probably anyone else who will advance his personal agenda. One week he's a demeaning dictator, the next begrudgingly helpful, and the next week you can't locate him. He will chastise you for a treatment plan and weeks later you discover that he's using the same approach. I've caught him in blatant lies which, he then attempts to manipulate and explain away as miscommunications."

Having finished his beer Ben stood up and paced the kitchen for the next 10 minutes providing his father with numerous examples of the doctor's contradictory behavior and odd if not inappropriate interactions with staff, patients, with Marni and himself. "The one word that I think well describes him is inconsistent, however, that one word really doesn't do justice to depicting his behavior."

"Have you mentioned any of this to the administrator?"

"On several occasions I have brought up my concerns regarding the doctor's relationship and behavior to me but I've come to the conclusion that Westergard, for whatever reasons, would rather ignore the problems and avoid any possible confrontation with the doctor."

"Might I venture an observation?"

Ben nodded affirmatively, "Please do."

"You might consider modifying the description to be inconsistently inconsistent. Is there a medical term or a specific malady for that?"

Ben sat down and pondered for several moments, "I hadn't thought of it in that manner but I believe that you could be right; that is a more apt description and no, I can't think of a definitive term or diagnosis."

"Are you worried about your job security Ben?"

Ben gave a noncommittal shrug.

"What are you planning to do?"

"I'm not sure. I have a one year contract that I will have fulfilled in early May. I've got a good track record and a boatload more experience which should expand my options. Thankfully I'm past being in denial hoping that his behaviors will change. I'm not about to go off the rails or do something rash, however, I'll be ready if push comes to shove. With your permission I'll use one of your famous sayings; I was looking for a job when I found this one."

"I've got another one that might fit the circumstances. This one I got from an old jarhead from Tennessee or maybe it was Kentucky, that I patched up on Okinawa; Church ain't over till the snakes are back in the bag."

Ben could only smirk, shake his head and hope that Edward Parker would live to be 100.

"Pie. It's time to sample your lady friend's pie."

Having retrieved the pie from the refrigerator Ben placed two handsomely sized wedges on plates and delivered them to the table with clean forks, and resumed his seat. They had both begun eating their pie when Ben heard a soft moan of satisfaction from his father, "This is excellent, a damn fine pie."

Ben's mouth was full so he just nodded enthusiastically in agreement.

"Ben, if you find a gal with a sparkle in her eye, is kind to dogs and strangers, possesses a sense of self-worth and who can bake your favorite pie then she's probably a keeper.

"Sage advice. Eat your pie."

SALTY

Weather forecasting has become performance art, where you can be wrong 90% of the time and still get paid. Forecasting human behavior and emotion is a whole different animal, or art form. Ben had grown to rely on Myra, the hospital receptionist, to forecast the general hospital mood and emotional status and he had rarely been disappointed. He sincerely attempted to be pragmatic about his environment, avoiding at all costs the appearance of gender bias. Having calculated that 93.75% of the employees were female, and having frequently observed the incontrovertible relationship between Myra's initial morning greeting and the general conduct of the predominately female hospital staff throughout a day, he felt relatively safe in its predictive value. She was his mood barometer, the most accurate that he had discovered. He had never mentioned this to another soul, shrewdly placing his life above unscientific investigation but clearly strong evidential proof.

There was a look of sadness, near grim resignation, on Myra's face before she looked up from the desk and saw it was Ben. She attempted a wan smile before asking, "You made it back in one piece. How was your time off?" The smile was slowly fading as she looked at him expectantly. Ben had witnessed this look and demeanor before, the first time when Myra and half of the hospital staff were late, thereby unsuccessful in purchasing a block of tickets for Cher's Farewell Tour when it was playing in Billings, June of 2003. However, he had also seen the 180 degree effect when Myra and the crew had secured their block of tickets for Cher's appearance in Saskatoon, Saskatchewan, six hours away on a good day. He chose not to press her until he had accumulated more background information.

"The time off was great, but the roads were crappy from day one on and absolutely foul coming back starting at Miles City. The last 40 miles, between Sunnvale and here, took me close to two hours last night."

"I thought they closed that road last night."

"Apparently they did but it was after I had headed out of Sunnvale. Sideways snow, lots of cross highway drifting. I nearly mired in on Stop Gap Pass. The mail truck was stuck tight at the top of the pass. I offered the driver a ride, but he said that he had radioed in and a state plow was headed out to help him. Glad to be back."

Ben was almost prepared to ask her, "Why so down in the mouth?" when Myra ventured, "Mr. Westergard would like to see you. He asked that when you arrived to have you wait in his office before heading down to the clinic." She appeared a bit embarrassed, her eyes unable to meet his, then resolutely gathered herself and said, "He'll be in any minute."

This, he thought, was indeed odd. Westergard normally did not make it in until 8:30 AM, 8 AM on occasion, and glancing at the wall clock behind Myra, Ben noted that it was 7:45 AM. Myra stood up, momentarily interrupting his train of thought. She walked over to the administrator's office, unlocked it and waved him in. Flatly she said, "I'll let Mr. Westergard know that you're waiting for him," and then returned to her chair at the reception window.

Ben plopped down into one of the two chairs against the wall facing Westergard's desk, dropping his coat in the other. He scanned the desk and thought that it was much too orderly for a guy; Westergard must sweep the paperwork off into a draw before leaving for the weekend. Outside it was still below freezing, the east facing window remained mostly frosted. The sun was obscured by a mottled sky of clouds and lightly falling snow. He was mulling Myra's disquieting manner when Westergard entered his office. He wondered what had happened, what he might have done to instigate an early morning meeting with his administrator, a notoriously irritable individual when under caffeinated and interacting with staff before 9 AM. Ben straightened himself, arose extending his right hand. Westergard grasped his hand, more firmly than Ben remembered of the past. He motioned to Ben to have a seat as he removed his bulky parka and closely matching gloves. After shaking out the parka, it was placed on a hanger and carefully hung behind the door. The gloves were placed side by side over individual pegs fastened to the back of the door. Fastidious? More obsessive compulsive then Ben had observed? Perhaps he had misinterpreted the clean desk.

"How was your time off?" Westergard asked as he pulled out his chair and sat down behind the desk.

At this time, slightly more nervous than curious, Ben answered, "Good, really good. It was good to have a little time off. Roads were a nightmare, but otherwise everything else was good." As he looked at Westergard he thought, "How many times had he used the word 'good'?"

Westergard sat upright, hands folded before him on the desk, staring to his right, out of his window. Ben watched him thinking that Westergard had probably not heard a word that he had said. Westergard appeared preoccupied, detached, probably prioritizing his thoughts, considering what he was about to say to Ben.   Ben's concern and imagination was ramping up, about to hit overdrive, maybe hyper-drive if he allowed it. What the hell was so pressing that it warranted a one on one meeting with the administrator before 8 in the morning, before the start of the business day. Christ this was not a good omen. He was wracking his brain, starting to notice the beginning of a small knot in his gut, trying to come up with a conceivable reason for the meeting when suddenly it hit him; he was getting fired. No, I can't get fired, I didn't do anything wrong. Or did I? Oh, shit, where was this coming from? What the hell did he do wrong? Did he piss someone off? Who did he piss off? Dr. Saroni? Christ, he was gone the whole 10 days. A patient? Did a patient file a complaint? Westergard? What would get him so riled up? How pissed off is he? Someone is obviously wrapped around the axel, but whom?

Ben began reviewing what transpired during the 10 days prior to leaving on vacation. What action or incident had been so flagrant or antagonistic to warrant getting canned? Was it sneaking into the kitchen, sharing some of the Christmas party baked goods with the night crew before the party? No, everyone involved could be trusted, plus they're just as guilty. Letting the stuporous drunk he had stitched up sleep it off in the waiting room instead of admitting him to the hospital? Maybe? No, that's been done on previous occasions. The two dead patients! That must be it. The two nursing home patients that had died and had to be stored outside in the shed in the subzero weather. All right, admittedly he had not been able to notify either Saroni or Westergard for three days because neither of them was in cell phone range and quite frankly, no one knew where they were. The coroner and undertaker were okay with it so what's the problem? There was no frickin' problem! At least none that he was aware of. Okay, Okay, for the time being he was making this the number one possibility.

The snowbird? Possibly the snowbird. The lady from Bedlam that he had never met, never treated, never even heard of, who called from Arizona demanding, not requesting, demanding that he call in an antibiotic to her pharmacy in Scottsdale in order to "nip her pending bronchitis in the bud." He had politely declined, recommending that she be evaluated by a provider in Scottsdale who could provide a proper physical exam. Shocked, he had been duly shocked, by the extensive four letter vocabulary that she had unleashed over the phone. Ben had politely thanked her for her opinions and continued support of the Bedlam Medical Center, wishing her a wonderful and healthy winter in Scottsdale. She must have exhausted her allotted cell phone minutes because the call had abruptly ended. This might constitute a problem if she called Westergard to complain. He decided this could be number two, maybe three.

Wait, the narcotics patient, of course. Dr. Saroni's patient who, similar to the Scottsdale patient had called the clinic, not requesting but demanding refills for his narcotics before Ben had left for home on Christmas eve day, before the previously well-advertised noon time closing of the clinic and local pharmacy. Ben had reviewed his chart, past prescriptions and discovered a pain control contract. He was not due for refills until December 30; therefore he was a week early. Ben also found that previous to that call, there had been frequent, documented early requests for refills. It appeared that a mere phone call accompanied by an absurd excuse, like "they fell out of my pocket into my ice fishing hole," or "I loaned my car to a friend, who is now in Arkansas and my medications are in the glove box," or perhaps the best one that Callie, the clinic nurse, had related to Ben was, "my dog ate them and we went to the veterinarian who pumped his stomach but couldn't save any drugs but saved the dog." Ben politely declined to refill the prescriptions, reminded him of the medication contract and that he was one week early for refills, and then recommended that he make an appointment for the next Monday when the doctor would be back in the clinic. Ben had refused again when the patient had shown up in the emergency room on Christmas Day. That guy might very well have complained to the doctor. A virtual toss up with Ms. Scottsdale, so consider them interchangeable as possible numbers two or three. Ben was sticking with the frozen nursing home patients as number one. He'd know soon enough.

Westergard cleared his throat. Ben snapped to attention, girding himself for the unknown, and anticipating the worst. "Ben, I have some news for you and there is no easy way of preparing you for it, and…" Oh god, he's going to fire me… "I'm sorry to have to be the one to tell you. Salty passed away while you were gone." There was a blank look on Ben's face. He was hearing the words, but they were not immediately sinking in. This wasn't what he was expecting. He suddenly experienced an exhilarating relief, then a plummeting free fall to a near crushing sense of guilt. What kind of friend allows his focus to become so selfish? His friend Salty had been the furthest thing from his thoughts.

Westergard quietly continued. Ben detected a tone of unexpected compassion and empathy which seemed somewhat alien when expressed by the usually staid and unemotional administrator. "I know that you had developed a rather close relationship with Salty, that's why I wanted to tell you in private."

Ben replied evenly, in a subdued voice, "Thank you, Mr. Westergard. This was very considerate of you. Would you mind telling me what happened? When did he die?"

"New Year's Eve. His passing was not witnessed. Just after midnight the ER received two victims of an MVA, a rollover just south of town. As near as the doctor and coroner can determine, while everyone was in the ER treating the patients, Salty was apparently able to transfer himself to his wheelchair, pushed himself out the front door and to the far west end of the parking lot. It was 25 below zero, crystal clear skies." At that time of night the front door was locked, allowing anyone to exit on his own, but requiring someone to "buzz" them back in. Westergard continued, "Salty chose a spot out past the street light, and set his wheel brakes. Sometime recently, probably around Christmas, someone must have smuggled in a fifth of his favorite whiskey. He consumed about half of the bottle. After the ER patients were treated and discharged, the doctor went home. The evening med pass had been completed at 10 PM so staff returned to the nursing station. The rest of the night was uneventful. When the day shift nurse arrived in the morning she found Salty, dead, dressed in a hospital gown, coat and bottle in his lap, sitting in his wheelchair. She called the doctor and sheriff's department who dispatched the coroner. The coroner and Saroni concluded he had died of acute cardio-pulmonary failure with hypothermia, congestive heart failure, and diabetes as the main contributing factors. The coroner conveniently overlooked the alcohol level, much to Saroni's displeasure, and released the body, sorry, I mean Salty, to the funeral home."

The administrator stated, "This was not an entirely spur of the moment decision on Salty's part. He left a note on his bed stand," handing Ben the note to read;

You folks were busy, so I went for a solo ride to watch the stars and bring in the New Year. Thanks to all of you for everything you have done for me and will continue to do for others. You all do yourselves proud. See ya when I see ya. Salty

Westergard reached over the desk and handed a manila envelope to Ben. "Salty left this in the draw of his bed stand. Ben immediately spied his name written on the envelope in large block letters.

"Any word of a service? As far as I know and Salty would admit to, he had no living relatives except for his estranged son, and he wasn't even sure where the son lived. Salty told all of his friends that he had a simple will requesting cremation and no services, including military." Ben allowed himself a smile as he added, "He wasn't particular as to where his ashes wound up, but I think he might not be too averse to being sprinkled in one of his favorite fishing holes."

"Ben, I'm not at all sure that will happen. No family was listed for emergency contact; however, someone in town must know how to contact the son. Salty's son showed up in town Saturday, contacted the funeral home director, and demanded Salty's ashes. Other than the rumor that the son had a few drinks at The Dirty Shame and then left town, I have no other information. Sorry. There's talk of some of his friends planning an informal memorial service sometime in the future, but I guess we'll have to wait and see."

"Thank you Mr. Westergard. I really appreciate everything you've done. Salty had a damn good run and obviously went out on his own terms." Ben held up the envelope, and nodded at Westergard. He was just managing to suppress a growing sense of sadness, realizing that he was not going to stifle his emotions much longer. A growing sense of loss was reminding him of his Uncle Griff, another of Ben's close eclectic characters now but a fond memory.

"You okay?"

"Yeah, I need to get down to the clinic," he hurriedly answered. "Thanks." Leaving the administrator's office, Ben was relieved to find Myra's chair empty. He headed down to the clinic. Once in his office he closed and locked the door. He used the Leatherman he kept in his desk and slit the top of the manila envelope. There were two additional smaller envelopes inside, each one labeled and each one contained something solid, unbendable. He opened and began reading the letter in the envelope labeled, "Read First."

Dear Ben, I needed to go on my own terms. I've become a tired, irritable, and handicapped old fart with an increasing reliance on the good will of others. I am unwilling to allow this to go on until I can't even wipe my own butt. I cannot begin to repay people's kindness. Worse, I can't tolerate my own growing disabilities and neediness. That butt wiping thing is looming large.

You have become a good friend, a shining example of what any man should hope for in a friend, a doctor and as a son. Your father did well by you. I believe you two are deserving of each other. You know it was just a matter of time before they started lopping off pieces to keep me alive. I've made my decision not to prolong the inevitable.

Yes, I've made a plan, as cliché as it sounds, to do it "my way." (God I hated that philandering wop bastard as a human being, but the SOB sure could sing.) I have ego enough to believe that you may be disappointed that I chose this way out, but I have confidence enough in you that you will not judge me for it.

Keep on with how you practice medicine and "treat people." People like and trust you. I have seen, heard about and greatly appreciate the care and compassion that you show to every patient, however, beware, for it may be your Achilles heel. Stay the course; lightening and romance will strike again. Have a couple of drinks on me. Stay well my young friend. Happy Trails.

Samuel Salty Solmenson

There were two old wooden bar tokens for The Dirty Shame Saloon taped to the bottom of the letter. Ben felt tears welling. His throat was constricted. He was taking deep breaths, concentrating on neatly opening the "Read Last" envelope as he felt himself starting to tremble. He ended up tearing the envelope to extract a greeting card. A blank greeting card which, on the front Salty had taped a picture of a hand displaying the thumbs up sign. Inside the card he read;

Ben, my good friend.

I present you with this small token of my unwavering and (un)dying appreciation and respect. You are an honorable man and a credit to all physician assistants.

Live Long, Live Well, Live Free.

Fair Winds and Following Seas

Salty had taped his bronze star to the inside of the card. Ben was shaking, his head bowed, cradled in his hands. He cried; unabashed, unapologetic, uncontrolled.

WHO KNEW?

"Oohhh, look at you, Ben Parker, all smiley and filled with vim and vigor." Marni had practically sprung into his office sporting a starched white blouse, stop light red jacket with a matching knee length skirt, nylons, with her sensible black low heeled shoes buffed to a shine. A thin gold necklace and pendent adorned her neck and a cameo was pinned above her left jacket pocket. She was smiling ear to ear.

Ben, his eyes betraying his surprise, assessed Marni's choice of attire, "Wow, looking good Marni but this is not exactly concierge medicine that we're providing here."

She sat down in lady like manner, setting her brief case on the floor beside her, crossing her legs at the ankle before giving Ben her undivided attention. She replied in a voice implying total confidence, "I am presenting myself in the best light possible today because Westergard and I are meeting to discuss the renewing of my contract.

"That should do it. Is your choice of blaze red carrying some subliminal message that I am not aware of? Is red his favorite color?"

"There is nothing subliminal, under the radar or about a favorite color. It screams power and my determination to exact what is fairly mine."

"I'm sure that Westergard will cower in your presence and acquiesce to your every demand."

"That my friend is precisely my intent but hey there, look at you. Sparkly disposition, sly smirk, there's something afoot. Did you have a good vacation?" She did not pause for his answer, "You must have because I heard tell that you bought Stella a package of Twinkies, Callie a box of dark chocolates and Myrna says that you're back to your old whistling self."

"What do you mean back to?"

"Ben, when you first got here you whistled constantly. Everyone knew where you were in the building so you were easy to track. Then you quit, as if someone had put a shock collar around your neck. I thought your whistling habit was an endearing trait and I kind of miss it."

He pondered her observation for a few moments, realized that she was correct and was about to change the subject...

"Ben, I'm sorry that your friend Salty is gone. He was a wonderful character and I know how close you two had become; are you okay?"

"Yeahhh, I'm okay Marni. Thanks for asking." Ben sounded wistful, "I should have realized that he was more depressed than what he let on."

"No Ben, you shouldn't have. Remember, I was with you making rounds at Christmas. Sad as it may be, Salty made a choice and I truthfully don't believe that any of us could have influenced him to do otherwise. He wanted peace and found it in his own way, intentional or not."

"I know Marni, yet I can't help but to think that I could have done something more. But you're right, at any rate, he went out by his own design; intentional or not." Ben was considering whether his and Marni's wording was

233

providing Salty permission for his choice to abandon them or expunging themselves of fault, perhaps both. "I will miss him, that old fart."

They both sat in silence for a minute lost in their own thoughts.

Ben spoke first, "You finally went on vacation last week; did you make it to Seattle?"

"Hell yes! We had a great time. The roads were good, slept in a few days, drove around sightseeing, went to visit Grandma Cappelleti's grave site, ate plenty of fresh seafood, drank some good wines and were overdosed with attention as his family feuded and fawned over us. We couldn't have asked for more, except maybe a few more days on our own and a little less family dysfunction. But tell me about yours." She shifted herself on her chair, waited expectantly, and when he did not immediately start recounting his vacation she started up again, "You cannot stop smiling, so what's up?" She paused and suddenly her face beamed and she blurted out, "You got laid! Yes, Ben Parker got himself laid!"

Ben had turned crimson, "No Marni, if it's any of your business."

"Okay then, you met someone and there is a high index of certainty that you will get laid."

Not to say that the subject of sex, to which Marni had so blatantly alluded, had not crossed his mind; Ben was trying to stay focused on the emotional aspect of his blossoming relationship rather than projecting on the physical possibilities. Yes, he hoped that eventually they might progress to nights of impassioned if not unbridled sexual adventures, however, that was a topic he was not about to broach with Marni. "Yes Marni, I met someone and yes we've been talking a lot, and yes I'm a bit taken with her." He was forcing himself to sound blasé.

"You've been smitten Ben Parker, smitten."

Knowing that Marni was right on the money with her declaration he chose not to admit to it at this juncture in time, rather he coolly said, "She's got potential. We'll talk about it later," He raised his hands in a protective "stop" position deferring what he knew would be an incessant stream of questions from his friend. "I know what's wrong with Saroni."

Marni leaned forward in her chair, a patronizing expression on her face, "What do you mean by what's wrong with Saroni?" Everything is wrong with Saroni."

Ben shook his head no, "That's not what I mean Marni. I know the cause of his behavior, his medical condition."

"What medical condition? He's a dickhead." She appeared genuinely puzzled.

"It was something my father said that started me thinking. I had…"

Marni raised her right index indicating that he should wait a minute. "Sorry to interrupt your stream of thought but before I forget to ask, how is your father?"

Ben smiled, "Good. He's his usual irascible self. We had a good visit, watched some football, cooked up some steaks and on another night some ribs, had a couple of beers, and had some good conversations." His was a smile of appreciation when he said, "Dad's a tough old bird."

"I'm happy to hear that you had a good visit. So you were saying…"

"Something my father had said. I had told him about Dr. Saroni's inconsistencies; his behavior towards medical staff, hospital protocols, patient treatment plans and unpredictability of fulfilling his appointments and responsibilities. About the periods of time he was surprisingly consistent and then an abrupt reversion to inconsistency. Even the periods of consistency were inconsistent in duration. Dad made the observation that Saroni wasn't merely inconsistent but inconsistently inconsistent. He joked that, "You medical folks must have some clue, some syndrome that you can hang on him, some name or diagnosis for what's ailing him. You've got medical jargon covering everything."

"I joked back with him that absolutely there had to be some medical condition that has a hallmark description of being inconsistently inconsistent."

"So should we be scouring Harrison's Internal Medicine or the DSM IV for our mystery malady?"

Ben continued on in an attempt to ignore her. "On my drive back I was thinking about what Dad had said and something suddenly dawned on me." He paused for effect, "Irregularly irregular is the hallmark description of what?"

Marni stared at him blankly.

"Irregularly irregular describes what? Come on, you know that."

"Atrial Fibrillation?"

"Right. Exactly. So relying on a process of deductive reasoning we could surmise that someone who is inconsistently inconsistent has…"

Again, Marni looked at him blankly, shrugging her shoulders.

Ben was matter of fact when he continued, "It stands to reason that if you are inconsistently inconsistent you have cerebral fibrillation."

Marin remained expressionless and Ben was beginning to slightly squirm in his chair when she suddenly burst out laughing, "Ben, there is no such thing as Cerebral Fibrillation. You cannot just make up a medical condition

236

for something that doesn't exist, or at least you wish to exist."

Ben was enjoying the moment but tried to appear disappointed as he defended his position. "What makes you so positive that cerebral fibrillation cannot exist? The malady befits the description. The hallmark signs and symptoms are certainly defined and cerebral fibrillation would seem an appropriate name for it."

Marni was vacillating between expressing exasperation or humor, "Maybe so, however, I defy you to find it in any medical resource book or journal."

"Then perhaps it should be. Why shouldn't we be credited for defining and naming a medical condition?"

"What do you mean we, Kemosabe? Don't get me involved in your harebrained schemes."

"You would be missing out on an incredible opportunity Marni. Just think, we might make it into the New England Journal of Medicine or at least honorable mention in some medical pamphlet; Rural PA's establish criteria for diagnosis of cerebral fibrillation, the cause of Inconsistently Inconsistent Behavioral Syndrome."

She was laughing when she told him, "You are more than half a bubble off plumb, Ben Parker. Maybe we should call it Saroni's Syndrome."

"I don't think that's the wise move here. With his ego he would probably try to take credit for the discovery. You need to stick with me Marni," he spread his arms out to their full span, "because the world is our oyster. Once we are accredited for this discovery and have established ourselves as credible researchers we can pursue grant opportunities to help find the cure for RCI."

"What the hell is RCI?"

"One of the most prolific and debilitating problems plaguing society which, has grown to near epidemic proportions within all levels of government. If we could discover a cure for that we would literally write our own tickets for life.

"And again, RCI is what?"

"Rectal Cranial Insertion Marni, RCI stands for Rectal Cranial Insertion."

Marni silently shuddered. "Let's stick with cerebral fibrillation for the time being and we'll worry about RCI and our road to fame and fortune after hospital rounds."

"Deal. I knew that I could count on you, Marni."

Marni giggled, "I'm so happy to have you around Ben. You do make life interesting."

KNUDSEN

Within the closed cab of a pickup sound was impeded, however, the relative quiet served well for observing human interaction which at best was humorously illuminating and at worst excruciatingly disturbing. Ben had just arrived, having parked in the hospital lot next to a mound of freshly plowed snow. Reaching to turn off the engine he observed a large, bearded man in dirty coveralls and plaid woolen hat, ear flaps loosely dangling, shouldering his way out of the hospital's main entrance. He was awkwardly balancing an armload of small potted plants and vases filled with colorful flowers while tenuously maintaining his footing on the ice slicked sidewalk. Ben shifted his gaze to his left and spied a small collection of similar vegetation that appeared to have been unceremoniously dumped in a snow bank adjacent to the sidewalk. Sudden movement from the main door split Ben's attention between the man seemingly headed towards this pile and Dwight Unger, the hospital maintenance man, now making a mad, haphazard dash toward the unknown man. Precariously slipping and sliding, Dwight made his way past, maneuvering himself into a position between the man and the pile of despoiled, rapidly wilting flowers entering the throes of a frozen death.

The outside temperature was still below zero and steady streams of exhaled vapor flowed from the mouths of the two men. Ben watched as their animated conversation exponentially escalated to what Ben feared would come to fisticuffs. He quickly turned off the truck and exited the cab in the hope of reaching and insinuating himself between the potential combatants before blows were struck. Just as he slammed shut the driver door a flash of hunter green caught his attention as Stella, the charge nurse, streaked along the sidewalk, planted herself sideways between the squared off males raising her outstretched arms, which, knowing Stella, was presumably more than mere symbolic gesture. Now there were three rising vapor trails. The man with the plants quickly pivoted, defiantly opened his arms sacrificing this multi-colored offering to the snow bank, then turned and shuffled flat footed back to the entrance door.

Ben trotted over to Dwight and Stella, mindful of the treacherous footing. They were picking vases and pots from the snow bank and gently brushing snow from the most current plant dumping. He silently joined their efforts concentrating on what he might save from the clutches of old man winter.

Gloved hands clamping the plants to his chest, Ben stood and looked at his co-workers, "Sooooo?"

"So, I'm freezing my butt out here, let's talk inside." Ben and Dwight fell in behind Stella and the three traipsed up to the entrance door, each carefully balancing their own armful of stiffening vegetation. She hip checked the handicapped access door activator and they filed in the building, past the nurses' station to the corner of the resident wings and into the large resident bath and shower room. The door automatically closed behind them enclosing them in a warm, damp, liniment scented shower facility. "Set everything over there," she motioned with a toss of her head toward a stainless counter against the tiled wall, "We'll see what we can save later."

Ben asked, "Now can you fill me in?"

It was Dwight that spoke, "He grew up in Bedlam. His name is Elgin Knudsen." Dwight pronounced it with a hard K rather than the silent K pronunciation that Ben had heard the many Knudsens in the community employ.

"Why does he pronounce it with the hard K?"

"Just to be ornery I suspect. There's a near blood feud with the other families who pronounce it with a silent K. He has a tendency to be contrary, as just witnessed by the destruction of his wife's plants and flowers."

Dwight was about to explain when Stella interrupted, "Knudsen is under the misconception that plants use oxygen and expel carbon dioxide, therefore all of those plants and flowers that people brought to his wife's hospital room were actually causing more harm than good, depleting oxygen and impeding Mrs. Knudsen's recovery. I attempted to tactfully explain the concept of photosynthesis but he stopped me cold. He said that he knew how photosynthesis works, that he definitively remembers his high school biology teacher, Mr. Teabury explaining O2 in, CO2 out and Mr. Teabury would not lead him astray; though I thought that I detected angry sarcasm."

Now Dwight interrupted and interjected, "Like I said, Elgin is ornery, actually angry might better describe his disposition, and contrary, both well-honed over the years. I believe that he is more contrary out of spite rather than stubbornness or stupidity but if it relates to Teabury …well, I'd bet that it's more a feeling of betrayal affecting his thinking."

There was a pause as both Ben and Stella stared at him incredulously. He stared back at them, "What?...I went to high school with him. I was a sophomore when he was a

241

senior. We played together on the football team. His parents were alcoholics and abused the kids. I'm surprised that any of them made it through high school."

Stella broke the silence, "I was just surprised that you had that much insight about him Dwight. Anything else?"

"He got a football scholarship to North Dakota State but ended up dropping out after a year. I think he was homesick for friends and his girlfriend. He was drafted into the army soon afterward and I'm pretty sure that he was still in Vietnam when his favorite science teacher, Mr. Teabury, poisoned half the football team with homemade hooch and then drove off of an 80 foot cliff into the river with a cheerleader who was wearing nothing but her sneakers and class ring. The cheerleader was Elgin's girlfriend."

"Jeez, Dwight, that's enough to jade anyone if not tip them over."

"That was the least of it Ben. He signed up for another tour, was seriously wounded, and returned to the states with a drug addiction and a heavy dose of paranoia."

Stella, a veteran herself, couldn't help herself, "Are you going to tell us that he has a membership in the Flat Earth Society?"

"No. He made it to Hawaii, Vietnam and Australia and didn't sail off the edge so I think that it's safe to say that there are no Flat Earth beliefs and apparently no tin foil under the hat, at least that I know of. He has, however, spouted some John Birch propaganda and believes that the Battle of the August Moon, where the Russians battled and beat the U.S. on the lunar surface, is real."

Ben broke in, "Really? A battle on the moon? Okay then, we know that he's got some issues but where has he been?" He turned to Stella, "Isn't his wife the swing bed

242

patient Saroni admitted here last Friday with the surgically repaired right tib-fib fractures, rib fractures, dislocated left shoulder and pneumonia?"

"Apparently he's been working in Alaska and just made it home last night. When he's gone his wife runs the ranch. She's pretty much on her own out there."

"No hired help?"

Dwight offered, "No hired help. They've got two boys in their early twenties that live at home but they're just about useless. I don't know how much truth there is to it but Knudsen and wife got together after he got back to the States and were married after he knocked her up." Stella gave him the stink eye. "Sorry, when she became large with child. They may be first cousins and that might help to explain why the boys seem to have the combined IQ of a two by four." Stella just shook her head.

Ben questioned, "So how was she injured?"

Stella shrugged and she and Ben resumed starring at Dwight as they listened.

Dwight prefaced his answer with, "Everything I have I got from her neighbor, Pete Anderson. She was feeding the cows."

"She got run over by a cow?"

"No, she got run over by her tractor and hay trailer."

"Who the hell was driving the tractor?"

"She was." Again, Stella and Ben just stared at Dwight who recognized their confusion and a need for an explanation. "There's an old technique that some of the ranchers use when they have to feed alone. You find a long stretch of field without any ditches, use some rope or bungee cords to tie off the steering wheel to keep it from turning and put the tractor or truck into low granny. Then you jump out, run back and climb on the trailer and start tossing off hay. You've got to keep an eye out ahead and

243

get back to your rig before you hit a rough patch or the end of the field. Then turn around and repeat. Apparently Mrs. Knudsen had tied off the tractor's steering wheel and put it in gear but slipped when getting off. She hit the ground hard and the rear tractor tire ran over her leg and then the trailer tires ran over her chest. Anderson found the tractor in the barrow pit on its side and cows out on the road. It had run the length of the field, through the barbwire fence and tipped over when it hit the ditch. He found her in the field and went to the house to call the ambulance. The boys were watching TV and chowing down on Fruit Loops."

Ben made the obvious conclusion, "So, in a nutshell, you're telling us that we're not dealing with the typical American family here."

"Bingo."

Stella pulled open the shower room door motioning them to exit, "Okay then, let's get out of here."

The three filed out of the shower room and almost instinctively lined up next to each other outside the door. Stella stood between Dwight to her left and Ben on her right. They had a premium vantage point, taking in the nurses' station which formed the junction of the resident and hospital hallways and the main lobby. Dr. Saroni had his back to the front counter of the nurses' station and was bent slightly backwards, any retreat now thwarted as Mr. Knudsen leaned in, his face well within the doctor's personal space, piercing eyes within hard facial features, sporting a thick growth of beard with patches of gray. Angry spittle flew from his mouth. From their viewing point they could see the doctor's cowering profile. Tara stood wide eyed in the back of the nurses' station clutching a patient chart to her chest.

"It's Knudsen, Kaa…nudsen, Kaa, fucking, nudsen. How fucking hard is it to pronounce my name right? What the Christ is so hard with that?" Mr. Knudsen leaned back, wiped his mouth on his sleeve, sneezed, retrieved a red bandana from the back pocket of his coveralls and violently blew his nose; it sounded as if an elk was bugling. Suddenly, a loud racket, a thud, followed by a high pitched squeal emitted from somewhere down in the hospital wing. Everyone in the general area of the nurses' station heard it and turned toward the patient hallway. Dr. Saroni and Mr. Knudsen were in a position to see down the hallway. Knudsen shook his head and gruffly yelled town the hallway, "For Christ's sake, cut the crap you two. Can't you morons stay out of trouble for five minutes? Pick your brother up off the floor and stay in your ma's room or out in the truck." Knudsen's attention continued to be riveted down the hallway.

Ben commented, as if the following silence called for casual observation, "Stella, I'm surprised to see you here on a Tuesday day shift."

"Myrna called off sick and fool that I am I answered the phone."

"Think what you would have missed. This just goes to show you that not all the excitement transpires in the ER on weekends."

She shot Ben a baleful glance, "Don't patronize me Ben. I'm still short on my morning coffee quota."

"Hey! Now! Not when you damn well feel like it!" Knudsen watched for another minute, appeared satisfied and turned his attention back to Saroni.

Ben, Stella and Dwight returned their focus back to the two men, Saroni now holding and reviewing the patient chart that Tara had been clutching. "When are you releasing my wife? I need her at home and frankly I'm not sure she's getting the best care here."

The doctor now seemed slightly more relaxed though defensive, "You are to be assured Mister Knudsen…"

"Jesus, that's Kaa nudsen! What do I…"

They could see Saroni backing up and heard him repeat, "Sorry Kaa nudsen, sorry Kaa nudsen…" as Elgin launched into another pronunciation diatribe.

Suddenly Mrs. Talmadge, who travels by the preferred nickname of Speed Queen, whizzed by, her motorized wheelchair whirring at high speed as she neatly swerved to avoid Ben's toes. She was bent forward in her chair however; it was indeterminate whether it was due to focused intent or her spinal kyphosis. The chair's control stick was directed by her right hand while her left hand thrust aloft a cane which she was pumping vertically up and down above her head. Stella nonchalantly stated, "Mrs. Tallmadge appears a might frisky this morning. Probably got a hold of some caffeinated coffee but I better check to see how much Ritalin she got at the morning med pass."

Dr. Saroni had apparently appeased Knudsen temporarily because Mr. Knudsen was calmer and Saroni was no longer shaking. "Well doc, how about me taking her home?"

"I see her for rounds shortly. Perhaps, maybe I discharge today."

Ben felt a nudge in the ribs from Stella and turned to his left in time to see the DON, Heidi Lafevbre emerging from her office across the hall and advancing toward the doctor and Mr. Knudsen at a brisk pace. She was a vision in bright pink scrubs. Tara had taken refuge within the supply and medication room and was sneaking furtive glances from the doorway.

Mr. Knudsen was quieter but his voice still carried well. "Ya know doc, I'm sure you're milkin' the insurance

246

for all it's worth but I think she can heal up at home just as well. Maybe better since she won't have the oxygen being sucked out of her room so she can't think straight and agrees to stay here."

For once Dr. Saroni looked utterly confused. "I do not know of this oxygen loss. As I say, maybe your wife discharged today."

Heidi Lafevbre had arrived at the doctor's side, "Dr. Saroni, may I have a brief word with you?" She beckoned him to follow and he complied, the two of them huddling back in front of her office doorway.

Tara darted back into the nurses' station and picked up a box of bakery confections, her sugar levels apparently tanking. From out of the blue, seemingly addressed to no one in particular, Mr. Knudsen posed a question, "Where the hell is this guy from?"

"Zimbabwe. I think Zimbabwe." Tara immediately fled, retreating back to her supply room sanctuary; hopefully thinking out of sight, out of mind.

For some inexplicable reason they continued to stand expectantly, awaiting the next interaction between Saroni and Knudsen. Perhaps morbid curiosity or a sense of guilty voyeurism kept them rooted in place. Ben looked to his left; Saroni and Lafevbre were in animated yet volume subdued conversation their body language indicating each with a stiffened resolve. He slowly panned clockwise. Tara slouched in the supply room shadows munching a frosted donut, Knudsen stood with his arms crossed upon his chest slowly rocking back and forth on his heels and then his vision settled on the Double Ought Boys, Misters Quigley and Kijek slowly advancing in his direction from the lobby aiming toward the residents' hallway to his right. Their walker legs appeared to lift and set down in unison as they moved past the nurses' station making a tediously slow but steady progress.

"Hiya doc, how're they hangin'?" It was Victor Kijek with a broad grin on his face; his dentures were apparently well adhered this morning. Ben could hear a barely suppressed snigger from Dwight on his far left. Kijek delightedly burst out with, "I woke up this morning with a stiffy. You know, a woody, a regular harpoon…" he was pointing at his crotch "…and Dule here…" he jerked his head in the direction of his roommate Dule Quigley "…is jealous and wants to know where he can get one." This was followed by some cackling laughter.

Dule countered with, "He lies more than a politician in heat. He knows damn well that his Johnson will be perennially drooping without a prostate."

Ben suggested without inflection, "Maybe your prostate regenerated Mr. Kijek. The human body sometimes has near magical properties." He gave a noncommittal shrug while remaining straight faced.

Kijek and Dule turned to each other with raised eyebrows and a surprised look. Dule shook his head as he looked back to Ben, "Kijek is full of crap. The only way that he'd have a woody is if he taped that shriveled worm to a Popsicle stick."

"You got anything in your medical bag of tricks to help me euthanize this asshole?" Kijek wobbled a little, free standing as he darted both forefingers at his roommate. "How about a scalpel, or…what do they call those things in prison? A shiv? Something I could use as a shiv on this dickhead?" Dule chortled, "And then I get to piss on your grave."

"More like dribble, you flaccid moron."

They continued down the hallway arguing, the clicking feet of their walkers repeating off of the walls.

Dwight leaned over and naively whispered, "You can't grow a new prostate, can you?"

Stella interceded, "Of course you can't. What are you doing Ben, feeding them that line of BS?"

"Those two wise asses are forever stirring someone's pot or pimping me about some ailment or bodily function, so I'm having a little fun with them, maybe keeping them off balance and on a new topic for the next 24 hours."

"You don't think that's a little mean spirited?"

Dwight observed, "They'll forget all about it by the time they've had lunch and found something new to insult each other over."

With some poignancy Stella retorted, "It's their peckers that don't work; their brains are fully functional."

"Okay, okay, sorry I said a thing. I've got to get back to work."

Stella stayed him with her hand on his arm and spoke softly, "Sorry Dwight, I didn't mean to sound so harsh. Stick around and let's see how the Saroni-Knudsen match shakes out. I think that it's an exercise in futility and I hate to say it but I bet the doctor caves in. He's a bully; however, in this case I think that he's being out bullied." She pronounced Knudsen appropriately. Dwight remained to watch.

Heidi disappeared back into her office and Dr. Saroni walked back to the front of the nurses' station where he sidled up to Mr. Knudsen. Mr. Knudsen had watched him approach without expression. "Let us see to your wife, examine her progress." Saroni quickly proceeded down the hospital hallway; Mr. Knudsen followed in the doctor's wake.

Dwight ventured, "What do you think Saroni and Heidi were discussing?"

Stella replied as a matter of fact, "I'm sure that she was trying to convince Saroni that sending Mrs. Knudsen home too soon was not in her or the hospital's best interest. She'll want to squeeze every blessed penny out of the patient or insurance carrier before she puts her blessing on discharging them. I'm pretty sure that she does it to impress Westergard. Heidi Lafevbre is not so much a patient advocate as a finance whore."

Ben knew that there was no love lost between Stella and the DON but wow, good for Stella for calling it like it is.

Dwight smiled as he declared, "This was exhausting, I need to get to work but now I'm thinking I need a nap first."

"Me too. I'm way behind but sometimes I thoroughly enjoy a little diversion from the norm. How about you Ben? Why are you here, I thought it was your day off?"

"I'm headed to Wynot to get a new heater core for the truck; this one is starting to leak. The hospital currier is out sick so I volunteered to take the X-ray films and drop them off to be read by the radiologist."

"You are such a boy scout Ben Parker; we need to get you a merit badge for services above and beyond." Stella and Dwight both laughed as Ben blushed.

"I'd settle for a little more pay and a lot more sanity, thank you. I'll see you two later."

Upon his return to Bedlam Ben swung into the hospital parking lot and as was his custom before going on his Tuesday night call at 1700 hours he stopped in to get a report or hand off from the doctor. About 95% of the time the doctor had already left by 1630 hours or earlier; he full well knew that Ben would stop in. The other 5% of the time

Saroni might be in the emergency room or otherwise preoccupied with a duty which he was rushing to complete, facilitating an earlier exit than his posted hours. As it turned out, today was not a 5% day. Ben knew a face to face report from the doctor was not to be expected and a phone call to his home would in most likelihood reach a recorded message. He stopped at the nurses' station; Stella was documenting in a patient chart and Ben waited patiently for her to briefly pause. She looked up expectant but tight lipped. He knew the answer before he asked.

"Hi Stella. Anything or anyone new that I need to be aware of?"

She replied flatly, "The doctor discharged Mrs. Knudsen home this afternoon."

As incredulous as he felt he held his tongue and reaction in check. He did not ask for details. "Anything else?"

"No, no new admissions. Everything else is copacetic."

Ben had an overwhelming desire to flee the building. "Thanks Stella. Who's on tonight?"

"That would be Karmma."

The disappointment that Ben and Stella were feeling was palpable. "Have a good evening Stella." He was already walking toward the exit when he heard, "You also."

As he gingerly walked across the icy parking lot he was seriously considering whether or not Dr. Saroni had an inflatable spine or any spine at all.

Thursday morning and having just arrived in his office Ben was hanging up his coat and hat when he heard raised voices out in the main hallway. As he made his way out of the office seeking the source of the disagreement he recognized the voices as Marni and Dr. Saroni. There was a mounting terseness in addition to the volume. By the time he emerged into the hallway the argument had escalated into a fully-fledged yelling match. An alarmed Callie stood in her doorway her hand covering her mouth. Several women from the business office had spilled out into the hallway and Ben could see Myrna at the far end of the corridor, arms folded across her chest looking on as a concerned observer. Drawing closer he was struck by Marni's "stand your ground" body language and the doctor's haranguing, condescending tone.

His anger was evident, perhaps from being challenged and his voice began to sputter, "You have not the authority...not entitled...to make this choice...this decision. Mine to make...to decide...you be insubordinate...you must confer...only to me. I...I am in power, empower...in charge here..."

Ben arrived at Marni's side just as she released both barrels of current and past pent up frustration, disappointment and resentment. He realized that he was too late to intervene.

"Actually I am qualified and authorized to evaluate, treat, and transfer a patient. I can and should contact the authorities if I suspect or have proof of physical abuse or sexual assault without having to contact you, which, is exactly what I did. We have a supervisory agreement but it doesn't require me to consult with you on every patient I see or every medical decision that I make in this hospital. For that matter, the chances of locating you for a consult when you are away from the hospital are slim to none."

Saroni stood stock still, mouth agape, as she stormed off toward her clinic office. Ben moved quickly to stay in step with her. "I don't need you to come to my rescue Parker; I can fight my own battles."

Ben could hear Saroni yelling at her, "I will see Westergard. I file grievance and you will see Westergard. You insubordinate. This I will not tolerate."

Saying nothing, he walked abreast of her to her office. She entered and he remained at the door as she flung her gloves and coat into the corner and plopped herself down into her office chair.   "What do you want Ben?" She continued to seethe.

"I know that you are perfectly capable of standing up for yourself. I wanted Saroni to know that you didn't stand alone and to maybe stop a nuclear explosion from happening."

Marni slapped the palm of her hand down on the desk, "That son of a bitch discharged that woman home to the care of a bully and abuser. She's still recovering from a trauma just to be traumatized again by her bastard of a husband and Saroni is more worried about covering his own ass because he's got no balls."

"What happened to Mrs. Knudsen, Marni?"

"Her leg is in a cast, her arm is in a sling, she's got pneumonia and broken ribs and the SOB husband wants her to resume some of the chores, the cooking and to cater to his whims and orders." Marni's recitation was speeding up to a near staccato. "She can't do it and he slapped her around and verbally abused her. Then he got drunk and punched and tossed her around. When he finally passed out she called a friend, packed a bag and her friend drove her here, to the ER. She literally cried for help. I evaluated her and she agreed to allow me to contact the sheriff's office. After I treated her the deputy interviewed her and she agreed to press charges. I called Sunnvale and got her transferred and admitted to a swing bed. Saroni thinks that I should have consulted with him and that I had no right to contact the sheriff's department."

"You did the right thing, Marni. You did what any good medical provider should have done."

"Now Saroni is going to whine to Westergard. Well, I'm good for that too."

"You don't have to go it alone Marni. You have a lot of support here in the hospital."

She was slowing down, composing herself, "I know Ben and I greatly appreciate that." She took a deep breath; let it out slowly as a crooked smile appeared. "You know, I'd offer to castrate Saroni but either he was born without testicles or someone beat me to it."

Ben laughed, "You're a wonder Marni Capelletti, and I am truly grateful to be on your good side."

She continued to smile and nodded as she declared, "It's what I keep telling people Ben; that you're much smarter than you appear to be."

THE RITES OF CANNABIS

When the phone rang it was obvious that Ben's declaration of sleeping with one eye open when on call was a bit exaggerated. Both eyes blinked open and as he bolted upright in his recliner the novel that had rested on his chest flipped closed and tumbled to the floor. He answered, "Hello," his voice slightly raspy from a Sunday after supper nap.

"Did I catch you at a bad time sleepy head," purred a female voice.

"Lindsay!" Ben straightened and adjusted himself in his chair and shook his head to free the cobwebs of sleep. "How are you?" He was gaining on his wakefulness. "How's my best gal?"

"Best gal? Since when do I have competition?"

Ooops; he began serious backpedaling to regain traction. "It was a slip of the tongue, an idiom blurted out by an idiot, I misspoke…there is no one else, only you. No one holds a cand…"

"You are so easy Ben Parker, like a big windup toy."

"How did you learn to press my buttons so quickly?"

He loved hearing her throaty laughter. "I had you pegged as soon as you called me within hours of me giving you my number."

"I didn't realize that I was so easy to read."

"Like a billboard, my sweet."

"I'm going to have to reassess my dating proclivities."

"Now would not be a good time to start. Were you sleeping Ben?"

"I was catching 40 winks. I had a long night last night but now I'm raring to go. So tell me how are you doing?"

"Busy. New semester and back to the school grind but the end is in sight. I'm thinking…" Ben's pager began its high pitched beeping.

"What's that noise Ben?"

"Ben Parker, please call the hospital."

"My pager. The hospital is trying to get a hold of me."

"Ben Parker, please call the hospital."

"Sorry, Lindsay, I've got to cut this short. Can I call you later?"

"Ben Parker, please call the hospital."

"I should hope that you would."

"Okay, I will. Sorry, I'll call you later. Bye Lindsay."

"Goodbye Ben. Be safe."

Ben dialed the hospital.

"Bedlam Medical Center, this is Becca Trebek RN. How may I help you?"

"You paged, Nurse Trebek?"

"Indeed I did PA Parker. Your services are requested. We've got a rollover

Immediately Ben's antennae heightened and his heart rate rose. "How many patients?"

"Just one, with a head injury."

"How soon will they be in?"

"She's already here."

"Okay, I'll be right in. Do we have a name or know anything about our patient?"

"Of course we do, it's Mrs. Haugen."

Wait. "Mrs. Haugen, the nursing home resident? How did she get involved in a rollover?"

Becca paused. "Yeah…I suppose that I should have clarified that a bit more. Mrs. Haugen rolled over, fell out of bed and hit her head but that wouldn't have got your heart racing."

"God dammit, Becca I…" Ben caught himself and curbed his tongue before saying something that he might later regret. "Is she on Coumadin?"

"Nope, you lucked out there."

"Any loss of consciousness?"

"Not to our knowledge."

"I'll be right in."

"Good, we were counting on your prompt response." Click.

He thought, "She's getting more obnoxiously familiar with every call."

"Any witness to her fall?"

"No Ben, she doesn't have a roommate. She's private pay so she has a single. Sheena heard her moan when she was walking down the hall."

"It's a little early for bedtime isn't it Becca?"

"Mrs. Haugen is ambulatory and spends most of her time alone and in her room."

Becca handed Ben a clipboard with Mr. Haugen's vital signs. They appeared to be within normal limits.

"How is she doing?"

"She appears stable. There's a little bump on her left forehead and some minor swelling to her left cheek but no bruises or skin breaks. She moved all of her extremities and did not seem to be in any pain."

"No complaints voiced?"

"Mrs. Haugen only speaks Norwegian and no one understands her."

"I'd forgotten that. Still no translator in town?"

"That would be a no. There used to be an older lady that spoke Norwegian who came in to visit the residents but she moved a year or so ago."

Ben was trying to recall any medical visits that he may have had with Mrs. Haugen. She was always stoic, relatively uncommunicative and her few responses had been in Norwegian. Outside of conducting the physical there had been little information garnered.

"We've been a little worried about her but; our concerns seem to fall on deaf ears."

"Who's ears?"

"Lafevbre and Saroni."

Ben nodded a silent "Of course it was." He was scanning her chart for medications and past medical history, "Remind me again about Mrs. Haugen's history here at the nursing home. Has she ever spoken any English at all?"

"Mrs. Haugen was admitted about two and one half years ago and yes, she spoke English. Her son was transferred from Minnesota to the MegaAgra plant east of town and moved her out here along with his family. Three months later the company had some problem in their Tokyo division and sent him over there to work. They put her in here before they left for Japan. We have Mrs. Haugen's daughter, a son, and a son and daughter in law on file as contacts. The married son has power of attorney."

"So when did she stop speaking English?"

"I think it was about a year and a half ago. Since the family went to Japan I think that she's only had one granddaughter visit in the past couple of years. She gets a call from Japan once or twice a month; otherwise I don't think that she has much contact with the outside world. Mrs. Haugen doesn't attend any of the social functions here, seems pretty withdrawn and her appetite is poor. I think that she's depressed."

"I'll head down to her room to evaluate her."

"Remember Ben, any resident fall with even minor injuries requires us to notify the family. I've checked the contact list and there are notes regarding the daughter and son here in the US. The daughter has apparently become estranged from the family and has requested that no contact be made. The unmarried son's number is no longer valid."

"That just leaves the son and daughter in law in Japan?"

"Fraid so. You know, Myrna is more familiar with Mrs. Haugen. Do you want me to give her a call?"

"Thanks, but let's hold off on disturbing Myrna's evening. I'll be back after I see Mrs. Haugen."

"Just one more thing Ben, I need to give you a heads up on Mr. Light Feather. At least one Sunday night each month Mr. Light Feather has his nephew and friends in for a pow wow and tonight's the night."

"And this is significant because…?"

"Because they lock the door or do something to it so it can't be opened by the nursing staff. Dwight has removed slide locks that they installed on two occasions. The other thing is that they burn something in there that smells an awful lot like weed." Ben's look said clarify. "You know; grass, pot, marijuana."

"How come this is the first that I'm hearing about it?"

"Timing? I don't know. We've complained to the DON on several occasions and she acts like we're imagining things. Lafevbre has said that she would look into it but…" Becca lifted her hands in question, "… who knows if she ever did."

"So nothing ever became of it?"

"Pretty much."

"Okay. When I'm finished with Mrs. Haugen I'll check into it. Remind me, what's the nephew's name?"

"Strong Tree. That's all I know."

Ben draped his stethoscope around his neck, retrieved the supply room otoscope and headed down the hall to Mrs. Haugen's room.

"What do you think, Ben?"

"I believe that Mrs. Haugen has a couple of contusions to her forehead and cheek. There's nothing that would prompt me to order imaging or labs. She appears a bit shaken and she's not responding or indicating that she understands English. I had to get a little inventive with the neuro exam but she'll do well with some ice and maybe a little ibuprofen."

"I'll get some ice and get her comfortable."

"Hold off a minute Becca. I need to review a couple of things in her chart." Before he sat down at the writing counter he slowly made a 360 degree scan of the nurses' station studying the counters. He spied Becca's personal DVD player, "What late night entertainment do we have tonight Nurse Trebek? A Paul Reubens to go?"

Becca blushed a bright red and Sheena sniggered. Retrieving her backpack, Becca pulled out a plastic movie case and waved it at him, "*Miss Congeniality*, Sandra Bullock. I learned my lesson."

Ben laughed as he took a seat and opened up Mrs. Haugen's chart, "Excellent choice, Becca." He studied the chart, reading the provider and nursing notes for the next 10 minutes. After looking up Myrna's home phone on the staff roster he dialed up her number and listened to her message machine. "Myrna, it's Ben Parker at the hospital. Nothing emergent; I had a quick question but it's not imperative that you call back. Have a good evening."

"Did you find something Ben?"

"Enough to indicate that some of the nurses' concerns and observations that were passed along were ignored or at least downplayed. It's not the time to point any fingers. We have to do the right thing now and make sure that we give her the help that she needs. I'm going to talk with her again and then you and Sheena can tuck her in."

Frail and withdrawn, Mrs. Haugen sat on the side of her bed. Her white terrycloth robe was pulled close about her shoulders and torso, her flowered flannel nightgown covered her legs to mid-shin. She held her legs tightly together, knees and ankles touching, the slippers on her feet barely reaching the floor. She stared down at her lap where her hands kneaded a lace handkerchief. Ben pulled her desk chair into the middle of the room and sat down across from Mrs. Haugen, keeping an appropriate distance between them. He lowered his shoulders and bent slightly forward so that their eyes were at the same level.

There was no pleading or hint of patronizing in his voice; she must have heard a genuine sense of empathy and humility, "Mrs. Haugen, I am sorry, deeply sorry for my inadequacies. I'm at a loss as to how to communicate with you and for this I must apologize. I don't know what to say, or how to say it, or what I might do to make things better for you. You deserve better but I don't know what I can do to help you."

She looked at him resignedly though he thought there was a fleeting glimmer of hope in her eyes. In a tired whisper she said, "Ask the right questions."

Ben was momentarily stunned, then sat back and processed her request. There was a plethora of pertinent questions that cycled through his mind, all within the brevity of one minute and then he leaned forward and quietly asked, "What do you miss the most?"

She stared directly at him, her eyes welling in tears and began to quietly cry.

"Everyting. I miss everyting."

On most evenings the town of Bedlam rolled up the sidewalks and turned off the lights after 6 PM, save the flickering neon of a tavern or the light over the mortuary door signaling someone's demise. In the Bedlam Medical center they waited until 8 PM to dim the hallway lights and tuck the nursing home residents in. The doors were shut as each resident had returned to his or her room. Solid and heavy, the doors were extra wide to accommodate wheelchairs, residents who ambulated with the aid of walkers, and ill patients being transferred via gurney. Per nursing home industry regulations the doors were manufactured to afford fire protection and privacy; heavy, easily swung, secure when closed, however, locking devices were not allowed. Ben stood unmoving, intently listening. His ear practically touched the door and he could hear several indistinct voices in conversation, punctuated by brief laughter. Movement at the nurses' station caught his attention and he briefly focused on Becca who was dangling a stethoscope from one hand and gesturing open handed with the other, "What do you think this thing is for?"

His olfactory sense was working overtime attempting to discern the specific pungent odor emitted by something burning within Mr. Light Feather's room. Ben was highly suspicious of an intermingling of burning sagebrush and marijuana. By any account neither was legal; no open flames or smoldering incense or the like were allowed in a resident's room and the smoking of cannabis was strictly forbidden on several levels. Mr. Light Feather's guests had apparently not been informed as to the rules and regulations of nursing home visitation or were blatantly disregarding them. Ben knew how strongly the Feds frowned upon cannabis in any shape or form and Medicare drove the bus.

Ben backed away and walked around the corner and by the nurses' station. He exited the hospital and stood in the frozen night ascertaining which window was Mr. Light Feather's. It was the first room on the left in the building's west wing and was opened approximately two inches above the sill. The blinds were drawn down even to the bottom of the window. He returned to the nurses' station where Becca and Sheena were sipping coffee and reading magazines. Looking up at Ben Becca asked, "So, what's the scouting report say chief?"

"I believe Mr. Light Feather's nephew and his five protégés are engaging in some unlawful practices."

"Was I right about the dope? The marijuana?"

"The odor is faint. I bet that they have a towel wedged against the bottom of the door. I think that I smell both sagebrush and marijuana."

Sheena looked a bit worried, "What about the sprinklers Ben? You know, with the smoke?"

"The smoke shouldn't trigger the sprinklers Sheena because it won't get hot enough but the smoke alarm would be sensitive to it. They probably removed the batteries to conduct their ritual smudging and pot party."

"So what do you want to do?"

"I'm going to knock on the door and discuss the matter with Mr. Strong Tree, who I believe to be the ringleader, for lack of a better term. Becca, I'll have you accompany me to witness the conversation. Sheena, if you would, I'd greatly appreciate it if you would put on your coat and stand just outside the entrance door and watch Mr. Light Feather's window. I'm going to knock on the door and I'm thinking that whatever they are smoking gets tossed out of the window. They'll probably open the window up more to air out the room and as soon as they do you come back in and you can return to your magazine."

Sheena glanced momentarily to Becca and then to Ben. She appeared a bit apprehensive, "Is this dangerous?"

"No, we're just covering the bases so we can submit a report to Westergard."

Becca chimed in, also addressing Sheena's question, "The only danger in this nursing home is getting run over by Mrs. Tallmadge or verbally eviscerated by Mrs. Milic."

"So what do you say Cagney and Lacy, ready to rock and roll?"

"Who?"

"Never mind. Sheena, grab your coat and we'll wait until you're out the door." Sheena retrieved her coat from the break room and walked through the doorway and into the night.

Ben and Becca quietly approached Mr. Light Feather's door and Ben positioned her off to the side. Rapping on the door loud enough to be heard over the voices within, he heard the room fall silent as he pushed against the door. There was no give. It had been locked or secured closed in some fashion or wedged shut. "Mr. Strong Tree, I'm sorry to interrupt but we need to talk." There was a distant murmur of voices and he heard the shuffling of feet. He thought that he recognized the rub of a window being raised in a cold stiffened casing. Someone approached the door from within. "Mr. Strong Tree, we need to talk."

"You are interrupting our ceremonial instruction. You have no authority and it is not to be tolerated."

Ben assumed that it was Strong Tree who was talking to him through the as yet closed door. "Again, my apologies. Am I talking to Mr. Strong Tree?"

"Who do you think you are interrupting our rituals?" The voice held a condescending if not provocative tone.

Ben's hackles were beginning to bristle; at least that's what he thought was causing the heat and hair arising on the back of his neck. "Mr. Strong Tree, I'm Ben Parker the physician assistant on call. You need to unlock, remove the wedge or remove what is barring this door and open it up. It's against regulations to physically prevent entrance to a resident's room."

"We have permission, a waiver from the administrator. We are not to be disturbed."

"I seriously doubt that. And it's against regulations to have an open flame or to burn anything within a residential room."

"The smudging is part of our ritual."

"Maybe sagebrush, but certainly not marijuana."

There was a pause. "Cannabis is a traditional part of our tribe's heritage and spirituality."

"Mr. Strong Tree, excuse the expression but you're blowing smoke up my skirt. I know for a fact that none of the tribes on the seven reservations in Montana have traditionally employed Cannabis in their religious or spiritual ceremonies." He was taking a wild stab at that being true.

Ben was met with silence.

"Okay then Mr. Strong Tree, let me give you a quick rundown of several of tonight's points of interest; one, there is no smoking in the building, two, there is no burning of incense, candles or any other material in a residential room, three, there is no use of Cannabis in any form in this building due to a strict adherence to Federal guidelines, four, you cannot barricade or bar entrance to a residential room, and five, visiting hours are now over for guests as well as family members. Please open the door."

"Westergard guaranteed that my uncle could conduct instruction and rituals in this facility and Dr. Saroni told my uncle that staying active and social interactions would help his physical and mental health. Take it up with them in the morning."

"I'm not disputing what may or may not help to maintain Mr. Light Feather's overall health and I will discuss all of this with Mr. Westergard in the morning. Right this minute I hold no reservations about contacting the sheriff's department and having them come immediately to discuss tonight's activities with you."

There was no verbal response, however, Ben heard a grunt as if someone was bending over and then noises emitting from the base of the door. The door then opened enough for Strong Tree and Ben to view each other eye to eye. Strong Tree's face was unrevealing though Ben could see that the slightly blood shot eyes were smoldering. The pungent odor was more intense, confirming Ben's suspicions and he noted cooler air escaping through the opened door.

"There will be no need to involve the sheriff's department this evening. You have made your point. We are done here for tonight…"

Ben had the feeling that Mr. Strong Tree had intended to say more but had decided not to further discuss or inflame the situation.

"Mr. Strong Tree, Mr. Light Feather is obviously free to conduct ceremonial rituals and teach his students; you just need to respect…"

"We are done here." He closed the door in Ben's face.

Becca mouthed the words, "Wow, that went well," and then made a pained face.

They walked over to the nurses' station.

"Becca, did you have a chance to figure out the time difference between here and Tokyo, Japan?"

"Fifteen hours, Ben. What's going to happen when Westergard hears about tonight?"

Ben stood silently calculating. "I need the phone number for Mrs. Haugen's son and daughter in law. I'm projecting it to be around noontime in Japan."

Becca was insistent, "What about Westergard? He's going to…"

"I will deal with Westergard tomorrow." He turned to Sheena, "Anything of interest happen outside of Mr. Light Feather's window?"

"Someone opened the window and something orange-red flew out with a bunch of sparks and then it hit the snow."

Mr. Light Feather's door opened and his five protégés filed out followed by Mr. Strong Tree who pulled shut the door. They silently walked out past the nurses' station without diverting their eyes and exited the hospital into a cold winter night.

"I'm going to write orders for serial neuro checks for Mrs. Haugen, and then call her family while you two tuck in Mr. Light Feather. And don't be looking for any leftover roaches or doobies to smoke during your break. Your luck might run out and tomorrow you have to randomly pee in a cup."

"Ben, don't you think that you may have taken more than a few liberties last evening with Dr. Saroni's patients? A phone call and a consult with the doctor would have been appropriate considering the circumstances. That in and of itself may have been enough to help avert the current situations that I am now forced to address."

If there was one thing that Ben had learned over the previous several months was that Jonathon Westergard was adroitly familiar with the subtleties of framing communication in the vaguest of terms. He believed that Westergard approached his administrative duties as a professional politician would his constituency; as that of the verbose yet well couched benevolent dictator. A chair had been offered, however, Ben had declined, choosing to stand. Westergard remained seated in his office chair. The soft whir of a personal space heater drifted up from beneath the desk. He had checked on Mrs. Haugen's status with Myrna when he first came to work at 0730 hours and had been informed that Dr. Saroni had met with the hospital administrator at 0645 hours; an ungodly early time for either of them.

Ben now speculated that Saroni's and Westergard's meeting was to discuss spin control and to designate a scapegoat; Saroni to save face and exert control and for Westergard it would be to mitigate financial impact and maintain community relations. He was certain that both entertained personal and joint agendas in addition to those hat had become evident to him. Westergard was charged with keeping the hospital solvent. Ben was not blind to the fact that by keeping private pay nursing home residents and their families satisfied Westergard garnered financial income far more rewarding for the facility than the per diem pittance that the state reimbursed for indigent or near indigent residents. It certainly did not justify the subverting of regulations or turning a blind eye. The bottom line for Ben was that he trusted neither of them.

"Last night I received two complaints from two separate family members. Mrs. Haugen's son called stating that you were harassing him and his wife and Mr. Strong Tree lodged a complaint that you were harassing and threatening Mr. Light Feather's well-being. As the hospital administrator I have to consider these accusations seriously. Would you care to respond to them?"

Whoa. This is taking a nasty turn. Ben was immediately on the defensive, though acknowledged that he needed to respond calmly and factually. "The hospital has a written policy that should a nursing home resident incur a fall with any degree of injury the family is to be notified."

"I'm aware of that; however, what did you say to Mrs. Haugen's son that may have prompted the complaint?"

Ben was surprised and then quickly surmised that a son's guilt played significantly into submitting the complaint. "I did not speak to the son. I talked with his wife who is also listed as an emergency contact. It was approximately noon time in Tokyo and her husband was at work. I informed her of Mrs. Haugen's fall and that she had suffered some minor bruising. I was asked how Mrs. Haugen was doing in general and then our discussion became more in depth. The daughter in law is the person who calls Mrs. Haugen every several weeks but she was genuinely surprised to hear what I had to say. I'll give you a little background. Mrs. Haugen was admitted here after a lifetime in a small Minnesota town heavily populated with people of Norwegian ancestry. Her husband died five years ago. She had to give up her house, lifelong friends and social life lines. She gave the son who is now in Japan control of her financial and medical power of attorney and he in turn managed to alienate the daughter and the other son. The grandchildren are scattered around Minnesota and the Midwest. Mrs. Haugen admits to feeling abandoned and being very lonely. She is dependent on strangers and generally depressed. Having withdrawn into her own little world she has reverted back to speaking only Norwegian because it gives her small comfort by embracing her past memories and home."

"The daughter in law was not aware of any of this?"

"She claims that she had no idea. Social services has never contacted or discussed it with her or her husband. Mrs. Haugen is old school. Her generation was essentially told not to discount or second guess what a doctor says, women played second fiddle to males and she in particular does not want to be a burden to her family or to anyone else."

"How did you come up with all of this?"

"I reviewed Mrs. Haugen's chart notes, both nursing and medical provider, plus she told me."

"You speak Norwegian?"

"No."

"I was under the impression that she only spoke Norwegian. So how did she communicate all this to you?"

"I asked her the right questions."

Westergard looked puzzled. Ben ignored it and continued. "I'm not quite sure what you or Dr. Saroni may or may not have promised Mr. Light Feather and his nephew Mr. Strong Tree, or how they might have interpreted it. I was polite and respectful to a rather hostile Strong Tree. The door was barricaded, they were burning materials in a residential room, they were smoking marijuana and it was past visitation hours. I believe that I had an obligation to address these infractions. I did nothing to jeopardize Mr. Light Feather's health and did not infringe on any legitimate religious or spiritual ritual or ceremony."

"Why didn't you present this to Dr. Saroni last night?"

"There was no medical emergency or change of admission status that warranted a phone call disturbing the doctor's evening and also due to the fact that he is not my direct supervisor; you are."

Westergard's face appeared to be questioning the statement.

"I've read my contract and the medical center by-laws. You are my direct supervisor. Dr. Saroni and I have a supervisory agreement as required by the State of Montana that addresses the parameters of medical practice and our cooperative relationship. We are supposed to work as a team, not a subservient hierarchy."

"That's a little harsh Ben."

"Sorry but that's how it's often been viewed and conducted by the doctor."

Placing his hands on the arms of his chair, Westergard shifted his weight, perhaps an unconscious attempt to make an uncomfortable meeting slightly less so. He stared out of his office window at a gray, overcast January morning, the eastern horizon just beginning to display hints of light. Ben assumed that his administrator was contemplating, forming his response. Westergard turned his head back to Ben, folding his hands together on top of the pristine desk blotter. "Thank you Mr. Parker. I will take all of this information under advisement."

It was a dismissive statement and Ben opened the office door and exited. He was left without a definitive impression of what Westergard was thinking, however, speculated that the administrator had not been prepared for what he had heard.

Saroni was waiting as Ben turned the corner from his clinic hallway into the main corridor and advanced up to him. "You insubordinate Parker. Like Capetli."

Ben realized that it was an attempt to pronounce Capelletti, Marni's last name. He chose not to correct the doctor. "What can I do for you Dr. Saroni?"

"I supervise, you obey. Simple, hokay?" He was emphatic as well as condescending.

"This is regarding?"

Saroni's voice was rising, "You too know well. You disobey me. Disrespect me."

"Again, in reference to?" Ben knew that he was baiting him but it was not in fun. For months the doctor had been accusatory and demanding, often demeaning, yet obtuse on so many levels, on too many occasions that it was time to hold his feet to the flames. Ben had no way of ascertaining if the doctor ever considered personal accountability. Immediately self-doubt was beginning to insinuate itself into his thought process but he fought it off. He was prepared to storm ahead either establishing a beachhead or meeting his Waterloo.

"All, everything." The doctor was defiant.

Ahhhh. Let's play the victim and riddle the antagonist with the shame and guilt shotgun affect. "Please

272

Dr. Saroni, an example." He could see color rising in Saroni's face.

"Disturbing my patients," the doctor's voice continued to rise, registering a higher pitch, "Harassing patient families. This reflects on me."

They were standing in close proximity to where Marni and the doctor had squared off for their verbal altercation. Ben suspected that Saroni wanted an audience when putting his perceived subordinates in their place. The big question was why the doctor would repeat an event that had turned out unfavorably for him less than a week ago. Callie, he observed, was sitting behind her desk staring at them through her office window, concern on her face. "I gather that you are referring to Mrs. Haugen and Mr. Light Feather? Hospital protocol requires us to contact a family member regarding Mrs. Haugen's fall and I felt a provider's responsibility to voice my concerns about her overall health. Regarding Mr. Light Feather's nephew, Mr. Strong Tree, he was jeopardizing this facility by ignoring hospital policies and regulations and frankly he was breaking the law with his use of marijuana." Ben paused but added before the doctor could respond, "There was no medical condition or emergency that warranted me calling you." Saroni started to speak, his face further reddening, when Ben interrupted, "Are you sure that you want to continue this out here in the hallway?"

Saroni sputtered and yelled, "Impudence. Disrespect. I can have you…"

Ben suddenly leaned forward throwing Saroni off guard. He quickly and intently whispered in the doctor's left ear, "Stop this now before you embarrass both of us." Resuming an erect posture Ben stared into Dr. Saroni's wide eyed look of surprise. He continued softly, "Would you like to adjourn to your or my office or discuss this with Mr. Westergard.?"

Saroni recovered quickly. In a normal voice he responded, "Westergard not care to hear."

"Okay then, Westergard's office it is." Ben sidestepped and walked by the doctor.

"Where you go?"

"Westergard's office."

"No need, he not care."

Ben kept walking.

"Stop. No need."

Ben turned and walked back positioning himself in front of Saroni, "Yes, there is a need. We have to sort this out here and now."

"Sort this out? Nothing here to sort."

"As a matter of fact we do. We have differences in our approach to patient care and interpreting the parameters of a supervision agreement. We've come to loggerheads."

"Loggerheads?"

"An impasse."

"What impasse? No impasse here. Hokay now, I command, you obey."

"It doesn't work that way sir."

"Doctor."

"Let's go visit Westergard; maybe we can settle a few things. Perhaps he might mediate."

"No Westergard, no mediate, no impasse. Hokay?"

"You bet. Maybe I'll have a short talk with Westergard alone, you know, maybe touch on moonlighting, random rescheduling, ER call, turfing patients and your unavailability for phone consults. Maybe mention all of your damn inconsistencies that everyone in the hospital has to deal with." Ben had blurted it out and immediately felt purged yet at the same time amazingly stupid having vented his frustrations on an unsympathetic ear. Well in for a penny in for pound. He had inadvertently gone "all in" and realized that he wasn't bluffing, but how would Saroni react?

Saroni's eyes were closed. Tight lipped, he looked as if he was having his genitals examined. He opened his eyes and spoke evenly, "No impasse, no loggerhead, no problem."

"Yes, there are several problems."

Saroni glanced upward, then side to side and then shrugged, "What problem? I see no problem. You have problems? I do not."

"Then why did you initiate this hallway confrontation?"

"What confrontation? No problem here."

"Suddenly we're good? Why? What has changed?"

"I not change. I am fine. Why you unhappy?"

Ben took a step back, scanned Saroni from his neatly combed hair down to his well shined black oxfords. He had assumed a composed posture and his face was placid, emotionless. The navy blue power tie was tightly knotted and his sky blue shirt and white lab coat were spotless. Sharply creased pants were cuffed just touching his shoe tops. His hands were now firmly secured behind his back. The doctor had reconstituted himself. Saroni and Westergard obviously had their own joint secret programs and agendas; however, Ben recognized that the doctor had an agenda which he did not want shared with Westergard. Today Ben had exposed and prodded a nerve. He was not naïve to the fact that his and Saroni's differences had not suddenly evaporated and that peace had been restored within the Bedlam Medical Center.

Saroni had called a stalemate for the time being. However, Ben was well aware that today's confrontation might only incite an escalation of the doctor's future attempts at control, manipulation and targeted humiliation. The doctor was a narcissist, a chauvinist and worse, a bully. Ben took little comfort in today's stalemate; Saroni would be inwardly fuming and was certain to unleash a future shit-storm at the first opportunity that presented itself. Is this what he truly wanted to deal with on a regular basis? It was demanding enough learning the practice of medicine without now ducking and dodging Saroni's indiscriminate slings and arrows or constantly watching one's back to avoid the well placed dagger.

The doctor now appeared smug as if he were now back in control, "We are done here."

Ben countered, "Not by a long shot." With an abrupt turn he headed back to his office thinking, "I better buy a helmet if I'm going to continue beating my head against the wall."

The clinic day was finished and Ben was not on call so he was headed out, looking forward to a night off. He glanced through the clinic office window and saw Callie waving him in. Poking his head in the partially opened door was not enough as she said, "Come in and shut the door."

Obliging her request he positioned himself in front of her desk, "What's so important Callie?"

She handed him a printed sheet of paper.

Giving it a cursory scan he looked at Callie curiously, "It's the call schedule. I've got a copy at home and in my office."

"Look at it again." She was firm, this was not a suggestion.

He set down his briefcase and studied the schedule more closely. "This is the quarterly call sheet but he's added the month of April."

"And…?"

His eyes sought out what Callie had been trying to alert him to and it finally registered. "Saroni swapped April weekends around and it appears that he's off for nine days." Ben appeared more pained than disappointed. "I had already cleared Easter weekend off and that Tuesday and Wednesday for my ACLS class."

"I knew that but he dropped this on my desk as he was leaving today. I don't know what to tell you."

"Saroni just can't help himself, can he? He has to be in control; he has to be a prick. Sorry, pardon my French."

"You're excused and I agree that he's a prick. You had plans for that weekend?"

Ben did not want to broadcast his private life. He had planned a quick trip out to Missoula to visit Lindsay and return in time for the Advanced Cardiac Life Support class being held in Slipknot. "Yeah, I had plans."

"Maybe you could talk with him?"

"Not after today's fiasco. This is the start of payback."

"Westergard?"

"They're in cahoots."

"Never been there, is it nice this time of year?" She could not say it without breaking out in a smile.

Ben couldn't help but to join in with a smile, "I'm beginning to think that it is."

"I guess that you're pretty much SOL."

"Shit out of luck is describing my future here mildly. See you Wednesday, Callie. I believe that tonight I have a hot date with a cold six pack.

"Hello?"

"Hi, Dad, how are you doing?"

"Ben?" His father sounded surprised, "To what do I owe for a Monday night call? Everything okay?"

"Yeah, I'm doing fine, Dad, but I wanted to run something by you."

"Sure thing. Are you sure everything's all right? You sound a little off."

"Yes, I'm okay. I just wanted your opinion on something. An outside perspective maybe."

"I'm all ears. What's up? What's on your mind?"

"Well," there was a prolonged pause, "It might involve the use of my old room for a little while."

WESTERGARD & LAFEVBRE

As regular as clockwork the fourth Tuesday would roll around and with almost the same regularity Ben would spend that evening in the emergency room. Tuesday nights the ER was usually populated by patients who had legitimate medical complaints. Often the demands of employment precluded a patient with a new onset, nonemergent problem from arriving during clinic hours, and just as often an injury or illness incurred or contracted over the previous weekend which, was not improving, would instigate a visit. Tuesday late night and early morning hour emergency room visits, for the most part, were infrequent.

The fourth Tuesday of the month was the traditionally appointed night for the Bedlam Medical Center Board of Trustee meeting. Usually scheduled to start at 1800 hours in the conference room of the hospital, the meetings were rarely controversial, contentious, or prolonged. Several board members vigilantly adhered to protocol and the advertised agenda, lest they miss a pre or post meeting cocktail. Tonight's actions had not strayed from the norm. Due to his Tuesday night call schedule corresponding with board meetings, Ben was rarely able to attend a meeting, despite an extended presence in the same building. It would be considered an occasion of note when he listened for a short period at the doorway of the conference room, however, the most likely scenario was missing the meeting in its entirety.

Not overly busy tonight with the number of patients, Ben had been kept occupied with protracted encounters, attending to a patient with a wrist fracture and another patient with a substantial forearm laceration, and a third with low back pain. The board meeting had been conducted in a timely manner, and the post board meeting, traditionally rotated between the local taverns, and had in all likelihood concluded. Board members were known to ignore unadvertised meeting law restrictions and while gathered in quorum numbers, hold informal, illegal, hospital business discussions over cocktails before adjourning completely for the night to their homes. He assumed that with the meeting over, Board members, administrative staff and the attendees from the general public had all migrated out of the building and eventually home. The patient hallway was dimmed and the ER, X-ray and ambulance entrance hallway was darkened, save the light emitting from the small office across the hallway from the ER. Ben sat at the desk, completing the documentation on his third and hopefully last patient of the evening. He glanced at his watch, noted 10:30 PM and thought, "I should be by 11." Having reviewed the text he was about to apply his signature when he interrupted himself as he felt a presence in the office doorway. It was Pammulla the charge nurse.

"Sorry to interrupt you, Ben," she offered apologetically, "I saw a light and thought someone had forgotten to shut it off."

"No, just me finishing up." He signed and dated at the bottom of the provider notes, collected and clipped the pages together. "I'm finished, so I'll get the light. If we're all done at this end," sweeping his right arm indicating the outside hallway and ER, "then I'm outta here." Pammulla gave thumbs up; Ben squared his hat on his head, picked up his jacket and flipped off the switch for the overhead. As the two of them headed quietly down the patient hallway he quietly asked, "How did the meeting go tonight?"

"Pretty cut and dried. More talk about telemedicine with a presentation scheduled for next month. Saroni gave his report and immediately left. Financial report. Administration report. Blah, blah, blah, same old, same old. Nothing that I heard was new and different."

Arriving at the nurses' station they parted ways while saying good night, Pammulla to check on the residents and CNAs while Ben dropped the ER paperwork into the designated basket. Putting on his jacket as he headed toward the exit door he was surprised to see Westergard locking up his office door.

"Busy night Ben?" Westergard inquired. His coat was draped over his left arm, gloves grasped in his left hand, keys being pocketed by his right.

"Three ER's," Ben replied, "nothing overly traumatic but they were time consuming."

"Well, time we both headed home. Have a good evening." Westergard was off with a purposeful bent.

Both men strode off in opposite directions, Ben to the west parking lot, Westergard towards the emergency room and out to the east parking area. Ben was almost to his truck when he realized he had left his cell phone and pager in his clinic office. He trotted back in, went directly to his office and retrieved the phone and pager setting on his disordered desk top. Feeling a bit guilty by leaving the paperwork and mail unaddressed, he promised himself, "Tomorrow. Tomorrow I'll clean up the pile." Then he plopped himself down in his chair and spent the next 20 minutes opening, reading and discarding non pertinent mail, reviewing printouts of Dr. Saroni's latest protocol changes and updates, and straightening out the remaining piles on the desk, because he knew "neatness counts." To someone.

He returned to the nurses' station to once again say goodnight and assure everyone that he was finally leaving. Pammulla was flipping through the pages of the ER paperwork, looked up and with an expansive smile warned, "Better get a move on and get some sleep before I call you back in." Before he could muster a retort she continued, "I don't see the green page, the treatment sheet with the stickers."

Ben stood thinking and said, "I know that I saw it. It's probably down in the ER office. I'll run down and get it."

"No. Go home, get some sleep. I've got all night to find it except for when I call you back in."

"You seem to forget Pammulla, that I've got a list of everyone's contact and home numbers."

"And you Ben need to come up with a new threat."

Ben saw one of the CNAs down a resident hallway, outside a resident's room, waving to gain their attention. He motioned and pointed for Pammulla's benefit and said, "One of your fans is requesting your presence. I'll go get the treatment sheet and drop it in the basket."

Ben switched on the overhead light of the small office and from his vantage point immediately spied the green treatment sheet covered with yellow supply stickers lying on the floor under the near corner of the desk. Stooping, he picked it up and exited while turning off the light. The darkened end of the building was silent as he extinguished the light. He thought he heard a very faint "yes" uttered by a male voice and then a distant moan. He stood in the silent darkness, listening intently for any additional sounds. Taking great care to walk as quietly as possible, he advanced to the X-ray room, slowly opened the door just as the low whirring of a cooling fan on the processor started up. A quick visual scan of the X-ray suite revealed no one and he heard no other sound but the fan. He withdrew from the doorway, closed the door and again moved quietly, stopping in the center of the hallway. There it was again, a muffled guttural moan. He was positive that he had heard the moan but now believed it to originate from the emergency room.

Ben looked around furtively, first taking in the darkened hallway, next outside the double glass doors to the cement receiving pad for the ambulance, then down the dimly lit hallway of hospital rooms. Seeing no one he approached the double solid wooden doors enclosing the emergency room and peered through a small observation window set at eye level in both doors. The room appeared pitch black. He partially opened the right door, quietly slipped in and eased the door closed behind him. He stood silently in the blackness allowing his eyes to slowly adjust. Faintly glowing red lights reminded him that a number of instruments were sitting in their charging cradles. A short stream of white light at chest height poked its way out of the wall near the far right corner. At floor level, in the same corner, a dim white light stretched out from what Ben recognized as the threshold of the doorway to the adjoining bathroom. His eyes continued to adjust however; he still could not see well enough to maneuver safely.

He could hear the muted tones of a woman's voice as he pulled a small penlight from his shirt pocket. Aiming it at the floor and using short bursts of light, he cautiously made his way towards the stream of white light. As he neared the light stream emitting from the wall he could discern the sound of water running in the restroom sink, the woman's voice now silent. Once arriving at the light source he ascertained it projected out from the restroom through a small hole in the wall. Ben realized the hole was in the access door of a stainless steel box installed in the wall. The box had opposing access doors, one in the restroom and one in the ER, so a patient providing a sample in the restroom could place a urine sample in the box and the nurse or lab tech could retrieve it while in the ER. He remembered the access door on the restroom side was missing as was the knob on the ER door. He positioned himself in front of the access door, bending at the knees until his right eye was horizontal to the approximate one centimeter in diameter hole. Carefully he levered his neck and head forward achieving a vantage point where he could visualize most of the restroom by moving his eye or slightly adjusting the angle of his head to accommodate his field of vision.

Ben immediately determined that there were two people in the restroom. Directly across from him the door leading from the restroom to the X-ray suite was closed. He became suddenly aware that he had been holding his breath when his reactive gasp with already full lungs almost initiated a cough. He slowly expelled his breath as he tried to suppress his surprise and process the view. Westergard stood, rather slumped, in the far corner. His eyes were closed, his normally imperturbable face appeared peaceful, a thin smile was evident, his body language said pleasantly drained. The stiffly ironed and starched white dress shirt was uncharacteristically wrinkled and completely unbuttoned; his ever present power necktie remained knotted, hanging loosely from neck down his chest and abdomen, the appearance mimicking that of a red arrow pointing to his flaccid penis. His pants lay bunched about his ankles exposing his reflectively white, near hairless legs. Ben noted Westergard wore tighty whities, no surprise there.

By shifting his head slightly to his left it allowed Ben to observe the profile of a woman standing in front of the sink. Heidi Lafevbre stood leaning over the sink facing the mirror. Her scrub top and bra off, her pendulous breasts slightly, rhythmically bouncing as she vigorously brushed her teeth. "Holy shit," Ben mouthed soundlessly, "Who would have dreamed this up?"

Ben stared, transfixed, until his attention was drawn back to Westergard when Ben heard him begin to softly laugh, with an apparent but horribly lame attempt at a French accent. His very nasal laugh climbed in scale. "Hunh, hunh, hunh, my cherie, my leetle kumquat. Your leeps, zey are so succulent, hunh, hunh. Your mouth, eet eeze so magical. Destiny, eet haz been so kind to us. Hunh, HUNH!"

Heidi had finished brushing her teeth and was now cupping water into her mouth to rinse. She reached for a paper towel and was drying her face as she spoke bluntly to Westergard. "Okay, snookums, destiny dictates that what's good for the gander is good for the goose." Looking left then right, Heidi studied her face in the mirror. Never known for mincing or being at a loss for words she continued, "Next time snookums we're headed to the clinic GYN room. I'm gonna lay back, feet up in the stirrups and let that French tongue of yours lick me till the cows come home."

She began to turn around to Westergard and that's when Ben saw the tattoo on her upper chest, extending down into her cleavage. The huge lips and extended tongue, undeniably the Rolling Stones logo. Having turned completely, she now stood facing Westergard, her left shoulder in full view. Just below her left shoulder, on her upper arm Ben observed three distinctly colored tattooed roses, red, yellow and black connected by a short green stem. It hit him immediately, as if an electric jolt or solid punch landed to his chest. Snookums! The tattoos! He almost audibly gasped, then suppressed a desire to shout. "Holy Christ, it's Deanna!" He thought, "Wow. Jake's long lost girlfriend, I've found my roommate's lost girlfriend." After all these years he trips over her in this out of the way dot on the map. Holy Christ. he repeated to himself. She suddenly disappeared from view, then reappeared, standing and slipping into her bra.

Ben quickly and quietly backed away, carefully making his way through and out of the trauma bay, near silence with the closing of the heavy wooden door. He immediately began to briskly walk away from the emergency room, feeling that he was gasping for breath as he made his way down the dimly lit hospital hallway. He stopped, thought better of his automatic reaction and restarted at a normal pace. Pretending nonchalance, he would stop, peer into a patient's room and continue on repeating the performance as he proceeded down the hall. As he neared the nurses' station, Pammulla, the charge nurse, looked up, a slightly surprised look, and then glanced at the clock on the wall.

"I thought you had already left," she declared.

"No, I found your treatment sheet." Ben was smoothing out the now crumpled green page he had been clenching in his fist throughout his voyeuristic experience. "I've been down in the X-ray reading room reviewing tonight's X-rays," he lied, "and then took a quick peek in on our patients."

"Did you turn out the lights?"

"Yes, the lights are out, everything locked down and good to go. "All qui…" he caught himself before uttering the fateful "Q" word, "all mellow on the Western Front." For some reason Ben felt the need to cover all bases, as if he, the interloper, were guilty of having exposed the couple's tryst and must now protect them from additional discovery or embarrassment. He knew it was not his responsibility and yet felt oddly responsible. Go figure.

"You spend an awful lot of time here after hours," she observed.

"Calmer here at night. Easier to catch up on charts and dictation. It's a good time to review, study the reference books, whatever. They say you never stop learning, so considering what little I do know I need all the extra help I can get muster up."

"So, did you learn anything worthwhile tonight?" asked Pammulla as she shuffled ER paperwork.

"Sometimes it's something mundane, sometimes something amazing if not electrifying. Whatever it is, you need to salt it away. You may never come across it again and you may not remember everything you need to know about it but you have to at least be able to recognize it and know who would be the best authority to consult with on it."

"So again, how about tonight in Bedlam? Did you learn anything amazing or electrifying?" She had stopped her paperwork shuffle and looked questionably at him.

Ben paused as if deep in thought, though he had already decided that the need for understatement was paramount. Smiling innocently he chose his words carefully as not to pique her curiosity, "Interesting, I would venture to say. Always a new discovery, or new information, though sometimes its value is unknown at the time. Tonight, I would categorize as surprising, though maybe more common than I once imagined. Coincidence may also play a role. Most certainly nothing that electrifies or is of earth shaking significance. Whether I ever see or hear of it again I believe that it warrants additional consideration, therefore I will file it away for a future date. Tonight I'm too tired to give it any additional thought."

"Quite the philosopher tonight Ben Parker," she stated, hiding a desire to question him more.

He shrugged his shoulders and said, "Definitely more luck than intellect. Thank you for your help tonight. See you later."

"I'll see what we can arrange. Even Tuesday does get a little crazy at times."

Ben smiled to himself as he headed out the door. Westergard and Lafevbre, that's about as crazy as it gets.

UNPLANNED BUT SCHEDULED

A slightly wavering but pleasant female voice singing a melody that Ben did not recognize with lyrics that he did not understand was literally floating over the nurses' station. As he approached the front counter Myrna emerged from the supply room and entered the nurses' station smiling at Ben. Upon his reaching the front counter he realized that the singer was none only but Mrs. Haugen who sat in a wheelchair on the opposite side of the station.

"What a nice surprise. When did this start?"

"Yesterday, at the morning church service; everyone that attended the Sunday service has commented on her voice. Personally I had forgotten all about her singing. This morning she walked down the hall, plunked herself down in the spare wheelchair and began serenading us."

"I'm taking a wild stab at it here but she's singing in Norwegian?"

"Yep. Singing in Norwegian and talking up a storm all week in English. Her son and daughter in law have called every day this week and the daughter in law in flying back sometime in the next few weeks though I'm attributing this radical change to something you said to her or that smack to the head jarred something loose. At any rate she's been in good spirits all week and we get entertained to boot."

"Obviously the head injury did it so don't be blaming me for the singing Norwegian."

"Actually this is one thing that you should take credit for. So what's on your plate today?"

"I wanted to catch up with Westergard this morning before I start in the clinic."

"Get in line Ben, Saroni is in with him now."

Ben had been dividing his attention between Myrna and the singing Norwegian and his full attention was now raptly centered on Myrna. "This morning?" He glanced at his watch, "It's barely 7:15; too early for either of them."

"The happy couple must have scheduled a breakfast date because they were both promptly here at seven. I really didn't notice which one brought the tea and scones and who brought the flowers."

Ben was having some trouble containing his pleasure at Myrna's appraisal of two of his least favorite people. "You're sounding a bit jaded this morning Myrna; have the boys done anything in particular to prick your enmity?"

"Hah, you're not the only one that reads the dictionary; does animosity, hostility, or rancor ring a bell?" Ben was duly impressed. "Anytime the two of them meet in Westergard's office this early in the day means that they have something or someone in their sights. Theirs is an unholy alliance."

"Not exactly Butch Cassidy and the Sundance Kid."

"I'm leaning towards Genghis Khan and Attila the Hun."

"Apropos."

"In some ways I've considered it a kind of man crush but realistically, as I mentioned, an unholy alliance by any other name."

"Any clue as to what they might be conspiring about today?"

Myrna unfolded her arms from over her chest, placed her hands on the counter and leaned in towards Ben, 'I don't have the faintest idea what those two jackals are up to this morning but I'd bet carrion is on the menu."

"Good morning Myra. You look nice today." Almost immediately Ben felt a twinge of regret having commented on her appearance lest she interpret his compliment as meaning that normally she did not. Of course in this day, age and political climate even remaining quietly neutral might be construed as grounds to incur someone's ire. She was a vision of blue green, or was it sea green; he was willing to settle on just plain turquoise. Ben had once speculated after observing her in a complete ruby red ensemble that she had other fully color coordinated outfits accessorized in the same hue; and he had been proven correct. Today Myra displayed finger nails, ring, bracelet, ear studs and pendent earrings all in turquoise along with the clasp for a matching scarf. Her facial makeup blended with the fashion theme exhibited by her jewelry, vest, skirt, pantyhose and shoes. Only her white blouse and gold wedding ring broke with today's color scheme.

The odor of a recently smoked cigarette was attempting to sneak its way through a veil of strong perfume. Her teeth looked unevenly white and Ben recognized that Myra was trying a home whitening process. "Why thank you Ben. Today is my tenth anniversary."

His luck was holding. "Congratulations, Myra, to you and your husband."

"Oh, no Ben. Today is my 10th anniversary for working here at the medical center."

He had yet to clear 10 months and was teetering on disillusionment, "Well, congratulations for that milestone as well. Is Mr. Westergard available, Myra?"

"I'm sorry Ben; he's in a meeting with Dr. Saroni."

"When will he be available?"

She looked at her scheduling book, "He's booked fairly solid this morning and has a luncheon meeting with the hospital board and after lunch a meeting with Heidi. How much time do you need with him Ben?"

"Just a few minutes should do the trick."

"I'll talk with him when he and the doctor are finished. We'll try to fit you in sometime this morning but if all else fails will late this afternoon work?"

"Sure, whenever you can work me in would be great but preferably today."

"Anything that you would care for me to pass on to Mr. Westergard?"

Ben knew that Myra was now fishing. Information to the medical center employees was a form of currency or capital, and gathering enough of the right capital creates a sense of control and a perceived increase in status. The control of the information stream and its sources was sacred to Myra and paramount in her world; and though it was still gossip Myra was queen. Her little office was gossip central, and as the recipient of large amounts of unsubstantiated rumor she dutifully acted as an information clearing house carefully doling out snippets from her large cache of capital, metering out doses according to friendship or association. Ben was usually cognizant of what he said, careful not to divulge motives or reasons, knowing full well that once transformed into capital they would never remain privileged communication.

"No, thanks any way. Please just give me a call if an opportunity presents itself."

"Ben, this is indeed your very lucky day. You have been picked to perform a magnanimous and selfless community service, which, many providers would gladly label a 'plum' assignment."

"Callie, when you are so effusive in your description and choose to so grandly embellish the positive aspects of an as yet undisclosed assignation I can only surmise that the duty is dangerously balanced at the edge of a yawning abyss. So let's can the flowery BS and give me the bottom line."

"Three young and innocent children have somewhere, somehow managed to have their scalps inhabited with head lice. Two are brothers living in the same household and the third is their best friend and neighbor. The lice were discovered over the weekend. The county public health nurse caught wind of it from the pharmacist technician at the Sunnvale Pharmacy and in turn she contacted the elementary school principle who dutifully reported said outbreak to the school district superintendent who declared that this growing plague posed a definitive health risk to all those placed under his direct oversight and with due diligence consulted with our very own administrator, the illustrious Jonathon Westergard who immediately called a Def Con one meeting with the Bedlam Medical Center Medical Director the omnipotent Dr. Arman Saroni. The consensus was to assign our very best person to investigate and mitigate this most insidious assault upon the community's health. You are therefore to be dispatched post haste to the Bedlam Elementary school to evaluate this lurking scourge, examine each and every one of the school children, our society's most precious resource, put an end to this scurrilous, looming pandemic and finally to assuage the insecurities and fears of the

Bedlam community thusly thwarting any growing and misguided rush to panic."

Ben stood motionless, inattentively staring off into the distance.

"Ben, did you hear what I said Ben?"

His body snapped to attention. "Okay, sorry Callie, could you please repeat that? I lost track after the public health nurse?"

"Why sure, anything for you Ben Parker... but not in this lifetime."

"I know that you spent some time writing that whole soliloquy out..."

"I slaved away for an entire 15 minutes."

"... obviously just for my benefit. Thank you; don't worry, I heard every word and I am greatly impressed by your mastery of the English language." He shook his head slowly while taking a deep breath, "And you say Westergard and Saroni put their blessing on this travesty of my time?"

"And it would seem to be with prejudice. Roxy, who drew the short straw, will accompany you in order to herd the 'lil chilen' into your waiting arms."

"How many of these blessed community resources am I to see?"

"I called the school and they're projecting around 48 to 50."

"Okey dokey, I'll get the Wood's lamp, a couple boxes of gloves and a full body condom."

"A what? Did you say full body condom? Remember where you're going Mr. Parker."

"Apparently I will be descending into the ring of hell where parents wished that they had bought condoms years ago."

"You, Ben Parker, are without fail destined for a fiery afterlife."

"You, Callie Jansen, are not the first to voice that opinion."

Ben knocked on Callie's window as he was passing the office and before he had passed she was flinging the door open. "Where have you been Ben? I've got a patient roomed for you."

"Completing your "plum" assignment in the land where lice fear to tread."

"What does that mean?"

"Not one. Not a single louse, nit or vague hint that any louse had stopped to graze upon a pediatric scalp."

Callie grimaced at the thought, "So what took you so long?"

"Yeaahhh," he drew it out sarcastically, "About those 48 or 50 smiley faced, innocent, little elementary school students begging to cooperate with me. Try 84 squirming, little banshees half of whom want to see a live louse and the other half crying hysterically out of fear that they have lice. Some of the whiny little hellions scratched their heads so vehemently that they had a couple of the teachers scratching their heads and demanding to be examined...And wipe that smug smile off of your face, Callie. From you even a feeble attempt at a sympathetic look would be more appropriate."

Now she was openly laughing, "Oh you poor man. Are you in pain? Were you physically assaulted or just emotionally traumatized? Ohhh, the horror. The horror."

Ben could not help himself but laugh along, "Truly an apocalyptic event Colonel Kurtz. Okay, what's my afternoon look like?"

Ben had just reviewed Durinda Dunkle's chart, knocked softly and entered the exam room.

"It's about time." There was a definite edge to her voice. He heard the comment as he was closing the door. Instead of responding Ben chose to ignore the implied reprimand and walked over to where she sat. The small exam room contained an exam table, a nondescript chair and a four legged wheeled stool topped with a swiveling cushion. She had chosen the nondescript chair. He introduced himself and she weakly accepted his extended hand. She wore several rings, none of which indicated that she was married and both wrists bore precious metal bracelets.

Ms. Dunkle, 38, was heavy and in the current vernacular, fluffy. Her jet black hair, cut in a page boy, only accentuated her moon face and jowly neck. The purple silk scarf that she was wearing to perhaps hide her neck was tied too tightly and only caused the skin folds of her neck to be more pronounced. She was outfitted in various shades of purple. A blouse fastened one button shy of the collar, sweater, skirt, belt and sharp toed, moderately heeled shoes that appeared much too small. He did not want to hazard a guess as to what hand tool had been employed to layer on her makeup. There was a smug look on her face that telegraphed to Ben that she thought that she knew something that he didn't. Ben found her perfume to be more overpowering than Myra's. Was she attempting to camouflage an as yet undetected odor?

Having seated himself on the stool, Ben opened her chart once again to the lab/imaging section. "Is it Miss or Mrs. Dunkle?"

"Mzzzzzz; that is Ms. Dunkle."

"Ms. Dunkle, I understand that you are here today to review your laboratory results."

"Exactly. That was the intent. In and out; not being double booked, shuffled about or left waiting for hours." Ben was about to interject an apology, however, was not allowed to interrupt. "This is my day off and you people have trifled with and wasted enough of my time so let's get this done." He was about to start when she pulled several pages from her handbag, a plus sized leather bag sufficient to stow a large breadbox or several weapons with ammunition, and waved the pages at him, "I had the nurse make me a couple of copies."

"You would like me to review them with you, correct?"

"She was bitingly snide, "If not, that would defeat the whole purpose of the appointment, would it not?"

He was having some trouble with her abrasiveness. "Your lipid panel or cholesterol…"

"I know that."

"Your lipid panel results are high across the board. The triglycerides, simply sug…"

"I know what they are."

"The triglycerides are so elevated that the LDL or bad cholesterol cannot be calculated…"

"I can see all of that. What about the glucose?"

"Your fasting glucose is 158 and you did state that you had been fasting for…"

"Yes, I was, so go on."

"Have you been diagnosed with diabetes or have any close blood relatives been diagnosed…"

"Diabetes? No. I don't have Diabetes, plain and simple. It's possible I may have inadvertently put some sweetener in my coffee that morning but I am not prone to making that type of mistake."

"So, what is it Ms. Dunkle; fasting or non-fasting?"

"Don't be getting snippy with me Dr. Parker."

"I should remind you once more that I am a physician assistant not a medical doctor, Ms. Dunkle."

"Maybe I'm talking to the wrong person."

"Perhaps you are Ms. Dunkle. You had an opportunity to see Dr. Saroni this morning and turned it down. "

"I had something important come up; besides, Dr Saroni isn't on my recommendation list."

"Let me hazard a guess here. You have several other stops to make during the week, correct?"

"That's an interesting but invasive question."

"I would say that it is a reasonable question given that your lab tests were ordered by a Physician in Sunnvale, you live in Bedlam, work in Wynot and have avoided filling out the health history intake form that every patient is given."

"You are somewhat of a smartass, aren't you?"

"A thorough smartass Ms. Dunkle. Now back to your labs. When we see cholesterol, triglyceride and glucose numbers as we see here," he pointed at the lab results on the page, "combined with a blood pressure of 162/98, a heart rate of 96, and with your weight and BMI, Body Mass Index, substantially elevated, you are at a much greater risk for developing Metabolic Syndrome, diabetes and future cardiac disease or events. I also need to make you aware of your TSH, thyroid stimulating hormone, being slightly elevated which, should also be monitored." Ms. Dunkle had made no attempt to interrupt, which surprised him. "One quick question if I may; what line of work are you in Ms. Dunkle?"

"What has that got to do with our appointment?"

"Mere curiosity. Please; humor me."

"I'm the new manager for office technology supplies and services at Office Grande in Wynot. I was transferred here two months ago to address personnel issues and marketing strategies."

Oh Christ, he thought, by this time her employees are either on the brink of mass exodus or plotting a coup de tat. Time to wrap it up; I don't really need to take any more of this crap today. "Is there anything else that I can do for you today Ms. Dunkle?" A polite and innocuous way of allowing her to gracefully extricate herself.

"Could you take a quick look at this?"

Before Ben could answer she had slipped her right arm out of her sweater and held it straight up beside her head revealing a sleeveless blouse and her right arm pit. An angry red, raised lump about the size of a quarter with a central whitish dot was evident; the lump was circumscribed with moderate redness approximately an inch in width. Ben hazarded a guess that by the considerable unshaven stubble that the area was very tender. He began a series of questions; when did she first notice it, is it painful, has it been draining, have you ever had something like this before?

"Yes, it's frickin' painful and why all the questions? Just tell me what it is and how to treat it."

He reached for some exam gloves.

"What are you doing?"

"I'm preparing to examine your lesion."

"Not on your life buster. You're not laying a hand on me let alone this thing you're calling a 'lesion,'" said with great distain. "It's painful enough without you probing around."

Ben replaced the exam gloves back into the box, "I highly recommend that if you are contemplating seeking a second opinion regarding your infection that you do it much sooner rather than later. He arose from his stool, "If that's all Ms. Dunkle I'll escort you to the main hallway."

"I'm sure that you have time for one more thing." Ms. Dunkle bent forward and with some difficulty and awkwardness began to remove or rather pry off a shoe. There were noticeable attempts to silence or stifle the grunts accompanying her efforts. Even with panty hose the shoe was wedged on tightly and the removal effort reminded him of leveraging a truck tire off of its rim. Ben knew that the closest tire iron was out in his truck. The shoe was suddenly freed and sheer momentum almost tipped her forward out of the chair. Internally he cringed at the sight of her toes; crossed, severely bent and malformed, and he imagined them literally screaming in pain as they were being crammed into the fashionably pointed shoes. Oh, lord, the price of vanity and trend setting footwear.

"What would you suggest for my toes?"

Ben pondered for a moment but then without hesitation said, "You might start by wearing sensible shoes."

Her response was near venomous, "You're saying that I'm not sensible?"

He was being led to slaughter yet persisted by upping the ante. "I'm not implying that at all, however, you have hammer, claw and mallet toes that often develop from wearing shoes that are ill fitting; too small or too narrow or a combination of both. Over a period of time your toes may become disfigured. I suggest that you purchase shoes that a salesperson has correctly fitted for you and schedule an appointment with a podiatrist."

She was silent and he surmised that additional steam was preparing to erupt from an internal geyser. Her face was a grim mask as she repositioned herself to force her shoe on.

"May I get you the name of a podiatrist in Wynot Ms. Dunkle?"

Through gritted teeth she stifled a grunt and then a forced, "If you wouldn't mind, that would be fine."

"You've avoided addressing the probable infection in your axilla so are you planning on seeing another medical provider to treat it?"

Durinda glared at him, "I haven't decided."

"While you're deciding I could write an antibiotic prescription for you to at least give the treatment a jump start. What say you?"

She had a wary look in her eye, "I suppose that would be alright but just an antibiotic mind you."

"I'll be right back." Ben left her struggling with the shoe, positive that if he ventured too close or made an offer to help that in all probability he would be struck forcibly on or about the head with said shoe.

Ms. Dunkle had successfully levered her shoe back on without incurring further injury and adjusted her clothing back to a normal state. Ben handed her the business card for a podiatrist in Wynot and then the prescription for Ciprofloxin adding some verbal information regarding its use and possible side effects, "I knew that; don't treat me like a moron."

"Actually I have a responsibility to depart this information for every prescription that I provide; moron or not." Surprisingly she did not react. "Someone needs to examine that lesion more closely and obtain a culture to determine what pathogen is growing. Whether you choose to come back here or not I would strongly suggest that you discuss with some provider how you should start dealing with your weight, glucose levels and cholesterol issues. If you choose to return I would again strongly suggest that you do so with some expediency. Either I, Marni Cappelletti or Dr. Saroni would be more than willing to see you."

301

Ben had no expectations that she would respond positively or return at a later date, however, was surprised when she said, "Thank you. I'll give it some consideration." Then Durinda Dunkle loudly and heavily clicked her heels out of the exam room and down the hallway. Ben felt a pang of sympathy for her toes.

He saw Callie advancing toward his office door, "So how did things go with Miss Dunkle?"

"That's 'Mzzzzzzz' Dunkle to be sure. She's doctor shopping."

"Doctor shopping?"

"Yep, doctor shopping, looking for a new primary care provider…" Ben sighed, "…and pity the poor provider that she finally decides on."

"I've got one more patient roomed for you." Callie anticipated Ben's next question, "A chief complaint of a non-productive cough for a week. No fever. Vitals look good. She was scheduled this morning but refused to see the doctor; said that she would come back to see you this afternoon. So there ya go Ben, you're building a fan club."

"Who is it?"

Callie responded coyly, " Daphne Donner."

Ben jumped up, grabbed his stethoscope and said, "Don't you dare move. You stay right here in case I need you." He gave her a "don't try to pull a fast one on me" squint as he brushed by. Quietly he knocked on the door and warily entered. Miss Donner was sitting on the exam table, hands folded on her lap. She was wearing a clinic gown and staring at the wall opposite where she was sitting. As she turned toward the door a broad smile, bordering on the seductive, enveloped her face. Ben was certainly not immune to attractive women with shapely bodies yet, knew that his admiration for the female anatomy and allure was strictly limited to outside of work.

Granted, Daphne was an attractive woman, however, her years of smoking and sun worshiping had prematurely aged her skin. When she smiled the wrinkles and crow feet of her face were more pronounced.

"Hello, Dr. Ben." Her voice was always slightly raspy, husky also worked, due to her smoking. She kind of shimmied all over when she greeted him and arched her back accentuating her bosom.

"Good afternoon, Miss Donner. It dawned on him that the gown was being worn backwards. Clinic gowns were designed to be worn open and tied off at the back; Daphne was wearing hers open to the front, loosely tied and barely covering her well-endowed breasts. He noted that her blouse and bra were lying on the nearby chair. Holding up his right forefinger, a motion indicating "one minute please," he also verbalized the same thought aloud. He backed out of the room and found Callie in his door way bracing herself with a hand on opposite sides of the frame. She had an innocent smile but impish eyes.

"Did you set me up Callie?" His question sounded stern.

The smile disappeared. "What do you mean Ben?"

"Did you have her remove her shirt and bra and put her into a gown, backwards in fact?"

Callie appeared genuinely shocked by the accusation, "No way in hell Ben. I like to tease you some but I wouldn't do that to you. I realize that Daphne has you on her need to do list but no, I did not set you up. Apparently Miss Donner has upped her game."

Ben had recognized his overreaction and now sounded contrite, "I am sorry, Callie. I might be a little testy this afternoon, however, you did not deserve that. Please go in and have Miss Donner get dressed. Assure her that I, rather, make that we, are positive that her breasts are spectacular but to evaluate her for a cough I will not need to view or come close to touching her bosom. When she's once again dressed please poke your head out of the door give me a nod and remain in the room until the exam is over."

Callie nodded her head then arched an eyebrow as she grinned, "Just can't trust yourself now can you Ben Parker?"

"Get the hell out of my sight before a file a harassment complaint." He was grinning as well.

"Good afternoon Ben. I'm glad that we could finally find a time convenient for both of us to meet. How has your day gone so far?"

"Swimmingly. I couldn't have asked for better." Ben did his utmost to sound upbeat rather than reveal his lurking sarcasm.

"Before we address why you wanted a meeting I would like to inform you that I have twice met with the board, once last Tuesday and again today, and we have unanimously determined that you own no culpability for either of the complaints registered against you. Social services, Dr. Saroni and Heidi Lafevbre have together discussed the issues surrounding Mrs. Haugen and I have met with Mr. Light Feather and Mr. Strong Tree to review and reinforce Bedlam Medical Center policies and regulations. That concludes that piece of business."

Westergard picked up a large document sized white envelope from atop his desk, stood and reached over his desk extending it to Ben. "Which brings us to my second order of business…" Ben stood and grasped the proffered envelope thinking that it probably contained his discharge paperwork, "…The board and I are aware that your first year's contract would be ending on May fourth so the board authorized extending your contract for another year. Everyone is happy, completely satisfied with your work, work ethic and engagement to the community. So review it and we can meet to discuss any concerns that you may have."

"Dr. Saroni was also completely satisfied?"

Westergard's smile never wavered, "Yes he is."

"He actually said that?"

"Dr. Saroni said that your work was adequate, more than adequate for the most part."

"Adequate?"

"More than adequate. You know Dr. Saroni and his penchant for the art of understatement and minimal verbiage."

Ben nodded as if affirming Westergard's unrealistic summation of Saroni's tendencies; if he were to assign a penchant for Dr. Saroni it would be the art of inconsistency and deceit. As if reciprocating Ben pulled a sealed standard size white envelope from the inside pocket of his white lab coat and reached over the desk offering it to Westergard. Westergard, who was slightly hesitant as if being served with a subpoena, accepted the envelope. He sat down and asked, "What's this Ben?"

"My resignation letter."

His eyes widened and with the exception of his lips forming a thin line there were no other signs of reaction. From the top draw of his desk he produced a slim silver letter opener and slit open the envelope.

February 02, 2004
Administrator, Mr. Jonathon Westergard
Bedlam Medical Center
210 North Fort Street
Bedlam, Montana, 59227

Dear Mr. Westergard,

I am submitting my resignation as a Practicing Physician Assistant Certified, employed at the Bedlam Medical Center, 210 North Fort Street, Bedlam Montana, 59227. Per my employment agreement, I am providing the required ninety (90) calendar days (plus) notice prior to ending my employment, effectively starting today, February 02, 2004. My employment agreement ends on May 04, 2004. I am submitting for five (5) PTO days preceding my last day of employment, therefore my last working day at the Bedlam Medical Center will be Thursday, April 29, 2004.

I thank you, the staff of Bedlam Medical Center, and the Bedlam Hospital District Board of Directors for the opportunity of having provided medical services to the community and its citizens.

Sincerely,
Ben G. Parker PA-C

Ben observed no discernible change in Westergard's expression as he refolded the letter and slid it back inside the envelope. He blew out a slow breath as he set the envelope down on his desk and did not say, "You caught me off guard," however; Ben thought that he detected a momentary downturn at the corners of his mouth. "I am sorry to hear this Ben. I thought that the Board's affirmation by extending your contract indicated that we were all pleased with you and your work."

"I am pleased and appreciative of the Board's vote of confidence and the offer of an extension of my working agreement, however, that is not enough to change my mind."

"If you don't mind me asking; what would be enough for you to change your mind?"

"Working with a Physician that believes in a team approach to patient care and provides mentorship at a higher level than the less than adequate support I've received from Dr. Saroni."

Westergard frowned, "Examples please. I'm not aware of Dr. Saroni being any less than fully engaged in supporting you and your practice."

"I'm not going to sit here and categorically list the problems I have had with the doctor. I've been in to see you on several occasions over the past nine months to discuss his behavior towards me, my colleague Marni Capelletti, and other hospital personnel so I can't accept that you were unaware of the problems."

"Apparently you did not register a strong enough complaint. You could have come in more often or perhaps been more adamant, and presented evidence."

"If that were truly the case I could have been in at least once a week. Dr. Saroni is not about to change and obviously given his new three year contract he has no impetus to alter his behavior. The politics of this hospital appear to be well entrenched and I choose to pursue my career at a different locale."

"Have you secured another position elsewhere?"

"No. To date I have not initiated a search for another position."

"I will give you a few days to review the new contract and reconsider before I inform the Board of your resignation."

"Thank you. I will review the contract offer; however, I do not believe that it will sway my decision."

"Surely that's your prerogative Ben. I will keep today's meeting confidential until the end of the week or when you return a signed contract."

Ben stood, walked to the side of Westergard's desk and offered his hand. Westergard shook it with his usual lack of enthusiasm and Ben exited the office.

Dictating patient encounters was always a tedious task and though he tried his hardest not to procrastinate, on most days he found himself talking into a recorder after clinic hours had ended. Today was no different as he sat facing the wall to his right reconstructing his clinic appointment with Durinda Dunkle and recording it for the transcriptionist to type into posterity. He was close to completion when he sensed someone behind him, shut off the recorder and spun his chair around. Callie was standing in his doorway and a quick glance at the wall clock told him that it was 1715 hours; the clinic was officially closed for the day.

"What the hell is going on? You resigned. You quit." She presented a mixture of anger and disappointment.

"Where did you hear that?" As he was thinking "Why am I hearing this?"

"Gossip central, where else? Is it true?"

Myra, of course. "No comment."

"And then again, five minutes later, from Heidi Lafevbre."

So much for the promise of confidentiality. Obviously, Westergard was a man untrue to his word; he and every other fucking politician that ever crawled out from under a rock. Fool me once shame on you, fool me twice shame on me. "No comment. I promise that we will talk tomorrow."

"Tomorrow is your day off."

"I'll make it a point to come in early before I go on call."

Callie turned around and left. Ben swiveled about, fumed for a minute, and continued his dictating.

Ben punched some numbers into the desk phone and waited for an answer.

"Hello."

"Marni, the deed is done; just like I discussed with you on Saturday."

"Oh, Ben," Marni sounded sad, "Are you okay?"

"I'm good but I'll call you tomorrow. I'll buy you lunch and fill you in then. Okay?"

"Okay, I'll talk to you tomorrow. Bye."

"Hi, Dad."

"Well?"

"See you on May 3."

"I'll leave the light on for you."

"Hello, this is Lindsay." Her voice was upbeat, welcoming.

"Hi, Lindsay, it's Ben."

"Ben! Oh good, I was just thinking about you."

"Lindsay, hear me out first and then we can talk about it." He took a quick breath and launched into it, "I hate to say this, so I'm just going to say it; they're not going to let me loose at Easter to come visit you but what does your date book look like for the first week of May? I just had my schedule open up…"

TRUTHS

"You might be interested in these Ben," Myrna handed Ben several postcards, "or have you already seen them?"

He shuffled through them rather quickly, "No I haven't," and then started over, examining the pictures more closely and reading the messages on the back. "These are from Mr. Smythe aren't they, our wandering escapee?"

Myrna laughed, "That's what everyone believes. That old scallywag is having some fun being on the lamb."

"When did these show up?"

"Myra dropped them off yesterday. She said they were in the hospital's post office box."

"They just showed up yesterday?" He shuffled through the cards again scanning the backs, "These were mailed every three or four weeks or so since he escaped."

"Eloped."

"Right, eloped. Since he pulled his disappearing act."

"Scuttlebutt has it that Kaplanic, the postmaster, had so many complaints lodged against him that the district finally sent investigators to the Bedlam post office and they found stacks of undelivered mail and magazines. Currently he's on leave."

"Couldn't have happened to a nicer guy."

"Agreed."

"Myrna, did you take a close look at these postcards? · Besides the short generic messages on the back?"

Ben handed them back as she replied, "They were all pictures of ships or such."

"These are not new postcards. He probably collected them when vacationing over the years. These are not just ships; they're WW II era submarines or their conning towers that are scattered around the United States at museums or memorials. Look here…" As she fanned them out Ben pointed, "…Pearl Harbor, Alabama, San Francisco, Michigan, Cleveland, Maine, Connecticut."

She was nodding with each reference.

"I'm of the opinion that he was a submariner in the war."

"I knew he was a Navy vet but that was the extent of it."

"And look at the post marks; they are all postmarked Great Falls. Mr. Smythe probably filled them out before he left and one of his cronies is mailing them in Draught or Compton or some other small town near here. Everything in this area is routed to Great Falls first."

"Jesus, that old fart thought of everything. I wonder where he ended up."

"Hopefully someplace that he's happily baiting a hook, sipping a cocktail and spending his cash."

"Amen to that. Ah oh, here comes our favorite doctor. How come he never puts his smiley face on anymore when you're around Ben?"

"Has anyone ever told you that you have a truly evil streak under that twisted smile?"

Dr. Saroni stopped at the counter, opened a hospital patient chart to the Lab/Imaging section and looked to Myrna with a dour expression, "Why no labs?"

"The ER labs are in there but the morning labs are not completed yet."

The doctor flipped back to the Admission History and Physical and looked disapprovingly at Ben, "You write note. You told to dictate and you write anyway. Insubordinate. No one can read writing."

"I've never had anyone complain about my handwriting being illegible."

Myrna chimed in, "I think Ben has very nice handwriting; easy to read."

The doctor's scowl could have stripped flesh off the bone. Myrna smiled back sweetly. The doctor turned back to Ben, "Dictate only. You must obey my order."

Ben redirected the topic, "Would you care to hear about our patient?"

Saroni picked up the chart and headed to the hospital hallway at a brisk pace.

"I would take that as a no Ben." The two of them followed though not at the same pace so as not to give the impression that they were too excited to be associated with the foul tempered doctor. Dr. Saroni had entered the room. Ben a few steps behind and followed by Myrna who had resisted Ben's attempts to usher her in before him. The patient, Mr. Kurt Gunderson, was sitting up, the head of the bed locked somewhere between 70 and 80 degrees. His color was much improved from the pasty white of last night when Ben had admitted him with an acute urinary tract infection and dehydration. Mr. Gunderson had a history of treatment for prostate cancer. An unruly shock of white hair topped his head and several days of grey stubble covered his cheeks and jaw line. For an 83 year old man he was maintaining a relatively good physical bearing. Saroni stood ramrod stiff, his hands clutching the patient chart behind his lower back. Mr. Gunderson was staring at him, hands calmly folded on his abdomen.

"And just who the hell are you?" Mr. Gunderson's face was devoid of expression.

Seemingly nonplussed, Dr. Saroni responded pompously, "I am Dr. Saroni. I am hospital chief of medicine. I am your doctor."

Turning his head towards Ben who was standing behind and to the doctor's right, Mr. Gunderson momentarily frowned and then replied, "No, no I don't believe that you are. I already have myself a fine doctor." He motioned towards Ben. To Saroni he continued, "So you can go."

Dr. Saroni's back stiffened almost imperceptivity, his lower lip moving up and down mimicking a guppy, "I am only doctor in hospital and you my patient. You feeling improved?"

"Let's start over." Mr. Gunderson smiled and said, "Just who the fuck are you and why is your English so fucking bad?"

Ben looked left, behind and past Saroni's back to Myrna whose lips were clamped shut and eyes wide open in surprise.

Saroni's voice quivered and a level of shrillness was evident, "I am Dr. Saroni. I run hospital. Parker not your doctor. I am the doctor and you must listen." His attempt at an authoritarian tone apparently did not command the effect that the doctor had anticipated.

"Well if you are running this show then it's a piss poor excuse of a hospital and if they got the likes of you running it they are in deep trouble. Find me another place to go or send me home." Mr. Gunderson closed his eyes to end the conversation. The doctor whirled around and Ben watched as he stormed out of the room, steam literally rising from the top of his head. That's when Ben noticed Heidi Lafevbre standing within the door way. She immediately exited. Mr. Gunderson opened his eyes, winked at Ben and smiled at Myrna.

Myrna said dryly, "Well that went well."

Ben directed his next comment to Mr. Gunderson, "If it was your intent to alienate Dr. Saroni and regain some sense of control of your current situation then you did a bang up job on the alienation aspect."

"Mr. Parker you are my physician. I've heard enough about Saroni to know that I will not allow him to be in charge of my care and that his arrogance and position holds no water with me."

"I need to remind you that I am a physician assistant, Mr. Gunderson."

"Mere semantics, my boy."

"Excuse us for a minute sir; we'll be right back." They exited the room and immediately ran into Dr. Saroni waiting in the hallway.

"You will transfer him out." Saroni started to walk away.

"You have no medical basis to transfer him. He's…"

"OUT! GONE! He will not stay."

"I consulted with Mr. Gunderson's urologist, Dr. Abernathy and he agreed with my proposed admission and treatment plan"

"You not call me."

"I did call you and you did not answer. I left messages with both your home and cell phone services."

Dr. Saroni ignored Ben, "Call urologist. Transfer patient."

"No, we have no reason to transfer him. We are perfectly capable of caring for him here."

"You insolent. You insubordinate. You not hear me. OUT! Send him out." Saroni walked away down the hospital corridor, Ben and Myrna headed the opposite way back to the nurses' station and Heidi Lafevbre stood rooted in stunned silence.

Myrna stood within the nurses' station and Ben leaned on his elbows atop the counter. "Myrna, you've lived in the area for many years; what do you know about Mr. Gunderson?"

"To start with the man has more money than God, though you wouldn't know it to look at or talk to him." Ben could not hide his surprise. Myrna motioned to the lobby with a sideways motion of her head. Turning in that direction Ben discovered that Heidi had caught Dr. Saroni in the lobby and they were having an animated conversation. "I'm sure that Heidi is attempting to convince our doctor that transferring Mr. Gunderson is not in the hospital's best interest."

Ben's curiosity was piqued, "And why is that Myrna?"

"Because every year an anonymous donor gives the hospital $150,000.00 dollars and everyone or at least I thought that everyone knew that the donor is Mr. Gunderson."

"So if the donation is anonymous how do you know that it's Mr. Gunderson?"

Myrna pointed a finger at Myra's office, "Because neither Westergard nor Myra can keep their mouths shut."

Ben thought to himself, "As I also had the unfortunate experience of learning." Out of the corner of his eye Ben noticed someone passing by the far end of the nurse's station. He turned in time to see Norman Strong Tree and their eyes met and held. Strong Tree's face

remained neutral but his eyes bored into Ben expressing
distain. Ben assumed an impassive demeanor and his eye
responded, "I've got you on my radar." As he walked
Strong Tree adjusted the strap on the duffle filled with Mr
Light Feather's dirty laundry, and Ben's gaze held on him
as he continued to the doorway and exited the building
Turning back to Myrna Ben came eye to eye with Dwight.

"Hiya doc, how's tricks today?"

"Starting off rather acrimoniously Dwight."

"Saroni on the warpath again? What else is new?"

Dr. Saroni ended his conversation with Heidi and
approached the nurses' station. Based on his scowl they
determined that he was not a happy camper. He literally
spat out, "Patient stay. No transfer, he is yours. You
patient." The doctor pivoted and moved off towards the
clinic hallway.

"Alright, now with that settled, Myrna you were
giving me some insight to Mr. Gunderson."

"Dwight is the person to ask Ben. He is a walking
encyclopedia of the people of Bedlam."

Ben turned to Dwight who merely shrugged his
shoulders in response, "How is it Dwight that you know so
many details about so many people in this town?"

Dwight let out a hearty laugh and then lowered his
voice to a more conspiratorial level, even though Myrna
and Ben were the only people within earshot. "I'm the
janitor Ben; a virtual nobody. The silent guy always in the
background, present but not really there. People talk and
most of them can't help but to talk about themselves or
their families or their neighbors or the guy or gal from
across town that they never met but screwed their
neighbor's spouse or was arrested again for drunk driving
or blew the kid's college fund in Vegas or when Dad died
buried him with his collection of *Playboy* magazines and a

bottle of his favorite hooch. They talk to someone and that someone has to top that story and so on and so on. People talk and I listen only they don't realize that I'm listening. I'm the invisible man who has astounding hearing and a steel trap memory."

"That my friend explains a great deal. Is there anything about Mr. Gunderson that you think would be pertinent to know?"

"Mr. Gunderson is a straight shooter, a truly nice person. I know that he has to be tough as nails but he is smart, good natured, a sharp businessman and stand-up guy for the community. He grew up in Bedlam or at least just outside of town on the family farm. His best friend was Stan Gephardt. They enlisted together in the Marine Corp just after Pearl Harbor; both fought and were seriously wounded on Guadalcanal. After the war they went to college at Montana State and afterwards went into business together. They invested in new harvesting technology, Canola Oil and buying and leasing railroad grain and tank cars. Gephardt died in the eighties as a result of his war wounds.

Gunderson's granddaughter went on a high school trip to Washington D.C. and snuck out with some classmates one night. She got separated and was assaulted and raped. The chaperone responsible for the girl was Mayor Boyle's wife who was passed out drunk in her hotel room. Mrs. Gunderson died of cancer years ago when an impaired doctor working at this hospital treated her for something that she did not have and missed the cancer all together. When it was finally diagnosed in Great Falls it was far too late for treatment. The doctor, who did not disclose a prior treatment for drug addiction in another state, was Boyle's cousin and was initially hired when Boyle sat on the hospital board. Mr. Gunderson's son in

317

law, a nice guy in his own right but very naïve, was set on making his own fortune without Gunderson's help. He unfortunately became involved neck deep in one of Krum's scams, lost all of their money and ultimately was going to take the fall for Krum's fraud. He committed suicide. For all of his tragedies and losses Mr. Gunderson keeps on going. He must be up for sainthood because a lesser man would have killed Krum and Boyle. Does that help at all Ben?"

Ben was speechless. He found it astonishing that anyone could remember that much information about a relative stranger and that the man in room four had suffered so many traumas in his life. His voice was subdued, "I had no idea Dwight, no clue that he carried that degree of burden. Thank you for the information; tragic as it is it might help."

Myrna had been silent and now quietly spoke, "Someday I hope to hear that Krum and Boyle met their demises in an excruciatingly painful manner. Dwight, you need to keep being the fly on the wall, it's a gift for the rest of us."

"So what's the story doc, are you shipping me out?"

"No such luck Mr. Gunderson. Like it or not you're stuck here with us."

Gunderson let out a low chortle, "You might have second thoughts about that in short order. Now then, what's your opinion of this Saroni fella? I'm of the mind that he's a dyed in the wool asshole, excuse my French." It must be a generational thing Ben thought because his father also had a proclivity for disparaging the French.

Ben viewed him curiously, "I had the opinion that you just met him."

"Correct but I've got ears. "Why do you think I called ahead to see who was on call?"

"I wasn't aware that you had."

"I may come across as a senile old geezer but there are a few functioning brain cells left."

"I don't doubt that for a minute."

"Besides, I talked with Salty and he spoke highly of you."

Ben was genuinely surprised, "You knew Salty?"

"Oh yeah, most of us area veterans grew up together or at least keep in touch."

"I'm sorry, I never saw you visiting."

"I didn't. Salty and I spoke on the phone a few times. I was in Colorado Springs during November and December visiting with my family."

"Salty was a good person; I miss him."

"Me too. He was a rascal, that one."

The two sat in silence.

"We're losing some good ones and the town just can't afford it." He sounded weary.

Ben treaded lightly, "How so Mr. Gunderson?"

"Growing up here in a small town you always had a couple of bullies and assholes, pardon my French, but every town did. For the most part you knew who they were and ignored them though once in a while they might push someone too far and a fist fight might ensue. People were more likely to take responsibility for their lives and actions. Over the years the number of miscreants seems to have grown and they have become more sophisticated in their forms of malfeasance. The townspeople are now less likely to protest the affronts and hold the perpetrators accountable. Ambivalence and apathy have come to permeate society and I am as guilty as the next man in my failure to arise to the occasion and to take positive action to rectify the situation. Apoplexy runs rampant."

Without knocking Heidi Lafevbre swept into the room and unceremoniously insinuated herself between Ben and Mr. Gunderson. "Good morning Mr. Gunderson, I'm Heidi Lafevbre the Director of Nursing here at the hospital and please consider me to be your direct liaison to Mr. Westergard our administrator. Is there anything that I can do to help, to make your stay with us more comfortable?"

Staring directly up into her face, into her eyes, he bluntly responded, "You Miss DON could start by brushing up on your manners. You interrupted the conversation I was having with Mr. Parker."

Ben could not see her face, however, definitely noticed the slight recoil of her body, " I, I am sorry, very sorry Mr. Gunderson, I…"

The old man held up his hand, palm out, to stop her and rotated his head and eyes to the rolling bedside table to his left. Ben followed his eyes as did Heidi to the almost untouched food tray that remained on the table. Something with the consistency of solidifying mush filled one bowl. A plastic bottle containing prune juice remained unopened. On a small plate a bran muffin sat with an indentation in the top as if someone had probed attempting to establish its degree of freshness. The water glass was empty.

"A sorry excuse for breakfast wouldn't you say doc?" His eyes reverted back to Heidi; he snorted and pointed at the tray, "Gruel and unusual treatment." Ben could not help but smile.

"I will get you whatever you would like to eat Mr. Gunderson."

Ben added, "Please, let's try to keep it relatively bland and see how well it's tolerated. We don't want to roil things up since we finally got his gut quieted down."

"Like it not Heidi, let's go with what the doc says."

Ben thought that he could see her back and shoulders stiffen.

"One last thing Heidi?"

"Of course Mr. Gunderson."

Kurt Gunderson brought attention to the entire room with a sweeping flourish of his arm that reminded Ben of how cold, austere and inhospitable all of the patient rooms looked and felt.

"Miss Lafevbre, I've lived in foxholes with better accommodations."

Heidi bowed her head, "I'm sorry to interrupt your conversation with Mr. Parker. I will return with a more appetizing meal and to discuss your other concerns." She turned heel and briskly walked out never having acknowledged Ben's presence.

Mr. Gunderson winked and said, "Do you have time to talk a while Mr. Parker?"

"I do Mr. Gunderson."

"Kurt."

"Ben."

"Pull up a chair Ben and set a spell. I'm sure that Nurse Ratchet won't be back for a while."

Depression. Depression. Depression. Depression. Ben looked up from reviewing his patient schedule; his face contorted in faux anguish and pleadingly asked Callie, "Is this it? Is this all you have for me Callie? Has my practice now been regulated to a single one word medical complaint?"

Without skipping a beat Callie swung her chair in order to face him and leaned back sweeping her hair behind her head with both hands as she responded without show of mercy, "Yes. Yes Ben this is your lot in life. Your destiny or fate or whatever catch phrase that you choose to describe it. We welcomed you here with open arms, invited you in nourished and supported you, shared your pain and empathized with you through your darkest hours as you navigated the denigration and insanities set forth by Dr Saroni. Then, at the least provocation you throw up your hands, toss in the towel, turn tail, and quit."

Ben was stunned into silence. That hurt, but in quick retrospect he realized that he probably had that coming.

"Oh for Christ sakes Ben." She was suddenly laughing, "Don't look so down in the mouth; I'm only kidding. Honestly, most of us are truly surprised that you hadn't unleashed a torrent of foul language or taken Saroni out to the maintenance shed and pummeled him senseless with those oversized hands of yours."

"You apparently have never witnessed the occasional blue cloud that forms over my house, truck or at other arbitrarily selected spots out of the public eye."

"Blue clouds?"

"You never heard of turning the air blue?"

"No."

"Ask your dad; I'll bet he's done it a time or two. I'm sorry Callie if I let you guys down but I will not subject myself to the potential of three more years of Saroni. I've attempted to mitigate the abuse; however, it's far too early in my career to sail on without benefit of a mentor with a working rudder."

"A mentor with a working rudder, that's definitely not Saroni."

"How about a rudderless mentor or maybe a mentoring rudder. Yes, I like that, a mentoring rudder; someone to guide you in the right direction. Saroni himself would appear rudderless, therefore unable to guide either him or me. Think of it as free word association. I like to make shit up that someone out there is bound to believe."

Callie just shook her head, "We already knew that about you Ben. Just to change the subject, you do remember that today is Psyche Friday, right?"

"Yeah, I know. Winter is now in its fifth month and unrelenting. People have cabin fever, seasonal depression, some with real depressive issues and I'm starting to think that some have designer depression."

Callie lifted and arched an eyebrow.

"I'm beginning to think that some of the lonely people that I see here are not clinically depressed but are genuinely in need of someone's attention, so they research various signs and symptoms to create their own personalized form of depression. Still others, because of some twisted reasoning want to claim depression in order to commiserate with friends who are actively being treated for depression. It's a strange new world out there."

"And thankfully Ben they are all yours. You do have a rather unique way of interpreting people Ben. Now, if you hadn't noticed I did toss in a sore throat and a skin infection."

"I hadn't got that far, but thank you."

"The kid with the skin infection was seen two weeks ago by Saroni. His mother has given permission for him to be seen without her being present and she was adamant that he was not to be scheduled again with the doctor."

"I promise not to gloat.

As Ben entered the exam room a young man, the patient chart indicated 16 years of age, immediately sprang up from his chair. He stood almost at attention in a buttoned down Navy blue chamois work shirt tucked into

323

clean blue jeans. His cowboy boots had the low heels and rounded toes of a steer wrestler or working hand. His eyes met Ben's. An expectant look filled a face dotted with a moderate case of teenage acne.

"Good afternoon, Paden McCabe. I'm Ben Parker the physician assistant on duty. I understand that you have an infection on your fingers that doesn't want to clear up. Let's have a look young man." Ben pulled on exam gloves as Paden held out his right hand. Several raised nodules on his index and middle fingers were evident; blister like lesions taut with cream colored pus and fluid. A couple of lesions on the index finger had begun to flatten, turn darker and were weeping fluid. He examined the rest of the young man's fingers and then his hands and forearms. "Have you noticed any pustules on other parts of your body Paden? The fact that it started on your forefinger or index finger and several days later appeared on the middle finger may indicate the possibility that it may spread elsewhere through direct or inadvertent contact.

Quite honestly I have never seen this type of infection. To date it's been resistant to two different antibiotics so I'm going to retrace your history and see what might have been missed." Ben spent the next 12 minutes taking a detailed history; the days prior to and after the infection broke out. "The only inordinate exposure or contact might be with the sheep that are lambing." He vaguely remembered some references that his friend and mentor Had Lantos had once made regarding diseases that humans could contract from livestock.

The young man's face suddenly projected angst and he literally squirmed as he sat. "Is there something that I'm missing here? Something that I'm not aware of?"

Paden's head was bowed when he shook a "no" but when he raised his head Ben could see glistening eyes. "I got asked to the Sadie Hawkins Dance."

Wow, I haven't heard of that dance for many, many years. Ben thought back to childhood when his father and he would read the Sunday comic strips together. "Do you know who Sadie Hawkins is, rather was?"

"Wasn't she a gay Montana congressman who wanted more women in the army and the right to drink alcohol?"

Ben tucked his lower lip under his upper front teeth and gave a slow noncommittal nod. What are they teaching these kids today? "I think that you may have her confused with a couple of other prominent women Paden. Sadie Hawkins was a character in an old comic strip called Lil Abner."

Paden glanced at Ben with a look that said who cares, "Whatever."

"We got off track for a minute Paden; you were saying that you were asked to the dance."

"Yes sir."

"Is there more?"

"I like her and I think that she likes me a lot."

"That's a good thing, yes?"

"Yeah...I think. Yes sir. I think...maybe...well, yes," he was now having a hard time getting the words out, almost stammering, "I...I might, well maybe I might get lucky and now..." his head swiveled back and forth as he built up nerve, finally pointed at his crotch and then there were tears.

Ben spoke softly, "Paden are you indicating that you touched your penis with those two fingers?"

He mumbled out, "Yes. Yes sir."

"When you urinated?"

"What?"

"When you went to the bathroom; when you peed?"

"Yes sir…and," he bowed his head in embarrassment.

"When you masturbated?"

"Oh jeeezzzz…Uh huh."

"Okay then. Have you seen any of these same lesions, bumps on your penis?"

He shook his head vehemently, "No sir."

"Alright. I'm going to make a quick phone call and I'll be right back, so hang tight. When I get back I'll examine you…" Paden audibly groaned. "Don't worry; it's just like your yearly sports physical."

"Hello?"

"Tucker, it's Ben Parker."

"Hola, Mr. Parker, what can I do for you this brisk winter day?"

"I've got a young man here with an infection on two fingers that I have never seen before. Nodules and weeping pustules which are apparently resistant to antibiotics. I've narrowed the possibilities of exposure and/or contact and one of them involves sheep."

"Orf, my good man. You may be looking at Orf."

"Have you seen it before Tucker?"

"Seen it? Hell, I've had it. Do you want me to stop by and take a peek?"

"If you have the time and inclination. There's one little hitch; the teenager is hoping to get intimate with a girl after an upcoming dance and is worried that he could pass it on. How communicable is Orf?" There was no immediate answer, "Hello? Hello Tucker?" No response, the connection was gone. Ben waited a minute, dialed back and listened to Tucker Lebek's phone message. Ben hung up the phone and headed back to the exam room hoping that Tucker would stop in before the sun went down.

There was a hard knock on the door and before Ben could answer Tucker Lebek, the veterinarian waltzed in and shut the door behind him. His work boots were well splattered with drying yellow slime and patches of cow manure. Poking out around the sunglasses propped atop his head his hair appeared to be statically charged. His upper cheeks were a ruddy red and his normally bulbous nose was a busy roadmap of intersecting red and blue veins and capillaries. A thick beard covered his jaw and lower cheeks and he had curled the tips of his mustache. In addition to a T-shirt he had added a tattered flannel shirt under the well-worn and calf diarrhea encrusted Carhart bib overalls. There was a broad smile on his face, "Hey doc, lost ya on the phone so since I was in the neighborhood..." Apparently he noticed Ben appraising his work attire and spread his arms out and turned side to side, "...scours, damn calves are full of it. He lifted an eyebrow and tilted his head to the right, "You do know what I'm talking about, right doc?"

"Yes, Tucker, I do know what scours is. You must be packing a few pounds of it on your shoes alone." Ben and Tucker shook hands and the veterinarian slapped him on the shoulder and turned his attention to the young patient sitting on the exam table.

"Hello Paden, let's see what you have there. Where's your rash, your infection Paden?"

Paden held his two infected fingers up. Tucker stepped over towards the uncertain teenager, "Hold them out and spread them apart." Lebek pulled his glasses out of his shirt pocket, began to slip them on, stopped and wiped the lenses on his shirt sleeve and then put them on. Without touching he began to examine the fingers now forming a vee. "Paden, you have Orf. Plain and simple. Antibiotics will have no effect unless you acquired a secondary bacterial infection and besides Mr. Parker tells me that you've already been on two separate courses of medication."

"What is Orf, Mr. Lebek? I never heard of it."

"It's a zoonotic disease, a virus that can be passed to humans by contact with infected domestic livestock. You weren't having your way with one of the ewes were you Paden?" Tucker sounded gruff but kidding, however, Ben was feeling some unease.

"Was I what?"

"Having your way, having carnal knowledge with one of those brown eyed sheep, you know, in the biblical sense?" Now he was sounding less gruff and trying to intone a more humorous note.

Suddenly realizing what Tucker Lebek was inferring Paden literally cried out, "No! No way! Not on your life! Are you fucking crazy? Oh, jeeezzzz, I'm so sorry; that just slipped out."

"I've been accused of worse and I deserved that. Sorry Paden. Do you have a bum lamb that you had sucking milk off of your fingers?"

Paden stilled looked shaken when he nodded yes, "Uh huh, yes."

You might have had an open cut on your finger and that's how it got passed on. I'll come out later and check the sheep. Do you know which ewe bummed the lamb?"

"Yes, number 82."

"Where's your dad?"

"He's working up in Alaska."

"Your mom?"

328

"She's doing the books for Mr. McGovern and helping out part time at his place."

"So you and your brother are managing most of the lambing?"

"Yes sir."

"Okay, you give your mother a call and tell her that I'll be out there sometime after five or six tonight."

"Yes sir."

"Paden, Mr. Parker mentioned that you were worried about something else; something to do with getting lucky with a special young lady. Tucker paused, "Are you worried about giving Orf to her?"

An embarrassed flush reddened his face as his head dipped down and he stared at his boots. He mumbled, "Yeah, yeah I guess."

"You been spanking the monkey, boy?"

Paden's head snapped up.

"Jerkin the gherkin, polishing the..."

The young man burst out in tears, started nodding his head and stammered, "I... I, ah... I guess so."

Ben was aghast and stepped up. "Enough Lebek, enough. You're embarrassing him and he already feels bad enough. You are not helping things."

Tucker pulled a bandana out of his back pocket and handed it to Paden. "I am sorry son. I'm sorry Paden, I was having a bit of fun with you and I went way overboard. I am sorry." His voice was gentle and calming. "Your fingers will heal just fine. You could put some bag balm or Butt paste on them but the big trick is to keep them covered and they will be healed up in two or three weeks. When is your big dance Paden?"

"The weekend before Easter." He was wiping his nose on a bandana that Ben had severe reservations as to where it had been.

329

"You'll be fine. If you have any questions or problems you get hold of Mr. Parker or you can call me."

Paden sniffed and nodded, "Yes sir."

"Just because a girl asks you to a dance young man does not necessarily mean that she wants to drop her knickers for you."

The young man looked up, "I wasn't expecting that, just hoping."

"I know your dad, Paden and I don't think that he would put his stamp of approval on your plan."

"It's not a plan, just... I was just wishing."

"Don't get me started on wishes. If she were to grant you your wish were you planning on using protection Paden?"

"Uh huh, I've got a rubber."

"A condom. Have you ever used one?"

Now Paden was defensive, "I don't think that you need an instruction book..."

"Where have you got this condom stashed; your wallet?"

"As if it's really your..."

"Show it to me." Tuckers tone inferred "don't trifle with me."

Paden pulled his wallet out of his back pocket and slid the condom package from an inner compartment. The outline of the rolled condom was impressed in the battered foil packaging.

Ben was trying his best not to laugh.

Tucker laughed outright, "That's been in there for a while; I'd bet you 'borrowed' it from your dad's dresser. There's a date on the package; what is it?"

Flipping the package over several times Paden finally located the date and smugly said, "It was made two years ago."

330

Tucker laughed again, "No Paden, that's the expiration date from two years ago. If you use that condom you're going to remember your Sadie Hawkins dance every time you change a diaper."

Paden sat silent and sullen.

"If Mr. Parker has no qualms how about we discuss this further when I come out to check on number 82 and her friends?"

"That would be good Mr. Lebek. Thank you." He arose and offered his infected right hand to Ben and quickly retracted it, "Sorry. Thanks for everything Mr. Parker."

"You are welcome Paden. Hold on a minute." Ben located some nonstick bandages and stretch gauze then dressed the two fingers. "Change the dressings daily or whenever they get wet or dirty. Please don't hesitate to call me if you need anything and please, at least listen to Mr. Lebek; he has some good advice."

"I will Mr. Parker. Thank you." He left the room but Lebek lingered behind.

"Bag balm? Butt paste? Really Tucker?"

Tucker shrugged, "Bag balm is good for anything except slicking down your hair and Boudreaux's Butt Paste treats the jock itch, cold sores, shingles or anything else you can name. Maybe it will do some good."

"Will it?"

A sly smile appeared, "It certainly won't hurt."

"I've got some literature on unplanned pregnancy and STD's if you want it. It's titled 'Wrap that Rascal.'"

Tucker laughed, "Thank you no. I think that I've got it covered. When I'm finished with young Paden he's going to want to join the priesthood."

"Be kind Tucker; you were once his age."

"I know; that's what worries me."

CONSEQUENCES

Sitting in the parking lot of Susie's Four S's, engine running, defroster on high, Ben watched as fits and starts of customers exited their vehicles, entered Susie's and then in short order exited the diner. Exhalation vapors streamed from cold lips as they gingerly traversed the frozen ground. Most were clutching plastic DVD cases; Susie was doing a brisk movie rental business this evening. It was currently between high school sports seasons and besides patronizing the local taverns or sitting at home playing Monopoly or Clue or Trivial Pursuit or watching TV, there were few other forms of entertainment in Bedlam on a Friday night. 9 PM was the bewitching hour for Fridays and at 8:45 Ben entered Susie's establishment, the customer traffic having come to an abrupt stop. The thin, smiling squeaky voiced blonde stood awaiting his order from behind the front counter and he observed two tables of diners concurrently standing, putting on their coats, hats and gloves as they prepared to leave. Susie stepped out of the swinging doors leading to the kitchen.

Her wide smile preceded her greeting, "Ben, you're cutting it close tonight."

"Hi Susie. I know that it's a little late but do you have a couple of minutes to talk? If not I…"

She produced her patented teasing grin of the temptress, "Nay, nay Ben Parker, I've always got time…"

she batted her eyelashes, "…or something of interest for you. Take a seat and I'll be right with you."

He came close to blushing but instead turned, walked over to the first booth and sat down. As he stared out at the two remaining customer vehicles warming up in the frigid night Ben removed his gloves and watch cap and set them on the bench seat. Red rear lights came on, then white back up lamps, and chugging plumes of exhaust became trails of white as the last groups of diners drove out of the parking lot. Susie slid into the opposite side of the booth.

Ben's attention turned to her, "Good to see you Susie, thanks for taking the time."

"There's an air of gravitas hanging over you tonight Ben. Is this when you announce that you are leaving Bedlam, profess your undying love for me and purpose that I close up shop, abandon my friends and relationships, cancel my library card and accompany you as you journey forth to god knows where, we solely dependent upon your good looks and sparkling personality to carry us through life?"

Ben's expression morphed from surprised to one of feigned hopefulness. "That wasn't exactly why I wanted to talk to you, however, since you brought it up, what do you think? You game? My extraordinarily good looks, inimitable sunny disposition and your bank account?"

Susie motioned to him by crooking and beckoning him with her right forefinger and a come- hither look as she stood and leaned over the table. Ben leaned forward hesitantly.

She punched him in the shoulder. "You son of a bitch. When were you going to tell me that you resigned from the hospital? Everyone in town knew it before I got wind of it this morning."

Ben rubbed his shoulder, "Jesus, Susie, you've got a hell of a jab there. Hell, if you weren't always off on some junket with Kimimela you'd be more in tune with the news of Bedlam."

"I didn't realize that you were so frail. Why are you leaving Ben?"

"I promise to tell you, but please, another night. Okay?"

"You hungry?"

"Yes, but that's not why I'm here. I'd like to ask you to consider an idea that I've been mulling over.

"That seems reasonable. Mull away, I'm all ears."

"I've got an old timer in the hospital right now who made a telling comment this morning. I believe him to be an honest man who lives simply and carries no high expectations or grand allusions of the world or those populating it. He is not the only patient, visitor or employee to have made this type of observation and it once again reminded me that addressing the issue would be a worthy venture to entertain if not pursue. This is a gentleman who fought in and survived the jungles of the South Pacific who stated, and I quote, "I've lived in foxholes with better accommodations.""

Susie covered her mouth to quiet herself from laughing out loud though her eyes revealed sympathy rather than humor.

"I know that he was grossly exaggerating and attempting to inject some levity, however, it made me take another look within the hospital and clinic and ask the question, 'What can we do to improve the environment for our sick or enfeebled patients along with the long term care residents.' Last fall, the hospital was going to hire that con artist Brother Marise and thankfully that came to a screeching halt. At least the Hospital Auxiliary is aware of he situation and has made the initial overtures to rectify it."

Susie's eyes did not leave his when she asked, "What are you proposing Ben?"

"That the one person in town that I know to have the energy, perseverance and expertise to address the problem help me devise a plan allowing her to design a course of action for the Hospital Auxiliary while maintaining Calistra Cartwright's secret identity."

"And why is it I think that you have already constructed a plan?"

"Because you are a brilliant and intuitive business woman and I am but a shallow, under achieving personage unworthy of standing in your shadow?"

Susie could not help but laugh, "You are a manipulative ass hat perhaps, but please, go on."

"It's not complete, not fleshed out; however, I do have some thoughts about a Plan A."

"Would you care to elaborate a bit on your unfleshed Plan A?"

"Well, since you brought it…"

The high pitched, frantic beeps of Ben's pager pierced the relative quiet of the diner followed by Becca's voice, "Ben Parker, please call the hospital. Ben Parker, please call the hospital."

"Sorry, Susie, duty calls. Would you at least consider the possibility?"

"Saved by the highly obnoxious squealing of your pager Ben Parker. I will consider it but I make no promises."

The pager squealed again followed by an announcement, "Ben Parker, please call the hospital. Ben Parker, please call the hospital."

As he slid out of the booth she reached out and laid her hand on his, "You have a good heart Ben, thanks for sharing it with me."

He produced a broad smile and his eyes sparked when he replied, "Ditto Susie. Call me at the hospital sometime if you would like a tour; I'll reserve you a foxhole."

Now finished with his ER patient note Ben flipped off the ER office light and quietly made his way down the dimly lit hospital hallway. The rooms were all dark, the current two hospital patients asleep and oblivious to his passing by. At the nurses' station he placed his paperwork in the appropriate basket. "Done," he said to no one in particular.

With a fork in her left hand Becca was picking at another contrived weight loss meal, advertised as delicious and appetizingly appealing as pictured on the cardboard packaging, as she made chart entries with her right. She stopped picking, grasped a white Styrofoam food container and slid it onto the upper counter, "Susie stopped by and dropped this off for you." Ben could see "Ben P." written on the lid in blue pastel magic marker. Becca leaned over and pointed at the "P." "She must be under the impression that there's more than one Ben working here."

Ben could always depend on Becca to comment on almost any observation that she made. Sometimes sarcastic, funny or astute she was often enough inappropriate, unwarranted or just plain inane. He chose to ignore her comment, "Thank you, Becca." After a brief struggle with a strip of scotch tape he was able to open the lid of the irritatingly squeaky container. Inside the top lid was a hand drawn rendition of a hand giving the thumbs up sign. Ben smiled. The box contained a Philly Cheese Steak and a huge portion of French Fries. He flipped over the top half of the steak bun and found a delicious appearing sandwich inclusive of the Swiss cheese, mushrooms and miracle whip which he preferred. Even without the drawn thumbs up sign he would have known her answer was yes merely by the fact that she had made the Philly Cheese Steak just the way he liked it.

"Hello?"

"Good morning Ben, it's Stella."

"Doesn't anyone stay home on Saturday morning, eat breakfast, and relax over coffee before they decide that an ER visit is a mandatory part of the day?" He was attempting to intone light sarcasm but wasn't sure that he had pulled it off.

"And a beautiful day in the neighborhood to you Mr. Rodgers."

Ben acknowledged to himself that he very likely missed the mark. He replied brightly, "Good morning Nurse Stella Rasniki, what may I do for you?"

"No ER. I repeat there is no ER patient. I've got a heads up for you Ben. Mrs. Betsy Comstock, Mr. Gunderson's daughter, and a close family friend, Mrs. Carmine Gephardt-Holtsman were in earlier to visit with your patient. They stepped out for breakfast and plan to return later to visit with you."

"Excellent. I was hoping the daughter would make it. How's Mr. Gunderson this morning?"

"He wanted me to give his compliments to the chef."

"Wow, that's a good sign. They must have discontinued the oatmeal."

"The "chef" told me that the DON gave her specific orders that Mr. Gunderson was to have anything that he wanted for breakfast. Can you explain that?"

Ben smiled to himself, "I believe that I can but we'll talk about it later. Suffice to say that Heidi has her own radar for patients with deep pockets."

"He's definitely feeling better, however, getting a bit antsy and I believe he's angling to get out of here."

"That's what I like to hear Stella. Are his labs back yet?"

"Trudi drew them but they're not ready yet."

"Okay, I'll be in; in about 20."

Stella said enthusiastically, "Great, I'm sure that I can have someone in the ER by the time you arrive."

"You Stella are always an absolute ray of sunshine."

"Thank you Ben, you bring the best out in me."

Ben laughed, "I'll see you in a bit."

The nurses' break room had been empty so Ben had seated the two women at the table, offering coffee before he dispensed himself a bottle of water from the vending machine. Mrs. Comstock and Mrs. Gephardt - Holtsman were close in stature but that is where the similarity ended. Mr. Gunderson's daughter was dressed conservatively in a grey jacket and skirt, her plain white blouse buttoned to the neck. Brown hair streaked with grey framed an anxious, make up free face. Numerous fine lines bracketed her mouth and brown eyes, evidence of life's stresses. Her best friend since child hood, Mrs. Gephardt - Holtsman, casual in dress and demeanor wore a flannel shirt unbuttoned at the neck, designer blue jeans and hiking boots. Her jet black hair fell to her shoulders and square framed glasses perched upon a thin nose made her face appear narrowed.

She wore minimal make up. Both women were in their early to mid-50s, plain but not unattractive.

Ben was about to start when Sydney entered from the back door letting in a short stream of cold air. She excused herself for the interruption, hung her coat on one of the wall hooks and exited into the hospital hallway, the smell of cigarette smoke still clinging to her. He took a swig of water and addressed the women sitting together across from him.

"Mr. Gunderson is making great progress. His vital signs are much improved, he is tolerating oral fluids very well, his urine is clearing, and labs indicate that the antibiotics and IV fluids have returned him to normal parameters. The initial minor confusion, nausea and vomiting at admission has completely resolved. As long as he continues to progress in this manner I would anticipate discharging him home tomorrow with a follow up appointment early next week with his urologist, Dr. Abernathy."

The two women looked elated. His daughter spoke first, "I plan on staying with him until he's back to 100%, if not longer. I will keep close tabs on him."

"And I anticipate staying a few days to help out and spend some time catching up with the two of them."

"Great. That's great. I'm glad that he will have someone around and I'm sure he'll appreciate having you two to visit with." I'd like to bring up another issue before you go back in to see him." Ben shifted in his seat as he gathered his thoughts on approaching the subject at hand. "I've had several opportunities for extended visits with your father," he looked at Mrs. Comstock and then to Mrs. Gephardt-Holtsman weighing if he should broach the entire subject at this time.

As if reading his mind Mrs. Comstock spoke up "Carmine virtually grew up with our family so just think o us as sisters and discuss anything that you care to."

"Actually Mr. Gunderson already gave me permission to share any of his information with either o you. I was considering how far I wanted to go with this."

"If it can help him then please tell us." Mrs Comstock was adamant.

"I perceive a sense of melancholy, some degree o depression and an underlying unrest and anger with you father. I am well aware of the tragedies that your family has suffered and I am sorry for your losses. Your father has ar unrelenting feeling that he has failed his family, that he has not been able to protect all of you. His self-imposed blame and guilt is compounded by a need to hold accountable those associated with your family's adversities and enac some form of revenge, a retribution against them. He struggles daily wrestling with his mores and values and his moral compass won't allow him to perpetrate or commit acts of physical aggression." Ben stopped to take a breath and evaluate the reactions of his audience.

"We know that Dad has held himself to blame for most everything and we haven't been able to convince him otherwise or come up with a solution that would free him from his guilt. He is a proud and stubborn man unwilling and unfortunately unable to forgive himself. I guess that we did not see the degree of anger; he's good at hiding some of his thoughts and feelings. The sum total of everything has taken a huge toll on all of us but Dad tries to shoulder the family burdens."

Mrs. Gephardt-Holtsman spoke, "The actions, inactions and conduct of Krum, the Boyles and to some extent the hospital at the time of and after the family's traumas were inexcusable, make that reprehensible.

340

Granted, the Gunderson's have always been a proud and somewhat stubborn group yet they have accepted that at some level family members were participants prior to each trauma. However, there was never any attempt to establish accountability or to institute punishment for the guilty parties. Mr. Gunderson, as well as his best friend my departed father, has never lifted a hand in anger or retaliation since the war and I believe that some form of non-violent retribution would have given him some degree of peace."

"I can't say that I can fully comprehend your sense of loss," Ben was quietly empathetic, "However, I can appreciate the frustration and anger you may feel regarding the indifference and guile with which you and your loved ones were treated. Mr. Gunderson appears to be especially impacted, almost believing himself emasculated by his inability to enact retribution. He may be so focused on his perceived guilt and inability to exact a physical atonement that he doesn't realize that he can empower himself to act in a more passive yet effective manner consistent with his beliefs."

His daughter responded, "Are you advocating that he try getting even with Krum and the Boyle's?"

"No I'm not advocating or inferring that any action be taken. I just know that there are numerous ways to skin a dead cat without you having to be the one that killed it."

The two women projected bewilderment and discomfort at his statement.

"Okay then, your right, that's a rather graphic and unsettling picture, sorry. I should have said there are numerous ways to catch a mouse without having to kill it." He waited to see if there was a different reaction.

Now Mrs. Gephardt-Holtsman spoke, "I'm not sure what your motive is Mr. Parker or what your objective may be."

Ben was now having reservations. Admittedly he hadn't anticipated either lady challenging him initially but obviously the lawyer had a more jaded view of the world. "Since I have been in Bedlam I have made some random observations and a few others not so randomly obtained. Purely observations that I would be willing to share if you are interested. I have absolutely nothing to gain from passing them on other than the personal satisfaction of knowing that they may in some way serve your family and this community well. It is purely coincidental, the chance meeting of Mr. Gunderson that prompted me to share the information at all."

"Mr. Parker, I'm not…"

Mrs. Comstock interrupted and interjected, "Let the man talk Carmine. You're always looking for ulterior motives or seeing and believing the worst in everyone. Dad has a good opinion of Mr. Parker and if he has information to put forward I'm leaning towards the old adage that the only thing necessary for the triumph of evil is for good men to do nothing. I for one would like to hear what he has to say."

Ben took that as a signal to begin, "Your father is a wealthy man, yes?"

"By most people's definition, yes."

"Would you say that he's a good conservator of the land?"

"Yes, definitely yes."

"Mrs. Gephardt - Holtsman you are an attorney; do you specialize in any specific branch of law?"

"Yes, I specialize in environmental law."

"Would that include Conservation Districts and Water Rights?"

"I have a modicum of knowledge in both."

"Do you own the property west of here across the highway from Sacajawea Park, the group of older buildings set back north of the highway?"

She looked at him warily, "Yes I do."

"Do you have water rights to Indian Creek?"

"Yes. I don't know how much but yes."

"Have you noticed less water in the stream?"

"Not personally but I've heard reports of less water due to the drought."

"Are you aware of a new subdivision northeast of your property and who owns and is promoting the properties?"

"Krum and Boyle." She sounded disdainful.

"Do you know who the ditch rider is for Indian Creek and the irrigators with water rights?

"No."

"Would it surprise you to know that he is a shirt-tail relative of Boyle?"

"Now you have my attention."

"Mrs. Gephardt- Holtsman…"

"How about we go with Betsy, Carmine and Ben?"

"Carmine, have you been considering converting your property to a gas mart and convenience store combination?"

"Hell no. Hold on a second please." She produced a pen and small notebook from her shirt pocket, "Okay, now I'm ready."

Ben began listing his observations of the past 10 months, fielding questions, asking questions and elaborating when asked. Has anyone but the ditch rider ever measured actual stream flow and water allotments? How would you feel about Sacajawea Park expanding for truck and RV parking? The obvious neglect of the Stenerud ranch and lost riparian areas. The involvement of Boyle's brother-in- law and his son the ditch rider in caretaking the Stenerud ranch. The three Stenerud siblings in Hawaii, New Jersey and Germany and Krum and Boyle's joint vacations to those three locales. The water shortage at Krum and Boyle's golf resort. The proposed lengthening of the airport runway to accommodate corporate jets. The fact that Petroski might balk at selling thus the hint of eminent domain to accommodate the expansion thereby removing Mr. Petroski's ranch and farm land out of production. What then happens to water allocated for that land? Clandestine pressuring, mitigating, leveraging, transferring, purchasing or stealing of water for sub divisions or a proposed golf resort on arid land with no readily accessible or substantial water resources. "I'm willing to bet that land and water are the two main controversial issues in Montana over the past 100 years." Ben decided to stop at this point and allow the ladies to consider the information.

"Are you proposing anything Ben?"

"No. No proposal, just observations that I thought I would forward on to some smart, intuitive, and caring people to think about."

Betsy laid her hands flat on the table top and rolled her neck and shoulders in an attempt to stretch out a muscle or two, "Carmine, when I was flying up here I was thinking about approaching Dad about investing some of the family money in land purchases in and around Bedlam and perhaps putting them into Conservation districts for future preservation."

"What a fabulous idea, Betsy. I'd be more than willing to help with that. We could secure water rights and usages, assure open lands, develop riparian areas, and maybe even lease ground at affordable rates to young ranching and farming families as conservators of the land."

"I don't know why I didn't think of it sooner Carmine. Stop the blight of overpriced subdivisions, thwart rising taxes for unwarranted infrastructure demands, maintain view sheds, develop riparian areas; there are a host of possibilities. Perhaps we can help slow the carpetbaggers and Philistines that are lining their pockets and undermining the environment at the expense of the community."

Ben could tell that the two women were having fun with the concept, as if two kids were playing roles in their own home grown play.

"Great ideas Betsy. Let's go share them with your dad. I'm sure that Mr. Parker has his work to do so we can talk with him later." She turned to Ben and said, "Thank you, Ben. Thank you for everything."

"Ben, my father's opinion of you was spot on. Thank you so very much. We can take it from here."

"It was a pleasure meeting both of you and we will talk again later. You two and Mr. Gunderson have certainly made my day.

They exited the break room, Betsy and Carmine headed towards Mr. Gunderson's room while Ben stood in the lobby contemplating whether to whistle *Sympathy for the Devil* by the Rolling Stones or *Good Vibrations* by the Beach Boys. He dismissed both as he headed out the door for home and to grab a quick lunch. Credence Clearwater Revival had come up like a shot in the dark and as he whistled *Up Around the Bend* he remembered some of the lyrics,

There's a place up ahead and I'm goin'
Just as fast as my feet can fly

Come away, come away if you're goin'
Leave the sinkin' ship behind
Come on the risin' wind
We're goin' up around the bend.

NOT QUITE SAINTLY

"Happy Saint Patrick's Day, Ben."

"And a Happy Saint Urho's day back atcha, Lindsay."

Her throaty laugh was music to his ears "Wasn't it yesterday that the Finlanders celebrated Saint Urho driving out the grasshoppers to save the grape vineyards?"

"Uh huh, pretty much any excuse for a parade and party."

"I'm not interrupting anything am I Ben? You're not on call are you?"

"No, I'm good; no make that great since you called. Technically I'm not on call but I told Marni that if the Irish got too unruly and filled the emergency room to give me a call."

"And have my Irish brethren been behaving themselves so far today?"

"Nothing catastrophic today, just a steady stream of minor, alcohol related medical emergencies and buckets of green vomit. Now, last night was a different story."

There was alarm in voice, "What happened last night Ben?"

He snorted a laugh, "Last night all hell broke loose. I'm not sure if your familiar with how the Fins and Irish of Butte would take Saint Urho's and Saint Patrick's Days to heart but they have toned down a bit. In comparison they

347

are mere pikers compared to the exuberance shown in Bedlam. For some reason that currently eludes me, the town of Bedlam has unofficially yet traditionally designated a 48 hour time frame to celebrate just about any and all Saints for whom someone has hoisted an alcoholic beverage."

"I guess that I'm not following you Ben. I'm only familiar with Saint Patrick and vaguely aware of Saint Urho."

"Right, and those were the two that I was in tune with, that is until last night. It's amazing the amount of information one can glean from an ER full of drunks however, I digress. The Finlanders began toasting Saint Urho yesterday and at noon their mini parade kicked off. By late afternoon some of the Irish were beginning to get a start on today's celebration. Did you know that the patron saint of Norway was Olaf II Haraldsson, a Viking warrior?"

"Well, no. I did not." Lindsay made the declaration in a way that invited Ben to continue.

"The Norwegians, of which there is a goodly population in this area and apparently not to be undone have their own celebration for Saint Olaf. Rather than waiting until his birthday in July, over the years the Norwegians have incorporated the honoring of Saint Olaf into the Urho/Patrick festivities. I have been duly informed that there is quite a bit of overlap between the Saintly celebrations vying for recognition and bar space."

"So you mentioned that all hell had broken loose?"

"Ohhhhhh yeah. The Fins, dressed in blue, white and some in purple, had rented the pavilion in the downtown square for their party and a good number of Irishmen clad in Kelly green with a sprinkling of Orange had joined in to communally celebrate Saint Urho's Day. Norwegians, not wanting to feel left out were in attendance

348

dressed appropriately in blue and red. A goodly number of town folk with other miscellaneous ethnic backgrounds had drifted away from their own parties and had begun mingling in the mix at the pavilion. The Dirty Shame Saloon hosted and the clientele hoisted drinks in honor of Saint Grobian, the patron saint of vulgar and crude people. Our local librarian had opened the library doors and offered up cookies and punch to honor Saint Leibowitz, a character from some science fiction novels. A group of women marched down Main Street with folding lawn chairs and then imbibed pre-mixed Margaritas to celebrate Saint Martha the Dominator. The small, local coven of Wiccans sipped wine and quietly demonstrated against Saint Walpurga, who I'm told is feted at the end of April on Walpurgis Night. Apparently the Wiccans take exception to this Saint's bias against, and here you may take your pick, rabies, whooping cough or witchcraft."

"Wow, you have an eclectic population in Bedlam."

"Boy howdy, we do. So, a rousing and good natured party was being enjoyed by all when several members of the large, normally docile unless inebriated and provoked, Norwegian contingency took offence to the Fins and Irish jokingly referring to them as fish eaters and noogins. This lead to a heated exchange of words and the resulting disparagement of Saint Urho and Saint Patrick inclusive of the ancestral shortcomings of Finish ice monkeys and the potato heads of Ireland." Ben let a laugh escape as he said, "And then the donnybrook was on."

Ben heard a gasp followed by, "Oh no. Oh, I'm just cringing here thinking about a crowd of drunks brawling in the square."

He laughed again and then caught himself, "Sorry, I realize that I'm laughing at their expense but I got called into the emergency room because Saint Urho, dressed in purple, some white with a purple robe, is brought in with his crumpled pointed hat under his arm, a profusely bleeding scalp wound and a couple of broken fingers from attempting to fend off Saint Patrick's wooden staff. Saint Olaf, wearing blue and red and a Viking helmet with a broken horn, limps in while throwing up bright green vomit. In addition he's got a black eye and for some reason Olaf is steadying himself with Saint Urho's full sized plastic pitchfork complete with a giant plastic grasshopper impaled on the tines. Saint Patrick was helped in while clutching his broken wooden staff and his right wrist which was whacked by Saint Olaf's wooden sword. There were dark stains on his green robes the result of his broken and bleeding nose.

These were just the luminaries. I had more than a dozen others who wandered or were helped in with contusions, lacerations, sprains, strains, bloody noses and a couple of missing teeth. The nurse made a call to the doctor who never answered so she alerted Marni who graciously came in to help. I made it to bed around 2:30."

"Oh Ben. You had a rough night, how has today been so far?"

"So far today most of the ER's have been intoxicated individuals suffering the aftermath of falls. Mainly minor lacerations, abrasions, contusions and sprains, and of course dehydration and extensive amounts of green tinged vomit laced with corned beef cabbage and other assorted green dyed food stuffs. We're hoping that we saw the worst of it last night."

"I hope so too, for your sake. Here's hoping that Marni has a quiet night and doesn't need to call you in for help."

"Now you've gone and done it Lindsay."

"What? What have I done?" She sounded genuinely alarmed.

"You invoked the "Q" word."

"The what word?"

"The "Q" word. Q...U...I...E...T. Of course it's superstition but all too often it rings prophetic. As soon as someone utters the "Q" word during your shift everything goes to hell in a hand basket." Ben was trying not to sound too serious.

"Well I'm sorry Ben; I was unaware." She sounded apologetic; however, there was a hint of disbelief in her tone. "Is there anything that I can do to undue this unfortunate slip of the tongue?" Now her apology sounded more insincere with a modicum of sarcasm.

"Human self-sacrifice is the only known means of reversal."

"That's not going to happen. Would dinner and an apple pie suffice?"

"In my world yes though I'm not sure that it would be enough for Marni if the fecal matter enters the oscillating device."

That evoked a loud laugh from Lindsay, "You know Ben that you have talked more about your patients tonight than any conversation that we've had since you left Missoula. Almost as if you were attempting to avoid talking about them. Why?"

"I don't know. I hadn't really thought about it or tried to make a conscious attempt at avoidance. I guess that I thought that you wouldn't really be interested."

"Ben Parker!" Oh crap he thought, she sounds upset. "The day that we met you coerced me into sitting down in your booth, listening to and then judging the merit of three patient encounters. Did I get up in the middle of them and leave because I was bored, or had had enough?"

"May I remind you that you were being paid?"

She sputtered, "No you may not and that has n•
bearing on this. You are incorrigible!"

He attempted to smooth things out, "You're right •
probably am. You were a trooper and listened to all o•
them. Okay, you're saying that you want me to relat•
stories about some of my patients?"

"Of course I do. I'm interested in what you do, how
your patients effect you, how you are. You have quite a•
impact on their lives and at times they must impact you a•
well."

Ben paused to contemplate what she had said, "•
can do that Lindsay. Please, keep in mind that not all of my
patients have odd complaints and that sometimes th•
outcomes are not pleasant or as expected."

"So cherry pick. They can't all have bad outcomes•
It can't be all trauma and pain. Remember, many of you•
patients will miss you when you leave."

You just had to toss that in he thought; he wa•
already accumulating guilt on a daily basis. "Give me •
minute to gather my thoughts." He had dozens of storie•
that immediately came to mind and decided on a few t•
start off with. "I had a 40-year-old woman in the clini•
complaining of neck pain. After a lengthy interview •
finally determined that the cause was from her lying on the
floor and using a Suzanne Somer's Thigh Master t•
exercise her neck and to get rid of an unattractive ski•
wattle below her chin. A woman in the ER stated that sh•
was a breach baby at birth so any medications that sh•
might receive would have the reverse effect.

There's a 38-year-old guy in town that shows u•
around once a week complaining of chest pain, shortness o•
breath and recites a plethora of cardiac signs and
symptoms. So far we've determined that there is absolutely•

352

nothing wrong with his heart or lungs. He only shows up when one particular nurse is on duty and he knows that legally we can't turn him away from a Critical Access Hospital Emergency Room. We have to evaluate him and once he has had his nurse fix he goes home. A local woman demanded a letter for the district court stating that she should be excused from jury duty because she suffers from the chronic health condition of high cholesterol."

"You're making these up, Ben. You're patronizing me and having fun at my expense." She sounded disappointed, if not offended.

"No! No, Lindsay, I would never do that to you. These are real patients. Okay, here's another one and I promise you I am not making it up."

"Okay, go ahead." It sounded tentative though hopeful.

"A month ago an overweight counselor of the Mormon church who was celebrating his fiftieth birthday suffered a massive heart attack immediately after filling his mouth with a massive forkful of frosted birthday cake. Why do I know that? Because what the EMT's couldn't dig out of his mouth we had to suction out to maintain an airway. In front of a fervently praying crowd of fellow church members we managed to revive him only to lose him before the Life Flight plane arrived. Better?"

"They don't necessarily need to die to make it believable but yes, better."

"On Valentine's Day a hysterical woman was brought into the ER from the reservation. She and her abusive ex-husband had been drinking in his pickup truck when they got into an argument. He pushed her out and drove forward running over her legs. Then he backed up running over her hips and pelvis and then rolled over her chest and shoulder before driving off. At the time we were experiencing a short period of warmer weather which had created melting snow, slush and a layer of mud. Amazingly she had been imbedded but cushioned by the soft snow and mud. She was covered in tire tracks, however, the only long lasting results were extensive bruising, global aches and pains and a severe hangover. A local man, whom the clinic nurse nicknamed Wildmeat, is obsessed with the length of his penis. For the past year, after using any number of on line or magazine advertised cream products and enhancement devices he measures and marks his perceived growth on a seamstress's tape measure. He comes in once a month to confirm the length of his penis and have the nurse record it into his chart. To date no one has laid eyes on his manhood and he appears entirely happy with his progress."

"I'm starting to warm to your stories again Dr. Parker."

"That's PA not MD young lady, so don't be planning any expensive weekend getaways. One last story for now. In early February there was a teenage boy that I diagnosed with Orf…"

Lindsay interrupted him, "What did you say? Orf? Really Ben." She sounded exasperated if not scolding. "Orf? How naïve to you think I am? Be serious."

"I am, honest."

"Orf? How do you spell it?"

"Orf. O…r…f, Orf. It's a skin infection caused by a virus that some domestic livestock can pass on to humans through contact with a cut or open wound. You may look it up or I'll send you information about it."

"What did you do to treat it?"

"Time. It's self-clearing but you have to keep it isolated because you could communicate it to another part of the body by contact."

"Was that a problem for him?"

"At first it was a huge cause of concern for him. A girl that he had a huge crush on had asked him to a Sadie Hawkins Day dance and that planted the seed that he was going to get lucky. The problem arose that he had touched his penis with the infected fingers."

"You can pass it on by mere touch?"

"I might be understating the degree of contact; after all he is a hormone charged teenage boy."

"So he was masturbating."

"No mincing words with you lady."

"So did his penis become infected?"

"No, it did not."

"Did you cure him?"

"As of last week it was almost completely resolved."

"When is Sadie Hawkins Day?"

"Usually in November."

"I mean the dance smarty-pants."

"April, I think."

"So he might get lucky."

"C'mon, he's 16."

"And men peak at 18."

"You're advocating for sex at 16?"

"I'm just messing with you Ben."

"You just can't help yourself, now can you Lindsay?"

"You didn't catch any of this Orf when you examined him, did you Ben?"

"No, I wear gloves."

"So there is nothing preventing you from getting lucky."

"Not to my knowledge. At least nothing health wise, therefore I'd say that I was limited only by opportunity."

"Opportunity is fickle. You never know when it might present itself."

Ben was silent, weighing his words carefully.

"I miss you Ben."

His train of thought abruptly took another track. "I miss you too, Lindsay. I'm really looking forward to seeing you in a couple of weeks."

She almost purred, "Yes, and you would not want to miss that opportunity, now would you Ben Parker."

Ben was momentarily tongue tied, "I'm sure... ahhh, ah I... I'm not, not one to miss an..."

"Sorry Ben, hold that thought, my daughter is calling me on my cell phone. I've got to take it. I really do miss you Ben. Please be safe and will you call me tomorrow?"

"Yes, I will call you tomorrow but answer me this before you go; Does opportunity knock more than once?"

"Opportunity waits for no man; however, you Ben Parker strike me as a lucky kind of guy. Good night Ben."

"Good night Lindsay." He looked at his watch to see if there was still time to go buy a lottery ticket.

APRIL FOOL

As prolonged and harsh as the past six months of winter weather had been, Ben was anticipating a two season year; winter and road construction. Winter had truly tried the patience of many; early October snows still waited to melt from under the layers of subsequent storms. Yesterday's record high temperature had succeeded in stirring up spring fever within an already restless populace and to appreciably accelerate the snow melt. Ben stood on his back steps watching as a few bold robins inspected the expanding brown patches of grass appearing in his swiftly dwindling backyard snow field. A few green shoots were beginning to tease their way up through the matted lawn. Cloudless and intensely blue, the morning sky was hopefully signaling a second day of, dare he say it, spring like weather.

A random memory sprang to mind reminding him of an early spring day when he was attending college at Montana State University in Bozeman. As he recalled, 1979 had seen an overly long and frigid winter. He, his roommate Jake Tabor and a naïve dorm neighbor from Seattle whom they had taken under their collective wing, piled into Jake's pickup truck, along with a case of beer, for a sightseeing trip. They drove around Southwest Montana pointing out historic sites and landmarks as the stock of beer was steadily consumed. Upon their return to Bozeman they had to explain to the excited, gullible, slightly inebriated and hormone charged city transplant that in the spring, leading up to Easter, a Ranch and Farm Supply outlet displaying a sign announcing in large letters "Chicks Are Here," did not constitute a plethora of lithesome, long legged coeds were on display and available. However, even in the frozen tundra and hinterlands of Montana hope springs eternal.

Turning the corner from the hospital wing into the lobby Ben had to circle wide to avoid running into a gaggle of employees clustered in front of Myra's reception window. This was not an uncommon sight, however, it usually denoted that some extraordinary event had taken place or was on the near horizon. He casually took up station in front of the community bulletin board to the right of Myra's office and nonchalantly began reviewing the postings. Knowing that his presence could not have gone unnoticed by all six of the women he was relying on the group's engagement in conversation to hold their undivided attention and allow him the freedom of eavesdropping without suspicion. Sometimes the most obvious is the most likely to be ignored.

As he scanned the notices Ben could hear them speaking in excitedly hushed, almost conspiratorial levels and he was positive that he heard one employee say, "Imagine, Calista Cartwright. How did they get her to come here?" Hearing the name he realized that Susie's planned presentation for the internal hospital renovation must be in the very near future. He began a closer examination of the notices in earnest. Community Easter Egg Hunt at Bedlam Municipal Park sponsored by K & B Resorts Inc., that smacked of Krum and Boyle once again insinuating themselves into the community's good graces, Memorial

Day Little Buckaroo Rodeo, a listing of Bedlam Churches celebrating Easter services and the times, Conservation District Banquet and Dance, Alcoholics Anonymous meetings, a listing of times, dates and where the meetings were to be held including the basement of the Rotary Club, American Legion Hall community room, BPOE Elks Hall cafeteria and the Bedlam Library. He noted that not one AA meeting was sponsored by a church group; apparently God's good will doesn't extend to week nights. Bedlam Medical Center, there it is.

Recalling that Brother Marise's poster was a production piece of color and cursive script Ben was struck with the simplicity of this announcement.

Bedlam Medical Center
Community Room
Please join your friends, neighbors and community
members on
Thursday, April 1 at 7 PM
An invitation to attend a presentation by
Calistra Cartwright Enterprises
"Creating Comfort within Function"
Sponsored by all who support our local hospital.

Ben thought "Oh, boy I'm glad that I checked the bulletin board today. If I had missed tonight Susie would have skinned me alive," even though there is a hospital full of employees that probably would have mentioned it at some time or other today. Tonight we will find out what's in store; if it's Susie Halverson that appears or will it be Calistra Cartwright who shows up, or both. He stepped back from the bulletin board, glanced at the ladies surrounding Myra's window and then walked off to his office.

He plopped down in his office chair and took a sip from his bottle of root beer. A letter addressed to the Bedlam Medical Center lay front and center on his desk blotter. The return address indicated that it was from CMS Centers for Medicare and Medicaid Services; Quality Safety and Oversight Compliance Division. It had been opened. Ben slid the documents out and found a yellow post it note stuck to the first page: "Sorry Ben, I opened this inadvertently. The business office had it in their pile before dropping it off yesterday afternoon. Callie."

Having peeled off the post it note he began reading. It was dated March 20 and announced that he, Benjamin Parker PA-C had been randomly selected for audit of his Critical Access Hospital, Rural Health Clinic and Nursing Home Facility Medicare charts. Comprised of several parts the audit would be focusing upon the key elements of compliance of documentation standards, application of clinical standards; evidence based diagnostic identifiers, as well as coding and reimbursement agreement. The audit would be conducted on April 1 at 11 AM by the consulting firm of Howard, Howard and Fine Inc., a CMS certified auditing entity. It additionally requested that the attached list of Medicare patients evaluated at the Bedlam Medical Center by Benjamin Parker PA-C be made available for the purposes of the audit. Ben glanced at the attached page and saw a list of 30 patient names with their date of birth and Medicare number included.

His phone receiver was clamped to his ear and Callie's number dialed, all in less than five seconds. "Good morning Ben, what can I do for you?"

"This letter from Medicare."

"Sorry Ben, I just found it yesterday afternoon just after you left. I've got Irene pulling nursing home and hospital charts and I've managed to collect all of the clinic charts. The conference room is reserved for the audit at 11."

"Nothing like a last minute warning. Have you had one of these audits here before?"

"Again, sorry for the late notice, Ben. Saroni was audited a while back. If I remember correctly it was his first year here in Bedlam and everything went fine. Relax, Ben, you're documentation is very good so you'll probably do fine as well...but you know the government."

Ben did not like that little addendum, "Sure, you know the government. Thanks, Callie, I'll see you in a bit." He hung up the phone feeling a small pit forming in his stomach. Then he noticed his clinic schedule was setting on the left side of the desk, its edge tucked under the border of the blotter. Scanning the patient list he was immediately struck by the names that he saw. Harmon Krum Jr., Durinda Dunkle, Herb Yablonski, nicknamed Wildmeat by the clinic staff due to his preoccupation with the length of his penis, Mrs. Milic, Daphne Donner, holy crap he thought, Martin Kaplanic the postmaster; all these before the audit at 11. In a near panic he covered the distance between his office and Callie's desk in record time.

Callie looked up at him from her chair, a pleasant smile enveloping her face, her hands folded and laying before her on the desktop. "More questions Ben?" she sounded as if she had been expecting his arrival.

His approach was calm and respectful, "Callie, I'm mildly curious here but how did I manage to have a clinic schedule composed almost exclusively of my least favorite, difficult or noncompliant patients?" He gave her a disarming smile and raised an eyebrow.

Callie was not falling for this faux persona. She replied sweetly, "Because Ben Parker, you are a caring, compassionate and interactive provider and these patients greatly relish and respect the opportunity of scheduling their time with you," she emphasized the you by unfolding her hands and gesturing as if presenting him with a cake, "soooo, suck it up, gear up, and man up 'cause we know you have the physical and mental wherewithal to handle all of these challenging cases."

Ben realized that he may have approached this matter in the wrong manner, "Callie, I am not going to see all of these whack jobs in one day. Switch some of them with a couple of Saroni's patients."

"Perhaps it slipped your mind Ben but Saroni is off today. He scheduled off and Marni is covering any of his patients that come in and the ER since you have the audit. Would you prefer me to turf them off on her?"

Ben closed his eyes in disappointment and then said sheepishly, "I forgot, damn it anyway. Okay, I'll see it through."

"That's our guy. I'll have Mr. Krum Junior ready in 10 minutes." She smiled up at him pleasantly but dismissively; in return he gritted his teeth, forced a tight lipped nod and left for his office. Ten minutes later she was in his office doorway, "Mr. Harmon Krum Junior is ready in Exam two. He is complaining of burning upon urination and some sort of discharge." She started to make an additional comment, caught herself, instead said, "Enjoy your day," turned on her heel and was gone.

Oh jeezz, he thought, the Krum kid must have gone trolling in uncharted territory. Ben resignedly arose and headed to his first patient. He slipped the chart from the file holder attached to the door, glanced at the vitals, allergies, medication list, chief complaint, knocked and then entered the room. Dwight Unger was slouched in the chair, his legs extended well out in front of him, holding a steaming cup of coffee in his hand, "Hiya, Doc. Callie sends her regards. April Fools'."

At 1050 hours Ben stopped short of the conference room door to read a simple black and white posting taped up at eye level. Heidi Lafevbre might very well come undone with this blatant disregard for her no tape regulation on doors and walls.

Medicare Chart Audit

M. Howard MD.

C. Howard MD.

L. Fine MD.

He took a deep breath, blew it out slowly as he made sure his shirt was tucked in, collar straight and fly zipped up tight, then knocked softly on the door. No one responded. He knocked again slightly harder and tentatively reached to push open the door. An audible click sounded, the door opened perhaps eight inches and Callie's face greeted him, a right forefinger pressed to her lips as a signal for quiet. She opened the door just enough to allow him to enter and she motioned for him to hug the wall. He slithered in and dutifully pressed his back against the west wall. The tables normally arranged in a large square for meetings were pushed up against the North and South walls. A single table to the east standing a few feet from the wall was covered with a white table cloth. Three chairs were equally spaced on the back side of the table. Folded triangular white cardboard name plaques identifying the doctors were set on the table in front of each of the three chairs. A lone folding chair was centered several feet in front of the table. In evidence were three moderately tall stacks of charts, one in front of each chair.

Callie whispered, "You're a few minutes early." She pointed to a closed door in the far corner of the room,

"The doctors are in the office. Wait outside and I'll let you know when they are ready."

Ben nodded silently. His level of unease was building now aggravating an already nervous stomach. This was far bigger than he had anticipated. Now leaning against the hallway wall he folded then unfolded his arms across his chest, periodically pushing off the wall before settling back against it. Don't worry, you documented well...probably with more information than needed...this is merely a formality...no worries...Christ, what if they find something...what are they going to find...what can they do if they do...what will...

The door opened perhaps half way and Callie poked her head out and waved him in with her hand, "They're ready for you Ben." He thought that her demeanor was so... solemn.

He placed his hands behind him flat against the wall and forced himself forward and walked through the door. In Ben's mind the term audit was a distant memory and inquisition had been substituted. The three interviewer chairs were now filled and Callie gave him a nudge towards the lone chair in front. Even in his nervous and distracted state he thought it slightly odd though not highly unusual that the three doctors did not look up; instead they held up charts, intently immersed in the review process and he was unable to see their faces. As he took his seat the doctors, all wearing full length lab coats, continued their focused chart review. Unnoticed by Ben a number of hospital employees had quietly filed into the room behind him; his full attention being focused either in his lap or on the three charts that the doctors were engrossed in. C. Howard MD made a strange whooping sound while fluttering his fingers, his hand flat on his head and suddenly all three doctors dropped the charts that they had been engrossed in,

364

lat on the table. He suddenly knew that he had been had as he saw that each doctor wore a full face mask; Curly Howard, Moe Howard, and Larry Fine were easily recognizable as the Three Stooges.

Ben sprang up from his chair and literally yelled, "God damn it." That is when he heard the laughter erupt behind him. He whipped around and saw Callie along with a dozen other coworkers.

"April Fools', Ben!" As it was chorused he felt his face flush from embarrassment and turned away to find the masks removed and Stella, Becca and Karmma smiling broadly. Marni exited the corner office and walked directly over to Ben. The laughter abated and stopped.

"You know Ben, red goes nicely with the white lab coat." He stiffly tolerated her effusive hug as she stated for all to hear, "You also know that we wouldn't do this if we didn't love you." Everyone laughed and applauded. "We're all aware that you are leaving us and had expressed the notion that you would prefer nothing in the way of a going away gathering, however, I ask, who are we to respect that type of a request? So today we are holding a luncheon honoring our favorite April Fool."

Ben stood silently and gazed about the room at the 17 people present, making that 18 as Dwight appeared in the doorway. "This is someone's brainchild, so who's behind this stunt?" All 18 attempted to look baffled as they looked around at each other, some shrugging, others glancing up at the ceiling, some attempting to hide smirks. He heard, "Wasn't me, don't look at me, no way and who me?" No one even hinted at laying claim. Realizing that his was a fruitless endeavor he acquiesced, "Okay, you got me good, I give you that. I'll go for the lunch but just this one time and just as long as no one says sorry to hear that you're abandoning ship." With a flourish he brought his

hands together as if begging alms, "As always, cas
donations are welcome."

Marni called out, "Bring on the food, let's eat."

"Ben, Mr. Norlund just died. The family is all her
at his bedside. Can you come up to confirm an
pronounce?"

"Sure thing, Myrna, I'll be right there." He hung u
the phone and looped his stethoscope around his neck as h
left his office, then briskly walked to the hospital hallwa
and to Mr. Norlund's room. Mr. Norlund was one of D
Saroni's patients and his death had been expected. Hi
extensive health issues had prompted ever more frequen
hospitalizations with a notable decline in stamina an
constitution after each discharge and subsequen
readmission. Once a robust and proud rancher he no
presented as a cachectic wisp of his former self. Whethe
singularly or in combination his myriad maladies ha
finally overwhelmed his frail and tenuous grasp of life
death was not at issue and never in doubt. Ben entered th
room quietly, a somber air caste over the family members
Three sons stood by stoically while Mr. Norlund's on
daughter, tears streaming, silently sat in a bedside chai
softly and lovingly stroking his hand with hers. Be
positioned himself on the opposite side of the bed of th
daughter and Myrna stood at the foot of the bed, patien
chart in hand.

Mr. Norlund's pallor, which for days had bee
ashen and recently begun to mottle, had taken on a slightl
bluish tint as had his lips. The eyelids remained open
lifeless eyes centered and fixed. Ben was left wondering i
Mr. Norlund's last vision was of a faded ceiling tile, a
family member leaning in or somewhere unfathomable
Gently, respectively, though methodically Ben examine

366

Mr. Norlund, finally listening to his heart and lungs and palpating for a carotid pulse. He looked over his left shoulder to the wall clock behind Myrna, into her eyes, and then scanned the faces of the family. Quietly he said, "Time of death 1456 hours." Myrna made note in the chart. Having bowed his head in a short silent prayer Ben now addressed the family as a whole, "I am truly sorry for your loss. Your father is a good man." He had interacted with the family periodically during the past four months, one on one and in varying combinations of the siblings yet found himself at a loss of adding anything additional let alone comforting. "If there is anything we can do to help please, do not hesitate to ask." Ben moved back allowing the family to gravitate to either side of their father.

Outside, in the hallway, Ben and Myrna conferred. "I'll write up the chart and discharge notes if you'll make the obligatory call to the donor bank, then I'm heading back to the clinic. If you would, call me when the mortician arrives and I'll sign his paperwork."

Myrna looked at Ben with a surprised look, "Ben, the Norlund family intends to take Mr. Norlund home for burial."

Looking confused Ben replied in disbelief, "I'm sorry, what was that you said?"

"The family will be taking the body home for burial," the tone was matter of fact; "It's a family tradition."

Ben was nodding his head now as if understanding her statement, "Sure thing Myrna. You almost had me there but enough with the April Fool jokes, especially that are in really bad taste."

Myrna was aghast, "This isn't a joke Ben. Honestly. The family traditionally buries their members at the ranch in a family plot. Please believe me this is not an April Fools' Day prank."

Ben was serious, "You're serious here? Not pulling my leg?"

"Dead serious," which almost caused her to cover her mouth, "We may be a little callous here at times with our black humor, however, I would not joke about this. Two years ago their mother died here in the hospital and the family took her home for burial. Of course the mode of transportation raised some eyebrows but yeh; they took her home for burial."

"What exactly raised some eyebrows?"

"After Mrs. Norlund was removed from the hospital, all quite legally have you, they sat her up in her favorite rocker in the back of the pickup, cinched her down good and tight, then drove her back to the ranch so that she could have a last tour of the area and view the sunset."

"Now you're just screwing with me."

"No, sirree. A couple of complaint calls were made to the sheriff's department and the sheriff gave them a stern warning, though he waited until they had made it home. Apparently he expressed in no uncertain terms that everything about their stunt was illegal, a public health hazard and frankly just plain disrespectful to the dead."

"Do you think that they took his reprimand to heart?"

"I'm betting that there's a truck with a rocking chair or recliner in the pickup bed lurking somewhere close by."

Shaking his head, Ben could only mutter, "Oh for Christ's sake."

"Jacob is the oldest and probably has the transport permit in hand. You only have to enter the date and sign it acknowledging that Mr. Norlund died. The county regulations only require the mortician and sheriff's epresentative to fill out and sign at the time of issuance but hey're ultimately responsible for the family's compliance."

"This is in lieu of a death certificate?"

"No, you or Saroni will fill out and submit the death certificate to the state. The transport permit is merely to llow the family to transport him out to the ranch."

"I had no idea that home burial was still in practice. believe you but I'm going to the nurses' station to make a quick call to the sheriff's department. You know, just for ny own curiosity and make sure that the Sheriff had indeed ssued a recent transport permit to the Norlunds."

Myrna shrugged, "Suit yourself, Ben. I'm going to help the family clean up Mr. Norlund and prepare him for discharge. I'll bring the transport permit to you at the nurses' station."

"Sheriff's department, Reilly McIntyre speaking. How may I help you?"

"Mr. McIntyre, this Ben Parker, the physician assistant over at the hospital."

"Yes Mr. Parker, is this an emergency?"

"No that's why I used the main number."

"Okay, good, what can I do for you?"

"Did you recently issue a transport permit to the Norlund family for home burial?"

"As a matter of fact, yes. Jacob Norlund and one of his brothers were in yesterday during my shift. The permit actually is issued through the mortuary and the sheriff's department sign's off on it. Did Mr. Norlund pass?"

"He did, this afternoon. I just wasn't aware of the transport permit or home burial process."

"Well Mr. Norlund's body is now classified as a Bio Hazard and has to be handled as Hazardous Waste. Those are the rules."

Ben was appalled; that statement was not even within the purview of black humor, "I'm sure that you meant to say; my condolences to the Norlund family and I'm sure his remains will be treated respectfully."

"Right, like you said, and as I said there are rules and regulations regarding a Bio Hazard. His body began decomposing the minute he died. Now, if you take into account what he died of it can add to the toxic load therefore, the potential of toxins, or toxic and infectious waste being released becomes of greater concern."

"You, Mr. McIntyre, must be a comforting voice for the people dialing 911." Ben could not staunch his sarcasm.

"Thank you, Mr. Parker, we try to provide a needed service to the community."

Ben thought it best not to ramp up the sarcasm and to change the subject. "Where can I get a copy of the statutes on transport permits and home burial?"

"I'd call Garcia."

"I'm sorry but who is Garcia?"

"Garcia, the undertaker."

"I thought that his name was Jerry Munson."

"Yeh, Jerry Munson. We call him Garcia."

"Out of curiosity how do you get Garcia from Munson?"

Reilly sounded exasperated, "Munson?... Jerry Munson?... Mortician?... The dead?... Grateful Dead?.. Jerry Garcia?... soooo, Garcia."

"Oh, well that makes perfect sense Reilly." His eyes rolled skyward. "Thank you for the information."

"Glad to be of service. Have a great day." Click.

Ben immediately began wondering how many of Bedlam's public servants and government employees came from the same gene pool. Since he was now officially a short timer he knew, and more importantly did not really care, that he was unlikely to discover which pool needed to be heavily chlorinated.

Standing against the back wall of the employee's cafeteria, a vantage point that Ben felt was unassuming yet gave him a bird's eye view of the entire crowd as they entered and of course, when they exited. The Boyles, Krums, Rosencrantzs, Westergards, Stalcups, Brennita Cogburn, Roberta Montessi, Father Stalbach, and numerous other luminaries or community members unknown to Ben had strolled in and found seating. Currently he was watching the members of the Hospital Board finding their reserved folding chairs in the front row. Someone gave him an elbow to the ribs and he discovered Marni standing next to him displaying a wide grin. "What's up with the Cheshire cat grin?"

"Oh, just in a good mood I guess. A little bird mentioned that you had something to do with putting this evening together."

Ben shook his head no, "No, your little bird must have been eating fermented berries and banged its head on something. I merely mentioned to Susie, who you know has quite the flair for design that the hospital still needed help with their interior make over. As luck would have it, when Susie was in California she had had a working relationship with this Calistra Cartwright woman."

"Sometimes a pat on the back is okay to accept."

"Point taken but I still defer the credit to Susie."

"Whatever."

The crowd was talkative and expectant having filled all of the seats at least 15 minutes ago, more patient than Ben would have anticipated for a group having sat through one of these presentations the previous fall. Tonight would be devoid of the pomp and contrived circumstance foisted upon them by Brother Marise and certainly less ostentatious considering Susie's approach to life. He espied Susie up at the podium in animated, seemingly friendly conversation with the president of the Hospital Auxiliary, the fund raising arm for the hospital's capital expenditures. No blue jeans tonight; she was dressed in a pastel green blouse and black knee length skirt. As usual she appeared comfortable and confident. The president moved behind the podium which was offset to the crowd's right of center and tapped on the microphone, several distinct static snaps emitting from the speaker system. She cleared her throat signaling the crowd to settle in and quiet down. A large projection screen located front and center suddenly lit up, filled with a photo of the Bedlam Medical Center.

"Good evening ladies and gentleman and honored guests. I am Wanda Delwhimple, president of the Bedlam Medical Center Women's Hospital Auxiliary." The crowd responded with light but appreciative applause. "For the past several years we have been contemplating and developing a plan as to how to address the pressing need for upgrading and updating the Hospital's internal plant. A plan to restructure, upgrade and rejuvenate..." Ben found himself partially disconnecting from the droning introduction, staring off into space as he awaited the main event, "...and now it is with great pleasure that I introduce to you one of our leading community business entrepreneurs who has graciously volunteered her time and inspiration to help in the development and facilitation of our undertaking; Bedlam's own Susie Halverson." Susie briskly moved to the podium thanking Mrs. Delwhimple and adjusted the microphone as the crowd applauded enthusiastically. Ben wondered how many of the men in the room were clapping because of Susie's volunteerism, because of her stunning good looks, physical attributes, or her vivacious, flirting personality, or because unknown to their spouses they had ordered a Paul Reubens to go and were greatly appreciative of the clandestine adult movie venue available in Susie's back room. Ben saw her steal a quick look to the far back corner and smile at Kimimela who was standing silently with her back to the wall. The applause finally abated.

She scanned the crowd and began, "Good evening, all. I am not here to sell you anything. I am not here tonight to present a sales pitch. My presence tonight is to help motivate a community to support and to invest their…"

Someone in the crowd interrupted by shouting out, "I thought that this thing was free!"

"Aha! A heckler." She looked very composed, "It's rather hard in a small town to remain an anonymous heckler, Peter Olsen."

"I'm, I'm not amom, amominous Susie Q, I'm sayin' don't be tryin' to sell us no bill a goods. I thought this thing tonight was free."

"Did anyone tell you to bring your checkbook, Peter?"

"No, but…"

"Did someone at the door demand a cover charge from you?"

"No, I got…"

Ben finally located a head of unruly hair slightly bowed and shaking no with his answers.

"Then, not to be rude and truly without the intent of offense Peter but put a sock in it."

The audience applauded.

"Okay, Peter, are we good to go?"

"Yes ma'am, no offense taken."

"Let's skip ahead. When I was in California I had the opportunity to work in the design industry and

373

developed a working relationship with Calistra Cartwright who provided me with quite the education. When I was approached in early February of this year to help develop a feasibility plan for reconstituting and enhancing the interior plant design of the hospital I soon realized that we would need more help and expertise. I contacted Calistra Cartwright Enterprises and without hesitation they agreed take on this project." Susie pointed to Peter Olsen. "Please listen up closely, Peter, as a pro bono community service. There will be no charge for the design work or oversight if the hospital and community decides to implement the project plans. And Peter, just to completely assuage your suspicions, Calistra Cartwright Enterprises has pledged $25,000 to the project should the hospital and town of Bedlam make the decision to go ahead with the upgrade."

The audience burst into applause and Peter Olsen was the first to take to his feet in appreciation.

"I promised the Auxiliary that we would have a preliminary presentation by the beginning of April and here we are, April 1st to introduce the project. Medicine advances, new technology is developed and implemented and we accept and embrace the changes. The Bedlam Medical center is 44 years old. We take for granted the advances in Medicine yet we stalemate change to the hospital facility itself. The best that we can do for the accessibility, functionality and comfort of our family members, neighbors, and community members is to place televisions in the rooms, coffee makers in the waiting rooms and to occasionally slap a new coat of the same old colored paint on the walls. It's time to approach the internal plant with new energy, new ideas and new concepts that create a patient friendly and healing environment."

"I am your liaison and I provide the ground floor information to the design team in California, who in turn as produced a video presentation for tonight. The design team expects and will relish your input and critiques. This is a community project so therefore a community wide planning Chautauqua and several public design reviews will be scheduled starting in middle to late May. As I stated previously, tonight's presentation is a video production, however, I and representatives of the design team will be attending future meetings and planning sessions. It is with great pleasure and enthusiasm that I introduce to you a close personal associate, friend, and confidant of Calistra Cartwright who will guide you through tonight's presentation. The first step towards enhancing your hospital is the infusion of new life with an inviting and well-structured design plan..." The screen changed from the Bedlam Medical Center to projecting the start of the video. "I introduce to you Natalie Thackert."

Ben stood in stunned silence, mouth agape, as a lithe, energetic appearing middle aged woman, strode confidently into view on the screen. "Oh Susie, what have you done? What devious or nefarious plot have you devised?" He devoted his attention back to the screen. Natalie was wearing her graying brown hair in a younger style, bangs pulled to the sides and ponytail, a friendly smile directed squarely at the camera, sporting a blouse, skirt, and vest ensemble with sensible shoes. A simple string of pearls adorned her neck. It was anyone's guess as to her real age but she appeared to be in her late 50s. He knew that she was not a day under 68.

For the next 40 minutes Ben watched, entirely enthralled with the woman on the screen. She was engaging, moved fluidly with great posture, spoke enthusiastically with perfect diction and enunciation and by her eye movements he was positive that she was well prepared and not reading off of a teleprompter. He had absolutely no idea that his mother held that level of confidence or stage presence. If this was her first time in front of a recording camera then she killed it, she was a natural. This woman he remembered as an aging flower child of the sixties, more engaged in social reform, environmental issues, gardening and tossing clay for a pottery kiln has found her stride as an interior design spokesperson. Ben found himself conflicted between pride, remorse, unresolved hurt and a lingering mistrust, reestablishing with some effort that their relationship was a work in progress.

With a warm smile and disarming demeanor Natalie Thackert concluded, "All of us here at Calistra Cartwright Enterprises thank you for the opportunity to work with the community of Bedlam on this most auspicious and inspiring challenge. Susie Halverson shall remain your local liaison in direct contact with Ms. Cartwright and her design team as we continue the planning process of design and implementation. Suggestion boxes will be placed within the hospital for any written ideas that you would care to submit and please, do not hesitate to contact the Women's Hospital Auxiliary or Susie Halverson if you have suggestions or comments that would contribute towards building a warm, welcoming and comforting hospital facility. Thank you and good night."

The presentation ended and the screen was fading out, the audience began to applaud, Wanda Delwhimple was upright and moving towards the podium when a still photo appeared on the screen. An older color photograph with two children astride bareback upon an unmistakable Appaloosa, a pigtailed blonde girl holding the reins and a crew cut boy peering over her shoulder. Both had broad smiles. The audience was continuing its applause, however, here were a few gestures and heads turned to the photograph.

Unconsciously he gasped, "Oh, for Christ's sake." Ben muttered softly, "What the fuck?" and then chuckled quietly.

Marni observed, "That's an interesting way to end a video presentation." She looked at Ben, "What's so funny?"

"Do you know what a turkey is?"

Hesitantly she responded, "A bird. Thanksgiving dinner? The national symbol for the United States Congress?"

Ben laughed, "Appropriate but not what I'm looking for. How about a hat trick?"

She looked confused, "I don't know; something a magician does in his show?"

"When a bowler rolls three consecutive strikes it's called a turkey and a hat trick is when a hockey player scores three goals in a game."

"Well, thank you for those important bits of trivia. Is there a point to this?"

Ben was staring at her face and then flipped his head towards the photo on the screen, "That horse up there?"

"Yeh."

"Mr. Pasacovich, our neighbor back home owned that horse. When it was born his daughter was two or three years old and heard the veterinarian say, 'You've got a good looking, healthy foal' and she could only pronounce foal as fool. Mr. Pasacovich, who at times has a somewhat warped sense of humor, named the horse 'Fool' before he gave it to his daughter."

"Ookayyyy..." Marni sounded and looked expectant.

"The girl on that horse…" he pointed at the photo, "…is his daughter, I'm guessing about eight years old. Care to take a guess at her name?"

She responded with an odd look and asked, "How in hell would…" then her eyes widened and she giggled as a thought struck her, "April. Is her name April?"

Ben nodded attempting to remain expressionless, "And the seven year old boy sitting behind her?"

Marni studied the photo, "You?" She sounded highly incredulous asking, "Is that you, Ben Parker?"

Ben cringed at how loud she had blurted out his name and made a sign with his hand to lower the volume. "Yep, that's me."

"How the hell did that picture wind up there?"

Trying to deflect her attention Ben countered with, "Today Callie got me with an April Fools' prank, and then you got me good with the April Fools' luncheon caper…"

"Whoa there, kemosabe, you can't…"

"I certainly can and will pin that fiasco on you," he again gestured at the screen, "and now this photograph. That's the turkey. That's the hat trick."

"And again I ask, how did that photo get to be part of tonight's presentation?"

Ben hesitated, knowing that this trick had to have been orchestrated by a two person conspiracy. Quickly mulling over his options he had to decide whether to implicate both suspected perpetrators and ultimately disclosing Susie's secret. He opted for one. "Natalie Thackert."

"The lady giving the presentation from Cartwright Enterprises? How would she…"

"Natalie Thackert is my mother."

Marni's jaw literally dropped open. She sputtered out, "You, you got a lot of 'splaining to do bub."

Ben's eyes had sought out and found Susie standing across the room. Maybe Susie sensed his stare boring into the side of her head or maybe it was sheer coincidence that she turned her head and that they locked eyes. She smiled mischievously as her eyes traveled over to the photograph. "Perhaps, but I'm not the only one."

EASTER TIMES THREE

Using both hands Ben deftly shaped the dampened and warm orthopedic splinting material to accommodate his patient's wrist and forearm. Finally shaped to his liking, he fitted it against the rolled gauze and cotton sleeve, which padded and protected the skin of the fractured right forearm. Karmma began to unroll and wrap elastic bandages to secure the splint in place starting at the palm and wrist leaving the thumb free and working her way up the forearm to just below the elbow. She applied two metal clips to anchor the end of the bandage and taped over them as a secondary lock. Ben checked the finger tips for sensitivity and capillary refill assuring adequate blood blow and then applied a sling for elevation, comfort and protection. The middle-aged female patient was forewarned that the splint would remain warm as the splinting material stiffened. Karmma and Ben tag teamed her with care .instructions, the appropriate use of pain medication, contact numbers for the orthopedist she would follow up with and the myriad of discharge paperwork that she and her husband were required to sign. Yes, the patient declared, the pain level was very tolerable and the couple's multiple "thank you" was effusive as they were walked out to the emergency room entrance.

Ben motioned for Karmma to accompany him to the X-ray viewing room. He pulled out a chair for her, slid an X-ray out of an oversized manila envelope and clipped it into place next to the image currently displayed on the viewer. Two different patients, same view of the right wrist. Karmma looked from one to the other and back again.

Ben asked, "Do you see the fracture line in the distal radius on each X-ray?"

Karmma tentatively pointed and traced a line with her finger on the left image and then repeated it on the right image.

"Exactly. Good eye, Karmma. A transverse, non-displaced fracture of the distal right radius."

She sounded slightly astonished when she observed, "They look almost exactly the same." Karmma pointed to left, "Our 8 AM patient" then to the right, "Our 2 PM patient who just left." Swiveling her head to her right at Ben who was leaning on the counter, "Two fractures almost exactly the same within six hours; are you anticipating a third one today, Ben?"

"No, I'm not. However, since it occurred to you, Karmma, are you referring to or invoking the rule of threes?"

"I'm not necessarily waving a red flag but maybe a yellow caution sign."

"There's no scientific evidence to support the Rule of Threes. You may interpret the concept as coincidence versus fate versus superstition but not as a certainty or phenomena with any scientific proof or credibility."

"So, I shouldn't expect a third Urinary Tract Infection though you saw one last night and again early this morning? Or another chest pain caused by acid reflux like the two so far today or a third sprained ankle since we treated one at 10 and then again at 12:30?"

"No. The first one would be chance occurrence and the second a coincidence. There is no astrological alignment of the stars, no foreshadowing of things to come. The second occurrence may leave some people with uncertainty; speculating that a third episode is a greater possibility. However, if that feeling of uncertainty is allowed to prevail then a perceived sense of certainty may overwhelm the mere possibility of chance therefore you believe in the probability of reoccurrence; hence the rule of threes."

"Wow, you've given this some thought. So, you categorically discount the Rule of Threes?"

"Small towns are a microcosm of what may transpire in a city emergency room. During a fast paced shift you might see several bloody noses, eye emergencies, GI bleeds, drug overdoses, or chest pains and it's not until the third or fourth one that you recognize that there have been that many multiple occurrences. We see pathology and trauma here; just not as often."

"How about deaths Ben? If there are two we know with regularity to expect a third one."

"If you project that it will transpire often enough then it becomes second nature; ingrained and expected. Therefore, when it does take place it reinforces the predictability."

"So, I ask again; do you believe in the Rule of Threes?"

"Karmma, you might as well ask me if I believe in the Easter bunny."

"Well do you? Believe in the Easter bunny?"

"Ask me tomorrow morning after I check the house for chocolate eggs and rabbit turds."

The gas pump shut off with an audible clunk as he released the handle and set the nozzle back into its holder. A receipt whirled out; he stuffed it in his pocket and walked over to the convenience store part of the Bedlam One Stop. Cool and still, the morning air held no hint of snow or foul weather; high cirrus clouds and two contrails white against an azure sky. Ben remembered Easter egg hunts during his childhood when the eggs were hidden in the darkness of early morning only to be covered by an errant snowstorm blowing in shortly after. That would send the Easter egg hiders scurrying, searching for eggs under several inches of snow with only a vague memory of where they were hidden or securing replacement eggs that could be hidden in plain sight on a leeward hillside or inside the hastily cleaned barn at the rodeo grounds.

Inside Ben bought the two local papers, a medium black coffee and deposited them on the checkout counter. A young woman, perhaps 20 or 21 and unfamiliar to Ben appeared and unenthusiastically positioned herself at the cash register. Short black hair streaked with pink topped a face heavily made up and left her ears exposed displaying multiple piercings. She wore a bright yellow long sleeved Bedlam One Stop uniform shirt unbuttoned to her breasts and what he could only conclude to be some form of shiny full body leotard. Her nails were painted pink and purple and the bases of her fingers had been tattooed with blue letters. He read the backs or her fingers: CLUE LESS. Her name badge introduced her as Lycra. Ben concluded that her mother must be very proud.

She did not bother to look at him as she rang up his merchandise, "This all?"

"Yes, thank you. I thought that Frank usually worked on holidays, Lycra?"

Lycra's head snapped over and she glared at him "That's Lie-Cee-Rah and Frank doesn't work her anymore."

Ben was surprised as he handed her a $10 bill "Since when? Frank was here two weeks ago."

"I don't know maybe a week? Maybe more? He up and quit and ran off with the skinny white blonde order gir from Susie's."

Now Ben's curiosity was fully engaged, "Wow, had no idea that he was thinking of leaving. Do you have any idea where he might have gone?"

"Do I look like I'm workin' in a friggin informatior booth buddy?" She was attempting to count out his change gave up and laid it out in a pile on the counter. "He probably went back to Pakistan or somewhere warm and opened up his own convenience store." She was not snide definitely caustic.

Ben silently counted his change, slid the bills and coins into his hand, into his pocket, picked up his coffee and papers and said, "Thank you Lycra, have a nice Easter."

She glared without correcting him.

Just as Ben opened his driver's side door his cell phone rang. Pulling it out of his coat pocket he looked around him to make sure he wasn't blocking anyone from accessing the gas pumps and remained standing outside of his truck. "Hello?"

"Hey dare, dis is Josie Rosencrantz and is dis Ben Parker?"

"Good morning, Mrs. Rosencrantz." Ben extended his left arm straight out pulling his coat sleeve back enough to see his watch; it was 7:45 AM. "You're up bright and early the Easter morning."

384

"Yes sirree. You betcha dare, Ben Parker, annuder fine lookin' Sunday in Bedlam. Coupla tings dare Ben Parker. You told me dat you would be skeedadling, movin' away in early May and me and my big guy will be in Nort Dakoda takin' in da Lac Aux Morts Lake Ice Breakup Festival again and I wanted to double check, ya know, so dat we got all da wires freed up 'cause ya know dat no one, at least no one dat I know wants ta see ya go, but iffin dats what cha got ta do den da best to ya though me and hubby want ta know if dares anyting we can do ta keep ya here young fella." Ben knew that with her lung capacity her hobby must be free diving.

"I appreciate that, Mrs. Rosencrantz, but no, I'll be packed up and on the road on Monday, May 3rd. I'll leave the keys in your mail slot and you can mail the security deposit to the address that I gave you. Outside of being kidnapped or struck by lightning I can't think of anything that would prevent me from leaving."

"Yah, jeezz, dats too bad dare Ben Parker boot doncha know dat God, hesa got dat uneek sense a humor and dem lightning bolts yoost come outa da blue."

"I'll keep on my toes Mrs. Rosencrantz."

"You yoost do dat, Ben Parker, now den, I wancha ta know dat cha need to come to da Easter Day Parade and da festivities oot at da Rodeo Grounds taday. Hoo boy we got da fun in store, yes sirree, you betcha Ben Parker, fun for da whole family, we got da kiddies parade and da Easter egg hunt and da Easter bonnet fashionable show and da bunny hop in da sack obstacle course anda, hoo boy ya, da fresh egg horse rider toss an a course a community pot luck. By golly dare Ben Parker you bring your appetite an we gots more food den you can shake da stick at.

"Sounds great, Mrs. Rosencrantz, I will try my best to make it. Out of curiosity I see that there's another Easter egg hunt in town; have you always had two egg hunts in Bedlam?"

"Holy jeezz no dare Ben Parker. No dis is da brains storm or such of dat Krum and da Mayor Boyle 'cause ya know dis is election year and dose two are a coupla doozers whose got ta sell dem folks dat day are da good guys peddlin' dare resorts and hoosin' projects."

"What's the candy drop that they're advertising?"

"Yah, yah, day got ol Buster Bannion an his crop dusta plane snookered inta flyin' over da park an droppin' candy an such to da kiddies sometin dat my big guy tinks issa boneheaded idea an I tend ta agree wid hubby when he tinks tings are off the kilter. Oh, hay dare Ben Parker, I gotta spread ta purple and pink frostin' on da fake chickin' fried rabbits' feet so gotta go." Click.

The first thing Ben thought, "Wow, I wonder how those go over with the kiddies?"

"Good morning, Mr. Parker."

Ben looked up from the chart to see who was offering up the cheery greeting, "Father Stalbach, good to see you sir. Easter mass today?"

"Yes, and a bountiful meal following mass to share with all of the residents."

The smile was genuine Ben had decided and obviously reassuring to his congregation. Father Stalbach used an index finger to focus Ben's attention by tapping on his white clerical collar. "I don't leave home without it, or…" he pulled a spare collar from his coat pocket covering his black clerical shirt, "this one, or the one I now keep as a second spare in my car."

Ben began laughing, "Glad to see that you are well prepared for any event Father Stalbach." He had a sudden thought, perhaps odd to some but to Ben it seemed easonable. He hesitated but then coached his words, "Father Stalbach, I'm not well versed in the traditions of clerical clothing in the Catholic Church and there is no intent to show disrespect but are clerical collars always white?"

The priest looked surprised.

"I mean, are you allowed to have different color collars for seasons or religious holidays? Maybe purple for Easter or red or green at Christmas? I know that there are other vestment colors other than black or white however, I was merely curious about the collar."

Without hesitation or inflection Father Stalbach responded evenly, "Traditionally the clerical collar has always been white and I would not anticipate that frivolous changes in the clerical wardrobe are forthcoming." He shifted gears and his smile reappeared, "Perhaps, Mr. Parker, you would like to join us today?"

"I must respectfully decline sir. I am again on call for the emergency room and would hate to interrupt your service if I were called out."

"Easter and spring are times of redemption, resurrection, of new life and rebirth. Attending worship with our congregation will provide you with an inner peace, a shared tranquility and bonding with your fellow parishioners that you may be missing in your life."

Ben thought that if anything the clergyman was persistent and maybe a bit judgmental. "No disrespect intended Father Stalbach but I have my own approach to my spirituality and higher power so I thank you anyway." Apparently, Ben was oblivious to how dismissive he had sounded.

There was an edge to Father Stalbach's voice, "Perhaps another time, Mr. Parker." He turned and walked towards the residents' dining hall and the seated congregants.

"Were you being flippant with the priest Ben?"

"No, Karmma, honestly I was just curious about the collars and then up front about how I choose to deal with my beliefs."

"I'm not so sure that he was accepting that excuse." Karmma's expression was one of concern, "Are you okay Ben? You seem a little irritable this morning."

Ben was quietly thoughtful for a minute, "I don' know...maybe. Pammula kept me hopping most of the night with ER patients so...yeah, I suppose that I might be tired and irritable. Maybe I've got some sort of short-timers syndrome." There was a degree of resignation in his voice.

Karmma frowned and blew out a breath before she asked, "Were things, ahhh, were things all that bad here in the hospital?"

"No, Karmma, you and rest of the crew are good people and great to work worth and I will miss all of you but... Saroni. He was my problem; the bane of my existence. I have to assume, no believe, that my tour of duty here in Bedlam with Saroni was my penance for past bad behaviors."

She laughed loud enough for several of the resident congregation who were not hearing impaired to turn their heads towards the nurses' station.

"Again, it was not my intent but..." now Ben sounded a bit facetious, "I'll say a little prayer for forgiveness."

"You, Mr. Parker, you would be further ahead to drop a 20 in the collection plate."

Slumped forward in his clinic office chair, Ben was taking a short nap when the desk phone awoke him, "Hello?" His voice was gravelly.

"Ben, it's Karmma, you sound a little grumpy. Did I wake you up?"

"I was closing my eyes for a few minutes, what's up?"

"I'm down in the emergency room. The ambulance, rescue truck and fire department are out east of town. A small plane crashed in an open field and there's some kind of fire. The number of victims is unknown."

"I'll meet you in the ER in a minute." Receiving a message of that gravity sends the adrenalin skyrocketing, the heart pumping, immediately clears the cobwebs of sleep, and initiates a spring, if not a turbo charging of one's step. Ben did not stop at the nurses' station where he saw Roxy with a phone cradled against her ear as she flipped a page on the clipboard she held at eye level, rather he briskly walked down to the emergency room doors. Upon entering the ER, he found Karmma and Tara already at work preparing the two trauma bays. "Have lab and imaging been notified?"

Tara waved her free arm, the other carrying pre-packaged sterile burn sheets, "Notified and on their way in."

"Do we have another nurse or aides available Karmma?"

"Pammula's husband answered the phone and promised to wake her and send her in. I've got Roxy calling the list to find some aides. I think I saw Dwight's truck pull up in the rear parking lot."

The emergency room dispatch monitor had been turned on and Ben heard static and a burst of garbled transmission, "Any additional information on what's going on? How many patients?"

"No information to add. All we've been hearing is that static and unintelligible words." Tara and Karmma continued to set up preassembled trauma and burn supplies and equipment in the big and little ER's as Ben laid out a tray of instruments for possible intubations, located his pocket calculator and quickly reviewed trauma and burn treatment protocols. The dispatch monitor continued to broadcast white noise, static, garbled messages with the occasional recognizable word or two.

"Karmma, line one. Karmma Mason, line one." The unmistakable tinny, static laced overhead announcement gave them all pause.

Karmma picked up the phone and pressed the blinking red light designating line one. "Hello this is Karmma Mason RN." Karmma listened intently as Tara and Ben stood by expectantly. "How many should we be expecting?" She was nodding her head and held up one finger to Tara and Ben, "ETA?" After a short pause Karmma looked over at the wall clock at the head of Bay one. "Okay, thanks…yeah…okay keep us posted" then she hung up. "Dispatch says that they're having some major radio communication problems. The ambulance is about to leave the scene with one patient on board, condition unknown. They cannot confirm how many patients may be coming in. The ambulance should be here in 10 to 12 minutes."

Roxy was at the ER doors, "Sienna, Sydney, and Pammula should be here in a couple of minutes and Sydney will cover the nurses' station." Ben and Karmma simultaneously said, "Thank you, Roxy."

Ben addressed the three nursing staff members. "Karmma if you would please bring Pammula up to speed and line out duties to your crew. I'll triage the patient coming in but depending on who and what injuries come in afterward we may have to change the game plan on the fly. Trauma and major burns to the trauma bays and the less badly injured we'll run through the little ER. Any walking wounded can be staged out in the hallway. Roxy, would you please call Wynot and Sunnvale and give them a heads up in case we need to transfer. You might try Marni as well but I think that she is out of town today. Are we good?"

Ben heard three "Yes." Karmma responded, "We're ready."

"Okay, let's get this done."

Karmma, Tara, Roxy, Pammula, Sienna, Sandi from the lab and Junie the X-ray technician stood forming an informal gauntlet on either side of the Emergency Department hallway, anxiously awaiting the arrival of their first patient. Dwight stood outside on the cement apron helping to guide the ambulance in after having locked open the entrance doors to the hallway. Ben stood in the doorway. The ambulance braked to a stop and Ben and Dwight swung open its rear doors. John Bersted stepped down quickly followed by Zina Crane. Having unlocked the gurney John began to roll it out of the ambulance as Zina and Ben positioned themselves to the right and Dwight on the left to help lift and balance it as John deployed the landing gear.

In the span of a few seconds Ben made an initial evaluation of the middle aged male patient immobilized on a spine board and strapped to the gurney. A cervical collar stabilized his neck, Kerlix bandage swaddled his forehead below a bald pate and an oxygen mask covered his nose and mouth. His right wrist and forearm were taped to a cardboard splint. From his mid-chest to his feet he was covered with a wool blanket. The man's eyes were open discriminately moving, he was talking though his words were indiscernible under the oxygen mask and he was waving his left hand in what Ben recognized as the straight forearmed, rotating open palm wave of a parade queen.

Ben stepped forward, peeled back the blanket, returned it to its original position, and lifted the oxygen mask so that he could understand the patient. "My name is Ben Parker and I'm the physician assistant on duty. Can you tell me your name sir?"

"I'm Buster Bannion and the faster you untie me and get me off this fucking plastic board the happier all of us will be."

Ben repositioned the oxygen mask back on Mr. Bannion's face. In those first few seconds Ben established his patient's ABC's; airway, breathing and circulation. The patient was conscious and alert, he was talking evenly therefore his air way was patent and he was breathing without distress and there did not appear to be any serious or distracting injuries indicative of blood loss. Ben nodded to the others, "Let's go." The ambulance driver, Dave Bushnell, had joined them and took the head of the gurney.

When they began rolling Mr. Bannion towards the ER Karmma stepped forward, "How many patients are coming in?"

Zina responded with, "Mr. Bannion is the only patient. He was the only occupant of the plane." One could sense a universal release of tension among the hospital staff. Karmma led the way as the gurney continued to the ER and Zina provided an initial report.

"Mr. Bannion reports no loss of consciousness. After impact he was able to extricate himself from the plane before it caught fire and started a small brush fire. No burns reported or observed. We found him alert and oriented sitting outside of the fire area smoking a cigarette. He complains of a minor headache and there is a five centimeter laceration to the right forehead, moderate right lower arm pain, minor right sided chest or rib pain, bilateral ankle and knee pain which he rates as two to three out of 10. No neck, back or abdominal pain. No shortness of breath. BP 144 over 88, heart rate of 86, respirations 18, SaO2 94% on six liters of Oxygen. Denies any alcohol or recreational drugs on board." Zina stepped over and whispered in Ben's ear, "Just a heads up, Ben, Highway Patrol will be here shortly to see this lucky son of a bitch." Ben did his best to hide a smile.

They turned the corner into the emergency room and Karmma directed the transfer of the patient onto the trauma gurney and began delegating responsibilities to the staff. John, Zina and Dave positioned themselves nearby at the counter anticipating that they may be needed to turn or position the patient. Ben wrote lab orders for Sandi, told Junie that he would complete the X-ray orders after his initial physical exam of Mr. Bannion and joined the EMT's and driver as he waited for the nurses to finish their work.

"Great report, Zina. Good job, everyone."

John leaned over to speak, his voice subdued so as not to carry, "We got called out and had no idea what we were in for. No one suspected that it was Buster's plane and I'm sure that everyone was relieved that it was not a mass casualty scenario. Truthfully, I have no clue how Buster got out of that plane; let alone survived. It's totaled and was pretty well engulfed in flames when we got there and it had started a brush fire. Earlier I was exiting Susie's shop and stood on the porch watching him start his candy drop run but I lost sight of him behind the trees across the road. He pulled up, circled around and turned to the east. Apparently, he felt the need to buzz the sheriff's department so he dropped down again and I lost sight of him. The next time I saw him he was headed east waggling his wings so I thought that he was just showing off. I found out later at the crash site that he had flown so low that he clipped the aerial atop the sheriff's antenna tower. He crashed in Krum's golf course and when we arrived the lucky son of a bitch was sitting outside of the brush fire area having a smoke."

Ben was watching the progress of the nursing staff while listening to John and just nodded, "You're right John. He is one lucky son of a bitch." He pushed himself away from the counter to start his physical evaluation on Buster Bannion, by everyone's consensus, one lucky son of a bitch.

"I'd like a cocktail or two if I stay."

Ben had just spent 90 minutes in the emergency room with Mr. Bannion and realized that any attempt to make rational headway would continue to be an uphill battle. "Sorry, Mr. Bannion, you've been given pain medication and secondly you have a probable concussion, so I'm sorry, no alcohol."

"Don't be sorry, Parker, just promise me my cocktails."

"And I suppose that you'll want smoking privileges as well?"

"That's a no brainer."

Ben had already concluded that a no brainer was who he was dealing with. He was beginning to worry that Mr. Bannion may have understated his use of alcohol when providing his medical and social history. "Would something adverse happen if you skipped those cocktails for a day or two?"

"I would get adversely irritated with you, other than that nothing."

Now sitting on the side of the ER gurney since he refused to lie down, Mr. Bannion had been deflecting all reasonable approaches by Ben and Karmma to convince him that admission to the hospital for continued treatment and monitoring was the most appropriate next step in his recovery.

"Mr. Bannion, please allow me to review your current health issues. You have a probable concussion, head laceration, and a fracture to the radius of your right arm just above the wrist. There was considerable impact resulting in extensive bruising to your chest wall and three rib fractures, relatively severe bilateral ankle sprains, contusions and swelling of both knees and a moderate sprain of the right knee. You are dehydrated and your oxygen level drops below 90% without supplemental oxygen. It would be to your benefit…"

"My benefit is to get the hell out of here, have some cocktails and a smoke and go to sleep in my own bed."

"I was going to say that it would be to your benefit for us to admit you, give you fluids, oxygen, some pain medication, monitor your cognitive and neurological condition for the next 24 hours and reevaluate at that time with the potential for discharge home."

"It was only a hard impact landing, not a plane crash, so what's the big …?"

Karmma interrupted, "Buster, hard impact landing or crash you are one lucky son of a bitch to have survived."

"I've augured in five planes and lived to tell the tale. Obviously, I bounce well and I'm a survivor."

Karmma had apparently expended all of her cordiality and good will, "I'm not at all sure that I'd be bragging about five plane crashes; it has a tendency to highlight your piloting deficiencies."

Buster stared at Karmma with surprise and fire in his eyes and then shifted his attention to Ben, "I don't need to take this abuse."

"True, however, if you decide to stay with us the abuse comes with a sponge bath."

An expression of distain filled Buster's face which was followed by a look of contemplation and then to Ben's surprise, "Okay. I'll give you 24 hours."

Karmma motioned to Ben and he followed her into the X-ray viewing room. Three X-ray images were hung side by side on the viewing screen; the same view taken of three separate patients. Ben had already concluded Karmma's intent, however, chose not to say anything.

"Ben."

"Karmma."

"Would you mind telling me what we are looking at?"

"If I'm not mistaken, Karmma, you have displayed the X-rays of three patients seen in our emergency room in less than 30 hours, all of whom suffered a non-displaced right distal radius fracture."

"And that Ben would prove beyond the shadow of a doubt that…"

"That the rule of threes truly does exist and is quietly residing in Bedlam, Montana."

"I rest my case."

Having competed Wednesday morning hospital rounds Ben returned to his office and found the message alert blinking on his desk phone. Tired, a little sleep deprived and only halfway through his week of ER call his office chair was a welcome sight though short respite. He pressed the playback button and picked up the phone receiver.

"Ben, it's John Bersted. I was supposed to give you a message last Sunday but it completely slipped my mind. My sister Paula has been in Minnesota caring for our aunt who fell and broke her hip. She's flying back May 3rd and wants you to come out to our place for dinner on Sunday the 9th. She apologizes for not having you out earlier but it's been a really hectic year. There, that's your formal invitation. Give me a call when you have time. Thanks, Ben."

Ben hung up the phone. Now he found himself in a quandary; was he more disappointed that he now had to turn down an invitation to a long promised great meal or that for the past year he had seen only the face of Paula Bersted, former rodeo and beauty queen and his shallow and shameless curiosity for what the rest of her looked like would forever remain unfulfilled. His phone rang momentarily taking him off the hook from confronting the truth.

"Hello, it's Ben."

Myrna's voice greeted him, "Chop, chop, Ben. You've got people waiting on you for that resident's discharge."

"Thank you, Myrna, I was having a moment of inner turmoil. I'll be right there."

"Good, glad I could help. We have enough turmoil around here without you adding to it. Bye."

"Is that Elvin Bishop that you're whistling there, Ben?" He heard Marni call out to him from her office, stopped abruptly, backed up two steps and pushed open the mostly closed door. Standing in the doorway Ben whistled a few more bars. "Fooled Around and Fell in Love, right?"

"Yes, Marni, you have a discerning ear."

"Out of curiosity, Ben, why is it that you only whistle?

"It's the only way that I can carry a tune. Once, when I was a kid, after church our neighbor Mr. Pasacovich joked that no one in the Parker family could carry a tune in a bucket so I started whistling and stuck with it."

"Well you're really good at it and obviously have a pretty large repertoire. Do you do any Bob Dylan?"

"Sorry to say no, Marni. I have a tough time trying to whistle off key."

"Oh, oucchhh. That's cold, Ben; you're a bit of a music snob, aren't you?"

"How can you say that with any conviction, Marni? You only know what you hear; not what you don't hear."

"I stand by my statement until proven otherwise."

"Standing is tiring enough; it's a good thing that you didn't threaten to hold your breath until proven otherwise."

"You're a little snot Parker, a plague upon you."

"How is your day going my friend?"

"A little slow today but I'm not complaining."

"I wanted to thank you again for offering to take my Friday night ER shift Marni; that was way above and beyond any expectations. I'd be more than happy to cover one of your Wednesday shifts for you."

"There are only a couple left before you abandon ship Ben."

"So, speak up now or you'll be SOL."

"I guess then that I'll be shit out of luck."

Ben sounded contrite, "I'm sorry to leave you alone here to work with Saroni but…"

"No buts, Ben," Marni's voice was forgiving, "We'll all miss you and I really do understand why you're making the leap."

"Look, I'll catch up with you at lunch time. I've got some people chomping at the bit so I have to get going."

"Where are you off to?"

"To discharge our Norwegian warbler, Mrs. Haugen. Her family is here to take her home to Minnesota."

"Good for her. I'll miss her singing but thankfully we still have you."

He grinned, "For only a couple more weeks. You better start auditioning new nursing home residents because I'm just about outta here."

Marni sniped, "You don't need to remind me. Like your ability to sing; keep it to yourself."

At 7 PM Ben crossed the threshold of Susie's 4 S's to pick up several preordered sandwiches and subs with which he was treating Marni and the Friday night hospital shift. He wanted to demonstrate his appreciation since Marni had volunteered to cover this shift; her gracious gesture provided an additional break to his long week of emergency room call. A young woman bearing a strong resemblance to Kimimela stood at the order counter patiently listening to four middle aged women verbally dissecting the merits of their individual orders. Ben leaned his lower back against the pickup counter and scanned the crowded dining room. Susie's was at near capacity and the noise level of conversing customers, the clatter of plates and silverware, and chair legs scuffing over the hard wood floor annoyingly distracting. There were several faces that he recognized occupying booths and tables but the two profiles in his direct vision that he remained focused upon were sitting opposite each other in a booth on the far west wall. The man and woman leaned slightly toward each other, the woman smiling, her hands cradling her coffee mug; the man talking animatedly and gesturing with his right hand, while holding his coffee mug in his left. Ben was surprised but not overly. He had noticed a developing connection between Dwight and Stella over the past several months and they appeared to be enjoying each other's company this evening.

"Ben." Susie's voice was behind him. He turned to see her smiling though somewhat harried face.

"Susie, you look a bit overwhelmed tonight. Are you okay?"

Her pastel purple hairnet was barely entrapping her bangs and she used her right thumb to tuck a few wild strands back under the elastic hem. "My kitchen help called in sick and as you can see I have a temporary replacement taking orders and working the floor."

"I heard that …" Ben hesitated searching his memory banks.

"Stephanie."

"Thank you. That Stephanie had run off with Frank from the One Stop; I had no clue." He turned his head towards the attractive raven haired girl at the order counter, "This young lady looks somewhat familiar."

"Kimimela's daughter. She volunteered to help out for a few days but needs to get back to school."

"Is there anything that I can do to help out Susie?"

"Thank you, Ben. I've got someone coming in any minute to help out. Sorry that I can't stay and chat but I've got to go rescue some French fries. We'll get to talk later." She whirled around and literally ran back through the kitchen doors.

Ben paid his bill and headed out to deliver tonight's meals on wheels.

400

The only light on in the house at 10 minutes to 11 was at the rear of the kitchen and Ben was beginning to doze off in his living room recliner. John Wayne's "The Searchers" was ending and the remnant of his beer was warm. Now in a transitional state between wakefulness and sleep Ben may have heard a vehicle door close and shortly after soft steps ascending the porch stairs. A soft but distinct knocking on his front door awakened him from his reverie, his threshold consciousness. He swung open the door and reached to his right to turn on the porch light.

"Leave the light off Ben," Susie's voice soft with her request.

Pushing open the screen door he could see Susie standing on the porch, her hands clasped together waist high. He stepped down to the porch and allowed the hydraulic closer to shut the door. "Susie, what an unexpected pleasure." Then the lateness of the evening dawned upon him, "Are you okay? Is there something wrong?"

She stepped forward and now they stood but a scant 12 inches apart, "I'm fine Ben, tired but fine."

There was enough light from a streetlight for Ben to make out her features and he could discern a smile on her face. "What's going on, Susie?"

"You're leaving town Ben, that's what's going on." She paused gathering her thoughts, "I believe that we have become good friends despite my incessant flirting and our verbal jousting and admittedly there is an attraction that neither of us can deny. Without sounding trite or maudlin…both of us realize that we care for each other and therein lies the rub. Neither of us will be satisfied unless something is resolved.

"Therein lies the rub? The lady doth protest too much, me thinks."

Susie caught him by surprise reaching up and with both hands grasping the back of his head and neck, standing on her tip toes and kissing him passionately full on the lips. Ben kissed her back with the same fervor. Their lips parted, her tongue sought out his and they were lost in the passion and intimacy of their prolonged kiss. His arms embraced her at her mid-back and they literally crushed themselves together. And then their lips separated. Ben could hear her catching her breath as he caught his own. Her cheek rubbed against his then she kissed him softly on the lips. Gently he brushed his lips on her nose and then her forehead as she released her grip on his neck. Her hands slid from his neck, patted his upper chest and then encircled his lower back. They continued to embrace for a minute and simultaneously let go and stepped back to eye each other.

"The only thing resolved, Susie, is that we want more than either of us is prepared to give."

"I've been waiting to do this since last summer, Ben, and I hold no regrets for having done it."

"Nor do I, Susie. Given another time, another set of circumstances we would have been a great match."

"We would have set Bedlam afire, Ben Parker."

In the near darkness he could see a broad smile, maybe a glisten rather than a mere glint in her eyes.

"You have my number, Ben?" The husky voice he loved caught for a moment.

Ben made a feeble attempt to laugh before he said, "I've had your number since the day we met, Susie Halverson."

In her exaggerated Texas twang she responded, "You do know how to sweet talk a girl, you good lookin' thang, you." And then she was gone.

"Hello? It's Ben."

"Good afternoon, Ben, it's Stella at the hospital."

"Hi Stella, and just as a point of interest, you are the only Stella that I know."

"Well then, hello it's the hospital."

"Okay, Stella, what may I do for you?"

"I have two individuals in the emergency room who are in need of your expertise."

"What medical malady has brought them to our doorstep?"

"A rather unique malady if you will or rather a unique predisposing action initiating said malady."

"Is this a riddle of some sort?"

"Have you ever seen the movie *Cool Hand Luke*?"

"The Paul Newman, George Kennedy, Dennis Hopper *Cool Hand Luke*?"

"Has there been a remake that I am happy not to have seen?"

"No, no remake."

"Do you remember when Paul Newman bet that he could eat 50 hard-boiled eggs?"

"Nobody can eat 50 eggs."

"There, yes, you've seen it. Well we have two gentlemen that watched the movie for the first time this past Wednesday night and spent Thursday and Friday collecting every colored hard boiled Easter egg they could lay their hands on. From what I can ascertain the eggs were up to two weeks old and mostly unrefrigerated however, our protagonists were not to be denied their inalienable right to reenact the scene last night."

"So, the ER is filled with hydrogen sulfide?"

"Farts are the least of their or our problems at the moment."

"Well there is always the chance of Salmonella so did you alert our lab tech yet?"

"On their way in."

"I will see you shortly."

"Thank you, Ben."

Stella met him in the hallway outside of the main emergency room, her hands behind her back. Ben eyed her suspiciously wondering what she was hiding back there.

"What were you whistling when you came through the door, Ben?"

"*Stuck in the Middle With You* by Stealers Wheel."

He began whistling the chorus again and Stella added the words aloud, "Clowns to the left of me, jokers to the right..." and Ben joined in. "Here I am, caught in the middle with you."

"How is it Stella that you managed to find the most oddball cases and patients for my first big weekend on call last Memorial Day as well as this, my last big holiday weekend here in Bedlam?"

"Because, Ben, we are of the same mindset. We are not necessarily adrenalin junkies but not adverse to the intricacies, absurdities, mysteries, and occasional insanity of the emergency room."

"Have we had the pleasure of previously treating either of these two individuals?"

"I think that we should title this case Beavis and Butthead meet the Easter Bunny."

Ben began laughing, "So these are my surprise guests, how apropos. For that I give you these." He handed Stella a small brown paper bag which she deftly plucked one handed from his grasp, quickly opened and peered inside, "Oh yes," she sounded extremely pleased, "Hostess Twinkies, Ho Hos and Cup Cakes! You know your way to a girl's heart, Ben Parker."

"To be exact, Stella, I know the way to your heart and taste buds. Shall we look in on our duo of misadventure?"

"Hold on a minute Ben. I have something for you."

Ben smiled, "You shouldn't have, Stella."

"Oh yes I should," she bought her arm out from behind her back. "You might want to slip into something· more comfortable before you see the boys." She handed him a pair of protective shoe covers, scrub pants and a trauma gown. "The boys are leaking heavily from both ends and it's getting deep in there." She pointed to the ER office, "Your dressing room. I'm getting a new set for myself and I'll meet you back here."

Five minutes later Ben and Stella were dressed in scrubs, booties and gowns and standing in the hallway outside the ER doors. Ben placed his hand on the door handle and began to pull it open, "After you, Nurse Rasniki."

"Thank you, Ben. Always the gentleman."

"Actually, Stella I thought that I'd see how your footing was before I ventured in." With that said Stella entered, Ben right on her heels thinking, "I hope the case of Beavis and Butthead meet the Easter Bunny is not the chance occurrence that leads up to the Rule of Threes."

ONE TASTY LUNCH

As he approached the Lieutenant Tyrell Masters Memorial Bridge from the north, Ben was trying to remember an old joke with a punch line of "just like de-ja vu, all over again." He couldn't remember the joke's content and then again he wasn't feeling the same as he had when he approached the bridge from the south a year ago. Instead of a white knuckled grip on the steering wheel, sweaty palms and heightened anxiety he was experiencing a niggling sense of unease. It was a considerable change in intensity from the usual signs and symptoms of his Gephyrophobia; his fear of bridges. Just prior to reaching the midpoint of the bridge he pulled onto the shoulder lane, slowed to a stop and turned off the ignition. He turned on the emergency flashers, confident of the wiring continuity to the U-Haul trailer. He was anticipating a new yet, undefined adventure as he left Bedlam and planned to repeat Uncle Griff's magical portent coin drop as a superstitious predictor of the next step in his career. Obviously the Kennedy Half Dollar dropped a year ago had created an enormous splash rather than slicing into the water edge first and vertical. As Uncle Griff predicted; big splash equals rough seas.

He checked his side mirror for traffic approaching from the rear, saw an empty bridge deck, exited the truck and walked across the cement roadway to the east side ailings of the bridge. At 0730 hours the sun had made a good head start in its overhead climb. Hands atop the ailing he felt calm. Ben was attributing his past year of stress and improved coping skills with the substantial lessening of his phobia's intensity. Thank you for that Bedlam.

At this point of the bridge the river flowed 60 feet below. Murky brown, the spring runoff was earlier and greater than what he remembered of early May of last year. The water was running faster and carrying more detritus from up river and the gradually slopping southern bank was covered by a noticeably higher level of water. Areas of river turbulence were pronounced where water surged around and eddied behind large boulders and where limbs and flotsam congregated along the shore. The surface was well illuminated by the sun, unlike last year when he dropped his coin from the bridge in the shadow of late afternoon.

Sliding his hand into his front pocket Ben reassured himself that his selected coin was safe and secure; another Kennedy Half dollar. He knew that Uncle Griff had related that the bigger the denomination the better but had not defined for what it would be better. Believing that last year's attempt had been a disservice to JFK he would repeat the superstitious act with another 50 cent piece with an eye for an Olympic caliber water entry.

As he stared down river, briefly daydreaming of the road ahead, he heard the distant guttural rumble of a Harley Davidson motorcycle exhaust and turned to look south. He spotted the motorcycle fast approaching and thought that you could not ask for a better day for an open air ride. The advancing bike was closing in on the bridge at a rapid rate of speed and Ben could make out a rider with a passenger seated head and shoulders above the helmetless rider. Now on the bridge deck the motorcycle downshifted and he heard the unmistakable rumble growing louder. Ben observed that the motorcycle was slowing and he could ascertain that the rider was male and passenger female. Within seconds they had come to a near stop in the middle of the northbound lane within six feet of him. Before the motorcycle was fully stopped the passenger's long legs, clad in black leather pants and wearing knee high boots with fashionable sturdy heels, were extended ready to be immediately planted on either side of the rear tire for stability. The rider kicked it out of gear and the rounded toes of his boots barely touched the bridge surface. His head swiveled towards Ben as he shut off the engine, "Did you have a breakdown buddy?"

To Ben the motorcycle was easily recognizable; a Harley Davidson Low Rider, maybe a '94 or '95, dark metallic green with thin scarlet piping on the fenders, frame and gas tank. The front forks had been extended and the rider had a unique up, back and downward curl to the handlebars. It had a low rider seat with an elevated passenger seat and a tall custom back rest cushioned throughout the low and mid-back. Even taking into account the elevated rear seat Ben estimated that it was not an illusion that the female passenger was at least six to eight inches taller than the man. He could also see that she was providing a good portion of the stability required to keep 650 or more pounds of motorcycle upright.

Ben was wearing his dark green Ray Bans which hid his eyes as he looked over the two riders. On first impression the rider was a mini spitting image of Hulk Hogan the wrestler, with very similar facial features, a red, white and blue do-rag covering his head, long blond hair over his ears and neck and blond horseshoe mustache. His eyes were hidden by mirrored wraparound sun glasses and a heavy gold chain was draped around his neck. A black leather vest hung open showing off well-muscled upper arms, forearms and a hairless chest. Several tattoos were in evidence on both arms and inked across his pectorals was, "Live to Ride. Ride to Live." He bent backward and then forward in a way that made Ben think that the rider was stretching out his back. Ben caught a glimpse of lettering on the back of the vest and thought that it said, "T-Rex MC." It had never dawned on Ben that a motorcycle club might be partial to flesh eating dinosaurs. The rider carried no excess fat in his abdomen and a thick, wide belt ringed his waist through the loops of his black leather pants. His hands were covered by fingerless black gloves with raised silver studs over the knuckles. With the temperature still hovering around 40 degrees Ben thought that the motorcyclist's shoulders, neck and upper chest were covered with fine goose bumps, the result of a cold morning ride but then he realized that they were slightly inflamed and more likely an anabolic steroid induced rash.

"No, I was taking a closer look at the effect of the spring runoff."

The rider raised the mirrored sunglasses and propped them against his forehead and suddenly his eyes widened in recognition, "Doc. Doc Parker, from the hospital. How the hell are you?" Ben was at a total loss, drawing a blank as to who this man was and as to why they should know each other. Then the light came on and Ben was stunned, wondering if this truly could be the same gentleman.

"Bruce Wayne?" He sounded hesitant. Ben was thinking what have you done to Woody Allen?

"Ha! Took you a minute but I knew that you'd figure it out. How are they hanging guy?"

Ben gathered his thoughts yet chose to reply generically, "Great. I'm doing just fine, Mr. Wayne. And you? It looks as if you've been…" he paused, "…busy over the past year."

"Call me Easy, as in Easy Money."

"That's an interesting nickname; where did that come from?"

"The club that I ride with. I do the club's books and the brothers thought that it was fitting."

Momentarily at a loss for words Ben was thinking that this is one hell of a change in life style for any one, let alone Bruce Wayne and how can he find out more about Mr. Wayne's, rather, Easy's transformation without coming off as too invasive or self-serving. He tilted his head up slightly to the left towards Easy Money's passenger and it was noted by Easy.

"Doc, this is my woman, Cahira. She tells me it means 'Irish woman warrior.'"

Ben smiled and said, "A pleasure to meet you Cahira."

She was gazing down river; her eyes shaded with rose colored wrap around glasses, and gave him an almost imperceptible nod, barely moving her mop of fiery red windswept hair. He thought that she was a handsome woman. Cahira wore no makeup, large concentrically ringed hoop earrings, a diamond nose stud and a small silver, maybe platinum ring piercing her lower lip. A wide woven leather collar encircled her neck. She was also bare armed and a black leather bustier accentuated an ample cleavage. Barb wire, vines, snakes and various wild flower tattoos encircled her upper arms. Her black leather pants fitted her like a second skin. She was a big boned girl who was well proportioned. Ben concluded that black was this couple's chosen hue and discounted that they leaned toward Goth.

"I hesitate to broach the subject Mr. Wayne…"

"Easy."

"Yes, Easy but you never made a return appointment and I wondered about how you were doing."

Easy gave an unforced laugh, "Yah, sorry about that Doc." He did not sound apologetic. Rather, his whole demeanor was relaxed and self-assured, a far cry different from their first meeting. "I did take you up on the dermatologist, only I saw her in her office in Billings and as you can see…" he held both his arms above his head, "…I replaced a couple of small ones with a whole lotta big ones." There was another spontaneous and relaxed laugh. "That's where I met Cahira. She wanted to have her former old man's name removed in order to make room for new tats." He swiveled his upper body and head around as he set his hand on her thigh, smiling up at her and she smiled back. "If you had seen us together back then you would have never dreamed that we were hooked up but for some reason we found each other; so I moved to Billings three weeks after I saw you. Cahira owns a motorcycle repair shop, a liquor store and a fitness center; she needed an accountant and I needed to get my life back. Nearly a year later we're together and I came back up to close out my life in Bedlam. I'm doing well. We're doing well and I'm glad to say thank you for nudging me along to get on track. Thank you, Ben." He slipped off his right glove, extended his hand and the two men shook.

Ben pointed at the scabbard mounted on the right front fork, "Is that what I think it is? A Winchester 1892?"

Easy smiled broadly, "Hey, Doc, you know your hardware."

I'm acquainted with a few guns and I recognized the big loop lever action. This was Steve McQueen's gun. I remember it from watching reruns of *Wanted Dead or Alive* with my dad."

"I never saw that show. This I noticed at a gun show and it called out my name. It's a Rossi Ranch Hand, the Winchester Mare's Leg chambered for a .45 caliber. Easy displayed no embarrassment when he added, "I'm a little guy who's running with a rough crowd who have their share of unsavory associations."

Ben shrugged, "Who am I to judge?"

"So, Doc, what are you doing out here? I assume that truck and trailer are yours?"

"Headed for greener pastures."

"You're leaving Bedlam?"

"In a nutshell, yes. Time to move on." Ben was choosing to provide generic and vague answers.

"Yah, likewise, who am I to judge."

They shook hands; Easy tugged his glove back on and pulled his glasses down from his forehead.

"Keep the shiny side up Easy." Ben nodded at Cahira who this time smiled back. Bruce Wayne kick started the Harley as Cahira stabilized it and Ben thought that they made a good team. The 88 cubic inch engine roared to life and they were off towards Bedlam. He watched as they sped off thinking back to a year ago, concluding that there was no way in hell that he would have seen this coming.

Stepping back to the bridge railing, Ben removed the half dollar from his pocket and positioned himself for optimal viewing as he prepared to drop the coin. A memory of Uncle Griff explaining the process of the coin drop popped into his head and prompted a smile as he held the coin out vertically between his right thumb and forefinger.

He let it drop and intently watched it plummet to the river. It disappeared into the murky depths, parting the surface as a scalpel would incise a plump abscess. He let out a loud "Yesssss!" as he danced a quick jig and then quickly looked around lest someone had witnessed this odd ceremony. Ben trotted over to his truck, climbed in, fastened his seatbelt and started the engine. Slipping the gear shift into second gear, he simultaneously scanned the roadway ahead and then looked into the driver's side mirror. The bridge deck was empty in both directions so he eased the truck out into the southbound lane. His rear view mirror was useless due to a full load in the pickup box and a U-Haul trailing behind, however, he made the mental reference that he was putting Bedlam in his rear view mirror.

Ben had parked on the north side of the street flanked by a young row of poplars, a future wind break for a small animal veterinarian clinic and dog park currently under construction. Larger towns and small cities throughout Montana, traditional hotbeds of cowboy culture, were feeling the influence of moneyed interlopers from both coasts. Western chic was infiltrating on all levels and pet care was not immune, therefore large animal veterinarians were being usurped by a growing number of veterinarians catering to only the pampered canines and felines of wealthy transplants. A few hundred yards down the road the corrals, show arenas and grandstands of the rodeo grounds and auction yard stood empty though later this month the entire area would be inundated with pickup trucks and horse trailers. Traveling venders with custom trailers crammed full with western clothing, hats and boots, ranch ware, souvenir plastic snakes and rubber tomahawks would be peddling their goods, while food vans hawked hotdogs, hamburgers, chili, ribs and beer as amplified country western music entertained the crowds of cowboys and cowgirls attending the Miles City Bucking Horse Sale. Ben thought almost wistfully that the Wild West became more tamer as commercialization continued to encroach.

He picked his cell phone up off of the bench seat with the intent of giving his father a quick heads up as to his anticipated arrival home. The phone had been shut off since he started the truck this morning and drove off from Bedlam. No sooner had he turned it back on than it rang with an incoming call.

"Hello?"

"Ben, where the hell are you?"

"Marni? Is that you? I've only been gone a few hours and already you miss me?"

"I repeat, where the hell are you?"

Ben smiled to himself as he opened the driver side door, climbed out onto terra firma, closed the door and leaned against it; phone still to his ear. "I'm leaning against my truck under a warm, cloudless sky, the sun beating down on my face with nary a care in the world."

"That's great but where are you exactly?"

"I'm staring at a silver lunch diner near the fair and rodeo grounds in Miles City. My father would take me to this diner if we came to the Bucking Horse Sale or were traveling further east. They've got the most consistently good mushroom, bacon cheeseburgers, fries and chocolate fraps. Did I mention that without fail the food was consistently great?"

"All well and good but..." there was a short pause, "...What in God's name is a frap?"

"The owner of the diner had moved out here years ago from Boston where a milkshake is a frappe' only they pronounce it frap, without any accent. Since Dad doesn't have a great affinity for the French he would never be able to bring himself to say Frappe', therefore he also called them fraps, like a good Bostonian. So, fraps they are."

"Thanks for that. Look, Westergard has been trying to call you all morning and leaving you messages. Now he's in a meeting with the hospital board and he asked me to call you. He'd like you to call him as soon as possible."

"I can't imagine that the two of us have much to talk about so please tell him that I'll call him after lunch and back on the road."

"Saroni was arrested in the emergency room parking lot this morning."

"What did you say?" Ben sounded genuinely confused.

"I said; Saroni was arrested this morning in the parking lot when he was coming to work. The word is that after he was handcuffed the area was swarmed with a virtual alphabet soup of law enforcement."

"Alphabet soup?"

"Yes, alphabet soup; DEA, FBI, ATF, MHP, BSD, SAG."

"Okay, excuse my ignorance here but the last three are…?"

"Montana Highway Patrol, Bedlam Sheriff's Department and State Attorney General's Office. You name it and they had someone wearing a blue windbreaker with some acronym printed on the back."

"The Attorney General's Office? Lawyers in windbreakers, not three piece suits? What has the world come to."

Marni ignored him. "Once they had him in custody they virtually stormed the hospital with search warrants, cordoned off all of the exits and one group questioned Westergard in his office."

"What have you been smoking, Marni? Are you suffering from reefer madness?" Ben was joking yet still sounded incredulous, "What in the hell could Saroni have done to bring the feds to Bedlam?"

"Well try this on. First off, Saroni is not Saroni. His real name is Guido Petracelli and he's from Tenafly, New Jersey."

"No shit? No, you're pulling my leg. What's really going on there?"

"Really, Ben, I'm not making this up. Guido Petracelli got booted out of some Caribbean Island medical school for cheating and selling dope and ended up in Miami working for years as a medical technician or something similar in a dermatology clinic owned by..."

She paused and Ben interrupted, "Dr. Arman Saroni?"

"You guessed it, Dr. Arman Saroni, originally from Cairo, Egypt. Guido's wife, Melina Hernandez, was the office manager for the real Dr. Saroni. The feds claim that Guido and Melina conspired to kidnap and murder the real Saroni and his wife. The pretext they used for explaining away the Saroni's disappearance was that the doctor and his wife had returned to Egypt due to a family emergency and once there decided not to return due to family responsibilities and the dermatology clinic's pending financial insolvency. Melina had forged documents giving her power of attorney to assume the clinics finances, close the clinic and sell off the Saroni's assets. Guido and Melina then assumed the Saroni's identities and decided to continue the charade someplace where they might anticipate much less scrutiny."

"Similar to the thought process that prompted the Unabomber to move to Lincoln, Montana?"

416

"Probably." Marni suddenly grew silent and then burst out in laughter. Ben waited and wondered patiently. Her laughter finally abated and sounded as if she was catching her breath between involuntary snorts of laughter."

"Are you okay? Got that out of your system, Marni?" He could hear her attempting to stifle the occasional snicker.

"Yes. Yes, I'm okay, Ben. I suddenly found this whole thing, the course of this morning's events to be extremely funny, so... so ironic, so... I guess freaking appropriate when it comes to Saroni... just so damn ludicrous. I think about your descriptions of dealing with him, Saroni or Guido or whomever, as the theatre of the absurd and his being inconsistently inconsistent and it all makes so much more sense to me now. Oh boy, howdy, I'm sure that there's a whole lot of finger pointing and blame association going on at the board meeting right now as to who and how Guido was vetted for the position. There's enough blame to go around that everyone should have a red face." She snorted out another laugh and grew quiet, "Ben, you had him pegged. You said that your gut told you that something was off about him and, Jesus, you were right. Are you feeling some sense of redemption with all this?"

Ben was quiet, staring down at the worn asphalt of the street, trying to assimilate what he had just heard. "I think that I'm still trying to digest everything that you've just told me. Definitely mixed thoughts...mixed emotions. Maybe a sense of relief that I was not imagining that something was off about him. Probably some level of happiness that the community is free of him and satisfaction, yes satisfaction, that he's about to pay dearly for his crimes. Wait, let's amend that; I'm feeling unbounded joy, ecstatic to hear that the son of a bitch got caught. I'm thinking that the asshole deserves to be drawn and quartered and to have his head stuck on the end of pike pole planted outside the hospital entrance."

He could hear Marni laughing again, "Don't hold back, Ben, and tell me how you really feel. I need…"

Ben interrupted her, "Wait a minute here; where the hell did you come up with all of this inside information. You weren't there when they arrested Saroni, I mean Guido?"

"Not where, Ben, but who. Who always provides us with insider information? Who just can't help themselves from divulging every iota of information whether or not it's confidential?"

"So Chatty Chuck was there."

"Correct. Our favorite highway patrolman was there and had been made privy to the investigations during the multi-agency meeting to plan the takedown."

"Now that makes more sense, continue, please."

"Where was I before I was so rudely interrupted? Oh yah, there's more. I need to tell you about Mr. Strong Tree and his associates. First Chatty Chuck gave us a brief bio on Mr. Strong Tree. He's originally from Browning or the Blackfeet Reservation. He's done time for drug possession, intent to sell, assault, aggravated assault, felony assault, breaking and entering, and firearm violations. That's one dangerous Jose that you were screwing with."

"I wasn't screwing with him but in retrospect I may have pissed him off to some degree."

"Ya think? Friday after his usual visit with Mr. Light Feather, Strong Tree was stopped along the highway by the Highway Patrol and whisked off to Billings and kept under wraps. Then that same day, after Light Feather's students left the hospital, they were picked up by various law enforcement agencies and taken to Billings. Everything was hush, hush. Today, after Saroni was arrested, the DEA, FBI, along with local and state law enforcement produced a warrant and searched Mr. Light Feather's room."

"Why were they searching the old man's room? What did they expect to find; a slightly confused old man, a burnt roach or dried sagebrush?"

Marni sounded exasperated, "Stop interrupting me and everything will be made clear."

"Sorry."

"So, they execute the warrant and search the room. Now I'm going to explain the whole system and keep in mind that poor old Mr. Light Feather is an innocent party to all of it. You remember that Strong Tree would collect and carry off Mr. Light Feather's clothes on a Friday and return the cleaned clothing the following Friday morning?"

Silence.

"Ben? You still there?"

"You told me not to interrupt. I thought that the question was rhetorical."

"It wasn't."

"Then yes, I remember about the laundry."

"Laundry wasn't the only thing being brought in on Fridays. Strong Tree was bringing drugs in with the clean clothing. Mr. Light Feather had a locked, decorative foot locker on the floor at the foot of the bed which, everyone thought held personal and ceremonial processions but as it turned out it belonged to Strong Tree. A removable tray on top hid five individual lock boxes. The premise of the operation was that Strong Tree would place drugs into each box along with payroll money for each junior medicine man, who were in fact drug dealers. They would pick up the drugs and their payroll money from their individual boxes during the Friday afternoon visit, in turn placing and locking up the money generated from the previous week's drug sales and any unsold drugs. When Strong Tree placed the new batch of drugs in he also removed the drug sale money and unsold drugs and placed them in the duffle along with whatever dirty laundry he collected. Then he would walk out of the hospital with the duffle bag. For appearances and the benefit of Light Feather, once a month they would hold a meeting in Light Feather's room under the guise of a spiritual ceremony or training session. Every Friday since last September drugs and money were deposited and exchanged by the parties and no one but those six Indians were any the wiser; that is until the DEA got a tip a few months ago and started an investigation."

"Jesus Christ, Marni. You're making this up, aren' you?" Ben shook his head, not in disbelief but rather in dawning realization, "No. No, because you really can' make this shit up. Who's going to believe that someone is running a drug ring through a rural Nursing Home? That takes a huge pair of brass balls; not only that but a whole lot of imagination to set it in motion."

"Westergard is a wreck. He denies any knowledge of Strong Tree's activities and is cooperating any way that he can."

"He doesn't have any alternative now does he?"

"There's some speculation in the rumor mill that Saroni might have known about it."

"Sounds reasonable." Ben sounded rather blasé.

"You don't sound overly surprised by that."

"Well, with what we now know about Saroni I'd say that he's fair game for anything that they want to hang on him. Wow, what a day for the little burg of Bedlam."

"And you thought that I had finished. I've got…"

"Hang on a sec…" There was a road grader being followed closely by a construction scraper rumbling towards him, still several hundred feet away so he pushed away from his street side door and walked around to the right front of his truck assuming a leaning position with his left chest and flank pressing against the quarter panel. The heavy equipment was making brisk progress and passed Ben's truck, the diesel engines overwhelming all other ambient sounds. A dust cloud followed, churned up by the huge tires Ben estimated to be at least eight feet tall. "Okay, now I can hear you so please go ahead; you've got more to share courtesy of Patrolman Chumura?"

"Oh yes, my friend, and this will also put a smile on your face."

"I already have a smile plastered on my face thanks to Guido Petracelli."

"Okay then, consider Westergard's message delivered. Have a good…"

"Whoa, hold your horses, Mrs. Capelletti. I never implied that I didn't want to hear the rest of the story. Please, regal me with Chatty Chuck's additional information."

"Sorry, you're breaking up, Parker. I can't hear you."

"Okay. I apologize, Marni, for being flippant and insincere. Please, I'd love to hear the rest of your recitation."

"Accepted, and don't let it happen again. So, this next information all transpired on Saturday and it's been held close to the vest by the local gendarmes. First I'll add a personal editorial; Saturday, May 1, the first Saturday in May, filled with many activities both in and out of town so therefore a damn good chance that a large number of the community would be out of town or glued to their television set. After all, you've got the Kentucky Derby, an away high school track meet in Lewistown, the state high school music assembly in Billings and most definitely the opening of Paddlefish season."

"Please, don't forget the Ice Breakup Festival at Lac Aux Morts Lake."

"Uh, huh, and that's where exactly?"

"Lac Aux Morts, North Dakota, of course. Josie Rosencrantz would never forgive you if you left out her favorite spring vacation spot."

"And the Ice Breakup Festival…"

"Don't forget that it's May Day. There are probably a number of May Day celebrations with people dancing around the May pole and expounding on socialistic manifestos…"

"Enough!" Marni sounded sharply peeved with Ben. He fell silent knowing that he may be pushing the boundaries of friendship. "With all this going on it would be a reasonable assumption that the high school would be vacant, at least that was the thought of the high school custodian who had been ill on Friday and thought that he would catch up on his work in an empty school."

"Your editorializing is now finished?"

"Yes. Now I'm reiterating Chatty Chuck's story."

"I would love to hear what Chuck Chumura had to say."

"It's not only what but how he said it. You know that Chuck gives us information, whether he's supposed to or not and he's usually cut and dried, no embellishment, no inferred emotion, however, this time he had a smile on his face. I believe that he took great joy in reiterating these particular facts."

Marini paused for effect and then began, "There were a few vehicles parked out front of the high school which, stands to reason since the team buses left at 6:30 AM. The custodian, for whom English is his second language, found two vehicles parked behind the gymnasium that he didn't readily recognize. The back door was locked but he has keys to every door to the school. He went in and heard a woman shrieking in the men's shower so he called the sheriff's department. The dispatcher may have misunderstood some of what the excited custodian had to say and a deputy was dispatched to thwart a possible murder in progress. Since the only nearby back up was the sheriff he responded as well. They discovered the football coach and the mayor's wife having vigorous and vociferous sex in the shower room and apparently both were greatly intoxicated. The deputy had a mind to let her go with a stern warning and take the coach to the station; however, the sheriff was leaning in the opposite direction. There's no love lost between the sheriff and the mayor and maybe the coach didn't give the deputy's nephew enough playing time. Perhaps the deputy had something to hang over the sheriff's head or chances are they both may have stepped in something in the past that neither of them wanted exposed to the light of day. So they compromised and brought both of the perpetrators in.

The sheriff was adamant that the two flagrant fornicators would be held until their respective spouses came in to post bail, after all they were a menace to the town's children and to society as a whole. They were being charged with Lewd and Lascivious Behavior, Indecent Exposure, Public Intoxication and Endangering the Welfare of a Child. Sheriff Fiskers was certainly inclined to make the mayor squirm, if not genuflect if there was to be any chance of keeping this quiet and the coach had finally pushed the limit of the sheriff's patience and good will. The coach's soon to be ex-wife declined the opportunity to come to his rescue. The mayor showed up and uncharacteristically lost his cool. He called his wife a drunken slut and that set off a flurry of foul exchanges with the fireworks resulting with him stomping out of the station declaring that a night in jail might do her some good. Mayor Boyle failed to notice that your buddy, that scum sucking newspaper reporter General Custer Junior had shown up after apparently monitoring his police scanner.

Had the mayor known this he might have taken a different tact because, as they say, hell hath no fury like a woman scorned. As purely a magnanimous gesture," Marni's voice was now dripping with sarcasm, "and of course without an underlying agenda, Whip Acres offered to post her bail. The still partially inebriated and incarcerated Mrs. Boyle decided to purge her conscience of a number of deep dark secrets that were tormenting her soul. In the presence of the sheriff and the representative of the *Bedlam Bulletin* she began divulging Mayor Boyle's and his partner Harmon Krum's financial improprieties, illegal activities and other suspect shenanigans. She wasn't just throwing them under the bus; she was bringing the building down on their heads. When she was finished venting her spleen and purging her soul the sheriff released her to her benefactor, General Custer." Marni seemed almost out of breath.

"What about the coach?"

"The coach remained overnight as a guest of the county and they let him post his own bail Sunday morning after he had sobered up."

"Oh boy, that must have chapped his fanny; what a quick turn of the screw. I guess even iconic figures can be viewed as toxic once they cross a certain line."

"That line being screwing the mayor's wife in the boy's shower room?"

"Uh huh, that would do it."

"The school board called an emergency meeting for tonight."

Ben sounded as if he was enjoying himself when he chidingly said, "Not only is his fanny chapped; now they're going to put him on the hot seat and fry it as well."

"You, Ben, always manage to paint such a splendid description that it's hard not to picture it."

"You're welcome. It's a gift."

"Stay tuned, this could really get interesting. So are you going to call Westergard now?"

"I suppose that he's pressuring you to cover for as long as it takes to locate a locum to take over?"

"Heidi is frantically making the calls as we speak. I told him I'd cover until tomorrow if needed."

"This is going to cost him dearly. Locum Tenens do not come cheap."

"I'll hazard a guess that the potential of gutting the budget is one of the reasons that he wants to talk to you. As an administrator how do you foresee your doctor being revealed as an imposter and alleged murderer?"

"Don't use gypsy fortune tellers to do your vetting. Oh, did you hear that?"

"What? Hear what?"

"My stomach telling me that it's time for lunch."

"You're killing me here. When are you going to call him?"

"Westergard does not deserve my respect or undivided attention. I'm not necessarily about to jump for joy because he's got his keister hanging out in the wind though by the same token I'm not going to jump at his demand for me to call him."

"I wouldn't exactly call it a demand."

"By his insistence and my interpretation of the context I wouldn't exactly call it a request. I had a year full of Westergard, Saroni, Lafevbre, hospital and town politics, lowlifes like Krum and his associates, sociopathic postal workers, a nursing home drug cartel and more psych patients than you can shake a stick at. I was looking forward to at least one day free of Bedlam and its associated insanity. Maybe I'm sitting on the pity pot but after a year I was hoping to have made more of a positive impact on the community and its health system."

"You, Ben Parker, either quietly or unknowingly and I'm not sure which, managed over the past year to stir up an unholy tempest and consequently the entire town of Bedlam is on the verge of a volcanic eruption. You've made an impact and I know that it's positive, even if a little upheaval is the side effect. What have you got to say for yourself?"

"Nice of you to say, thank you, but if I had been aware of what I'm being accused of having done I might say; I regret that I hadn't stirred the pot even more. Or maybe, my job here is done."

Marni laughed, "Sure, you light the fuses, run away and claim that 'it's not my fault.'"

"It's not, by any stretch of the imagination, my fault. If you had any degree of celestial awareness you would have observed that the planets have been aligning themselves all year into a perfect universal convergence ultimately creating an unavoidable cataclysmic or should I say karmaclysmic effect. By the way who won the pool on Saroni?"

"Don't keep dodging the subject at hand. When are you going to call Westergard?"

"I'd call Dwight before I would call Westergard; so who won the pool?"

"Dwight's pool on what country Saroni was from?"

"That would be the one."

"I might have heard Stella's name mentioned but I'm not sure; I'll have to ask Dwight. He's been around but watching from a safe distance."

Ben laughed boisterously, "Leave it to Stella. I remember her joking around one day that she thought that she had heard that accent outside of Fort Dix, New Jersey, when she was stationed there. I wonder if that's what she entered in the pool."

"Like I said, I'll have to check on that. So are you going to call Westergard?"

"Maybe, after lunch."

"What if he asks you to come back, what are you going to say?"

"I'll give it some thought...after lunch."

She sounded exasperated, "Jeeeezz, Ben, give me something to work with here."

"Marni, I am sorry that Westergard has designated you as his current go between," Ben's tone was patient and considerate, "however, frankly I have no sympathy for him, Lafevbre or for that matter the board. He hitched his wagon to the wrong horse. This may not be completely applicable here but as they say; his poor planning doesn't constitute an emergency for me."

"Enough with the platitudes. I understand Ben, believe me, I understand your reticence to deal with him but please, for my sake maybe you could give me something a little more concrete to tell him?"

"Have you got a pen and paper?"

"Why?"

"I'm going to dictate a short note that will have to tide him over until after lunch."

"Okay, dictate away."

"Verbatim please."

"All right, if you insist."

427

"Greetings, Snookums…"

"What was that? Did you say 'Snookums?'"

"S-N-O-O-K-U-M-S. Yes, greetings, Snookums, write it down."

"Okay, continue." Marni sounded very unsure of where this was headed.

"Message received, period. Currently on the road, period. Will call you…before…the cows come home, period. Viva la France, period. Sign it…never mind, sign it Ben Parker. That should do it."

"What in the hell is that note all about?"

"Do you think that Westergard wants me to come back to work in Bedlam?"

"That would be my guess. Now, about that cryptic note."

"If he's intent on trying to woo me back to Bedlam then this note will either stop everything dead in its tracks or sweeten the pot considerably."

"You're avoiding the issue; what does that note mean?"

"I promise that I will discuss it in detail. Right now I'm screwing with Westergard's head and you need to maintain plausible deniability."

"It's screwing with my head as well. I trust you; however, I am going to hold you to that promise." She paused and then voiced an observation, "You certainly are a man of secrets, Ben Parker, and somehow you always seem to have an ace in the hole."

"It's not sleight of hand, Marni. It's information and some information means leverage and some leverage may provide opportunity and in this case the opportunity is having some fun with Westergard."

"Is Westergard going to understand this note, Ben?"

"I'm counting on it."

"Is there any chance that I will receive some verbal abuse or worse?"

"He might need a little supplemental oxygen…" Ben paused, "…though he might pee his pants instead. Worst case scenario; his head might explode."

"Oh, it can't be that bad."

"Trust me Marni, Westergard is normally a composed, unemotional, in control bureaucrat but when you take into account his current situation this has the outside potential of making his head explode or causing him to cry like a little girl."

"Oh great, flying shrapnel or a blubbering spineless worm. Are you messing with me Ben?"

"Yes, I am, definitely. I wish that I had thought of the blubbering spineless worm, good one. Now go deliver the message. I'm going to hang up, head over to the diner, sit down in a booth and order a mushroom, bacon cheeseburger, fries and a chocolate frap. The food here has always been consistently great and I expect it to be consistently great today. I'm looking for one thing today to be consistent after being subjected to a year of inconsistency. After eating a leisurely lunch, perhaps emitting a satisfying belch or two, I'll be headed home to visit Dad and soon after I'll be off to Missoula and a long awaited hot date."

"You know getting lucky doesn't require a ring."

"Don't worry; I'll work up to it slowly."

The following silence made Ben a little uncomfortable.

"Call me, Ben, after you talk with Westergard and we can compare notes, no pun intended." There was another extended, awkward pause. "We all miss you, Ben."

"And this too shall pass."

Marni scolded him, "Don't you dare dismiss how some of us feel about you leaving."

"I'm not, Marni. Emotions have a tendency to temper and fade. Saying goodbye to a friend today doesn't preclude a happy reunion tomorrow."

"We won't hold our breath. I'll talk with you later bye."

Starting at his current position at his right front tire Ben began whistling the Hank Williams rendition of *Hey Good Lookin*, one of his father's favorites, as he proceeded to walk around the truck and trailer eying his tires bouncing his weight on the towing hitch and ending up at the driver's door. Opening the door, he rolled up the window, pushed the door lock down and reclosed the door Normally, he wouldn't worry about locking the truck up but he had cash and documents in the briefcase sitting on the passenger side floor and his Colt 1911 holstered and secreted behind the seat. As he headed across the dusty and sun warmed asphalt to the shining silver aluminum and chrome diner Ben reminded himself of a passing thought that he had had while driving down the interstate. You could choose to think of Bedlam in two different contexts as pandemonium, tumult and chaos, or an institution for the mentally ill, the insane. He had tossed it around in his head for a short while since he found both to be applicable to Bedlam, Montana, finally choosing the definition for the insane.

Climbing up the diner's steps Ben recalled a quote attributed to yet, never uttered by Albert Einstein, "Insanity is doing the same thing over and over again and expecting different results." Ben had chosen to do something different and was hoping, if not expecting, a different result.

ACKNOWLEDGEMENTS

"Your job is to write the book; we'll do the rest." The marching orders and rallying cry from my friends and supporters who quietly neglected to mention the myriad of additional and required responsibilities that they would incrementally foist upon me as the publishing process advanced. Who knew that publishing a book(s) demanded more effort and fortitude than a mere "labor of love." Firm though gentle prodding and instruction by my stalwart friends, the tag team of Judy Edwards and Clare Duignan (agent and editor), enabled us to navigate the process and produce both novels without debilitating injury or trauma. The creation and completion of this novel was also dependent upon several additional influential contributors who deserve more than mention but will currently have to settle with name recognition; Ginny Wilshire, my wife, friend, ardent supporter and toughest reviewer, Dale Hutchison, Peggy Putnam, Darrell Schulte, and Craig Larsen. Once again, a special thanks to Corey Hutchison, graphic designer extraordinaire, whose imagination and skill created a most intriguing cover art. A multitude of individual talents melded into a collective effort to produce this finished product; a heartfelt thank you to all.

ABOUT THE AUTHOR

Dana Harvey lives in Montana and enjoys the challenges of life in a rural state. Whether snowed in at -30 degrees or facing 100 degrees and a drought, there is always a story to be told. Dana is a physician assistant and has also served as an EMT, volunteer fireman and with Search and Rescue.

www.plausibleplots.com

9 780578 703718